WEAVER'S NEEDLE

ROBIN CAROLL

An Imprint of Barbour Publishing, Inc.

Print ISBN 978-1-63409-994-3

eBook Editions:
Adobe Digital Edition (.epub) 978-1-63409-996-7
Kindle and MobiPocket Edition (.prc) 978-1-63409-995-0

Cover design: Kirk DouPonce, DogEared Design

Published by Shiloh Run Press, an imprint of Barbour Publishing, Inc., P.O. Box 719, Uhrichsville, Ohio 44683, www.shilohrunpress.com

Our mission is to publish and distribute inspirational products offering exceptional value and biblical encouragement to the masses.

Printed in the United States of America.

Praise for *Weaver's Needle*

"A non-stop adventure of a treasure hunt in the vein of *National Treasure*—this time deep in the heart of the Superstition Mountains in Arizona. Filled with Caroll's trademark suspense, killer twists, and romance, there's everything to love in this book!"

—*New York Times* bestselling author Tosca Lee

"Join the excitement and danger as these two competitors test their courage, wits, and stamina in a search for both a newly discovered map to the mine and then for the mine itself. But the mine isn't the most important treasure to be discovered."

—Lorena McCourtney, *New York Times* bestselling author of *The Ivy Malone Mysteries*, the *Mac 'n' Ivy Mysteries*, and the *Cate Kinkaid Files*

"[Robin Caroll] seamlessly weaves the suspense, romance, faith, contemporary, and historical threads of this captivating story and draws a heartwarming outcome from an intriguing setting, fascinating characters, and impossible odds."

—Cynthia Ruchti, author of 20+ books, including *A Fragile Hope*

"*Weaver's Needle* is an exciting read with interesting characters you want to root for."

—Margaret Daley, author of *Her Baby Protector*

"Robin Caroll is a master at layering rich details with unexpected plot twists and likeable characters. Highly recommended!"

—Colleen Coble, *USA Today* bestselling author

"*Weaver's Needle* is a thrilling race—a page-turning, heart-slamming suspense story with enough romance to make you need a box of chocolate. Highly recommended!"

—Carrie Stuart Parks, award-winning author of *When Death Draws Near* and *Portrait of Vengeance*

"The research Caroll must have put into this book—particularly around the treasure hunting, legends and Native American culture—added a poignancy that caused this story to stand out among others in its class for me. *Weaver's Needle* is a true treasure. Her best yet! Don't miss it."

—Cheryl Wyatt, *USA Today* bestselling author of romance with virtue

"Each page is filled with mystery and lore that left me right alongside the hero and heroine as they raced to a solution in this whodunit. Filled with details that transported me to the setting, this is a book that romantic suspense lovers will inhale. A definite keeper on my shelf."

—Cara Putman, award-winning author of *Beyond Justice* and *Shadowed by Grace*

"Robin Caroll does it again! *Weaver's Needle* is a compelling combination of whodunit, treasure hunt, and romance. You'll be rooting for Landry Parker and Nickolai Baptiste from the first page to the last. Great fun!"

—Rick Acker, bestselling author of *The Enoch Effect* and *Death in the Mind's Eye*

"[*Weaver's Needle* is] a story full of symbolism as the hero and heroine's search for treasure leads them to the true gold hidden in each other. Simply put, I adore this story!"

—Dineen Miller, multi-published and award-winning author of *The Soul Saver* and *Winning Him Without Words*

"There's nothing I like reading more than a novel about a treasure hunt, and Robin Caroll delivers in this heart-pounding search for an old map and lost gold mine. If you enjoy romantic suspense, you'll love *Weaver's Needle*!"

—Melanie Dobson, award-winning author of *Chateau of Secrets* and *The Silent Order*

Dedication

In memory of my dad, Charlie Lacy Bridges.
I love and miss you.
Every.
Single.
Day.

Acknowledgments

They say it takes a village to raise a child—that's never been more true to bring a story into the hands of readers. My most heartfelt thanks to the entire Barbour team. From acquisitions to editing to marketing, every person has been such a pleasure to work with, and I greatly appreciate all the efforts and talents used to make *Weaver's Needle* the best it can be.

Huge thanks to my agent, Steve Laube, for your timeless efforts on my behalf and for your calming, logical presence in this industry. Your gentle guidance is such a welcome gift.

Thank you to my friend and mentor, Colleen Coble. Not only are you such a dear friend of my heart, but your advice, support, and encouragement are huge blessings in my life. Special thanks to Colleen and her sweet husband, Dave, who visited Apache Junction on my behalf and provided me with notes, impressions, smells, pictures, and videos. Thank you both for being my eyes, ears, and nose by proxy.

Thanks to "Sleeping Wolf" for answering my Native American questions and sharing your experience and culture with me. I apologize for any twisting of your customs and beliefs to best fit the need of my story.

A huge debt of gratitude to my friend Heather Tipton for reading this rough draft quickly and providing honest feedback and stretching me to take my characters even deeper. You push me to be a better writer, and I thank you so much!

Endless gratitude and love to my husband, Casey, and daughters Remington and Isabella, who helped calm my deadline panic, even finding us a hotel room with electricity during storms so I could finish tweaking this story to turn it in on time. I could not do this without each of you. You are my world.

To my sweet grandsons, Benton and Zayden. . .I love you both so much!

Special thanks to my circle of "author support": Pam Hillman, Tracey Justice, Ronie Kendig, Dineen Miller, Heather Tipton, and Cheryl Wyatt. You ladies bless me with your love, laughter, encouragement, friendship, and prayers.

Thank you to Pam Hillman and Becky Yauger for helping me brainstorm certain plot points in this story and characterization aspects. You both helped me so much.

All glory to my Lord and Savior, Jesus Christ. I am nothing without You, but I can do all things through YOU.

The Legend of the Dutchman's Lost Mine

In the rugged Superstition Mountains east of Phoenix, located somewhere in a twisted labyrinth of canyon juts, lies the Dutchman's Lost Mine. The Apache Indians—Shis-Inday or "Men of the Woods"—had a secret gold cave hidden in the mountains. These mountains were the home of their Thunder God, and they held the area in reverence.

As news of gold in the Superstition Mountains spread, fortune hunters came from around the world to search. The Apaches, fierce protectors of their Thunder God's mountain, killed everyone who dared trespass.

As legend goes, in 1871, two German adventurers, Jacob Waltz and Jacob Wisner, came to Arizona. Waltz met and fell in love with an Apache girl, Ken-tee. Her relatives soon became convinced she had betrayed the location of their secret mine. According to their ancient ones, the gold had been placed there by the Thunder God for them to use only in time of desperation. When Ken-tee led Waltz to the mine, and they returned to Phoenix with nearly $70,000 worth of gold, the tribe warriors raided within hours. While they murdered Ken-tee, the Apaches failed to kill the Dutchman Waltz.

When Waltz was eighty years old in 1890, he decided to hide the location of the mine. As legend tells it, when he had completed his mission, he told many that "you could drive a pack train over the entrance to the mine and never know it was there."

Several months after Waltz hid the mine, he contracted pneumonia.

His only reported friend was a bread baker from Louisiana named Julia Thomas. History records the great February 1891 flood, which bore down on Phoenix, as the most ruinous in the American Southwest. It is reported Waltz survived the flood by climbing into a small mesquite tree, where he was stranded until someone cut him loose and took him to Julia Thomas's home, who was known to take in victims of the flood.

Julia tried to nurse Jacob back to health, only he was so old and his body so feeble, he couldn't resist his illness. He died in degrees over the summer. In October 1891, he attempted to tell Julia exactly where the mine was hidden. It's recorded he said, ". . .the northwest corner of the Superstition Mountains. The key is a stripped paloverde tree with one limb left on, a pointing arm. It points away from the rock, about halfway from between it and the rock, and two hundred yards to the east. Take the trail in. I left a number of clues." After speaking these ominous directions, he died.

All the Dutchman's clues seem to focus around Weaver's Needle. . . .

Chapter One

Unless you get one of those miracles they're always talking about in church, I don't see how you'll be able to keep the business open into spring."

Landry leaned back in her father's old chair—it creaked, but it didn't comfort her as the sound usually did. "I don't understand."

Her best friend and accountant closed her attaché case then stood. "I'll send you the final audit report next week, but Landry, it doesn't look good." She gave a half smile and squeezed Landry's arm. "I know why you wanted to start your own business, and I understand. I do." Marcie shook her head. "But with taxes and rent and overhead. . .it's my professional opinion you've bitten off more than you can chew. I'm sorry."

Landry exhaled through her nose and stared out the dirty window into New Orleans's early February grime. Mardi Gras would come later in the month this year, but right now, it was only rainy and dismal out, just like her financial status. "No, the truth is what I need." She forced a returning smile. "I'll look over what you've given me, but will wait for your report before I meet with Dad's lawyer." How would she tell him that she'd single-handedly killed her father's dream in less than a year?

"Hang in there." Marcie walked out of Landry's office and into the hall. "Are we still working out later tonight?"

"I can't. I have a meeting."

Marcie sighed. "Landry. . ."

"No, I really do." She shifted scraps of paper around her desk until she found the pink slip. She carried it with her as she walked Marcie into the front room of the office. "A prospective client. Supposed to meet at her house at six this evening."

Marcie stopped and faced her. "Since when do you make house call appointments? Isn't that the point of having an office?"

Landry gave a humorless chuckle. "Apparently I need to take appointments any way I can."

Her friend didn't smile. "It doesn't sound safe. I don't like it."

This time, Landry really laughed. "You watch too many scary movies."

"No, I watch the news."

"You're beyond serious." Landry waved the pink note again. "Besides, it's Uptown. I think I'm safe."

"Where?"

"Right by Audubon Park, baby."

Marcie raised one eyebrow. "Who, pray tell, are you meeting there?"

"Probably someone who wants me to recover a piece of art their great-aunt somebody sold a hundred years ago." But Landry read the name off the note anyway, snorting. "A Winifred Winslet. Who names their kid Winifred?"

Marcie's eyes went wide, and she slowly shook her head. "Winifred Winslet? Are you kidding me?"

"Uh, no. Do you know her?"

Marcie rolled her eyes and set her case on the reception table. "You really should start watching the news yourself, girl. Winifred Winslet is wealthier than wealthy. Old money. She was born into it, then married Bartholomew Winslet and merged their companies into Winslet Industries. One of the largest private oil baron companies in the South." Marcie perched on the edge of the table. "How do you not know this?"

"I don't keep up with the society pages." But if the wealthy woman wanted to hire her, Landry sure wouldn't turn her away. Not when she needed the money so badly, according to Marcie, whom she trusted more than anyone else. "Socialites don't interest me."

"Two weeks ago, the Winslets were all over the front page of every paper." Marcie lowered her brows. "You really need to stay abreast of the news."

Yeah. Yeah. Yeah. She didn't have time to sit in front of what Dad always called the boob tube. "I'll start, I promise, but tell me why they were on the news."

"Bartholomew Winslet was murdered."

Landry sank onto the arm of the couch in the front room. "Murdered?"

"Yeah. A robbery gone wrong, so the news said."

"Maybe that's why she wants to meet with me." She'd never been hired to recover something that might be linked to a murder.

"I don't have a good feeling about this, Landry. The news said the police had no suspects. You shouldn't get involved."

Probably not. Then again, she was known for getting involved when she shouldn't. "Won't do any harm to just meet with the poor widow. Hear what she needs recovered. Maybe it's something totally unrelated to her husband's murder."

"Uh-huh." Marcie stood. "I don't like it."

Landry pushed to her feet and chuckled. "If I stayed home every time you got a bad feeling or didn't like a situation, I'd have been broke long before now."

"You aren't broke, Landry. It's your company. You need to sit down with the attorney and go over my report." Marcie grabbed her case. "I still can't figure out why he was so big on you opening your own business. You could've kept doing recovery work for the insurance company."

"Because that was Dad's job." While she'd done a remarkable job, the board of directors hadn't been too happy to find out she'd been doing Dad's job for him in his last months. Without notifying them.

But she hadn't had a choice. Not really.

Marcie smiled. "They should have hired you, and everyone knows it. You're good."

Probably, but she would've had to jump through hoops, and after her discharge, she refused to jump over anyone's hurdles again. "But not good enough." It hurt her to even consider defeat.

"You aren't a CEO, Landry. You excel as a recovery specialist. That's where your strength is."

She nodded and crossed her arms over her chest. "Thanks again for the audit."

Marcie paused at the door and pointed at her. "You be careful tonight."

Landry grinned. "Yes, ma'am."

"And call me when you get home."

"Yes, Mother."

"Joke all you want, but I'm serious."

Landry gave her friend a quick hug. "I'll be careful, and I'll call you when I get home. Okay?"

Marcie gave a curt nod then ducked into the mist.

After locking the front door, Landry returned to her office and slumped into the chair. She stared at the mementos of her life, all crammed into one bookcase. The Distinguished Service Medal she'd received just prior to her discharge from the army. The custom-made frame holding her military police badge. Photos of her mom and dad at her officer training graduation. Photos of Landry and her father.

Her eyes burned as she stared at the tattered remnants of her life. She leaned back in her chair—once her father's—and pinched the bridge of her nose. How had her life gotten so messed up? First, Mom died right after she relocated to her first base assignment. She finished up her obligations to the army then moved back home to New Orleans. Then two years ago, Dad's diagnosis.

It was hard to believe he'd been gone almost a year. Not a day went by that she didn't think of him. Miss him.

She swiped her face and glanced at the clock. With traffic being what it was, if she didn't leave now, she'd never make it to Mrs. Winslet's on time for their appointment.

Maybe, just maybe, this job would help her get the financial footing she needed.

God, I need a little direction down here in my life. I think I've made a mess of everything.

What now?

Nickolai sat in front of the clinic director's chair. He crossed his ankles. Straightened his legs out in front of him. Then crossed an ankle over his knee.

"Thank you for coming in, Mr. Baptiste." The doctor entered the office, shutting the door behind him.

Nickolai shot to his feet and extended his hand. "Of course."

After shaking Nickolai's hand, Dr. Bertrand waved him back to his chair as he sat behind the desk. "I suppose you're wondering why I called you in."

Nickolai nodded, jiggling his left leg so that his knee bounced rapidly.

The doctor opened a file on his desk, scanned, and then smiled. "I have good news. We've received approval to go forth with our plans to open a halfway house, so to speak, for some of the patients here."

Where was this going? Nickolai shifted in the chair. "I don't understand."

Dr. Bertrand smiled wider. "Some of our patients have responded very well to long-term treatment plans. Medication. Therapy. They've made great progress."

Nodding, Nickolai remained silent.

"It is our contention that some of these patients can become viable members of the community. . .society. In keeping with that theory, we asked to purchase a home just two blocks away. This home will be converted into a halfway house. For patients who exhibit the signs of possible success in society."

Silence thickened the director's office.

"For patients like Lisbeth."

Nickolai's heart thudded double time. "Lisbeth?" Her name caught sideways in his throat, nearly choking him.

"Yes." The doctor kept his focus on the file in front of him. "She's responded well to her medication. She's participating in therapy. She trusts me. And her medication seems to be working at the correct dosage." The doctor looked back at Nickolai. "I think she's a prime candidate for success in the program, and she will turn eighteen next year."

Lisbeth: out of this. . .this. . .institution. Nickolai almost couldn't imagine it. Yet, he could. He'd dreamt of this so many times, but each time, the doctors had advised against her being released.

"What about her being a danger to others? And herself?"

"As I said, her treatment—medication and therapy combined—has given every indication of working. It is my professional opinion that Lisbeth is a perfect candidate for the halfway house." The doctor closed the file. "She's bright, and I think she could be a viable, participating part of the community. It would be a waste not to try her in the program."

"I—I don't know what to say." It was a dream come true, but it also came with reservations. Justified ones. "You really think she's ready?"

"She hasn't tried to cut herself in months. Nor has she exhibited any type of violent behavior."

Was that only because the clinic limited her access to tools that could hurt herself or others?

"I'm more than pleased with her openness and honesty in therapy. She could be my poster child for psychosocial treatment success."

But what about. . . "And her fascination for fire?" Had that affinity responded well to treatment, too?

The doctor stopped smiling. "She has a tendency to focus on fire. Believes it's a source of power."

Hadn't that been what brought on her diagnosis to begin with? If she still liked fires. . .liked setting them and seeing the flames eat. . .

"Mr. Baptiste, as you know, there is no cure for schizophrenia. We work within the confines of medication and therapy such as psychosocial treatment, illness management skills, education, rehabilitation, and cognitive behavioral therapy." He tapped the closed file folder. "Taking all of that into consideration, I've selected four patients who I believe, in my professional opinion, are candidates with the highest potential to succeed in the halfway house program. Lisbeth is one of the four."

Just the chance for Lisbeth to be out and normal. . . "If you think she has a shot, let's go for it."

The doctor smiled and passed a piece of paper across the desk. "Here's the information as well as the tentative timeline. If all goes as projected, the house will be ready by early summer. Of course, we'll go over the authorization forms as the date to move draws nearer. For now, read over the information, and feel free to call me with any questions or other concerns."

Nickolai scanned the first two paragraphs but stopped on the third that had the breakdown of costs. He jerked his stare to the doctor. "Forty thousand a year?"

Dr. Bertrand nodded. "That includes room and board, and full-time, on-site medical personnel. That's a requirement for the program."

Forty thousand. "How much does our insurance cover?"

The doctor frowned. "As this is a trial program, private insurance companies provide no coverage allowance."

Forty thousand dollars. "What about state or federal funding?"

"I'm sorry. With the economy and the crackdown on welfare, Medicaid, and Medicare, there are no government funds for this particular program."

Forty-k. Nickolai tried to wrap his mind around the amount. That was more than he lived on in a year. "So, you're telling me that I'll have to pay the full forty thousand dollars?"

"If the lump sum is a problem, we have arranged with our board of directors to allow for a payment plan. Of course, that would include interest. I don't have that information on hand at the moment, but I can have a copy sent to you, if you'd like."

Forty thousand. "Please send me the information."

"I will." The doctor stood, extending his hand. "I appreciate you coming so quickly. We'll be talking more very soon."

Nickolai noticed the Rolex as he shook the man's hand. A watch probably worth at least a third of the needed forty thousand dollars. "Thank you. Can I see Lisbeth today?"

The director glanced at his watch. That very expensive watch. "She's in group therapy right now. You know how changes in the schedule can uproot not just Lisbeth, but the entire group. There are many in her group who aren't as stable as she has become."

"I understand." He didn't have time for a real visit anyway. He let the doctor escort him from the office.

"Thank you again for coming in so quickly, Mr. Baptiste. We'll be in touch very soon."

Nickolai gave a quick nod then headed into the parking lot. A heavy mist weighed on his shoulders as he climbed into the Ford F-250 diesel. He rested his forehead against the steering wheel and waited for the indicator light to go off so he could crank the engine.

Forty thousand dollars was a lot of money. Money he didn't have just sitting around.

He started the truck and stared out the windshield. A push of breeze clumped wet leaves against the edge of the concrete median.

The information stated the selected patients wouldn't be moved for at least sixty to ninety days. If he took every case offered and worked overtime, he might be able to come up with a down payment. Enough that he could qualify for the payment plan at least. Hopefully.

His iPhone chimed then flashed his appointment reminder on the screen. He had a meeting with a lady to discuss a job. She was wealthy. Recent widow. Maybe he could get a head start on that down payment. Maybe tonight.

Nickolai steered the truck into the road. He'd already loaded the lady's address into his GPS. He pushed the button, and the driving instructions popped on the screen. He'd arrive within ten minutes.

Images of Lisbeth before flitted across his memory. Her smile. Her hugs. Her dry sense of humor.

Forty thousand dollars was a lot of money, but his sister's recovery would be worth every single penny.

Chapter Two

Talk about living in the lap of luxury.

Landry parked her VW bug in the driveway of the Winslet house, hoping it wouldn't insult the manor's grounds with its well-worn aging. An elegant two-story house raised on low brick piers with a side-gabled roof sat back from the property line and boasted covered two-story galleries framed by columns supporting entablature. The facade openings were arranged asymmetrically. In one word. . . breathtaking.

Something Landry would never be able to afford. But she wasn't here to buy the house. She was here for a job.

The February wind danced through the overstated live oak trees surrounding the house as Landry made her way over the cobblestoned driveway. She carefully took the steps to the front door then took a deep breath, letting it out slowly before she jabbed the doorbell.

A moment passed. Two. Three.

The door swung open, revealing a man in jeans and a T-shirt. A very attractive man with cut muscles and a wide smile. "May I help you?"

"Um, I'm here to see Mrs. Winslet. I have an appointment."

"Right this way, Ms. Parker." He motioned her into the entry.

Her sneakers squealed against the waxed marble floors as she followed Mr. Handsome into the first room on the right from the foyer. A formal study, complete with mahogany built-in bookcases and marble-front fireplace, met her. Maybe she should have changed into something more professional.

He gestured to the seating options. "Please, make yourself

comfortable. Mrs. Winslet will be with you directly."

"Thank you," she said to his retreating back. She avoided the stiff-looking Queen Anne's high-back chair, instead choosing the formal and uncomfortable love seat that sat across the coffee table. Brocade fabric. No throw pillows.

Landry scoped out the room. No windows broke up the monotony of the white and wainscoting walls. A painting of a woman, as formal and stuffy as the room, stared down her nose from her place over the fireplace. All in all, it was probably one of the most unwelcoming places Landry had ever been inside.

"I apologize to have kept you waiting."

Landry stood as the lady entered. She was much younger than Landry had expected, probably no more than sixty. Definitely not more than sixty-five. Standing about five feet seven inches, tall for a lady, but with a slim build. She wore a tailored gray dress. Her silver-streaked hair looked as shiny as a child's. Her blue eyes were separated by the hawking of her nose, which stood out from her other features as if it'd been placed on her face by mistake.

"Please, sit." She perched on the edge of the chair, her legs tucked demurely against the piece of furniture, ankles crossed but not touching. "I'm Winifred Winslet. Thank you so much for coming."

"I'm so sorry for your recent loss." Her tongue thickened inside her mouth. Landry had to remind herself Mrs. Winslet was a potential client, nothing more.

"Thank you, dear."

Mr. Handsome returned, carrying a silver service. He set it on the marble table splitting the room in two.

Mrs. Winslet nodded at him, and he disappeared in silence, shutting the study door behind him.

"Would you like some coffee?"

"No. No, thank you." Caffeine this late in the day would keep her awake all night. She needed to get the conversation on track. "So, the message I received was you were interested in discussing my company's recovery of an item?"

"Not quite so fast, dear." The woman poured herself a teacup full of coffee then added a real lump of sugar and a splash of cream. She stirred it silently, not hitting the sides of the cup with the spoon. "Why don't we visit a bit first?"

Visit? This meeting was strange to begin with, and felt like it would get stranger still. Maybe Marcie had been right. "Mrs. Winslet, I don't mean to be rude, but I have limited time. If you'd kindly—"

The door opened, interrupting Landry's words and train of thought.

Mr. Handsome led another man into the room. He gestured for the other man to enter, handed two large envelopes to the mistress of the manor, and then left the three of them.

"Thank you for coming. Please, have a seat." Mrs. Winslet gestured to the space beside Landry.

The mass of a man sat, his weight shifting Landry toward him. Heat blazed in her cheeks. She lowered her gaze to the ornate rug lying under the coffee table, but she couldn't ignore her awareness of the man beside her.

He stood at least six feet something and was all muscle. All muscle. Even his neck bulged. Hair black as a raven's feathers. Strong jawline. He radiated strength and vitality.

"Since everyone's here, let me get to the heart of the matter. The reason I've asked you to come." Mrs. Winslet stood, hovering by the fireplace in her sensible low heels.

"As I'm sure you're both aware, my husband died recently. An unsolved murder. Messy business." She scrunched that big nose of hers. "Nevertheless, my husband was a collector. Of all sorts of antiques. Mainly documents. He has quite the collection, most loaned out to various museums, you understand, but worth quite a bit of money."

Landry remained silent, still very much aware of the man beside her. Who was he? Why was he here?

"In the weeks before my husband's demise, he arranged to purchase a new document for his collection. According to Bartholomew's notes, it contains information regarding an old legend set in the Superstition Mountains in Arizona."

The man shifted his weight. "The legend of the Dutchman's lost gold mine?"

Landry's stare locked on Mrs. Winslet. Everybody who worked in the recovery business knew about the legend.

"Yes. My husband purchased a document from a direct descendant of Julia Thomas. He believed the document had information regarding the lost mine."

The coldness in the widow's voice pricked the goose bumps on Landry's forearm to attention. "A map?"

Mrs. Winslet shrugged. Well, more like she raised a shoulder and tilted her head to meet it. "Bartholomew's notations indicate nothing more than his investigator had confirmed the document, a single piece of paper, was in fact owned at one time by Julia Thomas. The scientific dating of the document gave the same evidence."

"You're sure?" the muscled man asked.

Mrs. Winslet gave the exact look she wore in the painting on the wall. "Of course. Bartholomew would never have spent such an amount of money without proof of the document's authenticity."

Landry cut her eyes to the man, then back to Mrs. Winslet, who continued. "Whatever the document is, there is no doubt it was originally in Julia Thomas's possession." She straightened a crystal figurine sitting on the mantel.

A pause for effect? It worked. Landry met the man's inquisitive stare with one of her own.

"You're wondering how you fit in, yes?" Mrs. Winslet smiled at them. One of those high-society, polite smiles.

"The document's missing," Landry concluded.

"Yes, my dear. According to my husband's calendar, which has been verified by his secretary and assistant, he had an appointment to pick up the document. The plan was for him to take it directly to the bank and place it in a safety-deposit box. He had meetings scheduled later that week with various professionals regarding the document—appraiser, attorney, and so forth."

Made sense.

"Police have verified he obtained a document from the seller and paid for it. Unfortunately, he was murdered before he reached the bank." Her repeated coldness regarding her husband's death rubbed Landry wrong.

"He had the document on him when he was killed?" the man next to Landry asked.

Mrs. Winslet nodded. "I'd like it back. That's where you come in."

The man shook his head. "Ma'am, no disrespect, but this is a matter for the police. Even if the document were recovered privately, it's evidence in an open investigation."

Landry caught the slight fall of Mrs. Winslet's expression before she continued. "I understand that. The map is now my property; however, the police aren't actively working on locating the document. They're focused on the murder."

"As they should." He shook his head. "You can't just hire someone to recover an item stolen during a murder."

The man had a point, but Landry was the recovery specialist here. "Actually, you can. If the item is found, of course, it needs to be turned over to the police as evidence."

The man snorted and glared at her. "It's interfering in a police investigation."

Landry shrugged. "It's a gray area. Just like victims' families who don't believe the police are working fast enough and hire PIs to solve the crime. It happens all the time, and I think it's within a person's right to hire whomever they like to solve a crime or recover a lost or stolen item."

"And just what is your law enforcement background?" He crossed his arms over his chest, ignoring Mrs. Winslet.

"Army military police. Honorably discharged." She crossed her arms over her chest. "And yours, Mr. Legal Parameter?"

"New Orleans PD, nine years, Ms. Gray Area."

Mrs. Winslet cleared her throat. "Well, now that we're all aware of the details, here is why I called you." She handed each of them one of the large envelopes. "If you are interested, inside are copies of everything regarding the document and the case. Please, only open if you're truly interested in recovering the document on my behalf."

She was the recovery specialist. . .why did she give a copy to the cop? Landry stared at Mrs. Winslet, who took a breath before going on.

"Obviously, I want the item back. And quickly. I'm willing to pay a recovery fee in the amount of fifty thousand dollars."

Wow! Fifty grand wasn't exactly chump change. Before Landry could jump in and accept the job, Mrs. Winslet continued.

"If both of you choose to accept the challenge, please understand that I'll only pay one of you. Whoever recovers the document first and returns it to me—undamaged—will receive fifty thousand dollars. I will, of course, pay for all up-front hard costs, through my official representative, Stan Hauge."

A challenge? Landry stared at the man beside her. "Who are you?"

His eyes darkened by shades. "Nickolai Baptiste. And you are?"

Baptiste? Every pore of Landry's body went hot. Her mouth could barely form the words. "Landry. Landry Parker."

His facial features tightened. "Parker Recovery?"

She nodded.

He shot his glare to Mrs. Winslet. "What is this, some kind of joke?"

"I assure you both, this is no joke. I want the document recovered as quickly as possible." Her spine was as tight as the tension in the room.

Landry could barely concentrate with him sitting next to her. She knew who he was, of course, but had never met him in person. Did her only competitor in New Orleans have to be so drop-dead handsome? She shook her head and stood. "I'll accept the assignment, Mrs. Winslet." Gray area of the law and all. Fifty thousand would surely save her company.

He stood as well. "Wait a minute. Let's discuss this." He tapped the envelope against his hand. "You're pitting me against her?" He shook his head and smirked. "That's hardly fair. To her, I mean."

Smirked. He smirked! Landry clamped down the retort burning her tongue and lifted her chin. "Again, I'll accept the assignment, Mrs. Winslet."

The widow smiled. "I'd hoped you would, dear. All the information is there, along with my contact information and that of Mr. Hauge."

"Wait a minute." His jaw muscles popped.

"If you don't want the assignment, Mr. Baptiste, don't take it. If you do, I welcome the challenge." He had no idea how much she welcomed the challenge. She smiled at her new client. "I'll be in touch. Soon." Landry turned and left the room then exited the house, heading to her VW as quickly as possible.

Not fair? She'd show him. She'd find the stupid document first and beat him, earning the fifty grand. And the bragging rights.

Not fair. Indeed.

That was Landry Parker? His nemesis? Somehow he'd imagined her to be more—more—masculine? Nickolai couldn't exactly wrap his mind around that dark-haired, blue-eyed spitfire being a successful recovery specialist. She looked more like she belonged on a magazine cover than sitting beside him as his biggest competition in the state.

"I'll be in touch, too." He nodded at Mrs. Winslet, grabbed his own envelope, and followed Landry from the crazy widow's house. Pitting one against the other. . .he'd never heard of such. To top it off, the situation was as far left of legal as one could get without going right. That map—document—whatever it might be, was evidence in an open, ongoing murder investigation. To recover it and not turn it in to the police would be illegal. Interference.

"Hey, wait a minute." He bounded down the stairs, ignoring the late-winter breeze skittering around the box hedges. He approached the woman just as she reached her car. "Surely you're not going for this?"

"I am." She rested one foot on the driver's floorboard and pivoted, resting her arm on the hood of her beat-up little car. She looked him right in the eye without flinching. "I need the money and the job sounds reasonable."

"But it's evidence in a murder. Even if recovered, if it's not turned over to the police as evidence, that's interference in a police investigation. That's criminal." She'd been military police? Sure didn't act like it. Not even close. The law was the law—black and white, no muddying it up with gray areas.

She crossed her arms over her chest and leveled him with an icy stare from her big baby blues. "I don't recall Mrs. Winslet telling us what she planned to do with the document once she gets it. How do you know she isn't just trying to help the investigation along and intends to hand it over to the detective working her husband's case as soon as she has it?"

Nickolai ground his teeth. The woman was deliberately splitting hairs. "But she didn't say she was going to turn it in, either."

"Do you ask all your clients what they're going to do with their personal property that you recover? Does their answer dictate whether you take the job?"

Well. . .no.

Landry smiled as he hesitated. "Right. What I thought. But because you're an ex-cop, you're all wrapped up in the legalities. Fine. You do what you want. Me? That's a nice recovery fee." The challenge in her voice was unmistakable.

"But pitting us against each other? Doesn't that feel shady to you?" Couldn't she see the widow was playing them?

"No." She shrugged. "Look, if you don't want to do it, then don't. I'll have no problem finding the document without the interference. If you decide to take the assignment, great. I'll welcome the challenge."

Landry slipped behind the steering wheel. "Doesn't matter to me one way or the other. I intend to recover the document and collect the fifty thousand." She shut the door, right in his face.

With a wave, she started the engine and drove off, leaving him staring after her.

The woman was infuriating. Intending to recover the document even if he took the assignment? The cockiness…arrogance…confidence.

That fifty thousand would cover the expenses of his sister getting into the halfway house.

Little Miss Landry Parker intended to recover the document, did she? He'd see about that. Yes, sir, he'd just see about that.

The Foretelling

"N*ii nahii'maa at'e, ya nahiika'ee at'e.*" Gopan bowed his head against the fire's smoke.

The three shamans answered in unison. "Yes, the earth is our mother and the sky our father."

This was the Native American way. Their culture. Not a religion, but their beliefs and practices merging as an integral and seamless part of their very being. Who they were, at the core.

Gopan continued in his Apache language. "I come to ask for wisdom. Dreams have come to me. Dreams of Thunder God's anger. His wrath on our people."

The elder of the shamans, Paco, stood and faced the eastern sky. His Apache tongue split the silence of the range. "Hail to the East, to the new day. To the light. To the eagle. To insight. To the East, we call on you."

Nantan stood and raised his arms. "Hail to the South, to innocence. To trust. To the mouse. To the path home. To the South, we call on you."

The wind shifted directions, swirling the smoke.

Dyami joined the other two shamans, facing the west. "Hail to the West, to the darkened waters. To looking within. Home to black bear. To the medicine path. To the West, we call on you."

Gopan's pulse kicked up a notch. He stood, holding the pouch with the blue cornmeal, and faced the north. He raised his arms. "Hail to the North, home of the old ones, and those gone before. To the wisdom place. The place of snow leopard and white buffalo. To the North, we call on you."

All four men knelt as one. In the prone position, each blew into their medicine pouches. Paco's voice rang strong against the darkening sky. "And to mother earth, for the two and four leggeds. For those that fly or crawl and swim. For all children of the mother."

In unison, all four men stood. Nantan waved his arms above his head in a big circle. Another. Then another. "And to father sky. Thank you for this day."

Dyami raised his arms alongside Nantan. "Great Spirit, we ask for the explanation of the visions. We ask for meaning."

All four kissed their pouches then laid them in the weeds, as their ancestors before them had done. As was laid out in the sacred texts from the previous shamans of the tribe.

"So be it," said Paco.

"It is a good day to die," all four men whispered. "*Sadnleel da'ya'dee nzho.*" Long life, old age, everything good.

A star shot across the dusky sky.

The breeze kicked up, blowing the smoke across Gopan's face. He inhaled the smoke but closed his eyes against the burning.

Paco spoke softly. "*Indaa* comes."

Every muscle in Gopan's body tightened. What white person would come?

Chapter Three

"You're insane to take this case, you know that, right?" Marcie stabbed the air as she pointed at Landry.

Landry shook her head even as she looked over the documents from the envelope for the tenth time this Wednesday morning. "Look, fifty thousand would get the business back in the black."

Marcie raised her eyebrows.

"What? You didn't think I'd looked over the paperwork you left me? I did. I might not be great with numbers, but I saw the bottom line." Landry reorganized the documents spread out on the conference table in chronological order. Again.

"It's too dangerous, Landry."

"It's recovering a document."

"A document someone has already been murdered to get."

Landry shook her head and plopped down onto one of the chairs. "We don't know that's the reason Mr. Winslet was killed."

"Come on, don't play stupid with me," Marcie huffed as she sat on the edge of the scuffed table. "You know that's why he was murdered."

"Probably." Landry believed he was, but she didn't need to confirm her best friend's fears. "But I can handle myself, probably a lot better than my competition."

Nickolai Baptiste.

Visions of his dark hair...his piercing eyes...his smirk had invaded her sleep entirely too much last night. Maybe that's why she felt as she did. Restless and edgy.

"That's something else that bugs me—this whole competition

thing." Marcie's eyes widened as she spoke faster. "If you hire someone, hire them. You don't offer them a job, but only if they complete it before someone else. Especially when one of them has years more experience."

Landry sat up straight. "I'm just as qualified."

Marcie blushed. "I didn't say you weren't. I just pointed out that he has more experience than you do. I didn't imply he was better."

"Mmm-hmm." If her own best friend didn't think she could beat Nickolai, what did that say about her?

"Seriously, Landry." Marcie grabbed Landry's hand. "You know I think you're an awesome recovery specialist. Everybody who's ever hired you gives you nothing but glowing recommendations."

"But?"

"But this case is different. Homicide is involved." Marcie lowered her voice. "I'm scared for you."

Landry squeezed Marcie's hand. "I'll be fine. I know how to cover my six. I was trained by our military, you know."

"I still don't think you should take the case." Marcie eased off the table and smoothed her skirt.

"I've already taken it." Landry stood and spread her hands over the conference table. "These are all the documents Mrs. Winslet provided."

Marcie glanced over the papers. "Anything useful?"

Landry smiled. Marcie might not like it, but she was on board. "I'm working it just like Dad taught me, starting with the missing item and backtracking."

"Where, exactly, is that?"

"I know Mr. Winslet had it when he got out of his car, going toward the bank. It was gone when his body was discovered. That's a short period of time."

"Back up a minute and let my analytical thoughts get on the same page. How can you be sure he actually had it in his personal custody?"

Landry nodded. "Follow with me for a few minutes." She found a check stub and held it up. "Receipt of the cashier's check Mr. Winslet got from his bank the morning of January 18. Made out to one Joel Easton for a million dollars."

Marcie let out a slow whistle. "A million dollars? Yikes."

"But if the map is real and points to the lost mine, a million dollars is barely a drop in the bucket." The excitement bubbled in Landry's chest. A real treasure map.

"There's no proof that it's an authentic map."

"True. But think about it, Marcie. What if it is? Can you imagine the worth of what's hidden in the mountains? I doubt Mr. Winslet would pay a million dollars for something he didn't strongly believe was real."

"It's a long shot. A legend. Not a single shred of proof of there ever being a mine, much less a map to find it."

Landry leaned against the table and crossed her arms over her chest, staring at her friend.

"What? Accountants know how to Google, too." Marcie rested against the table as well, mimicking Landry's stance.

"It's been said that Jacob Waltz had a matchbox made from the highest-grade ore in his possession when he died. That might be your evidence." Landry chuckled at her friend's wrinkled nose. "Come on, Marcie, I don't have to find the mine or even believe the map is real. All I have to do is find the map and get it back to Mrs. Winslet and collect fifty grand. Easy-peasy." Well, not exactly, but Landry couldn't deny this case interested her more than any other had in quite some time.

A modern-day treasure hunt.

"I still don't like it."

"I know you don't." If there was one thing left in this life that Landry could count on, it was her best friend being overprotective of her. Marcie had always been a mother hen, but she was even more cautious since Landry's mom then dad had passed away. "And I love you for trying to watch over me, but I have a job to do."

Marcie sighed and slouched. "So I'm going to assume the police looked into the guy who sold the map?"

Grinning, Landry lifted a sheet of paper and read. "Joel Easton, thirty-two, from Phoenix, Arizona. Not married, no children. Lives alone. By profession, he's a landscaper who—"

"A landscaper? In Phoenix?"

"Apparently." Landry chuckled. "Maybe that's why he had to sell the map. I'm guessing landscapers don't make a lot of money in Arizona."

"Okay, go on with what you were saying."

Landry read aloud. "According to the police report Mrs. Winslet provided, on January 18, Joel Easton met with Bartholomew Winslet at the Le Pavillon Hotel on Poydras Street at precisely 10:45 a.m. Security camera footage of the downtown hotel shows Mr. Winslet taking something, looking at it, then slipping it into what appears to be a protective sleeve before placing it in his briefcase. He gave Mr. Easton the cashier's check, and the men shook hands. While Mr. Winslet finished his cup of coffee, Mr. Easton crossed the lobby and got into the elevator at 10:58. Security cameras followed him entering his room on the third floor of the hotel at 11:02."

Landry flipped the page and paced slowly as she read. Whoever had compiled the documentation had been very thorough in creating a timeline. "Mr. Winslet left the hotel at approximately 11:05 and got into his waiting car. Mr. Easton checked out at the front desk at 11:22. He left the hotel, having the concierge hail a taxi for him."

Landry turned to the next page and kept reading. "According to the taxi driver's log, he drove Mr. Easton to the airport, dropping him off at exactly 11:58. Easton boarded his flight to home in Arizona at 12:30 p.m. He had a forty-five-minute layover at DFW, and landed on time in Arizona." She stopped and set the papers in place on the table. "So, yes, the police checked him out and his alibi is tight. If he had anything to do with Mr. Winslet's murder, he had to hire someone to do it."

"Do the police think that's a possibility?"

"They wouldn't tell anyone if they did, Marcie." Landry sat back down in one of the chairs and looked up at her best friend. "But if he was a suspect in any way, I'm pretty sure they'd have sent at least one detective to Arizona to follow up, and they didn't. They did their questioning by phone. They didn't even have local police question Easton in person."

"What about you? Do you think he might be involved?" Marcie sat on the edge of the table, her posture rigid. . .perfect.

"I don't know." Landry chewed her bottom lip as she scanned the information before her. "I know a million dollars sounds like a lot of money, and it is, but if the map was real. . .it could be worth a lot more."

"What are you thinking?"

"I've put out a couple of feelers in the art world. Word on the street is the map is available again for sale on the black market."

Marcie's eyes widened. "Joel Easton?"

Landry shook her head. "He's not the one listing it, but the description is the exact same as Easton's—word for word. Black market art sales are usually so convoluted that you don't really know who you're doing business with until you meet them face-to-face." She took a deep breath, bracing for the argument she knew would come. "I set up a meeting with the potential seller. In Apache Junction. On Friday."

"You're going to Arizona? You're going to meet with this person who deals in the black market?"

"Yes." Landry swallowed. "Mrs. Winslet's vice president made the arrangements and is accompanying me. We fly out tomorrow afternoon. But don't worry: I won't be unchaperoned, Mom."

Marcie shook her head. "But. . .whoever has that map had to be involved with Mr. Winslet's murder. There's no other way they could have it to sell. I don't like it."

That was the mountain Landry had to climb. "I'm just going to see if this is legit. Someone could've seen the news about Winslet's murder and decided to try and make a little money. They could be faking having anything."

"If it's a fake, how would they even know about the map?"

"You'd be amazed how fast details like that spread throughout the antiques and collections community. And the description matches Easton's, so it could've been copied."

Marcie's frown said it all.

"Gee, thanks for the vote of confidence in my abilities."

"It's not that."

Landry tapped her fingers on the table. "Then what? I'm serious, Marcie. If you doubt my ability to do this, then just tell me."

"I know you can do anything you set your mind to, Landry."

"Don't sugarcoat what you think. You know me better than that." Landry couldn't accept fake flattery, no matter who dished it out.

"I'm not sugarcoating anything. I'm just saying that this is a dangerous case and there's no guarantee you'll locate the map." Marcie held up her hands in front of her, as if to ward off Landry's argument. "Not because I think Nickolai Baptiste will find it first. What if the map is gone? Where neither one of you can find it. What if it's destroyed? You can't help that."

True. But, still. . .

Marcie continued, obviously on a roll. "You don't have a contract with Mrs. Winslet, you don't have a retainer. All your up-front hard costs are covered, sure, but what about your time? This isn't even your standard mode of business. Everything about this case feels wrong."

"I know it's not how I normally agree to cases, but the income from this one case alone is equivalent to at least a dozen or more of my regular ones."

"That's not an excuse, Landry." Marcie's stare could melt glaciers, and she locked it on Landry. "So why did you jump on this case?"

"I need the money."

"Your business does, but I'm not buying that's your motivation." Marcie stood, her stare burning.

Landry refused to shift in her seat. "I don't want to lose Dad's business. I can't fail him. This is his legacy."

"Baloney. You're his legacy." Marcie leaned against the table, not taking her gaze from Landry.

Silence hung as heavy in the office as the dark clouds settling over New Orleans.

Finally, Marcie straightened and headed for the office door. As she reached the doorway, she turned and faced Landry. "If you're being honest, I bet you don't know exactly why you took the case. I'm pretty sure, however, you'll need to figure it out sooner rather than later. For yourself." She flashed a quick smile. "I love you, ya know."

Landry smiled back. "Love you back. I'll call you later." She watched her best friend retreat then glanced down at the documents on the desk.

Why had she taken the case? The money Mrs. Winslet promised? The challenge Nickolai threw at her?

Or was it something else? The good Lord knew she didn't have time to figure it out at the moment. She needed to concentrate on the case.

Chapter Four

Maddening. Just maddening.

Nickolai gripped his cell phone tighter. The longer he sat on hold, the more he told himself doing anything at all on this case was a bad idea. He looked out the front windshield of his truck, staring at the facility his sister had called home for the last couple of years.

"Hey, Baptiste. Haven't heard from you in a month of Sundays. How are you?" Chris Graze's voice was as big as his personality.

"Doing well. Enjoyed the Saints' games this season, even though we didn't do as well as I'd hoped. At least we beat those Cowboys."

Chris chuckled. "Yeah, yeah. . .rub it in. Missed watching games with you, bro." The laughter left his voice.

Nickolai swallowed and ran his knuckles over the steering wheel. "Same." And he did miss his former partner. More than he'd realized.

"Hey, man, I get it. I was there."

Yes, he'd been there on the day Nickolai had almost died. If it hadn't been for Chris's fast action. . .

"I have a feeling you didn't call me to talk football." Chris snatched him back to the present.

"No, although I do love rubbing it in your face that we beat you."

"I know you do."

Nickolai chuckled. "I do have a favor."

"Don't you always?" The familiar easiness between them had returned.

"This one should be easy enough."

Chris snorted. "You always say that. What is it?"

"The Bartholomew Winslet homicide."

Chris whistled. "Nothing like jumping to the top of the ladder, huh, Baptiste? I can't tell you much on that one, my friend. The captain is leading the investigation himself. I don't even have access to a lot of the file."

Money did grease the wheels of justice, that was for sure. "I've got a lot on the case already. I just need to know what angles y'all are working on recovering the map."

"Map?" Keyboard tapping sounded over the connection. "Oh. The alleged missing document." It wasn't just his former partner's wording that came out stiff and awkward—his whole tone changed.

"Alleged?"

"Yeah. According to the widow, he picked up an expensive document, but it wasn't recovered when his body was discovered."

Nickolai flipped through the envelope Mrs. Winslet had prepared for him. He scanned the information again. Something didn't feel right. "Chris, the hotel security camera showed Winslet putting it in his briefcase before he left. If it wasn't found on his body, wouldn't you say it was taken? That it's missing?"

"Maybe not. Could be that he put it somewhere else after he left the hotel. Or it was left in his car."

Something didn't sound right with his old partner, either. "Are you kidding me? Le Pavillon Hotel security tape shows him leaving the hotel with the briefcase at 11:05. The statement from his driver said he had the briefcase when he got out of the car at 11:32 at the corner since the front of the Crescent Bank was blocked by the armored car. His body was found at 11:42 by one of the guards from the armored company. No briefcase was found next to his body. What other explanation is there?"

"How're you getting all this information, Nick?"

"Let's just say someone's interested, and I'm poking around a little." Which was true. He hadn't decided for sure whether to take the case. "Are you saying Winslet's driver is a suspect?" Which was logical. He flipped through the papers spread over the front seat of his truck. "Miles Lewis."

"I can only tell you what's documented." More tapping sounded; then Chris cleared his throat. "At the moment, we're working many angles. We don't have a specific list of suspects. You know the drill. . . ."

He did, which was why he understood Chris wanted to tell him more but couldn't volunteer anything. "Anything else you have on Lewis?"

"According to notes, Lewis's statement that he was driving around the block during the actual time of murder was verified by GPS on Winslet's vehicle."

So the driver wasn't a suspect. He was, however, the last person to see and talk with the victim. "What about the seller? Joel Easton in Arizona?"

"He was interviewed over the phone and his alibi was verified."

"Are there any notes about his interview? His background? Is he even legitimate?" Come on, there had to be something in the file that Nickolai didn't have.

"I don't have any of that information. I told you, it's not my case." The unspoken warning was right there, where Nickolai could almost touch it.

"Just a couple more questions, Chris."

The sigh over the connection revealed a lot. A whole lot. "Make it fast, Baptiste."

"Is there a theory about the armored car? Was it coincidence that it was parked there, or was it at its regular time to be at the bank?"

The pause was heavy. "According to the notes I have access to, it was the normal time for the truck to be there. The driver courier of the truck was questioned, but he saw nothing." Another pause. "The truck's officer, upon exiting the bank, noticed Winslet on the sidewalk. He's the one who called it in to 911."

Interesting.

"If that's all, I've got to go."

"Sure. Thanks."

"Hey, no problem. Let's get together soon, yeah?"

"Sure." Nickolai ended the call and stared at the papers from the envelope. It didn't make sense.

He should call Mrs. Winslet and tell her he couldn't take the case, that it was a police homicide investigation. He should call Landry Parker and warn her not to interfere in the investigation, either.

No, he should turn down the case and mind his own business, period.

But something about Chris Graze's voice. . .it was more than just the captain heading up the investigation. Something was sure off about the investigation—he felt it in his gut, and his gut was rarely wrong. He'd work the case just as he had when he was on the force—start with the victim at the time of death and move back from then. That meant the driver, Miles Lewis.

Nickolai located the paper Mrs. Winslet had compiled of people associated with her husband and their business then dialed the number for Miles Lewis.

"Hello?" The answering voice didn't sound much older than Nickolai's thirty-four, which was a little surprising to him. For some reason, Nickolai had assumed Winslet's driver would be older.

Nickolai cleared his throat. "Miles Lewis?"

"Who is asking?" The defensiveness came across clearly in those three, very proper, words.

"I'm Nickolai Baptiste. Mrs. Winslet gave me your name and number as I'm working for her." Maybe.

"Yes. She informed me that some people might be contacting me in regards to Mr. Winslet's passing." People. Him and Landry Parker.

Nickolai reached for his notebook and a pen. "I understand you were Mr. Winslet's driver?"

"I drive for both Mr. and Mrs. Winslet."

Might better be specific with this one. "You were driving Mr.

Winslet the day he was killed?"

"I was."

He paused, waiting, but Lewis didn't elaborate. Nickolai detested these kinds of interrogations. They were like getting a root canal. He'd have to walk the driver through the information. "Can you tell me what time you and Mr. Winslet arrived at the Pavillon Hotel?"

"I dropped him off at 10:32 that morning. Before you ask, I know the exact time as we had just left the bank down the street."

Where he got the cashier's check for Easton. "Did you enter the hotel with him?"

"I did not. Mr. Winslet instructed me to wait for him, so I parked in the hotel's lot until he called and asked me to pick him up at the front door."

"Which was when?"

"He called me at almost straight up eleven. I had to make a block to pick him up at the front entrance approximately five minutes later."

Nickolai grabbed the page Mrs. Winslet had included in the packet. According to the statements given by the waitress at the Crystal Room inside the hotel and the hotel's doorman, Lewis picked up Winslet at 11:05.

"So he gets in the car. Did he say anything to you?"

"Of course. I may be just a driver in your eyes, sir, but I liked Mr. Winslet and we spoke as friends."

A bit too defensive? "My apologies. What did he say?"

"He informed me that he had obtained the map he had purchased, was excited to have it authenticated, and instructed me to go straight to his bank."

"And you did?"

"Of course."

Nickolai swallowed the sigh. "But when you got there. . ."

"There was an armored truck parked in front where I would

normally let Mr. Winslet out. I asked Mr. Winslet if he would like me to drive around the block to give the armored vehicle time to move, and he agreed."

"So you drove around the block?"

"I did. The truck was still there, so I made another circle."

"And the truck was still there?"

"Yes. Mr. Winslet had a lunch meeting scheduled at noon, to which he didn't want to be late as punctuality was a pet peeve of his, so he asked me to let him out at the corner of Poydras and Loyola. I did." Lewis's voice hitched on the last two words.

"Did he have his briefcase with the map in it when he got out?"

"Of course. That was his whole purpose in going to the bank—to put the map in his safety-deposit box until he could give it to his appraiser."

"I have to be sure, Mr. Lewis—you're positive he had the briefcase with him when he exited the car?"

"I am more than sure, sir. I am two hundred percent positive. He had it in his left hand as he got out of the car because I held his right hand to assist him."

"So you helped him out of the car, then what?"

Lewis let out a dry cough. "Mr. Winslet told me he wouldn't be but a few moments and he walked toward the bank. Cars honked behind me and the armored truck was still in its place, so I got back in the car and pulled out. I intended to continue circling the block until Mr. Winslet exited the bank."

"And you did?"

"Yes, sir. I did. Three times." Which the car's GPS verified. "I had just pulled around for the fourth time when I noticed a crowd of people near the front of the bank. I pulled up to park, but the ambulance arrived. I whipped around in front of the armored truck still there, parked, and rushed toward the crowd. They had just put Mr. Winslet on the stretcher." Emotion filled the man's voice.

Nickolai understood. Better than most. "According to the police report, you spoke to the officers from the eighth district who arrived on the scene?"

"I did, then later went down to the station to sign my statement."

Which Nickolai had a copy of, but it wasn't much help. "I have a copy of your statement, Mr. Lewis."

"Then I'm not sure why we're having this discussion, Mr. Baptiste."

Nickolai wasn't exactly certain himself. "Can you think of anyone who wanted to harm Mr. Winslet?"

"No, sir. Bartholomew Winslet was one of the kindest, most gentle, generous men I have been fortunate enough to know. Do not misunderstand, he was smart and didn't allow himself to be taken advantage of, by no means, but his compassion and bigheartedness were very ingrained into who he was as a person. Publicly and privately."

Spoken as a friend, not an employee. Nickolai made a note. "Mr. Lewis, do you believe, then, that his murder had to do with the map more than him as a person?"

"The police didn't ask me that."

Nickolai stared out the truck window and waited, holding his breath. A moment passed. Then another.

"I do. I believe he was murdered to get the map."

Nickolai exhaled slowly. "Do you know who all knew he was going to pick up the map that morning?"

"His wife. Me, of course. The appraiser." A pause. "I would imagine his assistant and his secretary. Maybe someone else, but none that I'm aware of."

Nickolai wrote as quickly as Lewis spoke.

"The seller, obviously, and whomever they told. I would assume a significant other or relative, but I don't know. I would hope. . ."

"You would hope what, Mr. Lewis?"

"I would hope that the seller wouldn't have told the other interested party."

This was new. "Other interested party?"

"The other person who had been bidding on the map."

Nickolai's gut tightened, just as it had back when he'd been Chris's partner. "There was another person bidding on the map?"

"Indeed. Mr. Winslet almost had the map for eight hundred thousand, until the other bidder came in at nine. Mr. Winslet had to jump to a million dollars to secure the map."

Nickolai flipped through the papers he'd gotten from Mrs. Winslet. "I don't have any of that information. Did you tell this to the police?"

"No. They didn't ask me, so I didn't think it important. Is it?"

Probably. At the very least, it gave him another suspect. "Maybe. Do you know this other bidder's name?"

"I'm sorry, no. Mr. Winslet didn't know. Well, if he did, he never told me. He had simply expressed frustration in the price acceleration because of the bidder. The seller even made a point of telling Mr. Winslet that the other bidder was local to him, so he wouldn't have to worry about security in delivery. That's why Mr. Winslet paid for his travel expenses."

The seller would know who this other bidder was and if he, in fact, knew who Winslet was. Nickolai's "sixth sense" kicked in, and despite his best effort, excitement rose within his chest. He thanked Lewis for his time then called the number listed for Joel Easton. He received a recording that the cell phone number he dialed was unreachable. Had Easton used a burner phone? Very sketchy, but he glanced at the time on his cell.

He'd call this evening and see what he could find out. Depending on what he learned, he'd decide whether or not to actually take the case.

There was no denying his interest was piqued. Especially with the new information about the other bidder. And there was the money. . .no one could deny the payday on this one job alone was about what he normally made in a year.

He shoved the papers back into the envelope and stashed it in the console before climbing out of the truck. After locking the door, he made clean strides across the parking lot. This always felt like the longest walk ever. Like what he imagined a death row inmate's walk to the executioner's room would be.

Which was silly because he was only going to visit his sister. The only problem was, he didn't know which sister he'd see.

On one hand, there was his sweet Lisbeth. A decade and a half younger than him, Lisbeth had been his parents' midlife surprise, but she'd been the apple of their eye. Strong willed, determined, but she wrapped their dad around her little finger and only had to smile to get him to do whatever she wanted. She'd barely reached puberty when she'd begun to change.

And that was the other Lisbeth. The one who'd become more sullen. Withdrawn. Sulking. Then out-and-out rudeness. Hard for Mom and Dad to control. She'd cut herself. Nickolai had been convinced she'd only hurt herself to manipulate their parents. He'd already been a cop for many years, had extensive training. He'd seen it all. Thought he knew it all.

He'd been wrong. Dead wrong. And his mistake had cost his parents their lives.

"Good morning, Mr. Baptiste."

The front desk receptionist never failed to greet him as soon as he entered. His returning smile was automatic. "How's my sister this morning?"

"She's doing very well."

Despite himself, Nickolai let out the breath he hadn't realized he'd been holding; yet, he did the same thing every week.

"Go ahead down to the visiting room and I'll let the nurse know you're here."

Nodding his thanks, he did as instructed, just like he had every week for the past eight years. The routine remained constant, only Lisbeth's mood changed from week to week.

He took a seat in the chair he always sat in then decided to change and moved to the love seat where Lisbeth usually sat.

The door opened, and a nurse led his sister into the room.

Lisbeth was beautiful, but then again, she always had been. Long, wavy black hair that matched her dark, almond-shaped eyes. Today, though, there was a brightness to her eyes. And more pink in her cheeks.

She rushed toward him. Froze as her gaze darted from the chair to the love seat. Back to the chair.

Nickolai stood but didn't speak. If Dr. Bertrand thought she was a candidate for moving into a halfway house, a shift in their weekly seating arrangements shouldn't put her into a tailspin. If it did, he just saved himself forty thousand big ones.

The corners of Lisbeth's mouth turned up; then she flung her arms around his neck and hugged him tight. "Hey, Nicky."

He slowly hugged her back. It'd been a long time since she'd called him Nicky. "Hey, squirt." He kissed the top of her head. "How are you?"

"Good." She pulled back and sat on the love seat but left enough room for him to sit beside her.

He did, staring at her. Had she been this lively last week? Had she been improving every week and he just didn't notice?

"How's everything going?" He smiled as he asked.

"Good. Did you talk with Dr. Bertrand? Did he tell you about me getting to move?"

Ahh. So that was it. Nickolai didn't know how he felt about the good doctor telling her about the halfway house. What if he couldn't come up with the money? Wouldn't such a disappointment cause a major setback in Lisbeth's progress?

"He mentioned it." Nickolai proceeded with caution. "What do you think?"

"What do I think?" Her eyes lit up like he hadn't seen in years. Almost like he remembered them from Christmas when she was ten and she'd gotten the ten-speed she'd had her heart set on. "It's getting out of here, Nicky. It's a chance at a life. A real one, not a hospital one. What do you think I think?" Her giggle was infectious.

He hated to rain on her parade, but he needed to see her reaction.

"Do you think you're ready? Really?"

A shadow dropped over her eyes. "I'm doing everything I'm supposed to do. I take my medication without fighting them. I go to therapy. I talk about my feelings." Her eyes filled with moisture. "I'm doing my best to get better, Nicky. I think I am. Really, I do."

His heart thumped against his rib cage, and he pulled her against him and held her. He could feel her heart racing against his. He kissed her forehead. "Then I'm excited for you, Lisbeth."

And he'd do whatever it took to make it happen.

Chapter Five

"Thank you for meeting with me." Landry tried hard not to size up the woman in front of her, but she was failing miserably.

"Of course." Monica Courtland, Bartholomew Winslet's assistant, was about thirty-five, give or take a few years, stood maybe five feet tall, and wore her long blond hair back in a severe bun. Her eyes were overshadowed by the bulky, black-framed glasses perched on the bridge of her nose. "We're all trying to adjust to Mr. Winslet being gone."

"I understand." Landry wanted to be sympathetic, but it was hard to do when the entire offices of Winslet Industries seemed to have not missed a beat with its leader passing mere weeks ago.

Monica sat down behind her desk, her posture more rigid than Marcie's. "How may I help you?"

The preliminary introductions and polite exchanges were obviously concluded. Thank goodness Mrs. Winslet had let all the employees know she expected full cooperation from all of them regarding the investigation—from the police and the individuals she'd hired independently. Landry pulled out her iPhone and scanned her notes one last time. Quickly. "I see that you verified Mr. Winslet had arranged an appointment with his document appraiser for the week after he acquired the map. This was a common practice of his?" He would need an appraisal to carry insurance on it. "I mean, to acquire without an appraisal already in hand?" Seemed a little foolhardy for a man with Winslet's means and apparent habit of purchasing very expensive items.

Monica's smile strained. Maybe her bun was pulled back too tightly. "Mr. Winslet was a collector, as I'm sure you're aware. He collected various pieces of art, as well as rare documents of great historical value. While ideal to have each item appraised prior to acquisition, there have been times that the practicality of such couldn't be met."

The man owned—and had loaned out to various museums—works from some of the most notable artists of all time: Picasso, Van Gogh, Rene Magritte, Rembrandt. . .even a da Vinci. "Can you give me an example? Aside from this map?"

Monica flashed that polite smile of hers as she moved to her computer. "He has amassed previously unpublished writings of the likes of Benjamin Franklin and Edgar Allan Poe. Each of those, he had the source researched and verified. The documents themselves couldn't be appraised until three days after purchase." She typed on her keyboard then stared at her monitor. "When he acquired a rare additional page to the 1620 Mayflower Compact, he knew the seller personally. He waited two weeks to have that one appraised." She tapped her fingers over the keys again. "Just last year, he acquired an early version of the American's Creed by William Tyler Page penned in 1917. While he knew the seller by reputation, he had to wait days for his appraiser to return from vacation to review the document."

Landry nodded. She knew who Franklin and Poe were, for sure, but neither was as interesting as a real treasure map. "Did Mr. Winslet always use the same appraiser?"

"I've never known him to use anyone but Trenton Godfrey." She typed on the keyboard and squinted at the monitor. "And according to the records and insurance policies, all have Mr. Godfrey listed as the appraiser. Do you need his number?"

"No, thank you." She had it in the massive information file from Mrs. Winslet. "Can you tell me if it was Mr. Winslet's habit to put items he purchased in the bank's safety-deposit boxes until it could be appraised? At the same bank?"

Monica tilted her head. "Yes. He took no chances with such

important parts of our culture. Our patriotism. Mankind's history."

Except he'd taken a chance with the map. This one time.

"I understand Mr. Winslet had a lunch meeting scheduled here at the office for the day he died. Who was that with?"

"Phillip Fontenot." She didn't have to look up that name on the computer.

"That name's not familiar to me." She'd read the name in the file but couldn't place him. Landry leaned forward, resting her elbow casually on the desk. "Who's he?"

"Mr. Fontenot is Mr. Winslet's best friend, and he sits on the board here. He came here all the time to visit, even when there wasn't a board meeting." The emotionless mask slipped, and Monica's eyes glistened with moisture. "Those two laugh so loudly, even with the door shut." She smiled, easing the harshness of her face. "It's like they're college boys again when they're together."

Interesting. Everything Landry had read about Mr. Winslet gave no indication he was anything but mature, driven, determined, and rich. Her mental image of him didn't extend to acting like a boy. "So they had a lunch date that day?"

Monica nodded. "Mr. Winslet had it on his calendar for noon in his private suite here."

"Was that common?"

"Very. Mr. Winslet conducted business at various restaurants around town, but lunches with his personal friends were served here."

"Was that very often?"

Monica tapped on her keyboard again. "Looks like at least a couple of times a month."

So, common. *Think, Landry, think.* She needed to cover every person who was in contact with Winslet, or supposed to be, for the day he died. "Was Mr. Fontenot on time for lunch that day?"

"Let me check the key code log. . . . Every person who visits above the second floor is given a specific code to open the door to the area they're authorized to go to on that day," Monica explained. She pushed her glasses back up the bridge of her nose. "Looks like Mr. Fontenot accessed the private suite at approximately 11:45."

Monica peered over her computer screen at Landry. "I remember Mr. Fontenot's reaction when we received the call." She shook her head. "He was devastated. Almost broke down. Immediately left to go to Mrs. Winslet."

Just like Marcie had done when Landry's father had died. The value of friends. . . Landry didn't know what she would've done had Marcie not been there to keep her from falling apart.

"If there's nothing else, I should get back to work," Monica said.

"Can you tell me who Mr. Winslet depended on most in the company?"

"That's hard to say. There are several top executives who Mr. Winslet consulted with on a daily basis." The formality of Monica's tone was a little too much.

Landry smiled. "I'm sure there are." She leaned closer toward the desk. "You and I both know that the assistants are the ones who know everything. Am I right?"

Monica's cheeks pinked as she smiled and glanced at the floor. "Well, there's Mrs. Winslet, of course. She's the co-CEO." She leaned a little forward herself. "I guess she's the sole CEO now."

Landry nodded. "I suppose."

"Mr. Fontenot, of course, as well as the other board members."

"Are there many of them?" Landry interrupted.

Monica shook her head. "Aside from the Winslets, there's Mr. Fontenot, two of Mrs. Winslet's cousins, and Paul York."

"I've not met Mr. York." Truth be told, the name didn't even ring a bell with Landry. She didn't think she'd even read it in the packet from Mrs. Winslet.

"Oh, no one has. At least, not in person." Monica rested back in her chair. "He's a hermit. He videoconferences in for the board meetings."

Landry filed that little tidbit away. "Anybody else Mr. Winslet depended on?"

"Mr. Hauge, of course."

"Stan Hauge?" The VP Mrs. Winslet assigned to assist on the investigation. She was supposed to meet him here in a few minutes.

"Yes. Stan is a good man. Loyal. He looked after Mr. Winslet as best he could."

Odd phrasing. "What do you mean?"

"Oh, for the last several months, he'd been trying to take on more and more of Mr. Winslet's daily work. Kept telling Mr. Winslet that he worked too hard and should take some time off or retire and travel with Mrs. Winslet."

Very interesting. "But Mr. Hauge isn't on the board, is he?" He wouldn't be eligible to take over if something happened to Bartholomew if he wasn't a board member.

"Oh, no. He's just been with the company for a really long time." Monica glanced at her watch. "I don't mean to rush you, but I have a conference call in ten minutes that I need to prepare for."

"Of course." Landry stood. "Thank you for your time and information."

Monica stood as well, moving from behind her desk and gently leading Landry to the elevator. "Of course. If you need any further information, you know where to find me."

The elevator dinged and the doors opened, as if on cue. Maybe the CEO's assistant had a special button that could call the elevator to the floor immediately.

She stepped inside and smiled as the doors closed, Monica still standing in front of the elevator. Landry tried to recall everything in the packet on Monica Courtland. Just the barest of facts. She couldn't help but wonder how Monica and Winslet had gotten along. She was his personal assistant, after all, yet she didn't seem too terribly broken up when talking about him today. Wouldn't they have been a little less formal with one another? Surely she had to care about him. Maybe this was how she handled the grief.

Landry stepped off the elevator to find a man with thinning gray hair in a tired business suit waiting on her. "Ms. Parker?"

"Yes?"

"I'm Stan Hauge."

She felt a little guilty for probing Monica about him, but not too much. It was, after all, her job. In a way. "Nice to meet you." She shook his hand. Despite looking like a congenial grandfather, his handshake was firm.

He walked toward the front door of Winslet Industries. "I've made our hotel reservations in Arizona. I'm sorry to say there's a marathon in town so options for accommodations were very limited. We'll be staying at the Apache Junction Motel." His brow furrowed and nose wrinkled.

Landry held back the grin. "That's okay. Anything with a bed is fine." She'd stayed in some pretty rough places before, but clearly Stan wasn't accustomed to less than five stars.

"Well, they say the rooms have clean and comfortable beds." He smiled easily at her. "I've arranged for a rental as well. A nice sedan."

Landry stopped walking. "You can have the sedan. I'll need a Jeep or truck, whichever they have." She'd done her research and knew the terrain of some of the areas she might need to check out. A sedan would not do. "Besides, no offense, but I work best on my own."

Stan looked a little concerned but nodded. "I'll make the additional reservation before we leave. I apologize for the late flight as well, but there were some matters I needed to clear up here before leaving." He pushed open the front glass door and motioned Landry ahead of him.

"Not a problem. I can get a good night's rest and be ready to hit the ground running in the morning." She turned and shook his hand again. "Then I'll just see you at the airport this afternoon."

"What do you mean they're flying to Phoenix this afternoon?" Nickolai pressed the cell tighter against his cheek.

"Ms. Parker has a legitimate lead there, so she and my representative will be flying out this afternoon." Mrs. Winslet sounded so smug, or maybe she was just used to being in the know about everything. A lot of wealthy people had that attitude—force of habit. "Have you decided to take the job as well, Mr. Baptiste?"

No. Yes. Maybe. He'd tried to call Easton several times last night and this morning to no avail. He'd even called his landlord, who informed Nickolai that Easton had moved out a week ago and left no forwarding address. Might look suspicious, but he'd just taken in a million dollars. No reason to think he wouldn't improve his living situation.

"Mr. Baptiste?" Mrs. Winslet's tone made it clear she expected an answer.

He rolled his eyes, and his gaze landed on a picture propped on the end table—he and Lisbeth, taken just before she'd been admitted. Her arms were wrapped around his waist, her head resting against his chest. Both of them smiling brightly for the camera. He groaned silently. "Yes, ma'am. I was calling to let you know I'm heading to Phoenix myself. I, too, have a lead."

Something about the police not knowing about the second bidder—or Chris not giving him the information—made Nickolai's gut tighten. In his experience, his gut was usually on to something. He crossed the room to his hall closet and pulled out his duffel bag.

"Unfortunately, I don't think my representative can get you on their flight. Would you like him to get you on the first one in the morning if possible?"

He did a quick mental calculation. If he drove hard, he could get there in less than twenty-four hours. Probably closer to twenty, which would put him and Landry Parker on even footing, so to speak. "No, ma'am. I'd prefer to drive. I like to have my truck."

"Then I'll notify Stan to reserve you a room at the hotel that will serve as a central location while there."

"That's fine. He can call me with the information." He headed to the bedroom, threw the duffel on the bed, and started grabbing clothes from his closet to cram inside the bag.

"I look forward to hearing from you, Mr. Baptiste."

Nickolai tossed his phone on the bed and finished packing, his mind jumbled as he made a mental note to call the hospital and check on Lisbeth before heading out of town. First he needed to talk to his former partner.

Chris answered his cell on the second ring. "Two calls in one day. I'm impressed, Baptiste." He sounded much more relaxed than he had at the office.

"Yeah, well, I have a couple more questions before I leave town."

"Where are you going, my man?"

"Arizona."

Nickolai could feel the tension seeping over the line.

"Why are you going to Arizona?"

"The case." Nickolai only gave a short pause as he sat on the edge of his bed. "Easton's in the wind, Chris. I think he used a burner to contact Winslet and the police. He's moved out from his apartment, left no forwarding address, and when I called his place of employment, he quit before he came to New Orleans."

"Wouldn't you? I mean, if you were about to score a million big ones, wouldn't you quit your job?"

"Not until I had the money in hand. Neither would you."

Chris laughed. "That's cuz we're cynical, man. We've seen too much of the ugly."

"Maybe so." Did he show his hand? Maybe chance it? Nickolai stood and grabbed his duffel and carried it to the living room. He set it on the coffee table while he searched the hall closet for his jacket.

"What else?"

He grabbed his Windbreaker and shoved it into the outside pocket of the duffel. "What do you mean?"

"Come on, Baptiste. This is me you're talking to. What else do you have?"

"Look, I don't want to step on any toes in the department."

"I got you, Nickolai."

Yeah, this was Chris. His partner. His friend. Nickolai dropped to the couch. "There was another bidder on the map."

The slow intake of Chris's breath said it all. The police didn't know. "Who?"

"I don't know. Someone local to Easton. Jumped the price up to the million Winslet had to pay."

"How do you know this?"

"I interviewed Winslet's driver, Miles Lewis."

"I didn't read anything about that in the case notes."

"Then it was missed." Nickolai stood and paced the worn carpet of his living room. "Chris, what's going on with this case?"

"All I know is that the first responders called it in as usual. It was assigned to the dynamic duo." Benton Miller and Zayden Miller—not related—had earned the nickname by their highest-in-the-department homicides solved percentage.

Nickolai liked and respected both young men. "I can't believe they wouldn't have gotten the information in questioning. I didn't have to push Lewis hard to get the info."

"That's just it. The case was assigned to them, but before they could interview anyone besides the driver and officer with the armored truck, Captain Palmer took over the investigation."

That was very unusual. "Did he give any reason why?" Nickolai stopped pacing and leaned against the back of the recliner.

Chris snorted. "You know Palmer, he's a jerk. He just announced he'd be overseeing the investigation and that was that. He had a couple of uniforms type up the statements from everyone he interviewed. That's pretty much all the paperwork that's in the files."

Kid Palmer was more than a jerk. . .he embodied the definition of narcissist. Everyone in the eighth district knew he had his eye on the political arena and dared anyone to get in his way. Was it just the Winslet name, with all the money and power that came with it, that had pulled him to take over the case, or was there something else?

"Miller and Miller were pretty miffed to have the case pulled from them, that's for sure."

They were younger, new detectives who wanted to make names for themselves. But they played by the book. "I can imagine. Any chance they're working off the books?" It's what Nickolai would do. Matter of fact, he and Chris had done that very thing several times in their nine-year partnership.

"Officially? No, of course not."

Which meant they were. "Maybe I'll call them when I get back in town. Been a while since I've seen the dynamic duo. I think we're due for catching up."

"Hey, I think we should get together for a few drinks and catching up. When you get home, of course."

"Sounds like a plan." Nickolai scooped up his duffel bag.

"You take care, Baptiste."

Nickolai held the phone tighter. The message was deeper than the words themselves. "I will."

"And call if you need me. I mean that."

"Thanks." Nickolai let out a steadying breath. "I'll call you when I get back to town."

He slipped his cell into his back jean pocket, locked the front door, and headed to his truck. He'd left the envelope filled with papers in there. Nickolai tossed his duffel into the backseat of the extended cab and climbed behind the steering wheel. He set his cell's mapping GPS to Apache Junction, Arizona. It showed a driving time of twenty-two hours, forty-seven minutes. Good thing he'd just had the oil changed last week.

Starting the truck's engine, he had but one last thought: he'd gotten information the police didn't have that was relatively easy to get, but he knew no one else had spoken with Miles Lewis in the last twenty-four hours. Knowing that, he couldn't help but wonder: What was Landry Parker's lead that was taking her to Arizona?

Chapter Six

"This cannot be the only establishment that has any vacancies." Stan Hauge slammed the door to the sedan and stared at the Apache Junction Motel.

Landry pressed her lips together as she shut the door to the rental Jeep and leaned against it. Even in the dark of night, the motel looked, at best, like a hokey, run-down, sad place. Two rows of buildings with the parking lot between them boasted plain cream walls with terra-cotta-colored accents. While she had no problem with the accommodations, she could only imagine the offensiveness Stan felt. On the plane ride and layover, she'd gotten to know him just a little, enough to recognize he'd become accustomed to the finer aspects of life, courtesy of Winslet Industries.

"You said there was a marathon going on this weekend?" Landry slipped her purse's strap over her shoulder and moved toward the motel office door. The bag was a little heavier than usual since she'd pulled her 9mm out of her checked bag as soon as she'd gotten the Jeep.

"This is ridiculous. We can't stay here. It's probably infested with roaches." Stan's lip curled as he spoke.

Landry pushed down the laugh. "Aw, come on, it isn't that bad. Just needs a little updating, but it looks clean."

"Looks like it needs to be condemned," he muttered under his breath, but he followed her into the office.

She smiled as a bell over the door announced their late arrival, then stopped so suddenly that Stan bumped into her.

Nickolai Baptiste stood, a duffel bag on the floor beside his chair.

"I was about to give up on y'all making it."

Why was he here? Better yet, how did he get here before her?

Stan stepped around her. "Forgive my tardiness. I didn't realize we had to wait for a shuttle to take us from the concourse to the rental agency. There were complications there." He pulled out a credit card and advanced to the counter to speak to the older woman leaning there who was watching their interaction with great interest.

Landry turned her back to the woman and Stan and collided with Nickolai's smug expression. "I thought you weren't taking the case."

He shrugged. "Changed my mind."

"Funny how money can compromise someone's ideals and perception." She'd seen it many times over in her military career. Good, honest soldiers who'd gone down the slippery slope of exchanging their moral fortitude to cash in on a little good fortune. Ruining their careers and their lives.

He narrowed his eyes. "I'm not compromising anything."

Yeah. Sure. Right. "What happened to interfering in a police investigation?"

"I've checked in with the police about the case. I was a detective there for almost a decade, remember?"

Great. So he'd have inside information that she didn't have access to. "Glad you got that all worked out with your conscience."

He opened his mouth, but Stan rejoined them. He handed them their keys. Real keys, not electronic cards. "Our rooms are all next to each other." He paused, looking from Landry to Nickolai, then back to Landry. "I'll take the room in the middle as we'll use it as the base of operations, if we need it."

Landry took the key Stan offered her and mumbled thanks.

Nickolai broke eye contact with Landry and accepted his key from Stan. "How does a base of operations work, exactly?" He fell into step beside Stan, leaving Landry to trail them.

She turned and smiled at the lady behind the counter. "Thank you, ma'am."

The woman's face lit up as she returned the smile. "You're welcome. You have a good night."

Landry followed Stan and Nickolai into the parking lot. Of course, his truck was just two spaces from where she'd parked the Jeep. How had she not recognized it? She needed to get to the top of her game.

"So any on-site expenses, you just let me know and I'll take care of them," Stan was saying as Landry stepped up next to him. "I'm here to assist in any way I can, and to liaise with Winifred as needed, of course."

"I don't expect I'll be needing any assistance." Nickolai wore his cockiness as shamelessly as his smugness.

But he'd missed the casualness of Stan's reference to Mrs. Winslet. His boss, but there was a softness to his tone as he'd said her name. Not exactly a caress, but a slow gentleness. Interesting. Landry smiled as sweetly as she could muster, considering her exhaustion from a long day of traveling and the frustration of seeing her competition. "If you gentlemen will excuse me, I'm going to call it a night. I have some things to do yet and a busy day tomorrow." Without waiting for an answer, she climbed into the Jeep and started it.

She checked the number of the motel room, did a quick scan to see where it was located, and then drove the short way to park in front of the door. She'd barely parked and opened the back door to grab her suitcase when Nickolai appeared at her side. "Would you like me to help you with that?"

She slammed the back door shut and locked the Jeep. "No, thanks. I've got it." She eyed his duffel slung over his shoulder. "Do you need any help with that?"

He smiled, nearly disarming her with its high wattage. "I'm good."

"Well then, good night." She marched to the door and unlocked it before stepping inside. She pulled the door shut and locked the door as quickly as she could muster, thankful all the while for the darkness of night that hid the blush burning her cheeks. She flipped on the lights. Tossed her purse on the table.

Why did the man infuriate her so?

Before she could answer herself, her cell phone chimed. She grinned at the caller ID. "Hey, Marcie."

"You were supposed to call when you got settled in."

"I actually just stepped into my motel room." She flung her bag on the dresser beside the television set.

"How is it?"

Landry glanced around. The room was bigger than she'd imagined. Clean. Stan would be happy—not a roach in sight. "Good."

"You sound tired."

"I am. The flight was uneventful, but long. The layover was brutally boring. Had a snafu at the rental place, but got it all ironed out." She sat down in the chair, kicked off her shoes, and propped her feet up on the edge of the bed. "Then we get here and guess who's waiting on us?"

"Who?"

"Nickolai Baptiste."

Marcie's quick intake came loudly over the connection. "Well, isn't that interesting? I thought you said he wasn't going to take the case."

"That's what I asked him. Apparently, he changed his mind."

"Money often has a way of doing that."

Landry pulled the band from her hair and rubbed her head, loosening her curls. "That's exactly what I said."

"What time is your appointment tomorrow?"

"I'm supposed to meet with the seller at twelve thirty." Landry grabbed her notebook—a gift from her father—and opened it to her notes.

"What's this person's name again?"

Landry smiled to herself. "They don't give out names, Marcie. He'll know me because I'll be wearing a red flannel shirt and my hair in a ponytail."

"I still don't like this."

"We're meeting in a very public place. Cobb's Restaurant, a few blocks from the motel. It's a family diner–type of place and should be pretty busy during lunchtime. Especially with all the people in town for the marathon."

"I don't like it."

Landry chuckled. "I know you don't, but it must be done. Just think, Marcie, it could all be over with tomorrow. If the map's real, I get it, return it to Mrs. Winslet, and collect fifty g's." And leave Nickolai Baptiste eating the dust in her wake.

"How will you know if the map's real?"

"Of course there's no way to know if it's really real until an appraiser checks it out, but I did my research. There are a few things I know to look for." Her friend in the art world had been kind enough to get a detailed description from the original seller's correspondence with Mr. Winslet.

"Okay. But if you think it's real, how do you plan to get it to bring it to Mrs. Winslet?"

"A minor detail, Marcie. I can always call in the local police here." It shouldn't come to that. Once she felt like she was looking at the real map, she planned to pull her gun and credentials and that usually had the criminals running off and leaving whatever she wanted. She wouldn't, however, advise Marcie of such.

"Sounds too dangerous. Remember, Mr. Winslet was murdered for this."

"I'll be careful. I promise."

"You and I have very different definitions of being careful."

Landry laughed. "I'll call you tomorrow. I need to unpack and take a shower. Flying makes me feel grimy."

Now it was Marcie's turn to chuckle. "Okay. Call me if anything else comes up."

Landry disconnected the call, stood, and stretched. Her muscles complained about the flight and lack of activity. She should take a quick jog. Just to get a feel for the area and get enough exercise that she'd be able to get some sleep. Maybe if she exerted herself enough she would be too tired to think about Nickolai Baptiste.

Doubtful, but she could try.

The nerve of Landry Parker: implying money would shift the direction of his moral compass.

Nickolai tossed his shaving kit on the bathroom counter. If he found even the slightest connection with anything here to the murder investigation, he'd call the police captain himself, no matter how much he personally disliked the man.

Compromising ideals? He didn't compromise on anything, but especially not on anything that could cast a shadow on his integrity. He shook his head as he set his duffel on the table and sat in the chair, not sure what to do with himself. Nickolai had tried to locate Joel Easton several times while he'd waited for Stan Hauge and her to show up. No luck.

His cell phone rang. He checked the caller ID and let out a breath. Earlier, he'd texted a woman he'd gone out with a couple of times. She was a PI, handled mostly divorce dirt, but she was thorough and honest. Even though they hadn't connected, they'd remained friends. "Hi, EmmaGrace. Thanks for getting back to me so quickly."

"Yeah, you owe me for this one, Nick."

His gut tightened. "Yeah?"

"Yeah. Finally found your Joel Easton."

Nickolai remained silent. EmmaGrace liked to do things her way, in her time. That included relaying information. He grabbed a pen and the notepad.

"Easton hasn't made any significant purchases since returning to Arizona. However, my sources tell me you should check out Ironwood Cancer and Research Center in Gilbert."

"Gilbert, Arizona?"

"It's twenty-something minutes from Apache Junction where Easton lived."

"Okay. Who should I check for there? Easton?"

"Yes, but not Joel. Look for an Abigail Easton."

Easton had never married. "Sister?"

"Mother."

"Ah." He wrote notes quickly. "Thanks, EmmaGrace."

"Just remember, you owe me, Nick."

He tapped the pen on the notepad. His mom had cancer. That could explain a lot. A whole lot.

Nickolai opened his phone's GPS and searched for the name of the cancer place. In seconds he had the full address of the facility. He'd be making a trip to Gilbert bright and early in the morning.

Nickolai turned the television on and flipped through the channels. Nothing held his interest. Too much driving. He dropped to the worn carpet and did a couple reps of push-ups. As usual, his right shoulder seized. No matter how much physical therapy he tortured himself with, or how hard he worked to keep his range of motion at the highest level, it was no match for the wad of scar tissue balled between his shoulder joint and collarbone.

Maybe some fresh air would help clear his mind. At least enough that he could take a hot shower and crash. Some nights, that was the best he could do—wear himself out entirely so he had no choice but to sleep, even if it was the most restless sleep known to man. The worst nights always ended with his nightmare of flames jerking him awake.

He opened the door. It might be February, but Arizona was about the same as New Orleans this year. He slipped on his light jacket. He locked the door behind him and stepped around a patio chair. Every room had a plastic chair sitting by the door, cluttering the walkway. He noticed both Stan and Landry had their curtains drawn. Good. Better for safety that way.

Nickolai took in a deep breath. The spicy scent of creosote and sage bushes assaulted him, but in a strangely comforting manner. Almost familiar. He turned and headed toward the road, Apache Trail. There was quite a bit of traffic, probably not usual for a regular Thursday night. But with the marathon. . .

He turned right, to the empty dirt parking lot beside the motel. There were no security or streetlights burning, but the Arizona sky blazed with stars and the Taurus the Bull constellation, and an almost full moon, giving Nickolai plenty of light for his walk. After all, he'd heard the horror stories about snakes in the area, and he wasn't keen on meeting one face-to-face his first night here.

Picking up his pace, Nickolai walked along the back of the motel's rooms. He took note of access to the rooms, a habit he couldn't shake after so many years on the police force. The air-conditioning units were definitely the biggest point of vulnerability. He made long strides down the back row of the motel. The cool air did seem to clear his mind. Maybe now a hot shower would relax him enough for sleep to come.

Nickolai went around the back side of the motel and moved quickly toward his room. Only then did he notice a figure in the shadows. Was that someone by the Jeep Landry had rented?

He crouched and moved closer. Silently. Stealthily. He couldn't see the figure anymore. Where had he gone? Nickolai risked straightening. An unmistakable coldness crept over him as a voice from behind him said, "Who are you, and what are you doing by my Jeep?"

He whipped around. Froze. Landry stood facing him, a 9mm looking comfortable in her hands. "You!" She lowered her weapon and glared at him. "What are you doing creeping around out here?"

"What are you doing with a gun?"

Even in the dark he could make out her widened eyes. "Seriously? Don't you carry?"

"Usually." His Beretta was in his jacket pocket, but he wouldn't pull it unless absolutely necessary. Especially since. . .

"So what are you doing by my Jeep?"

"I saw you but didn't know it was you. I thought it was somebody else, so I was checking it out for you."

She crossed her arms over her chest. "Who else would it be?"

"I don't know. That's why I was checking it out." Did she have to be so insufferably annoying? "What are you doing out here?"

"Not that it's any of your business, but after a day of traveling, I needed to stretch a little, so I took a quick jog. What are you doing out here?"

"Same thing."

"Oh. Well." She glanced around, cleared her throat, and then took a step toward the row of rooms. "I guess that's it, then. Stay away from my Jeep."

He shook his head and smiled to himself in the dark. "No problem. Good night."

"Yeah. Good night." She brushed past him and unlocked her room. She cut a glance at him over her shoulder before she hustled the door shut behind her.

Nickolai dug out his room key from his pocket, resisting the urge to peek at the window as he passed her room. He needed to do what he came here to do then get as far away from Landry Parker as possible.

Chapter Seven

Late for a sale? Even in the black market world, being late to a sell-meet was considered bad form.

Cobb's Restaurant and Lounge was smaller than she'd imagined, but its red walls and friendly staff welcomed her. She especially liked the chicken curtains, which she knew her mom would've just had a fit over. Loving roosters and hens both, Mom had had quite a collection. From dish towels to salt and pepper shakers, as long as there was a chicken present, Mom would love it.

Landry glanced around the restaurant again. It'd filled up fast. People in for the marathon, the waitress had told her when she'd requested a table in the corner. She'd been early for the meeting, of course. Picking out the best and most private table, she set her cell phone in her front pocket so she could record without being obvious, and watched every person who came into the restaurant. She checked the time again: 12:35. Officially five minutes late.

Very bad form for a seller. He was either new to the game or would turn out to be a no-show. Neither boded well for a successful recovery plan.

The waitress appeared. "Would you like another Dr Pepper?"

Landry shook her head. "No thanks. I'm good for now."

The waitress shrugged and hurried away. The noise level continued to rise, nearly giving Landry a headache. Or maybe it was the climate change. She pinched the bridge of her nose.

"Are you the one here about the map?" A man plopped down on the opposite side of the booth. The black vinyl creaked under his weight.

Landry sat up straight, taking in every detail of the man across from her. Maybe twenty-five years old. Grease-weighted black hair hung in waves down his back. Acne-pocked face and sunken eyes that were wide and glassy, yet dull. Cracked lips. Cigarette smoke–stained teeth.

"And you are?" Landry leaned forward and pressed the record button discreetly on her cell.

"My name's not important."

"It is if I'm doing business with you." She straightened, pushing her posture to be like Marcie's. "I'm Landry Parker." She forced herself to extend her hand over the table.

He hesitated then shook her hand and withdrew his quickly, but not before she spied the tattoo on his wrist of a skull and crossbones. "I'm Allen. Allen Edgar."

The name slipped off his tongue easily. Either it was his real name or he had a lot of practice in giving an alias.

Landry would just bet it was his real name. "So, Allen. About that map."

"Do you have the hundred grand? That's a bargain, you know. The mine is worth a lot more."

The waitress appeared at the table. "Can I get you something?"

"No. No." He dropped his head.

Ah, so he was local enough that he was afraid of being recognized. Landry shook her head at the waitress. "We're good. Thank you."

When the waitress had left, Landry focused back on Allen. "Did you bring the map?"

He lifted his head. "Not until you have the money."

She smiled. "You requested cash. That's a lot of cash to carry around."

"Like I said, it's a steal."

"I don't want to take the map until I pay for it, of course. I just need to verify it before I go to the bank and get the cash." She leaned back against the booth, shifting to try to make sure her phone recorded well. "You can't expect me to pay that much money for something without seeing even a glimpse of it."

"That's a bargain price."

This runaround needed to come to a screeching halt. Now. "If you really have the map, yes, it's a good price, but if you don't have the map, then you aren't getting a dime."

He stared at her with hooded eyes.

She didn't blink. Didn't even breathe.

"Well, I guess I can let you look at it." He glanced around the restaurant. "For just a minute. Until you pay me."

She nodded slowly, not breaking eye contact with him. "You have it, here, Allen?"

"Just outside. In my car." He jerked his head toward the window with the chicken curtains. The parking lot sat just beyond them. He moved to stand. "Come on."

Landry slipped out of the booth, stopping her waitress on the way out. "I'll be right back. Hold my booth, please." She gave the waitress a ten then followed Allen out of the restaurant. When she'd arrived, there had been several cars in the lot but plenty of empty spaces. Now the parking was full. She was a little relieved that it was daylight as she trailed him to his car. That was her whole point in talking to the waitress—so Allen knew someone expected her back inside.

She worked to keep up the conversation. "So, where did you get the map?"

He shrugged and led her toward a well-used, road-worn old Ford Mustang. "A friend of a friend of a friend. You know how it goes."

She did, but not in the way he meant. "So you got it and posted it for sale?" She kept herself on alert and aware of her surroundings. Walking between cars parked too close together, she made sure to leave herself plenty of distance from him.

He stopped at the Mustang and opened the trunk with the key. "It's here."

Landry approached cautiously as he pulled out a folder from a backpack. The edges of the folder had definitely seen better days.

Much better days. He opened the folder and pulled out a piece of paper about eleven inches by fourteen.

She took a step closer. "May I see it?"

He hesitated then handed it to her. She leaned in to inspect it, but also to allow her cell to focus. At least, she hoped it was still on and would get a shot of the map. She held it almost directly in front of the camera, inspecting it for Allen's benefit.

Cream parchment-feeling paper. . .yellowed, but by color, not by age. Black marks, trails of dashes. Writing in black ink, but hard to decipher. Landry could make out the words *willow, first water, weaver's needle*—

Allen snatched the map out of her hands. "You've seen enough."

She needed to decide how to play this. Clearly, the map was a copy, and not even a good one. Just a photocopy. While horrified that someone would risk damaging the original by using a copier, she could understand someone not wanting Allen Edgar to carry around the original. No doubt he was nothing more than a delivery person. If she called him on the copy, he might spook and she'd lose her only lead at this point.

On the other hand, if she promised to give up the money on just a copy, the seller might think she was an idiot and give her a copy instead of the original. Or give her nothing.

"So, the money?" Allen clearly didn't care about her internal dilemma.

"Where's the original?"

"This is it." He tapped the folder where he put the paper. He shoved it all back into the backpack in the trunk and slammed the lid.

"That's a copy."

"It's the map."

Clearly, he didn't understand. "That's a copy of the map. That's not the original."

Confusion sank into every pockmark on his face. "It's the map."

Oh. Mercy. He didn't understand. She hadn't considered this possibility. "The description you posted was for the original map, not a copy."

He shook his head. "Look, you know how to reach me. You've seen it. One of these went for a million dollars, so a hundred grand is a steal. When you get the money, let me know." He brushed past her to the driver's door and climbed behind the wheel. "You have until five tomorrow afternoon, and then I'll relist it and sell it to someone else." He started the car and squealed off, his tires kicking up a few loose rocks in his wake.

Great. Now what?

Landry pulled out the phone from her pocket, stopped the recording, and saved it. She started it, fast-forwarding to the map. She hit PAUSE. It looked almost as clear on the phone's video as it had on the copy she'd held. At least she had that.

But precious little else at the moment.

She trudged back into the restaurant, and thankfully, her booth still sat empty, save for her Dr Pepper getting watered down. She stared at the picture.

"That must be a popular thing these days." The waitress stood by the edge of the booth, looking over Landry's shoulder.

"Really? Why's that?"

"Another guy had one just like that in here earlier this week."

Had Allen suckered in someone? "Just like this?"

The waitress nodded. "But it looked really old. It was in one of those plastic, protective sleeves."

Like the original would be. Landry tried not to appear too excited. "Are you sure?"

"Yeah." She straightened. "He tried really hard to be secretive about it. As soon as I would walk over, he'd try to cover it up." She chuckled. "As if I would want another map of the Superstitions. Everybody knows how to find Weaver's Needle."

"Do you know who he was?"

The waitress shook her head. "Not from around here, that much I know. There are a lot of people in town for the marathon this week, though."

Disappointment threatened to strangle Landry. "Do you remember what he looked like? Anything distinguishing about him?"

The waitress shifted her small tray to the other hip. "He was older. Maybe sixty or so? I'm not really good with ages. He was going bald. What hair he had left was gray and really thin."

"Nothing else?"

"Sorry, we were really busy that day. He paid in cash. Only left me a ten percent tip. Oh, he asked me where he could buy a tent and supplies."

"Oh?"

"Yeah. He said he planned on camping out in the Superstition area." The waitress shrugged. "I told him to try Stop N Shop Military Surplus just down the road."

"Thanks." Landry left a hefty tip and slipped out. She needed to see about some camping supplies.

He couldn't ask for a more beautiful afternoon. Seemed like everyone and their brother was in town for the marathon this weekend. Everywhere around Apache Junction this morning had been buzzing about the event's festivities that would kick off this evening. They'd sure put up enough signs on every street corner in town. Guess it was their annual big event, bringing in tourist money.

To Nickolai, that meant it brought in more crime. He always hated Mardi Gras at home. People going crazy, doing the stupidest stunts they'd never even dream of doing except during carnival season. There were no off-duty officers in New Orleans during Mardi Gras. It was all hands on deck, 24-7.

Nickolai drove the thirty minutes to Gilbert, Arizona, with his truck windows down. The fresh air kept him focused. He certainly hadn't slept well last night. He wanted to blame his sleeplessness on the sounds of motel room doors slamming and the occasional outburst of laughter, but in truth, it was the memory of Landry Parker pulling a gun on him that had him tossing and turning. The bed had been extremely comfortable at the motel, but not enough to cull the image of Landry's stare from his mind. He'd seen her briefly this morning at the Starbucks down the road, but she'd driven off before he'd even gotten his coffee. Probably best. He had his own plans for the day.

Plans that currently had him exiting off the 202 Loop in Gilbert.

A couple more turns and he pulled into the parking lot of the Ironwood Cancer and Research Center. Nickolai strode in through the front glass doors as if he belonged. A young receptionist looked up from her computer screen. Not a single blond hair moved out of place. "Hello. May I help you?"

"Yes, ma'am. I'm here to see Mrs. Abigail Easton."

She tilted her head to the side and gave a puzzled smile. "Are you family?"

And here's where it got dicey. He smiled and lowered his gaze to meet hers over the modern counter space. "I actually need to see Joel, her son. I understand he's here with her."

She glanced at her computer monitor and typed on a flat keyboard that made no sound. "Why, yes, Mr. Easton is having an early dinner with his mother in her room."

He smiled. "Good, then I had the right information." Nickolai leaned forward and spoke in a stage whisper. "I was worried I'd messed up the time and Joel would be most upset with me."

She returned his smile. "I can't imagine Mr. Easton being upset. He's so kind and gentle."

"Well, when it comes to his mom, of course." Nickolai hoped he wasn't off base.

The receptionist nodded. "Her room is right down this hall, take the first right, then it's the second door on your left." She pointed him in the right direction. "Her name is on the door. You won't miss it."

He nodded. "Thank you, ma'am." Nickolai hurried off the way she'd pointed, before she realized he had never met Joel Easton, had no clue if he was kind and gentle when it came to his mother, and had no business here.

Except that he did.

Nickolai hesitated just outside the door to Mrs. Easton's room. Intrusion was rude, no matter how justified. He knocked softly and heard the muffled response to enter. He knocked again, just a little harder. Again came the response from inside. He remained in the hall.

The door opened, and Joel Easton stood in the doorway. "Yes?" He looked exactly as he had in the picture taken as a still from the hotel's surveillance video.

"Mr. Easton, I'm Nickolai Baptiste from New Orleans, looking into the details of Bartholomew Winslet's murder." It was times like these that he wished he still had a badge to pull.

Joel glanced over his shoulder. "I'll just be a minute, Momma." He joined Nickolai in the hall, pulling her bedroom door closed behind him. "What are you doing here? I've told the police everything I know already."

"I'm actually focusing more on the map as I believe it's the motive for Mr. Winslet's murder." Nickolai noticed the two nurses staring at them from down the hall. "Is there a place we can speak privately?"

Joel nodded. He led Nickolai down another hall and out a side door. He turned as soon as they cleared the sidewalk, moving to a set of benches almost behind the building. "I don't know what I can do to help you." He sat on one of the benches.

"You can answer a couple of questions for me. How did you get the map?" Nickolai pulled out the small notebook from his back pocket. They said you could take the guy off the force but could never get the force out of the guy. He sat on the other bench, facing Easton.

"It's been in my family for generations. You know about the legend, right?"

Nickolai cocked his head. He did, of course, but he wanted to hear it from Easton's angle.

Easton sighed. "Long story short: The one person who had found the mine was dying. He was taken to Julia Thomas's house for her to try and nurse him back to health. She tried to help him, so he drew her a rough map to the mine. He died. Julia Thomas was my ancestor. The map's been handed down in the family."

"So why not have it authenticated a long time ago?"

"Seriously, man? Because then everyone could find the mine."

Nickolai would come back around to that one. "Why did you sell it now?"

Easton flicked his hand toward the building. "My mom. There's a new treatment plan going on here, with some really promising results. But it doesn't come cheap. To get her on the plan, I had to get a lot of money fast." He shrugged. "That's all I had. I sold it and everything I had to get her the treatment, and in just a week, I can see her progress, so it was worth it."

This was way too familiar. Nickolai shifted on the hard bench, looking anywhere but at Easton. He and the man seemed to have too much in common at the moment as Nickolai forced himself not to think about Lisbeth and why, exactly, he'd taken this case.

A bird hopped on the ground near the concrete curb.

Nickolai stared at his notes. "Why not uncover the mine a long time ago?" Like back before the Superstitions had been incorporated into the National Park Service so it was government owned. Now, if any gold or anything was found, it would be the property of the United States government.

Easton stared at the bird, hopping along, pecking at little specks on the ground. "We've all looked. At least I know my uncles did. And my grandfather. He searched so hard that my grandmother threatened to divorce him if he didn't stop."

"Then maybe the map isn't real?"

"I can't say for sure, of course, but we've traced it all the way back to Julia. There's no reason to believe it's not real."

"Except that no one can actually find the mine." Many believe there was never a mine to find—that the gold attributed to the mine was actually derived from the Peraltas Cache.

Easton clapped his hands, and the bird flew off. "Because it's hidden well and even with the map, it's vague. You still have to actually figure the map out. Old Dutchman wasn't going to make it easy to find, even on his deathbed, when he drew it out for Julia."

"Do you have a copy of the map? Not the original, of course, but a copy?" It would help to have an idea what it looked like.

Easton dipped his head for a moment. "I did, but when I sold all my furniture and moved, it was lost." He stared at Nickolai. "Sorry I'm not much help."

Never mind, a copy of the map wasn't the issue. "What can you tell me about the other bidder?"

"Other bidder?"

"The one bidding for the map against Mr. Winslet. Who was he?"

Easton's cheeks turned pink.

"He has a motive to kill Winslet for the map. I need a name." Nickolai might not be a detective anymore, but he'd perfected the intimidating tone.

"There isn't one."

Nickolai leaned forward. "What?"

"My buddy hacked into Art Source and created a profile of an opposing bidder." Easton sat up straight and crossed his arms over his chest. "I'm not proud of what I did, but I needed to get the price up to be able to afford Mom's treatment."

"Who is Art Source?"

Easton brushed invisible crumbs from his lap. "The company that listed the map for sale. All the buyers there are verified, so it's a legitimate place to sell, even if their fee is crazy."

"Fee?"

"Art Source gets a percentage of the selling cost. Four percent. Well, four percent of a million dollars is forty grand, so you can see why I needed to get Mr. Winslet to pay the highest price possible."

Nickolai wanted to be outraged, but he couldn't muster the emotion. "So this friend of yours who hacked into Art Source. . .he knew about the final bid?"

"Of course. That was the whole point in him hacking."

Years of experience screamed inside Nickolai. "He just hacked for you, as a favor?"

"Well, I gave him some money."

"How much?"

"Ten grand."

Nickolai tightened his grip on the pen. The guy knew Easton had gotten a million for the map. Knew Easton had paid a forty-thousand-dollar fee to the company. And Easton assumed ten thousand would be enough for his friend who made it all possible? Nickolai knew better. Friendships in illegal activities did have limits. "What's his name? Did he know when you were meeting Winslet to give him the map?"

Easton hesitated.

"Look, I'm trying to keep you in the clear here, but you've got to help me. The person who killed Winslet knew when he picked up the map. Knew it in enough time to plan to steal it. If you know anything... you don't want to be charged with obstruction of justice, do you?" He hadn't exactly said he was with the police. He'd only implied.

"Allen wouldn't do that. Besides, he didn't go to Louisiana."

Allen. "Are you sure about that? Positive?"

Easton's eyes widened a little. "You don't know Allen. He rarely gets out of his mom's basement. She has to force him to shower. The guy's a hermit."

Classic. "I'll check it out here, and if he never left, then no one in New Orleans has to know, okay? Give me his full name."

"Allen Edgar."

"His address?" Nickolai scribbled as Easton gave the information.

Easton stood. "That's all I know. I need to get back inside."

Nickolai stood as well and handed his business card to the other man. "Call me if you think of anything else about the case."

Easton nodded.

"I hope your mother continues to get better."

Just like he hoped for the best with Lisbeth.

The Preparation

I know that with the help of the spirits I can do and I will do. I depend on the Creator and spirits. Everything they show me is for the people's protection. Oh, Grandfather, I am so weak and pitiful. Help me for the sake of your people." Gopan lifted his head from his prayer. His fingers trembled slightly as he stood, carefully lifting the pipe he'd chosen.

His pipe's stem had been hand-hollowed—a representation of man being hollow to allow the breath of the Creator to move through without any restrictions. The prayers through the pipe were sent on the wings of the spirit directly to the source, the Great Mystery, so as to be heard clearly. The pipe, like the ritual Gopan was about to undergo, was holy and sacred.

He slowly offered the pipe to the north. Then the south, followed by the east and west. Each time, Gopan took one step to turn, lifted the pipe, and nodded. When he finished, he directed it to the sky father above and the earth mother below.

The medicine man extended his hands. Their traditions were part of who they were in the past, who they were today, and who they would be until the end of days.

Gopan's heart fluttered as he presented the pipe to the medicine man. He touched the elder man's hands and then brought the pipe back to his chest. Slowly. Reverently. He repeated his movements again. And a third time.

And the final, fourth time.

The medicine man accepted the pipe, also accepting the responsibility for Gopan's journey to speak to the spiritual beings.

The altar had already been prepared with prayer flags, a piece of flannel cloth, and the chokecherry tree, used because they represent the bittersweet nature of life. They are the blood of life, the blood that ties the tribe together and unifies the world family. The cherry itself, representing the pituitary gland that allows the travel from the physical into the spiritual world and back. The tobacco ties on a continuous string, with specific colors in a particular order, fluttered in the Arizona breeze.

Gopan ran a finger over the items laid out on the altar: an eagle feather that represents the eagle who carries prayers as he soars to the highest heaven, who can see great distances, and who can communicate between the physical and spiritual worlds; a peace of a conch shell that represents the ocean, which is the salt of life and reflective of mankind's beginnings; and a blanket for his protection on his vision quest.

The sun dipped, signaling the onset of sunset. Gopan moved to the seven large stones he'd gathered. On each, he made a circle with the clay paint. The circle representing the loop of life—no beginning or end. . .the beginning of cellular consciousness. It represented the light that enters into that cell.

Gopan and the medicine man moved, placing the stones into the fire pit prepared and lit hours ago. The fire would burn for the duration of Gopan's journey. All the elements were represented: earth, fire, water, and air.

Today was a good day to speak to the Great Spirit.

Chapter Eight

Yep, a total waste of time." Landry sat in the plastic chair outside her motel room, talking to Marcie on the phone while watching the groups of people mill about the parking lot. "But the good news is I got a couple of decent screenshots of the copy of the map."

"Why is that good news?"

"Because now I know what it looks like." Well, that and. . .it was a treasure map, even if it was a copy.

"Good. I mean, since you've got no more leads there, you'll be heading home soon. Tomorrow?"

"Actually, I talked to a salesman at that military surplus store." She resisted the urge to shake her head as a couple of men in those skintight jogging shorts nodded at her. Landry stood and ducked into her motel room. "He remembered the man and the map. He confirmed it's most likely the original. He said the man bought a tent and camping gear and mentioned camping near Weaver's Needle. That's pretty much where the map shows the location of the mine to be."

"You're going to go look for this man? Is Nickolai still there?"

"I have to check it out, Marcie. I was hired to recover the map. That means even if I have to follow someone into the mountains."

"You need to be really careful, Landry."

"I will. You know I will."

"You didn't answer me about Nickolai."

No, she hadn't. She tried not to think about him. "Well, I pulled my gun on him last night."

"What?" Landry would give a nickel to see her best friend right now.

She could imagine it well: her green cat eyes wide, her almost porcelain skin turning pink, and Marcie would fluff the tips of her red pixie-cut hair.

"Hey, he was skulking around my rental. I didn't know it was him. It was dark."

"Oh, mercy, Landry."

"It's fine. He's fine. Whatever."

"Did he meet your fake seller?"

"No. I didn't share the information with him, and he didn't follow me or anything."

"So what's he doing there?"

"I don't know." That question had been bugging Landry. He'd been gone by the time she'd gotten back from her bomb of a meeting, and she had no clue what lead he was following.

Marcie laughed.

"What?"

"I bet that's driving you up a wall—not knowing what he's doing."

"He is my competition here, Marcie. If he recovers the map first, he gets the fifty-thousand-dollar recovery fee."

Marcie sobered. "I know. Do you have any other leads?"

"No." That really bummed her more than she cared to admit. "Allen Edgar is a big fat dead end, but it led me to the conclusion that the real map is here."

"You really think you'll find this guy who has the map?"

"I'm going to try my hardest, that's for sure." She had fifty thousand reasons to try.

"What are you going to do when you find him? I doubt he'll just hand over the map."

Landry was pleased to hear her bestie say *when* instead of *if*. "Well, all those insurance frauds weren't exactly happy to see me show up to take the piece of art they'd filed a claim for. I have my ways."

"You need to be careful, Landry."

"I will, and, yes, I will call you tonight when I'm safely tucked into bed."

Marcie snorted then hung up.

Landry stretched. She grabbed her notebook and read the words she'd been able to make out on the map. She opened the browser on her phone and searched for First Water and Superstition Mountains. Apparently, First Water was a trailhead of the Dutchman hiking trail.

Landry opened the best still shot she'd grabbed of the map and studied it. There wasn't a big *X* marking a spot, but there was one area darker with an odd circle. For the time being, she was going to use that as an indication of where the mine could be.

Her breath caught for a minute. Where the mine could be. All her life, Landry had been a sucker for puzzles and riddles. A treasure map was the biggest puzzle there was, and the legend of the Dutchman's Lost Mine was one of the most complex of riddles.

She studied the picture again. First Water was farther from where the circle was marked than some other notations. Weaver's Needle was the closest to the circle that she could read.

Landry ran another search on her phone. This time for Weaver's Needle. She needed to print the picture she had.

After locking her motel room, she headed to the office. The little bell sounded as she entered. The lady who'd checked them in stood and moved away from the desk.

In the corner was a rack holding maps and pamphlets of local sites to see. She grabbed the map of the mountains and surrounding area. "How much for the map?"

"Two dollars."

Landry handed the lady two bills then leaned on the worn counter. "I was wondering if you had a printer I could use? I need to make a couple of copies from a picture on my phone."

The woman stopped smiling.

"I'd be more than happy to pay for the copies, of course." Landry smiled wider.

The woman hesitated before dipping her chin in a brief nod. "We have one." She tipped her head toward the printer sitting on the desk behind the counter.

Landry sent up a silent prayer of thanks as she saw the Wi-Fi icon on the front of the printer. She searched for available printers on her cell and, once connected, sent the two photos. She pulled two dollars out of her pocket and passed them to the lady.

The woman took the money before lifting the copies off the printer tray. She paused as she looked at them. "What are these?"

"Do you recognize any of the landmarks there?"

The woman continued to study the top picture. Her brow furrowed. "These dashes look like the hiking trails along the Superstitions." She glanced at Landry. "Are you going hiking?"

"I was thinking about doing a little looking around."

She shoved the copies at Landry. "Let me guess: You thought you'd poke around and find that gold mine, right?" She shook her head. "Don't you think if that mine was there it would've been found by now? People like you come in all the time, thinking they've found something nobody else thought of. They all leave empty-handed."

Landry smiled despite her dismay. "Thank you for the copies." She headed to the rented Jeep. Maybe no one had found the mine because they didn't know where to look. Maybe this map, one from the man who actually knew the mine's location, was the key.

Or maybe she was just caught up in the excitement of a treasure hunt.

Still, it wouldn't hurt to just check things out.

Stan stood outside his motel room as she jumped into the Jeep. She gave him a wave as she drove by. Better he think she was chasing a lead rather than a ghost. Traffic was light at a little after three.

Using her phone's GPS app, she drove the short distance out of town toward the Superstition Mountains. Before she even arrived, she could see the distinctive peaks of Weaver's Needle. She turned onto one of the dusty access roads to the hiking trails.

Boom!

The Jeep jerked to the right. Hard.

Landry eased on the brake as she fought to keep the steering wheel from turning, praying as she struggled. She coaxed the Jeep to the side of the road, shut off the engine, and jumped out. Walking around the vehicle, she spied the culprit—back right tire was flat. Must've been a blowout or something.

She sighed then went to work removing the spare tire from the back of the Jeep. Even though it was February, the late-afternoon Arizona sun beat down on her as she struggled to remove the lug nuts. Dust from the dirt road rose and settled on her perspiring face. She wiped her forehead with her shirtsleeve and worked on setting the jack.

After walking the tire off, she slipped the spare on and spun the lug nuts. A very welcome breeze brought the cloying sweetness of local flowers, but the blunt, camphor scent of the creosote filled Landry's senses. She worked swiftly, ignoring the ache in her arms. Marcie had been right, as usual, and she needed to be more committed to their gym dates.

Landry put the jack in the back of the Jeep and moved to the tire. She ran her hands along the treads. Nothing to indicate a blowout. Her fingers found a cut on the sidewall. She inspected it closer. Definitely a slit, made with a knife or something like that. Nothing a rock on a dirt road could've done.

Her tire had been intentionally slit.

This could be laughable.

Nickolai had taken so many routes to the address for Edgar, only to go five or ten miles and see a ROAD CLOSED sign due to the marathon starting early in the morning. He'd been rerouted and turned around so many times, it was a miracle he wasn't totally lost by now.

Actually, he had no idea where he was, but thanks to his GPS, he at least had an idea of which way to go. This time, when the automated voice announced they were rerouting, he selected the option of least traffic rather than fastest route. Surely that would avoid the closed roads.

He could hope.

But now, following the "least traffic" directions, he'd looped around to where he thought he could be back in Apache Junction in less than ten minutes. Maybe. At least there was a lot less traffic. Okay, almost no traffic. He would find—

"Recalculating."

What? He hadn't turned. Hadn't even taken a big curve. He slowed down. Maybe the cell's GPS glitched. He slowed further as he approached a dirt road. He eased toward it and noticed. . .

Landry Parker?

He rolled his truck to a stop and put it in PARK. Landry had the back door of the Jeep open and was bent over a tire lying on the ground. He jumped out of the truck. "Hey, let me get that for you."

She paused, turning. Her eyes narrowed. "You."

He moved to grab the tire.

She stepped in front of him. "No, thank you. I've got it." She nudged him aside, grabbed the tire, and slung it in the back of the Jeep.

The hardness in her voice made him take a step back. Sure, they were competitors, so to speak, but she seemed more annoyed than usual.

She slammed the door shut and turned to glare at him, hands on hips. "Did you think a flat tire would have me whimpering? Scare me off the case? Not hardly."

"What are you talking about?"

"The flat." She jabbed her thumb over her shoulder toward the Jeep. "A slit in the sidewall. Did you think it would stop me? Make me quit the case?" She snorted. "I've had worse done to me to make me back off. Didn't work then and it won't work now."

Wait. "You think I had something to do with a flat tire?" She had to be kidding.

She shrugged. "You were the one sneaking around the Jeep last night."

"You're serious? You think I would give you a flat?" What kind of man did she think he was?

Her glare didn't lessen. "From the start, you tried to discourage me from taking the case."

"I thought this was a matter for the police to handle."

She popped her fists back on her hips. "Yet, here you are, working the case. For someone who thinks this is a matter for the police to handle, you're sure a long way from home, following leads. A little suspicious, wouldn't you say?"

"I just. . ." He couldn't say anything, because if the tables were turned, he'd think the same thing. Well, not that he'd think she'd slit his tire, but him just showing up after he'd been so adamant at the Winslet house did look suspicious. He couldn't very well tell her what he knew, though, not without tipping his hand.

She waited a minute then shook her head. "Yeah. What I thought." She dug keys out of the front pocket of her jeans. "Look, you aren't going to discourage me. A flat tire is nothing. Just do your thing and let me do mine."

"I didn't slit your tire." She needed to understand that he didn't play dirty, even when pitted against her. Competition was one thing, but he'd never stoop to slitting a lady's tire. He needed her to know that.

"If you say so." She opened the door to the Jeep. "Just stay out of my way and I'll stay out of yours, okay?" She didn't wait for a reply, just slammed the door, cranked the engine, and sped off, leaving him standing in the dust kicked up from her tires.

Nickolai stared after her, blinking repeatedly to clear the dirt from his eyes. He couldn't believe she hadn't been willing to listen, to believe him. He'd dealt with her type before—determined to prove themselves in a man's world. Usually with a big ole chip on their shoulder.

Only, he didn't think she had a chip on her shoulder. She might have been blunt with her suspicions, but she hadn't been arrogant or rude. She'd actually been reasonable and basically called him to a truce.

He got into his truck and clicked on his seat belt, sure of one thing: no matter how much he didn't want to respect Landry Parker, he did.

Might as well try to get to Allen Edgar's house again. Give himself a little space from Miss Parker. She could infuriate him like few others, and he didn't want to think about what that might mean.

Surprisingly, his GPS had no more glitches and directed him right to the address for Edgar's mother, where Easton had assured Nickolai he'd be. He knocked firmly on the door.

A woman, about seventy or so, with gray hair sticking out at odd angles answered. "Yes?"

Nickolai plastered on his most reassuring smile. "Hello, ma'am. Sorry to bother you this late in the afternoon, but I need to speak to your son, Allen. Is he home?"

She looked him up, then down, then up again. "What's this about?"

"I want to discuss with him a possible job opportunity using his advanced computer skills." Wasn't lying—if he was able to hack like Easton claimed, Edgar would have a skill set.

She smiled and opened the door. "Of course. Come in." She pointed at a door just off the kitchen. "He's down in his room in the basement. Just go on down."

Nickolai nodded. "Thank you." That was easier than he'd expected. Mom would probably love him to get a job and get out of her basement. He descended the worn carpeted stairs until he reached the bottom.

A man—kid, actually—matching Easton's description of the hacker jumped off the futon, nearly knocking his laptop to the floor. "What are you doing down here?"

Interesting he was more concerned about what Nickolai was doing in his room rather than who he was. "I need to talk to you about your extracurricular computer activities." He advanced toward Edgar.

The pasty color of Edgar's face paled, if that was even possible. "I don't know what you're talking about."

"I think you do. You see, I've already talked with Joel, who told me all about your hacking skills." Nickolai took two steps toward him.

The kid nearly stumbled back onto the futon.

Nickolai played his hunch. "And I know you're the one who stole the copy of the map from Joel."

Edgar's eyes widened.

Bingo!

"That's between you and Joel. I just care about the map."

The kid walked sideways to get away from Nickolai. "Look, I still have it. I haven't sold it yet. She hasn't come up with the money."

Wait. She? "Did you try to sell it? The copy?"

He stopped moving. "It's the map, man. Why are you and her so hung up on it being a copy? It's the exact same as the one sold for a million bucks."

Nickolai tried to follow the kid's thought train, but it was a bumpy ride. "Who is her?"

"The chick I met earlier at the bar and grill. From the website where I listed the map."

"You listed the copy?"

Edgar sighed. "It's the map."

"So you say. When did you list it?"

He shrugged. "Not even a week ago. The pretty lady's the only one who replied even though I discounted the price to a hundred grand. That's a steal when the other guy paid a million."

"The other guy. . ." Nickolai relaxed his stance, hoping to reassure the kid and keep him talking. "What do you know about him?"

The kid crossed his arms over his chest. "Not much. Apparently he's loaded. I mean, he forked out a cool mil for that old map that you can't even read all that great."

"Do you know who he is?"

Edgar shook his head. "Some rich guy in Louisiana, I think. I'm not real sure. Joel could tell you more about him. He met him and all. I just bid against him in the system to get him up to a million dollars because that's what Joel needed."

Clearly, he wasn't the murderer nor did he have the original map.

Truth be told, Nickolai wasn't all that sure the kid could find his way out of his mother's basement without help.

"But I have the copy of what he gave the man. If she doesn't come through with the hundred grand, I'll sell it to you for even less."

"Who is this woman?"

Edgar's eyes lit up. "I only know her as buyer2409, but man, she's fine."

If she was who he thought she was, Nickolai would have to agree. "Long black hair with smoldering eyes?"

"That's her. Drives that rented Jeep and looks like she could be a yoga instructor."

Landry.

"She's so fine, I was tempted to let her have the map for less than the hundred thousand. I might yet, if she calls me back."

"I wouldn't hold my breath, kid." Nickolai shook his head as he turned and headed up the basement stairs.

If Landry had found Allen Edgar and his copy of the map before him, what other angles was she working that he didn't know about yet?

Chapter Nine

Go Home.

Landry stared at the letter-sized paper with the magazine letters cut out and pasted on the page. Little tendrils of ice spread out from her spine despite the warm Arizona temperature. She'd been in some dicey situations before but had never been threatened directly. Well, this wasn't exactly a threat, per se, but the message came through loud and clear.

"It was taped on your door." Stan crossed his arms and peered around her motel room, as if the person who'd left the papers might be lurking in the corners. "Whatever you and Mr. Baptiste are doing is ruffling feathers around here."

That was true. The serviceman at the local tire shop had confirmed that there was almost no way the Jeep's tire could have been punctured where it was during normal driving. It'd been punctured to give her a flat, slow enough that she'd be out somewhere and probably stranded. And now this note. . .

God, I could really use some wisdom and discernment about now.

She'd only met with Allen Edgar here, and he didn't seem the threatening warning letter type. She'd spoken to the waitress and the salesman at the military store, but neither was personally vested in the map. Which meant, Nickolai had to be onto something. But the letter was on her door. Could there have been a mistake? The rooms were all side by side, so it was possible it was put on the wrong door. What angle was Nickolai working?

"Have you concluded all you need to do here?"

"I'm still following a few leads. Strong ones." Going home wasn't an option for her. Not now when someone wanted them gone badly enough to leave a warning note on her door. "You didn't hear anyone outside?"

Stan shook his head and sat in the chair at the little table in front of the window, opposite where Landry stood. "I knew nothing until I came out to get my phone charger out of the car and saw it. You drove up not even fifteen minutes later." He stared out the window into the darkening space. "I can't imagine what could be keeping the police."

If he expected a response in less than fifteen minutes for a non-emergency call, his interaction with police must greatly be on a whole different level than what Landry had experienced. Or Apache Junction had a much better response time than New Orleans, which was entirely possible, but with the marathon. . .

"I can call some of the other hotels and see if they've had any vacancies come up. Perhaps you'd feel a bit safer in a different venue."

"I'm fine here." She set the paper on the table and dropped into the other chair. "This doesn't scare me, Stan." If anything, it meant someone—she or Nickolai—was rattling the right cages.

Stan looked out the window again then stood, crossing his arms over his chest. "Well, I doubt we'll be here much longer anyway, so I guess we're good to stay put. I'll check with Mr. Baptiste when he returns."

"If he'd feel safer moving, I'm fine staying here alone." Actually, she preferred it.

The outside lights of the motel flickered on. Landry could almost hear the hum from inside her room.

"Oh, I couldn't allow that. Wini—er, Mrs. Winslet wouldn't stand for that. No, indeed."

"Then we'll be fine here."

"I'm sure—" He leaned toward the window. "Oh, here are the police." He opened the door and stepped outside.

Landry grabbed the note and followed the older man as he greeted the two men in their blue officer uniforms.

"I was about to call back and see what could be keeping you." Stan stood in front of the police cruiser.

The officer who shut the driver's door glared at Stan in the setting sun. "Sir, all nonemergency calls are addressed by priority. There were no injuries or harm in this case, so naturally, it didn't take as high priority as a break-in and robbery of someone's home."

"We were threatened." Stan looked as indignant as he sounded.

Time to avert. Landry moved around Stan. "Here's the offending letter." She held out the paper to the older of the two officers. "It was taped to my motel room door."

The man didn't take the offered note, just stared at it in Landry's hand. "Hmm, that's not much of a threat." He glanced at his partner, who peered over his shoulder.

"Yeah, it's more of a suggestion, I'd say." The younger officer met Landry's stare and winked at her. "Not a threat of any kind." He actually winked at her!

Landry forced her tone to be even. "And while I do perceive the note to be an implied threat, I'm not frightened in the least."

"Have you received anything else? Any obscene phone calls? Other notes?" the officer asked as he swatted a bug flying near his ear.

Landry shook her head and glanced at Stan.

"We haven't received anything else that I'm aware of, but more could follow, of course." Stan rose to his full six-foot-something height, actually looking taller with the straightening. Landry was impressed.

"But I'm sure you'll be leaving soon anyway, right?" the older officer interjected.

Landry's spine went more rigid than Marcie's perfect posture. "No, we haven't made plans to leave yet." She glared at the man who'd had the nerve to wink at her.

The older man opened his mouth, but his words were stolen by the rumbling of Nickolai's truck as he pulled alongside the cruiser. The headlights went out just before the engine turned off.

"What's going on?" Nickolai joined the odd little group on the motel room's sidewalk.

Landry handed him the note. "Stan found this taped to my motel room door."

"Apparently the little lady thinks it's a threat," the winking officer said.

She balled her hands into tight fists at her sides. "Obviously it's an implied threat, even if you haven't been properly trained to identify it as such, but it doesn't scare me." She shook her head—if only she could dismiss the backward officers as easily—and looked at Nickolai. "Stan found it and called the police to file a report before I got back to the motel."

"It's a threat." Stan nudged past them to Nickolai. "You're a cop. It's a threat, right?"

"You're a police officer?" the older of the uniformed men asked.

"Retired." Nickolai looked up from the note and met Landry's stare. "Stan found this on your door?"

She nodded. The intensity of his scrutiny did strange things to her. Things that felt really unfamiliar and made her seem weaker than she was. Landry cleared her throat. "But it could have been put on the wrong door, or it could be meant for all of us."

The older officer took the note right out of Nickolai's hand. "There are a lot of you out-of-state folk in town for the marathon. Some locals might be put out because of your presence. Nothing personal."

Landry had had about enough. She put her fists on her hips. "I would think that the influx of tourists for the marathon would be a real boost to the economy here in Apache Junction."

"Are you in tourism?" the younger officer winked at her again.

If he didn't stop winking at her. . .

"I'm former military police." That usually shut up guys like him.

"Really?" Apparently it didn't work on this one.

"Yes, really." Landry shifted, turning away from the young cop and focusing on the older one who seemed to be sizing up Nickolai.

"What, exactly, are you three in town for? Apparently none of you were participating in the marathon." The older officer handed the note to the young jerk, telling him to bag it as evidence.

"We're just—" Stan began.

"Does the motel have security cameras?" Nickolai interrupted.

The older officer put his hands on his gear belt. "We'll speak to the motel owner soon. For now, we need to file this report." He nodded to the younger officer. "Get their names, addresses, contact information, and take their statements. I'll visit with the owner." He turned and strode across the parking lot toward the motel office.

Nickolai followed.

Landry moved to as well, but the winking officer blocked her path. "Now, let me get the information for the report. Let's start with your name."

She gritted her teeth as she watched Nickolai fall into step alongside the seasoned officer. Unfair that he would get the intel and she had to stay here with the flirt.

"Is she always such a fireball?" The uniformed officer smiled at Nickolai. His teeth were illuminated blue by the neon light blasting from outside the motel office's window.

"Who, Landry?" Nickolai couldn't stop the returning grin.

"Guess she keeps you on your toes, huh?"

"I guess you could say that." On his toes and with his eyes wide open.

The officer chuckled and stopped just outside the motel office, holding out his hand. "Officer Brian Hogan."

"Nickolai Baptiste."

"Baptiste?"

Nickolai nodded, used to those outside of the New Orleans area having trouble with his last name. "I'm from Louisiana."

"I see. Guess that's where you were on the force?"

"Detective. Retired after nine years."

Hogan would understand. He would get it. Most cops did. If a cop retired before hitting tenure, there was a reason. Usually a reason that no one wanted to discuss.

Hogan swatted a mosquito and changed the subject. "Look, I'll be honest, I think that note was a prank, at best. Local kids messing with out-of-towners. But I have to ask, why are you here? It's obvious you didn't come for the marathon."

After years of being on the force and reading people's evasive answers, Nickolai understood the officer's inquiry. But also after being a detective trained in picking up subtle clues in others, he sensed there was more to the cop's probing. The question was, which gut feeling should he go with?

Best to just give the information that they'd find out soon enough on their own. "Landry Parker and I are both recovery specialists."

"Recovery specialists, huh?"

"Yes. We recover items for clients." No point in mentioning they didn't work together. Nickolai conjured up a mental image of Landry's face if she thought he'd implied she worked for him. He could imagine the fury she'd reflect and he almost laughed.

"What kind of items do you recover?" Hogan smacked a mosquito on his neck.

"Sometimes it's a missing will when someone dies. Or a piece of artwork that fell into the wrong hands. Documents. Deeds. Just about anything of value."

"I see. What are you trying to recover here?"

"I'm not at liberty to discuss that at the moment." Nickolai hated keeping information from the police; it went against his very being, but he had no choice.

Hogan let out a harrumph. "I see." He turned his back to Nickolai and jerked open the motel office door.

Although uninvited and clearly dismissed, Nickolai followed anyway. Unless Hogan told him to leave, Nickolai would do the job Mrs. Winslet had hired him to do.

Hired them to do.

The man behind the counter half smiled, half grimaced at Hogan as he stood. "Officer. What can I do for you?"

"How's business, Kohl?" Hogan leaned against the counter.

"Can't complain. The marathon almost put us at capacity."

The woman who'd checked them into the motel yesterday came from the back room and hovered just behind the man.

"You know, if you weren't so strict with all your rules and regulations..."

The man behind the counter shook his head. "It's what keeps my place off your worry list, Officer Hogan."

"Well, speaking of that"—Hogan glanced over his shoulder and made brief eye contact with Nickolai before turning back to Kohl—"I'm here to take a formal report. One of your guests seems to have received a possibly threatening letter put on their room door. You wouldn't know anything about that, would you?"

"Of course not." Kohl's face turned red.

"How about you, Margaret? You know anything about a menacing note on one of the room doors?"

"Of course she doesn't," Kohl answered before she could open her mouth.

"I appreciate your assertion, Kohl, but I was asking Margaret."

The man's face deepened into a crimson color, but he just nodded at the woman. "As my husband said, I know nothing about any letter. What did it say?"

Her husband frowned at her then Hogan. "Yes, what did it say?"

"It said 'Go home.'" Nickolai hated stepping on the cop's toes, but he wanted to see their reactions.

Both husband's and wife's eyes widened. "W–what?" Kohl sputtered. "Of course we wouldn't have anything to do with that. Why would we try to get guests to leave? This is how we live."

Hogan held up his hands as if to ward off the accusation. "So no one else has reported getting a letter like that? Or any prank calls? Anything else?"

Kohl shook his head. "Of course not. Nothing. We would have called anything like that in and reported it to the police."

Nickolai would have to tell Hogan about the flat tire. But not in front of Kohl and Margaret.

"Whose room?" his wife asked.

Nickolai held his tongue, hoping Hogan would offer up the information. As owners of the motel, they deserved to know. They'd find out anyway.

"The lady with this gentleman's group."

"Miss Parker," the woman barely whispered, but she still drew a glare from her husband.

"You know her?" Hogan asked.

The woman ignored her husband and approached the edge of the counter. "Yes. She's very polite." She cut her eyes to her husband. "Considerate. She came in to make copies earlier."

"Copies?" Hogan shot Nickolai a quick look. "Of what?"

"She had pictures of the map on her phone. She made a couple of copies and left."

Nickolai's pulse kicked into overdrive. Map?

"You let her make copies here?" No mistaking the irritation in Kohl's voice as he all but barked at his wife.

"She paid for them, of course." Margaret ducked her head. "I wouldn't have let her make copies otherwise."

Hogan tapped the counter. "A map? Of what?"

"The Superstitions." She curled up her lip. "She's searching for the lost mine." Margaret shook her head. "I thought she had more sense than that. Although, she did have a map I've never seen before. I could make out Weaver's Needle and a couple of other landmarks." She shot a stare at her husband, who continued glaring, then spoke to Hogan. "Not that I really looked, but some things just jump out at you."

"Of course. You couldn't help recognizing such prominent marks."

"Did she tell you where she got these pictures and what she was going to do?" Nickolai's question earned him a warning glance from Hogan.

"She didn't say," Margaret answered.

"There, she doesn't know anything more." Kohl effectively cut his wife off. She retreated a step, then another, back from the counter.

"Do you have any security cameras on the property?" Hogan asked.

Kohl nodded. "I'm not sure if that room is in the frame, though."

"Can we look?" Hogan pressed.

Kohl hesitated but waved Hogan behind the counter. Nickolai turned and pretended to be reading the bulletin board as the two men left. Once they were in the back room, their voices muffled by the distance, Nickolai smiled at Margaret.

She smiled back, a little shyly. "I hope Miss Parker wasn't frightened off. She is a very nice lady."

"Oh, it didn't scare her off. We aren't checking out."

Her smile widened. "Good. My husband. . .he doesn't like it when guests leave abruptly."

Nickolai leaned on the counter and flashed the biggest smile he could muster. "We won't leave until we're finished here." He lowered his voice to what he hoped sounded like a secret-between-friends whisper. "Hey, no one else happened to be in the office when Landry was in here making her copies, was there?"

She shook her head. "Only me up here. Vanessa was in the back, getting her orders."

"Vanessa?"

"She's our afternoon housekeeper."

"Oh." He straightened and looked at the doorway where Hogan and Kohl had disappeared. Their voices were a bit closer sounding. "Did she see the copies Landry made?"

Margaret wrinkled her brow. "I didn't show them to her."

Show them. . . Nickolai tilted his head. "Do you have copies of what she made?"

Her face whitened then reddened. No matter what came out of

her mouth, Nickolai knew she had copies.

"Well. . .the printer kept a record, and when I printed out the report at the end of the day, well, they printed out."

"Where are they?" Nickolai could make out Hogan's tone of displeasure.

Margaret, too, heard them. She reached under the counter and grabbed papers then pushed them into Nickolai's hands. "Here. These are the copies. Vanessa wanted a set for her boyfriend because he collects things like that, she said."

Nickolai inhaled quickly as Hogan and Kohl returned.

"You can't see the doors to the rooms you three are staying in," Hogan announced.

"Did your other friend find you? When he arrived this morning, the rooms on either side of you and Miss Parker were already taken, so I had to put him on the other side," Margaret said. "He asked what room Mr. Hauge and you and Miss Parker were in. Of course, I wouldn't tell him, but he said that was okay, that he would call Mr. Hauge."

"Who is this?" Hogan asked.

Kohl moved his hand over the guest register. "I'm not sure we should give you this information without a warrant."

Hogan shrugged. "I can get one. Of course, if I do that, it might hit the press that your guests have received threatening letters here at the motel. Taped right to the room door."

Kohl didn't hesitate. He glanced at the ledger. "Phillip. Phillip Font-e-not."

Nickolai didn't recognize the name from the packet, but with a surname of Fontenot, the man was definitely from south Louisiana.

Who was Phillip Fontenot, and what was he doing here?

Chapter Ten

"Miss Parker, why didn't you mention the map before?"

Landry pushed off from the edge of the bed where she'd sat and stared at the police officer who'd barged into her motel room with Nickolai in tow. He looked even more annoyed than before he'd gone to speak to the motel's owner.

Well, that was okay because she was annoyed as well. With Mister Winky, sitting at the table with Stan, who seemed to think she and Stan were afraid of their own shadows, she just wanted the report filed and everybody out of her motel room. "I didn't think it relevant."

"That's really for the police to decide, Miss Parker." He wore smugness as comfortably as his badge and uniform. "Can you give me a copy of this map? Margaret, the nice lady in the office whose husband happens to own the motel, said you made a copy in the office."

She could, of course, but she wasn't willing. No way would she let Nickolai even see a copy of the map. She was not in the habit of sharing information, especially when there was fifty grand up for grabs. "I'm sorry, but no."

"No?"

She shook her head then glanced at Nickolai. Would Mr. Black-and-White back his brothers in blue in order to get a look at the map?

But he surprised her. "I don't think the map itself is important, Officer Hogan." Nickolai eased down on the long counter holding the television.

Would wonders never cease? Landry could hug him at this moment, even if he was her competitor and she didn't trust him.

"Oh, you don't, do you?" the older cop asked Nickolai as he leaned against the wall behind the door.

The motel room felt too crowded. The air seemed stale, even though the door had been cracked about an inch. Just enough to let a mosquito in that continued to buzz about, annoying Landry even more. Nickolai and the officer had shut it when they entered. She felt as prickly as the cactus growing outside.

"I just realized the note is actually the second threat against Landry."

She crossed her arms over her chest to keep herself in check. What?

"The tire on her rental was punctured, flattening it while she was out today." Nickolai shot her a sheepish glance.

Forget hugging him—she wanted to throttle him.

"Is that so, Miss Parker?"

"Yes, it was a slow leak in the tire from a puncture." She glared at Nickolai, who wouldn't meet her stare. "And I don't think it's a coincidence that I caught him sneaking around my rental last night. Perfect time to puncture the tire."

That got his attention. Nickolai's head popped up. "I told you, I had nothing to do with your flat tire."

"Why is this the first I'm hearing of this?" Stan asked. Worry lined his face like tire tread.

Officer Winky held up his hand. "Wait a minute." He looked at Landry. "You had a flat tire today?"

"Yes." Better just to answer yes or no.

"You'd better get this down," the older officer told Winky.

Winky flipped pages in his notebook and looked at Landry. "You believe the tire was punctured? On purpose?"

She nodded.

The older officer—Hogan, Nickolai had called him—cleared his throat. "Why would you say that, Miss Parker?"

"Because of its location." She caught the look the two local cops exchanged and sighed. "As well as that's what the serviceman told me when I took it in to be repaired."

"You think Mr. Bap-tees could be responsible?" Winky gave Nickolai the stink eye before scribbling in his little spiral notebook. Maybe he wasn't all bad.

"I caught him sneaking around the Jeep last night." She smiled at Nickolai.

"I wasn't sneaking around, I already told you. And you didn't need to pull a gun on me."

"Whoa! A gun?" Officer Hogan pushed off the wall, straightening as he stared at Landry. "You have a gun? You better explain."

"Of course I have a gun. I also have a concealed carry permit as well. I am retired military police, well trained in firearms." This was getting old very fast.

"She declared it at the airport and showed her credentials." Stan traced the edge of the table in front of him.

"If you two work together, why would you think he'd give you a flat?" Officer Hogan asked.

Heat rose up the back of Landry's neck. "We don't work together. We're competitors."

"Are you now?" Officer Hogan faced Nickolai. "I think you'd best explain, Mr. Baptiste."

He told them they worked together? Oh, this was rich. "Yes, please do explain, Nickolai. I can't wait to hear this." She sat on the edge of the bed and stared up at him. Working together? Not even.

Nickolai's face reddened. "I meant that we were working on the same case, which we are." He sent Landry a stare that dared her to defy him.

But that's one of the things she did best. She smiled at Officer Winky. "Nickolai and I were offered the same job. Whoever recovers the item and returns it to the client is actually paid the recovery fee. So, you see, we are pitted against each other. I don't want him to succeed any more than he wants me to." She turned her smile to Nickolai. "Although, I don't resort to flat tires and menacing notes to obtain my goal."

"Oh, so now I not only gave you a flat, but I also left a stupid note on your door?" Nickolai shook his head. "I don't think so, lady."

"Hold up, there. She does have a legitimate concern." Officer Hogan rested his hands on his belt rig. "You are competing for a job, you were seen around her rental before the slow leak that caused her flat, and you did mislead me about Miss Parker's and your working relationship." He turned back to Landry. "What time did you leave before this note was found?"

"Around four-ish. I had my flat, changed it, and I should mention Nickolai just happened to be out on that exact road just minutes after I changed the tire. Almost like he knew there'd be trouble and maybe he followed me or something."

"I didn't follow you, because I didn't mess with the tire."

Officer Hogan shook his head. "Just hold up, there, Mr. Baptiste. What road was this?"

"North Apache Trail."

"Heading toward the Superstition Mountains?"

Landry hated to confirm in front of Nickolai, but she had no choice. She nodded.

"I was—" Nickolai started.

Officer Hogan cut him off with a snap of his fingers. "Now, Miss Parker, what did you do after you changed the tire?"

"I told Nickolai to do his thing and let me do mine; then I headed back into town. I stopped off at the tire store over on East Apache Trail because it was open the latest. Bob was the gentleman who fixed the tire and confirmed it was a deliberate puncture."

"Bob's a good guy," Winky volunteered.

Hogan nodded. "Then what did you do?"

"They were closing up when I paid, so that was about six. I came back here, intending to ask Stan if he'd like to grab supper, but he showed me the note and he'd already called you."

Stan nodded. "I found the note around five or five thirty, when I went out to the car to retrieve my charger. I saw the note and called the police. Landry showed up here about fifteen minutes later, and I showed it to her."

"I see." Hogan rested his hands on his belt rig again as he faced Nickolai. "Where were you today?"

Oh, this was going to be really good. Landry looked at Nickolai and raised an eyebrow.

Every line in his handsome face screamed he didn't want to say anything in front of her. She hadn't wanted to announce where she'd been, either, or anything about the map in front of him. Turnabout was fair play, right?

"I was in Gilbert at about four, so I guess I left here around three thirty. I left there around five or so. I got turned around with the roads closed for the marathon and my GPS and ended up next to a dirt road where I saw Landry changing her flat. I pulled up behind her and offered to help, but she accused me of puncturing her tire." He stopped telling his story long enough to glare at her. "Which I didn't do, and I explained that to her. She sped off. I reset my GPS and made it to where I was going. I was there until I drove up here at the motel and saw the police car."

"Gilbert, eh? What were you doing there?" Hogan pressed.

Landry was curious about that herself.

And Nickolai knew it. He flipped his glance from her to Hogan. "I was meeting someone in conjunction with the case."

Hogan followed Nickolai's slow gaze to Landry. "I see. Perhaps we should step outside and question you, Mr. Baptiste."

Nickolai didn't wait for a discussion. He took the three steps to the motel room door and opened it. Hogan followed, as did Officer Winky. Landry wanted to, desperately, but figured she'd be shut out. The police might need to question Nickolai, but since he was a retired cop, they'd still side with him ultimately. She did the same with military.

Stan's cell phone beeped. He checked it. Stood. "Sorry. He's called five times. I'd better call him back." He stepped outside into the night.

Finally alone, Landry plopped down on the bed. Gilbert. Who was in Gilbert that had any relation to the case?

"Joel Easton."

The officer with Hogan wrote the name in his notebook.

"How does he tie into the case?" Hogan asked.

"I'm not at liberty to discuss the details of the case, I'm sure you understand, but he was critical to my follow-up."

Stan stepped out of Landry's room, phone pressed to his ear. He unlocked his room and stepped across the threshold and shut the door behind him.

Hogan shook his head. "All this is linked to a murder back in New Orleans?"

Nickolai resisted the urge to correct the man's pronunciation of his home that came out as New Or-leans. It was a common mistake, of course, but still nerve grating. "It might be. The NOLA Police Department is working the case and hasn't made any statement regarding anything concrete."

That was ambiguous, he knew, but he didn't have a choice. He couldn't betray his partner's confidence by sharing what he knew about the case. Especially since the commander was heading up the investigation.

"I see." Hogan leaned against the hood of the cruiser and stared at him in the flickering security light of the motel. "I suppose we can call the New Or-leans Police Department and see what they'll tell us."

Nickolai's stomach tightened into a ball. This could and would be very bad for him. For Chris. For the case and the investigation. But, was Hogan really going to call, or was it just a bluff for Nickolai to volunteer more information? He didn't know for certain, but he had to play his hunch. "You can. I can give you the direct number so you don't have to go through the switchboard and the four times of transferring." He forced the chuckle. "You know how that is."

Hogan laughed, too. "Yeah, I do know. Ours is the same way."

Nickolai hated having to manipulate a fellow officer, but in this case. . .

"Look, I don't think you punctured Miss Parker's tire or left that note, but someone did." Hogan nodded at the other officer. "What about Mr. Hauge?"

"No, sir. He's here as a representative of their client. It's not logical that he'd write the note then call us to report it."

Nickolai wanted to laugh at the mental image of Stan cutting out letters from a magazine or newspaper and gluing them to the paper then taping it to Landry's door.

"If you aren't responsible, and Mr. Hauge isn't responsible, then there's someone out there who has made two different acts against Miss Parker." Hogan looked at Landry's closed door. "I don't want there to be a third one."

"Me, either." Nickolai, too, stared at Landry's door. He knew he hadn't done anything toward her, and he was pretty certain Stan hadn't. Whose feathers had she ruffled? He knew she'd talked with Allen Edgar, but he hardly seemed the type to threaten someone. Especially someone he hoped would give him money for something. "Do you think it's possible the motel owners or the maid could be the culprits?"

"Motive?" Hogan asked.

"They had copies of the map. Maybe they want to scare Landry off because they want to try their hand at finding the mine."

Hogan and the younger cop both laughed. Nickolai didn't see the humor. He shifted his weight from one foot to the other, then back again.

"Every local has grown up hearing that legend. Whether our families believed it or not, they told the story. I don't know of a kid who grew up in these parts who hasn't looked for the mine." Hogan shook his head. "Nobody's found anything. Even if they had, it'd be property of the feds now."

"This is a new map. One that is from a direct descendant of Julia Thomas." Nickolai could kick himself. He hadn't planned on sharing that much information.

But the younger cop just laughed. "A new map crops up every couple of years, touted as being the one that'll lead you straight to the mine."

Hogan chuckled as well. "Even with those new maps, no one's ever found even a speck of gold."

Nickolai wasn't entirely sure about that. If someone did find some little bits of gold, they wouldn't automatically say anything if they knew they'd have to turn it over to the government. Illegal, yes, but many people would just hide the gold and go on their merry way. With all the "sell your gold for cash" places all over these days, selling it wouldn't be an issue.

"Maybe she talked to someone who she offended," Nickolai suggested.

The younger cop flipped through his notebook. "The only person she reported speaking to was Allen Edgar."

Nickolai nodded. "Yes. I spoke with him earlier myself. I didn't see a threat, but I wasn't looking for him in that way, so I might have missed any warning signs." Unlikely, but he'd missed signs before. Like the night he hadn't realized his perp was carrying.

"We'll run a check and then talk to him."

That she'd gotten photos of the map, which without taking the time to really study them still looked pretty detailed to him, impressed Nickolai. "I can talk to her and see if she's been working any other angles. Just like she didn't realize the motel kept copies of the map that she'd made, or that the maid had been in the back, she might've said something to someone without realizing."

"You think she'll tell you?" Hogan asked. "No offense, but it looks to me like the little lady isn't too keen on you."

"I don't think she likes you much at all," the younger cop agreed. That there was hope in his voice annoyed Nickolai, although he couldn't understand why.

"We're competitors. Back home, we're the only local recovery specialists. Over the years, she's taken business from me, and me from her." He shrugged. "I guess we're about even, but this case. . .the fee is quite large and we both want it."

"So why do you think she'll tell you anything?" Hogan pressed.

"I don't know that she will. But I think if I come clean with what I know and share information with her, she might slip up and share with me. Or she might tell me once I point out that she may have put herself in crosshairs without meaning to."

"Good luck with that." Hogan grunted and handed Nickolai a business card. "We'll get the report made. Call us if anything else happens or if you learn something new."

"I will." Nickolai slipped the business card into his back pocket and shook the cops' hands. "I appreciate your time and attention on this."

"We'll be in touch."

Nickolai watched the cruiser pull out of the parking lot. He turned to head to his room when he noticed a man approach Stan's door. He had to be a little older than Stan himself, spreading bald spot on the very top of his silver hair, and a full but manicured beard. He knocked on the door.

Stan opened the door, and the man entered before the door slammed shut. Stan hadn't noticed Nickolai outside.

Who was the man? Was he the Phillip Fontenot the front desk had mentioned? Just how did he connect to them, and was he a possible threat to Landry?

The Message

Gopan entered the lodge tent, already sweating. He moved to the medicine man and took the pipe offered. He closed his eyes and inhaled. Deeply. The rich tobacco made him a little light-headed. That was good. He was ready for his journey. Enlightenment would come, he knew it. Felt it deep in his chest.

He finished smoking with the medicine man and stood. The earth trembled a little under his feet as he made his way out of the tent. He wove a little, his steps unsure. Gopan slowed his pace as he moved to the altar.

Lifting his own pipe, he offered it up toward the sky then dumped the tobacco from inside. He cleaned out the pipe with the cloth laid out for that purpose. The world shifted and he closed his eyes, steadying himself on the altar he'd made. Slow breaths in through his nose. Long exhale through his mouth.

In. Out.

Deep in.

Slow out.

Gopan opened his eyes and lifted the leather pouch. He offered it skyward then withdrew a pinch of sage that he slipped into the pipe. Always a little sage to keep everything out—physically and spiritually, as was the tribe's tradition. Their ancestors had passed down the rituals from generation to generation. Their customs seated deep into their very being.

Taking his pipe, he ducked back into the purification lodge tent. The medicine man's helpers moved as one to sit cross-legged around the floor, each in a certain place. As if tied together, all moved in one direction.

The medicine man took Gopan by the hand to the west end of the lodge. He motioned for him to undress and sit in front of the roaring fire. Heat licked Gopan's face as he sat, naked, in front of the fire and other warriors of his tribe. His heart raced as he watched the medicine man take his place directly opposite Gopan, across the fire from him. Looking at the medicine man through the dancing flames, his vision blurred.

In a booming voice, the medicine man announced to all in the purification lodge tent the importance of Gopan's placement. He explained the west represented the spirits, the thunder beings of their Superstitions who controlled the wind, the rain, the lightning, and the thunder.

Murmurs of prayers began. Gopan sat in complete darkness, save for the fire shooting higher and filling the tent with such intense heat, he wondered if he might pass out. He knew water, rocks, and air were also in the lodge: all the elements so all the spirits could enter.

He closed his eyes as they began, as one, to sway. The medicine man called for the Great Spirit to come to Gopan. To talk to him. To give him message and meaning.

Swaying. Rocking. He felt like the whole world moved with him. Sweat covered him. He licked his lips, tasting the salt. He thirsted but knew he wouldn't drink. Not for a long time yet.

His stomach lurched, the sweetness of the tobacco hung in the air. . .the smoke filled his lungs. Gopan wanted to cough, to retch, but he kept swaying. Concentrated on every sensation.

The dirt of the purification lodge tent beneath him clung to him, glued to his flesh with his own sweat. The strands of his loose hair stuck to his back.

Still he swayed with the others.

His face burned. His lips cracked. His head was too heavy for his neck. He released the muscles in his neck and his head fell backward.

Gopan kept his eyes closed and kept rocking, his head hanging with his face skyward.

Then everyone stopped moving. Silence prevailed as the medicine man appeared to Gopan's right.

Gopan took the man's hand and stood, shaking. He nearly fell, but the medicine man, while old and frail in appearance, had a strong grip and kept Gopan upright. He led him from the purification lodge tent.

The medicine man led him to a sacred place selected for Gopan's journey. A helper followed, carrying the items the elder would need to secure Gopan's quest.

He took the prayer flags Gopan had prepared and placed one in each direction, positioning Gopan in the center. Then he took the tobacco ties and unwound them, laying them ceremoniously along the ground, building the protected area. The entire tribe knew that once Gopan was in the center, nothing bad could enter the center, only good.

Gopan bit his bottom lip as he thought he saw several horrific things dancing around the circle, but listened as the medicine man announced nothing could enter the center except the things from the Great Spirit.

The medicine man finished the ties then laid out the chokecherry branch, the flannel, the conch shell, and the eagle feather. His voice warbled as he instructed Gopan.

"Remain in this center for three days. Pray hard for your life tonight. Pray for direction on the second. Pray for the Great Spirit's protection on the third." He handed Gopan his pipe. "Do not set down your pipe because this represents the Great Mystery. Never let it down or allow it to come apart."

Gopan nodded and took his pipe, holding it so tight he thought he might crack it.

"Pray. And pray. And pray."

Gopan again nodded, the gusting air of the evening cooling his burning skin.

"You are to have no food or water. You have your nakedness, your blanket, your pipe, and your prayers."

Gopan nodded, the outline of the medicine man blurring as he stepped farther from the circle. He knew the medicine man and all his helpers would be back at the purification lodge tent, praying for Gopan's quest. They wouldn't stop until he returned. That comforted him.

"Listen for the Great Spirit. The Thunder God."

The medicine man was gone.

Gopan lifted his pipe to the sky and, in the dark, began to chant and pray as instructed.

Chapter Eleven

Landry stepped through the wall of steam coming from the bathroom. The chillier air of the motel room cooled her damp skin, making her feel more refreshed than the hot shower had. It'd been a long day and exhaustion pulled at her, but she wasn't tired. Drained, yes. . .tired, no. Her mind wouldn't stop reviewing the case. She'd even read the entire book of Romans in the Bible to try to calm herself. It didn't work. Her mind kept going back to the case.

She rubbed the towel over her head then finger-combed her damp hair before quickly running a long braid down the back to keep it out of her face. She pulled out the envelope with all the case documents and spread them out on the other bed in the motel room. As if she hadn't studied them to the point of memorization. Nothing in the paperwork shined any light on why someone in Apache Junction wanted her gone.

Unless her copy of the map was the reason. Or someone didn't like her knowing the map was here and the man who had it was camping out in the Superstitions, looking for the mine. She didn't think Nickolai knew about the man. She could ask, of course, but she didn't know if she trusted him.

Did he puncture the Jeep's tire? Did he leave the note taped to her door?

She just didn't know him well enough to tell. She knew him by reputation, but that wasn't always factual. Wasn't she a prime example of how reputations sometimes twisted the truth?

Landry couldn't picture him cutting out letters from a newspaper or magazine and gluing them to a piece of paper to tape on a door. He seemed more direct than that. More. . .in-your-face type.

She plopped onto the other bed and rested her head against the headboard.

"I don't believe for a minute that she sent you here to check up on me." Stan's angry voice came through the motel's thin walls.

"Doesn't really matter what you believe, Stan. I'm here and expect an update."

Landry didn't recognize the other man's voice but knew it wasn't Nickolai or either of the policemen who'd taken their statements. She knew she shouldn't eavesdrop, but their voices were so clear.

"I don't owe you an update."

She didn't think Stan could get that annoyed to sound so angry.

"As long as this expedition is on Winslet Industries' dime, you do."

"Winifred doesn't need your permission to spend her own money."

Go, Stan! Landry smiled as she imagined Stan's posture at the moment. He was probably standing ramrod straight, feet spread about two feet or so apart, with his eyes narrowed and face reddening by the minute.

One of the men in the adjacent room let out a half snort, half chuckle. Landry couldn't tell if it was Stan or not but recognized there was no humor in the sound.

"She doesn't, of course, but I'm here to look after her financial interests and make sure these two specialists aren't taking advantage of her."

"We both know you'd like to look after more than her financial interests."

Landry turned and placed her ear against the wall. This was getting really interesting, really fast.

"At least I had the decency to wait until she was single, unlike you." The stranger's voice bit out each word with such savageness.

Whoa! Stan and Mrs. Winslet? Wow.

The air conditioner kicked on, filling the room with a solid hum.

Landry sighed, resisting the urge to jump up and shut off the unit so she could continue listening to Stan and the mystery man's conversation. Especially now when the good secrets were being thrown out there.

Her father would be so disappointed.

That was enough to push Landry to her feet to study the papers laid out on the bed, and away from the air conditioner controls. How many times had he drilled into her head that learning something by accident wasn't real investigating. Real investigation came from working the clues and following the item to be recovered.

She paced in front of the bed, scanning everything she'd looked at over and over already. She had to be missing something. What?

Her cell rang. Before she even checked the caller ID, she knew who it was. She'd forgotten to call her best friend. Sheepishly, she answered. "Hey, Marcie."

"Nice to know you're alive, at least. Not that I've been worried or anything."

"I'm sorry, Marcie. So much happened today." Even though she knew Marcie would flip out, Landry gave her a complete rundown of her day, ending just as she ran out of breath.

"I knew it was dangerous. Now are you ready to come home?"

"No."

"No?"

"If everything here was really a dead end, I don't think I'd be getting warnings to leave." Landry stared at the bed with all the paperwork laid out. "I just need to find the man in the mountains with the map." Had she missed anything in the file?

"What about Nickolai? Do you really think he could be responsible?"

"I can't see him doing the note, but what if the incidents aren't related?" Yeah, this made sense. Talking out loud always made things more coherent to Landry. Maybe she should just talk to herself more. "What if he wanted to get me off the case so he punctured the tire? The guy at the repair shop said it looked like whoever did it intended for it to be a slow leak and not cause a blowout." Yeah, Nickolai didn't seem the type to want her hurt. Just slowed down and maybe scared off. "Nickolai did come by after I'd changed the tire, which is suspicious, but proves if he did do it, he didn't mean for me to be stranded or anything."

"Then why do it?"

"To scare me off the case."

"With a flat tire?"

Landry chuckled. "For some women, that would scare them. A flat tire out in the middle of nowhere in a strange place with no one to call."

"Doesn't know you very well, but I'd be freaked. How would he know that you wouldn't just be driving around town?"

"I think maybe he followed me." That was the only thing that made sense.

"Okay, let's say he did puncture your tire to discourage you and then followed you, but you'd already changed the tire. Now what about the note?"

"I've been thinking about it. What if the woman in the motel office told someone about the map I made a copy of? She clearly recognized the area, realized it was a map to the mine, but did admit she'd never seen one like it before. If she thought it might be a map that really did show where the lost mine is, maybe she and her husband want to go look for the treasure themselves."

"So they put a note on your door telling you to go home? Wouldn't they like to keep the business?"

Landry sat down on the edge of her bed. "Maybe that's the perfect way to throw suspicion off of them. They could always argue that they'd never do such a thing because they don't want to lose business."

"Maybe."

Yes! If Marcie couldn't shoot holes in her theory, then nobody could. "Which means, maybe the map really is authentic and leads to the lost mine." Landry's pulse raced in time with the adrenaline pulsating through her chest.

"You really aren't going to give up looking for the actual mine, are you?" Marcie's voice carried the tone of defeat.

"I have to, Marc. I just have to. There's a man out there already hunting it, but with the real map. If I find him, I recover the map and get the recovery fee from Mrs. Winslet. But if I happen to find the mine, too. . .well, I'm sure there would be some compensation for finding it."

Thank You, Lord, for leading me on the right track in this case.

Nickolai studied Stan's closed door. Curtains were drawn, so he couldn't see the men inside. Was the man who'd entered the Phillip Fontenot whom Margaret had mentioned? He should just go knock on the door and find out, but he realized he really had no business asking Stan Hauge anything. The man owed him no explanations.

Neither did Landry, for that matter.

His gaze drifted to her room. Did she really think he'd puncture her tire and leave menacing notes for her? Despite his best efforts to assure her he wasn't responsible, she still looked at him with those accusing stares. Then again, she really didn't know him, so it was reasonable that she would question his intent.

He didn't know her at all, either, for that matter. Perhaps it was time for them to put their competition aside and get to know one another. Especially with more than just idle threats against them. They needed to be able to trust each other, not try to sabotage the other's progress.

Taking a deep breath, Nickolai knocked on her door before he could convince himself this was a bad idea.

He heard her lean against the door; then it swung open. "What's wrong?" She clenched her cell phone in her hand. Her wet hair hung in a thick braid that swept over her shoulder. Lisbeth used to wear her hair like that when she was younger.

"Nothing new. I just thought. . ." He paused, feeling a bit like a high school sophomore asking a girl out on a date for the first time.

"I was wondering if you were hungry and wanted to go get something to eat."

She stared at him with those sultry eyes of hers. They widened and her mouth stayed clamped shut.

"I mean, I heard you tell the police you were going to ask Stan if he wanted to grab something to eat, but then everything went crazy." Now he really felt like a boy with his first crush, the way he was stumbling over his own words. Not that Landry Parker wasn't attractive, she was more than just stunning, but. . . "I think maybe it's time we got to know each other a little better. More than just sizing up our competition. Don't you think?"

"Yes. No. Hang on. Give me a second, okay?" She shut the door before he could answer.

He could make out her muffled voice as he stood on the sidewalk. Waiting.

This was a bad idea. He should just grab a sandwich and head back to his room, go over what he knew about the case. Try to figure everything out. He didn't—

The door opened and Landry stood there. She'd changed into a different shirt. "Sure. Let's go. Where should we eat?"

He hadn't gotten that far because he hadn't really thought the whole thing through. He hadn't really even considered that she'd agree to go with him. His mind went over all the flyers he'd found in his motel room. Nothing too fancy. Simple so they could talk. "Um, I heard the Handlebar Pub and Grill has some really good burgers and an outdoor patio."

"Okay."

He led the way to his truck as several other guests in the parking lot slammed trunks, car doors, and motel room doors. Bursts of laughter filled the air. The parking lot was fuller than before, probably because the marathon ran in the morning.

Nickolai approached the passenger side of his Ford, moving to open Landry's door for her. He shut it after she climbed in, and moved to the driver's side. Maybe he should've just unlocked it with the remote and let her get in by herself? This wasn't a date. Oh, man. . .did he mislead her into thinking it was?

Opening doors for ladies was just habit. His mother had taught him that no Southern gentleman would ever allow a lady to open a door in his presence.

But he didn't want her to get the wrong idea.

He gave himself a mental shake as he slid behind the steering wheel. She knew this wasn't a date. If she'd thought that, there was no way she would've agreed to come. Nickolai cranked the truck's diesel engine.

The restaurant wasn't far, but the strained silence thickened the air. Loose gravel in the parking lot crunched under the truck's tires. The side of the building had lively cactus plants painted on the side. Landry burst out of the truck as soon as he parked.

Maybe she didn't like having doors opened for her, but most Southern ladies did. If she resented it, that was her problem. His momma raised him right.

He missed her and Dad so much. Every. Single. Day.

Nickolai followed Landry into the Handlebar Pub and Grill. They were immediately greeted by a young lady who, following Landry's request, sat them at a table on the patio. As was a habit from his law enforcement training, he took stock of his surroundings.

The temperature had dropped a little, so it was cool and quite comfortable. The bugs seemed to leave the patio alone. White Christmas-style lights draped from various pergolas created a "ceiling" in the area that was larger than he'd imagined. While other patrons sat at several of the glass-top tables with cushioned chairs, there was good spacing between the tables. Plenty of semiprivacy in order to talk, but not too intimate.

Perfect.

A waitress came immediately with menus, welcomed them, and took their soft drink orders then left. Nickolai studied the menu in silence.

"Oh my. The grilled mahi fillet sounds amazing. I didn't realize how hungry I am." Landry probably didn't even realize she smiled as she read the menu.

She was even prettier when she smiled, and totally unaware of how beautiful she looked in the soft glow of the lights overhead and curling around the pergola posts.

Nickolai's mouth went dry in that moment. Luckily, the waitress returned with their drinks to take their order. Landry quickly ordered the fillet and handed her menu to the waitress.

"And what'll you have, sir?"

"What do you recommend?" He didn't even remember what he'd seen on the menu that sounded good. Landry Parker distracted him, and suddenly, more so.

"I'm partial to our green chili burger. That's an eight-ounce, free-range beef patty with two strips of thick-cut bacon, roasted green chilies, pepper jack cheese, and chipotle aioli on a fresh bakery bun. We cook just about everything on an outside grill, and much of our food is smoked with pecan wood. It really adds a lot of flavor to all our entrées."

"That burger sounds perfect. That's what I'll have." He handed her the menu.

"Um, the pecan wood?" Landry asked the waitress. "It's just used for smoking, right? I have an allergy to tree nuts, but it's only if I ingest any."

"Yes, ma'am. It's just used for smoking. Will that be okay?"

"That's fine. Thank you."

Alone again, Nickolai stared at Landry across the table. He'd have to start the conversation sometime. "So, I just thought it would be a good idea to sit down and get to know each other better. More than as competition or as an adversary."

"I'll be honest with you, I wasn't too keen on coming, but I happened to be on the phone with my friend who thought it was a good idea." She took a sip of her soda.

Thank goodness for her friend, then. "Well, I'm glad you came. So how did you get into the recovery business?"

"I was in the army. Military police. I was good in the investigation parts of my job. Really good."

"So why would you leave? I mean, couldn't you have re-upped?"

"I could have, but my mother became ill suddenly and died soon after her diagnosis. It took us all by surprise."

"I'm so sorry. I lost both my parents without warning. I still miss them every day."

She nodded. "After Mom died, I finished my current obligation to the army then went back to New Orleans to be with my dad. He was in the recovery business. Insurance recovery." She stared into her glass, stirring her straw absentmindedly.

"I'd heard he was good." Nickolai wasn't making that up.

"He was the best. Everyone said so."

Nickolai knew bits and pieces of the story. . .her dad was a recovery specialist for a large insurance company and was well respected in the field, but something happened and Landry took over the reins of the business. There was a lot of speculation as to what happened, but either way, everyone knew the insurance company was very upset and her father lost his job. Probably a lot more personal information than what Landry would be willing to share with him right now. He could understand.

"I was New Orleans PD for nine years before I left." He changed the subject to give her time to compose herself and not push himself as prying. "Earned my gold shield and loved it." His mouth quirked. "Had some success with investigations, too."

"So why'd you leave?"

Even after four years, talking about it still put a lump the size of a mountain in his throat. "I was shot."

Her eyes went wide. "You were shot?"

He nodded. "My partner and I were chasing a suspect in an alley behind the French Quarter. A shopkeeper had been robbed at knifepoint. I made sure to keep enough distance so he couldn't turn and stab me, but when he was cornered, he turned and shot me. I never even had time to draw."

"You were expecting a knife, not a gun."

"I should have expected anything and been prepared for everything."

"Yeah." She nodded and took another sip. "How bad was it?" Her question came out softly. . .caring and gentle.

It'd been a long time since he talked about this to someone outside of Chris and the medical team. Longer still to discuss it with a woman.

"I'm sorry. That's too personal."

Surprisingly, he wanted to share this with her. "No, it's okay." He pointed to the knot of scar tissue that wedged hidden in his right shoulder area. "Here."

She winced. "Not a through and through."

He shook his head. "I wish." That she understood warmed him. Then again, she was former MP. There were a lot of parallels between them. He sighed. "It was deep enough that even with more PT than I would wish on my worst enemy, I know I'm never going to be back to one hundred percent."

Unfortunately, that gunshot not only marked the end of his law enforcement career, it also marked the end of everything normal in his life.

The waitress arrived with their supper. The amazing aroma hit him as she set his plate in front of him. His stomach growled in response. After making sure they had everything they needed, the waitress refilled their drinks and rushed off.

"If it tastes even half as good as it looks and smells, this is gonna be good." He smiled at her.

"Oh yes." She smiled back. "Would you like to pray?"

What? He shook his head.

"Okay. I will." She ducked her head. "Dear Lord, thank You for this meal and the hands that prepared it. Use it to nourish our bodies, and use our bodies to Your will. In Jesus' name we pray, amen."

Chapter Twelve

"Oh, this does taste as good as it smells." Landry savored the fillet, the rich flavors filling her senses. "The pecan wood really adds a whole other level of zest. This is wonderful. Do you want a bite?"

He shook his head. "This burger's out-of-this-world good, and it's huge. I might not be able to finish it all."

That burger did look great. "Can you cut me off a little bite, just so I can taste it?"

He nodded, but not before she'd caught the surprise on his face. Perhaps she'd made this too personal. She hadn't meant to, but considering the information they'd shared, she hadn't thought twice about it coming off as too familiar with him.

Now she felt awkward. This wasn't a date, for goodness' sake, but she'd made it feel like one. *God, what am I doing?*

Nickolai cut off a piece of his burger and slipped it onto the edge of her plate.

"Thanks." Landry could barely get the word out. She should've stayed with her gut instinct and said no when he asked her to come. But no. She'd had to listen to Marcie tell her this was a good idea. She hadn't taken the time to really think it through.

She needed to walk them back to the zone where they belonged. Back to even footing. "I guess you probably heard that soon after my mom died, my dad was diagnosed with Alzheimer's. That's the most horrible disease." She swallowed the bite of burger, which despite being amazing, caught in the back of her throat. Landry took a long drink of her soda.

"I'm so sorry."

"It wasn't so bad at first. He'd forget little things like leaving the stove on. Or forgetting where he left the cup of coffee he'd just poured. I'd tease him and we'd laugh." She paused and forced herself to finish the fillet. The memory of her dad's day-to-day loss of memory would haunt her forever.

"I've heard how awful it is, not just for the victim, but for the family as well."

"It is. Soon he started forgetting work stuff. Like not remembering what to fill out on a form he'd actually helped create. Forgetting where to find the case worker's information in the file. Not knowing what job he'd already accepted." She could never explain how she felt like she died a little every day when she saw her dad and witnessed him struggle to remember. That was the worst of it—that he knew he was supposed to know something but couldn't yank it from his memory bank.

"I can't imagine." Nickolai wiped his mouth and set aside his now empty plate. "And I'm sorry I keep apologizing. I hated everyone's sympathy after getting shot but knew they just didn't know what else to say."

"I know. It's hard. You want to reach out to someone and let them know you care, but you don't know what to say. 'I'm sorry' seems so insignificant because when it's said to you, it feels flat." She clamped her hand over her mouth. Had she really admitted that? Out loud? To him?

He chuckled. "Don't get embarrassed. That's the truth. I feel the same way. But when we tell it to someone else, we don't mean it to be trivial."

She nodded and smiled, grateful. Then it struck her—Nickolai Baptiste wasn't quite the arrogant monster she'd made him out to be in her mind. To tell the truth, she'd actually been enjoying tonight. Yes, the food was amazing and the restaurant ambiance and service was outstanding, but the company and conversation was just as welcoming.

She didn't know whether that was a good thing. . .or bad. Oh, Lord. . .

Time to change the subject. "If I'm not being too nosy, after you were shot, you couldn't stay on the force?"

"They offered me a desk job while recovering, but it was too frustrating to watch my best friend partnered up with someone else and getting to do the job I loved."

"So you left."

He nodded and took a drink of his soda. "I did the whole feeling sorry for myself bit for several weeks; then my dad kinda kicked me in the behind. Told me I'd wallowed around long enough and it was time for me to find something else to do with my life instead of moping and making everyone around me miserable."

Landry chuckled. Her dad would've done the same thing.

Nickolai laughed, too. "I was being quite pitiful. My mother felt sorry for me, but my dad had had enough."

"My dad was the same way. He'd let me pout and kick the couch for a day or so, but then tell me to get over it. No matter what it was."

"Yep." He ran a hand over his beard that he kept trimmed and neat. "So, I saw a notice in one of my law enforcement magazines about a recovery specialist online course. I figured I'd take it just to get Dad off my case." The corners of his mouth lifted, just a hint.

His smile could be quite disarming. Landry reached for her glass.

"Ended up really enjoying the course. When it was over, I talked to Dad and a couple of other people who knew about business plans and the like, and well, one thing led to another, and that's how We Find It was born."

"Cute name, by the way. Always wondered how you came up with it."

"I didn't. My little sister did."

The waitress appeared at the table with their check. Both of them reached for it. Nickolai tugged a little harder. "I asked you to come, remember?"

"But. . ." That sounded way too much like a date. While the thought didn't cause her to shiver as it would've before they'd eaten and talked, she still didn't want that to be misconstrued.

"How about I get this one, and you can get the next?"

She nodded, surprised how the implication that there'd be another shared meal warmed her.

The waitress grinned at Landry as she took Nickolai's credit card and rushed away.

Landry's cell rang. Even without the special ring tone, she knew it was Marcie. "I'm sorry, but if I don't answer this, she'll send out the SWAT team."

He nodded.

"Hello, Marcie."

"Why didn't you call me when you got back?"

"We're waiting on the check and then will head back to the motel." Landry pushed the button to lower the volume. She had a pretty good idea what her best friend's response was going to be.

"You're still with Nickolai Baptiste? You left over two hours ago!"

Had it really been that long? The time had flown by. "Oh, the food is delicious here. I had the mahi fillet, and it was out of this world." She smiled at Nickolai and made a she's-going-on-and-on gesture. He smiled back.

"You're still right there with him?"

"Yes. I'll call you later. Bye, Marcie." She disconnected the call, her cheeks burning.

The waitress appeared with Nickolai's receipt and card, thanked them, and then waggled her brows at Landry before leaving again.

"I'm guessing that was your best friend on the phone?" Nickolai signed the receipt before slipping his credit card back into his wallet.

"Yes. Marcie. She's like a mother hen, always worrying about me." She dropped her phone into her purse and stood.

He motioned her to lead the way. "It's nice to have someone like that. My partner worries about me."

She couldn't imagine a guy calling Nickolai and giving him grief over being out with her for over two hours. She snorted a little at the thought.

"What?" Nickolai stepped around her to open the door.

"Just having a hard time imagining your partner being the worrywart Marcie is."

"Chris isn't a worrywart so much as just being there for the hard stuff." He stopped at the passenger side of the truck, unlocked it, and opened the door for her. "I went through a lot of hard stuff, and his logic and reasoning really helped." He shut the door behind her.

Landry fastened her seat belt and took a quick second to check her reflection in the visor's mirror before flipping it up. It'd been a long time since a man had opened doors for her. Her daddy had always done that, but since he'd died, no one. Then again, she hadn't really given anyone the opportunity to, either. It was nice. She'd kind of missed it.

Nickolai slipped behind the steering wheel. "And your friend is the one who convinced you to come tonight, so she has that going for her. In my opinion, of course." He chuckled as he waited for the diesel's light to go off.

"Oh, Marcie's the best. Sometimes her worrying can be trying, but for the most part, I love that about her. It's nice to know someone's thinking about me and worrying about my happiness and safety."

He cranked the engine and then cracked the back windows. He turned and faced her. "Speaking of safety, I'm being one hundred percent honest with you, Landry. I didn't have anything to do with your tire or that note."

The sincerity of his voice was matched by the seriousness of his expression lit by the dashboard glow. It hit her—with all this man had been through, petty games to discourage her weren't in his playbook.

"I know. I'm sorry for jumping to the wrong conclusions."

"I can understand why you might think that, after I was such an arrogant jerk at Mrs. Winslet's."

She laughed. "You were a jerk."

He laughed with her. "Well, you surprised me. You weren't what I expected." He put the truck in DRIVE and eased out of the parking lot.

"Why? What did you expect? A ghoul with horns?"

He laughed harder. "Well, you are my competitor, you know."

"Yeah. I'd pictured you with horns, too." She chuckled.

Funny, she didn't see him that way anymore. It was nice and comfortable between them. As much as she might hate to admit it, she enjoyed his company. Teasing and all.

"Horns, huh?" Nickolai eased onto the main road, slipping into the traffic. Everyone and their brother seemed to be on the road. The marathon, of course.

"Sorry." Landry chuckled.

He liked how she let out little snorts when she laughed. It was cute. Endearing. Just like her.

Whoa! There must've been more than chipotle aioli on his burger.

The traffic halted. He eased the truck to a stop behind the car in front of him. Then he noticed the flashers.

"Wonder what's going on?" Landry sat forward and leaned right, then left, peering out the windshield.

Now he remembered, and groaned. "I saw a flyer about the runners participating in the marathon tomorrow being recognized tonight at some sort of ceremony. That's why so many of the roads were closed early today."

She sat back against the seat and cracked her window a little. A part-spicy, part-flowery, part-muskiness aroma rode under his nose on the gentle evening breeze. Her perfume or shampoo or something, but the smell was definitely right for her.

He needed to get his thoughts back on track. Focus. Nickolai put the truck in PARK and popped on his flashers, like most all the other vehicles on the road. "Okay, let's go ahead and get it over with. Let's talk about the case."

"And we were getting along so well, too." But she smiled.

"I'll start. Before we left, I spoke with my partner—er, former partner, to see what the police have on the case. The Winslet murder is big because the head of the whole criminal investigations division, the captain himself, is overseeing the investigation."

"I'm assuming that's unusual?"

He nodded. "Very. So the Winslet name and money must really be big."

"I know. One of us is making someone really nervous. I guess that would be me since I seem to be the target." She shook her head. "But I can't imagine any of my leads motivating someone to puncture my tire or risk taping a note to my door."

"Yeah, I can't see Allen Edgar risking being caught. He'd be terrified."

"Right." She stiffened and twisted, putting her back against the door. "Wait. How do you know about Allen?"

"I met him. Talked to him."

"You followed me?" Her indignation was as visible as her rising anger.

"No." He needed to calm her quickly or they would undo all the easiness between them. He'd have to put his cards on the table. "I spoke with Joel Easton. He told me about his and Allen's plot to raise the buying price on Winslet. When Joel said he'd lost the photocopy of the map, I realized Allen probably took it, which he did. When I talked to him, he said he'd tried to sell it to a beautiful woman, and I figured out it was you. How did you find him?"

"He had copied and pasted the exact listing from Art Source onto a black market of the art world site, so I thought whoever had the map had come back here to resell it." She relaxed a little. "They had a plot to raise the selling price on Winslet?"

Ahh, she hadn't known that. Well, it would build their trust for him to be able to share the information with her. He told her about talking with the driver and the other bidder, the hack, but also Easton's motives.

"Wow, that's pretty devious, but I can understand. If there had been a chance to cure my dad, I probably would've done the same thing." She chewed her bottom lip and sat back against the cushion.

Nickolai couldn't argue. He'd probably do the same if he could cure Lisbeth. In a way, he already had compromised his normal stance by taking the case, just so he could afford to get her into that halfway house.

"We both agree it's probably not Allen."

He shook his head. "I'd guess not, but I've been wrong before. Still, I'm not sure what he would gain by trying to scare you off."

"It's not logical. He wants me to pay one hundred thousand dollars for that copy of the map. I can't see him wanting me to leave before he got some money."

"That was my thinking as well." Nickolai swallowed. He had informed her of what he knew about her lead, shared on a lead he had that she didn't. Now was the tough part. He swallowed. "I think maybe you're a target because of the copy of the map you have."

Again her eyes widened. "What?"

He raised his hands in mock surrender. "I'm not following you. I'm not stalking you."

"Then how do you know what I have?"

Transparency and honesty were his best options here. He reached into the console and handed her the copies he had from Margaret. "Because the printer recorded a copy when you made your copies. It's easy to print off another copy or two." Maybe even three in this case.

She took the papers, shaking her head. "And I thought she was so nice. Even felt sorry for her because I think her husband treats her like a second-class citizen." She set the copies on top of the console. "Aside from that, I can't see her stabbing my tire or putting the note on my door. Maybe I'm wrong, but she seems too mousy and timid for that."

"I agree, on all counts." Traffic was still stalled. "Did you know there was a housekeeper in the back of the office when you were in there? A lady named Vanessa?"

Those amazing eyes of hers widened again. "No. Did you talk with her? Could she be capable of everything?"

He shrugged. "I haven't got to talk to her yet. She had already gone home by the time I spoke with Kohl and Margaret in the office. That's the owners' names, in case they didn't tell you. Anyway, it's not just her we need to talk to. Apparently Margaret made a copy for Vanessa's boyfriend because Vanessa asked for it. She said her boyfriend collected stuff like that."

Landry shook her head. "Unbelievable."

"I know. I can't wait to get his information from Vanessa tomorrow and pay him a visit." Cars began to move. Nickolai turned off his hazard lights and pulled the truck out of PARK.

"Oh, I'm going with you." She paused. "I mean, I'm going to talk to him as well, so maybe we could talk with him together."

He hid his smile with the turn of his head. "Sure. Something else. When I was in the office, Kohl mentioned that a Phillip Fontenot had arrived and asked about our group."

"That's who was arguing with Stan!"

"What?"

She told him what she'd overheard from Stan and another man arguing in his motel room. "Of course, I didn't want to pry, so I don't know any more than that. Now that I know it was Phillip. . . according to Monica Courtland, Bartholomew's assistant, Phillip and Bartholomew were best friends. They even had a lunch date scheduled for the day Bartholomew died."

"So you spoke with the assistant?" Good work. He hadn't gotten around to it yet.

"I went to see her. At first, it was odd, because she said everyone was broken up about Winslet's death, but it looked pretty much like business as usual around Winslet Industries. At least to me."

"What was your impression of her?" Nickolai followed the line of cars inching forward.

"Old beyond her years, and I don't mean in a good, mature type of way. I mean in the lacking fun way." Landry smiled and shrugged. "She came across as uptight. Maybe it was from her years of working for such an older executive like Winslet."

"Wonder what her story is. I might need to call my partner and see if there's anything about her in the case file." Hopefully, Chris could access that information, or give him some background on the girl.

Landry nodded. "But she was very clear on the relationship between Bartholomew and Phillip. According to her comments, they were best buds. She said when Phillip came to the office for lunch, as was pretty common, Bartholomew lost his formal manner."

"And now he's here."

"Even more, Stan thinks Phillip has a crush on Winifred, and Phillip didn't deny it."

Nickolai resisted making a face. "Really?"

"Yeah. Here's one even better. According to Phillip's response, Stan has a crush on Winifred that was apparent before Bartholomew died."

"That is interesting." Could be a good motive to murder Winslet. Two men interested in the man's wife?

"I'm thinking we need to talk to Stan and Phillip."

He nodded. "And I was thinking..." The traffic began to move at a much better pace. "Maybe we should drive out toward the Superstitions. See if we can make out any of the landmarks from the picture you got." This was it...the true test of faith. If she agreed, they'd made progress, and that would make him happier than he cared to admit.

But if she said no...

Nickolai held his breath and waited for an answer.

Chapter Thirteen

Should she agree or refuse? Should she tell him about the man going camping? Wasn't that the million-dollar question?

Landry snorted at herself. More like the fifty-thousand-dollar question.

"Or, if you'd rather not..." The dejection in his expression filled her with unexpected smugness.

She didn't think that was considered becoming in anyone. She cleared her throat. "I was just wondering if it would be better for us to find this Phillip first. . . ." She checked the time illuminated on the dashboard. "Since it's dark out."

He nodded.

"Unless you'd rather do it separately. I mean, I just thought since we were both going to find him anyway..." Goodness, she tripped over her own tongue, which annoyed her all the more.

"No, I think we should. I mean, we need to find out who's behind these stunts."

She smiled, warmed. "Good. Then we agree. We'll find Phillip tonight, then maybe drive out to the Superstitions tomorrow. Actually, I think the map is in the Superstitions."

"Really?" He shot her a quizzical look.

"Yeah. The waitress saw a man with the original map. In a protective sleeve. He went to the military surplus store and bought a tent and other camping supplies. She recognized the area as Weaver's Needle."

"And you weren't going to tell me?" Nickolai grinned. "You little sneak."

"Like you would've told me before tonight?"

He shook his head. "No, I guess I wouldn't have."

She rolled down her window a little more as he picked up speed. The cool evening air filled the truck's cab with a most comfortable crispness. Landry closed her eyes and laid her head back on the headrest. It had been a while since she'd been just this. . .relaxed when working a case. Maybe it had something to do with Nickolai Baptiste. Maybe not. Maybe she was just flat-out exhausted with worry about the business and her dad's legacy and making everything work out. Or maybe, just maybe, she'd accepted that she had to give it all to God and stop taking the worry and fear back. Last night, she'd done just that. Today had been a good day, overall, despite flat tires and ominous notes.

"Um, Landry?" Nickolai's voice was edged with importance.

She sat upright. "What?"

"My brakes are out." He pumped the brake pedal. It went all the way to the floor. Again. Again.

And again.

Minutes stood still as her consciousness and emotions and rational thoughts all collided.

"What?" She gripped the dashboard and stared out the front windshield. Cars stopped at the red light about five hundred yards in front of them. The stoplight sat at the bottom of a pretty good-sized hill.

"Behind us," Nickolai ground out.

In that split second, she realized the cab of the truck was lit up from more than the dashboard. She turned. Made out the eighteen-wheeler bearing down on them. Faced front—four hundred yards.

There was no shoulder.

Her heart pounded. The tangy taste of metal filled her mouth. *Oh, God, please help us. Please let that truck stop.*

Three hundred yards.

Traffic flashed by in the opposite lane.

Nickolai rolled down all four windows.

No place to go.

Two hundred yards.

No options.

"Brace yourself." Nickolai laid on the horn.

No one could move anyway. Landry gripped the console with her left hand and the door armrest bar with her right.

One hundred yards and gaining.

Landry closed her eyes and prayed.

She registered the sound of the eighteen-wheeler's brakes squealing just before the loud crunch of metal echoed inside the cabin. She slammed backward then was instantly flung forward. Landry opened her eyes and gritted her teeth, clenching her hold on the console and bar tighter.

As if in slow motion, she swayed as the truck turned almost 180 degrees to the right. The trucker's grill ground with Nickolai's bumper.

Landry's muscles tensed as momentum shook her, knocking her against the passenger door. She registered the jolt of pain in her shoulder a nanosecond before the side of her head grazed the locked and tightened seat belt. Her head rolled back against the headrest.

Time froze. Her senses, overloaded. The swooshing of air as it sliced through the cabin filled her head. The wind caressed her face—cold, and oddly, comforting. Headlights from vehicles split the darkness of night. Her hands cramped against the smooth leather of the truck's interior.

Everything went silent and still. No breeze, no movement, no sound. Her chest tightened: no oxygen, no air—her lungs seized, not inhaling. Just Landry's heartbeat pounding in her head.

Da-dun. Da-dun. Da-dun.

She opened her mouth and sucked in air. Everything erupted at once.

Cold encapsulated her. Shivers vibrated through her. Goose bumps pimpled her flesh. Screams registered. Cries. Lights flashed. Clicks.

"Landry, Landry. . .are you okay?" Nickolai's voice cut through everything else.

"Yes. I'm all right." At least, she was pretty sure she didn't have any broken bones. Not that she could feel at the moment.

Nickolai reached over and released her seat belt. "Breathe slowly. It's the adrenaline rushing. Give yourself a minute."

She inhaled through her nose. Exhaled through her mouth.

He opened his door. Light flooded the truck's cabin.

She blinked, finally releasing her death grip on the truck. Her hands alternated between cramping and shaking. *Lord!*

He opened her door. She hadn't even registered that he'd gotten out of the driver's seat. "Come on, let's make sure you're okay." He took her elbow and helped ease her out of the truck. She wobbled for a minute; then his chest was against her back and his arms on either side of her. His breath grazed the side of her face and neck. "You just need to get your footing. Does anything hurt?"

She couldn't think. Couldn't process. The musky scent of his cologne permeated her personal space. It was a familiar fragrance, but she couldn't place it at the moment. Her gaze went to Nickolai's truck. The front end looked like it had maybe grazed a tree or pole, but the back end's bumper was gone. It wasn't on the ground. . .oh. She saw it—attached to the front grill of the eighteen-wheeler.

God, thank You. Thank You. Thank You. Only You kept us alive.

"Landry?" She could feel Nickolai's chest move as he said her name.

Giving herself a mental shake, she straightened, pushing off from leaning into his strength. "I'm fine." She did a quick mental evaluation of self: legs okay, arms okay, back okay. . .only her right shoulder and right side of her head hurt. And her neck, a little. The pain in her shoulder throbbed, while her head and neck just ached.

"Are you sure?" Concern thickened his voice.

She nodded then immediately regretted it. "My shoulder hurts, and my head and neck ache, but my shoulder really hurts."

"You must've hit it against the door." He handed her the straps of her purse then led her tenderly to the side of the road.

A woman screamed as the truck driver approached. "You idiot. You could've killed us all. What, were you texting?" she snarled at the truck driver.

"It's not his fault. It was me. My—"

She glared at Nickolai and Landry, cutting him off. "Oh, were you playing kissy face? Good thing my kids weren't in the car with me. I've called the police."

"I'm sorry. My brakes went out. The pedal went all the way to the floor." Nickolai didn't engage in any confrontation. His voice remained steady and neutral. "Are you hurt, ma'am?"

"I'm fine, except where the seat belt dug into my shoulder." The woman crossed her arms over her chest.

Landry could empathize. Her shoulder was killing her now. Hot pain shot down her arm.

"I didn't see everyone stopping." The driver of the eighteen-wheeler's shaggy beard bounced as he spoke. "Are you okay?" He posed the question to all three of them, but his gaze rested on Landry.

Before anyone could answer, the whir of sirens filled the air as a fire truck and ambulance pulled up. How could she not have heard them approaching?

"You need to have your shoulder looked at." Nickolai led her toward the ambulance. He faced the woman who'd been driving the car in front of them. "You, too. Just to make sure you're okay." He quickly filled in the EMTs then turned back as a police cruiser whipped in behind the fire truck.

Landry started to follow him, but the EMT eased her onto the back of the ambulance beside the other woman.

"Let me take a look at this shoulder."

All thoughts of Nickolai or the accident fled as he touched the exact spot on her shoulder that sent bolts of red, shooting pain down her arm.

Oh, Lord, help me.

She had to be okay.

Even in the dark and from about a couple of hundred feet away, Nickolai watched her face go from pale to white as the paramedic examined her shoulder. It took every ounce of his self-control not to run over to the back of the ambulance. That, and the uniformed officer pushing for answers hovering by them.

The area of the road was lit up like daylight with the cruiser's spotlight shining on the group of them hovering around the uniformed officer.

"You said you didn't have enough time to stop?" the officer asked the driver of the eighteen-wheeler.

"I didn't. I didn't see the line of traffic stopping. It just did. Next thing I knew, I slammed into the truck in front of me, which propelled them into the car in front of them. Luckily the light had already changed by then and the car in front of that one sped out of the way."

"Lucky for them indeed." The uniformed officer jotted notes on the accident report form attached onto the clipboard.

"It's not his fault," Nickolai interrupted.

"Oh yeah? Got your license and registration?"

Nickolai handed the cop his driver's license. "Nickolai Baptiste. The registration is in my truck console. My brakes went out. I had no choice but to hit the car in front of me." He nodded at the trucker. "I wasn't able to stop, so neither was he."

"Had your brakes been squealing? Feeling a little mushy when you pressed on the pedal for a while?"

"No, sir. They were fine earlier. Not a hint of a problem."

"I see." No, he didn't, but Nickolai didn't feel like going into much more with the young cop who definitely fit the stereotype of an egotistical narcissist who got into law enforcement for the power, not to actually serve the people. Such a constant frustration to the good cops out there who had to deal with negativity based on behavior like this one's.

"You're a long way from New Or-leans, Mr. Baptiste. You here for the marathon?"

Swallowing the long, exasperating sigh begging to be exhaled, Nickolai explained who he was, why he was in town, and again, slower this time, explained that his truck's brakes had gone out. The cop took down the information then handed Nickolai's license back to him. "Recovery specialist working a case here, huh?"

It was times such as these that Nickolai longed to have his badge again, just to avoid going through the silly rigmarole that this traffic unni would put him through. He quickly gave the condensed version, finishing up with mentioning Officer Hogan by name.

"I'll check in with him when I get done with my report. You say your brakes didn't work?"

Nickolai nodded. "Not at all." And that was extremely strange. He intended to go back to where he'd parked at the restaurant and see if there was brake fluid on the ground. Same thing with where he'd parked at the motel.

"Did you try pumping the pedal? Sometimes that can do it."

"No pumping on newer model vehicles equipped with ABS, which my truck has." Nickolai ground his teeth.

"Huh. I see." Clearly he didn't, but he wrote on his form anyway.

Nickolai shifted, staring at the ambulance. The doors still stood open, but they'd moved Landry inside, so he couldn't see her. Was she hurt more than she'd let on? More than she'd known? His gut tightened and twisted. If she was seriously injured while he was driving. . .

"You are aware that the law requires drivers to maintain complete control of their vehicle at all times, correct?" the officer asked the truck driver. "And that hitting a vehicle in the rear is a clear indication that you were not in complete control of your vehicle."

The trucker nodded. "I should've been able to stop."

Nickolai turned back to the officer. "But he didn't see me stopping because my brakes were out, so how would he know? Due to the steepness of the road toward the traffic light, and having no brakes to even slow down, our speed increased. This put more space between myself and the eighteen-wheeler, so naturally he would assume we were accelerating, not coming to a stop." Nickolai knew how hard it would be if this accident was a black mark on the trucker's record. He might lose his CDL, but he would definitely lose his job. Trucking companies had gotten too bad a rap for a long time, and the insurance on the big rigs alone cut deep into profits.

"You an expert in vehicular accidents now?" the officer asked Nickolai, glaring the entire time.

"No, sir, but I can't even be sure if I didn't hit the car in front of me before I was hit." He straightened as the lady who'd been driving the car he'd hit strode toward them from the ambulance. "It was nobody's fault. . .that's why they're called accidents."

The cop didn't even have a chance to ask the lady anything as she joined them. She held out papers to him. "My name is Molly Berringing. Here is a copy of my driver's license and my vehicle registration. I'm the one who called and reported the accident."

He took them from her and slid them under the clip. "Thank—"

"I was sitting at the red light, late because of the road being closed because of the marathon kickoff tonight. I'd forgotten this part of Apache Trail would be closed during the opening ceremony and I'd just needed to run to the store and pick up another loaf of bread. If I'd gone to the grocery on the other side of town, I wouldn't have been caught in the traffic jam, nor this wreck."

"Ms. Berringing—"

"It's Molly. I'm divorced. A single mom to my sweet little Ashland and Ashley. Thank goodness they're at their dad's right now and weren't in the car. They could've been killed."

"Molly," the officer interrupted. "Tell me what happened, please. You were sitting at the red light. . . ."

"Right. I knew the light was about to turn green because I come this way from work every day. Anyway, something told me to look in my rearview mirror right at that moment. That never happens to me, really, getting funny feelings like that."

"So you looked in your rearview mirror?"

Nickolai pressed his lips together to hold in the smile. At least the officer could understand frustration. Welcome to his world.

She nodded. "I saw that pickup truck heading right toward me, and that big old eighteen-wheeler barreling down right behind him."

That wasn't right. Nickolai interrupted her. "He wasn't really barreling down—"

"Please, Mr. Baptiste. I'm taking Mis—er, Molly Berringing's statement." The officer smiled at her. "Go ahead, ma'am."

The trucker locked stares with Nickolai then rolled his eyes.

"As I was saying." She shot Nickolai a warning to keep quiet. "I saw them both bearing down on me, and I thought, 'Lord, You gotta save me.'" She nodded. "I saw the yellow light on the other side and knew the light was about to turn green, but wasn't sure it'd turn in enough time."

He glanced back to the ambulance. Landry sat on the back, her right arm in a sling. One of the paramedics was still with her.

"I knew I was gonna get hit and I was terrified. I mean, that's a big truck and an even bigger eighteen-wheeler. I just knew I was a goner, so I started praying and praying."

"I bet." The officer shot Nickolai a hard look.

"I was praying, too, ma'am," the trucker offered softly.

"Well, He must've heard our prayers," Molly said, "because just as those trucks hit and hit me and I started to slam into the car in front of me, the light had changed and those cars sped off, so I didn't hit anything." She narrowed her eyes at Nickolai. "I was just rear-ended. Good thing my kids weren't in that backseat, mister, or you and I would be having a totally different conversation right now."

"Yes, ma'am." No sense riling her up even more. Besides, he noticed Landry making her way toward them. He moved to intercept her. "Are you okay?"

She fell into step beside him. "Bad bruise on my shoulder from hitting the truck door. Minor whiplash on my neck."

"And they aren't taking you to the hospital?" What kind of two-bit town was this?

"I declined. I'm fine. I told the EMT if I showed any of the symptoms we discussed, I'd go to the emergency room." She let him hold her left elbow and guide her.

"You should've gone with them." While her color had improved a little, she was still too pale.

"I'm fine." She smiled.

"Ma'am, you were the passenger in the Ford truck?" Officer Friendly had noticed her. He must have liked what he saw, because Nickolai would swear he puffed his chest out more than he already had inflated himself.

She nodded. "Landry Parker."

Nickolai took a step closer to her.

His movement wasn't missed by the cop, who raised his brows at Landry. "Are you from New Or-leans as well?"

She flashed him a smile so brilliant, it pierced the night. "I am, sir."

"What can you tell me about the accident?"

"I wasn't paying attention to the road, enjoying the cool evening when Nickolai informed me that the brakes in the truck were gone. I looked over and saw that the pedal had gone all the way to the floor."

"I'm sure you were frightened. What did you do?" Even the cop's voice came out softer when he talked to Landry.

She seemed to have that effect on people.

"He warned me about the truck coming up from behind, and the stoplight in front of us. We both realized there was no shoulder and that there was a steady stream of oncoming traffic. We truly had nowhere to go."

The cop nodded, not even making notes.

Nickolai and the trucker met gazes again, this time grinning.

"Naturally, we knew we had to do something. Nickolai rolled down the windows in the truck and laid on the horn. After that, it's a little blurry as to what happened. It all went so fast. We hit and were hit, almost at the same time." She gestured to the sling. "I was slammed against the door, and I hit my head against the back of the seat."

"Are you going to the hospital?" the police officer asked her.

She shook her head. "I think I'll be okay." She smiled at him. "I promised to go if I felt even the slightest bit like I needed to."

The cop smiled at her. "You watch yourself, Ms. Parker. Whiplash can creep up on you."

"I will. Thank you."

The cop turned his gaze on Nickolai. "Why did you let your windows down?"

"To reduce glass being broken and cutting us and others."

"Pretty clever, wouldn't you say?" Landry smiled.

The cop ignored her question and turned to Molly. "Did you hear his horn?"

Her expression clearly said she had. Nickolai would bet that she hadn't noticed him or the eighteen-wheeler heading toward her until she heard the horn.

She shrugged. "There was so much going on, I really don't recall."

Two regular tow trucks and one designed for a big rig pulled up.

"I see." The cop slipped his pen into his shirt pocket. "I have all of your information. Your vehicles will be towed to this garage." He handed out business cards. "I'll file my report and be in touch within twenty-four hours." He turned and headed to his cruiser. The spotlight on top of his car went dark.

"What are we supposed to do?" the trucker asked.

Molly smirked. "My sister will be here any minute. I called her before I left the ambulance."

Landry smiled at the trucker. "I called our friend from the ambulance as well. I'm sure he'll be more than pleased to drop you off."

"I'm not from here. I was just passing through. I need to call my boss."

"Look, why don't you ride with us to the motel? From what

Wedgwood Baptist Church

000010007793
ADETUTU, OLOLADE
4116 William Fleming Ct
Apt C
Fort Worth TX 76115
469-994-5092
ololadetutu@gmail.com
Date: 02/17/2019

03/03/19 The fire in ember 15694
03/03/19 Called to protect 20274
03/03/19 The lady of Tarpon Springs 20275
03/03/19 Jerusalem's queen. a novel of Salome Alexandra 20391
03/03/19 With this pledge 20477
03/10/19...Wanted: a superhero to save the world 20360
03/10/19...Weaver's needle 19752
03/10/19...Just joking 5 18590
03/10/19...Momentum [CD] CD 165

I understand, there aren't many rooms available in town with the marathon going on. If they're all booked, you can crash on my other bed." Nickolai already felt bad enough that the trucker was involved in the accident at all, knowing all that he did.

"Thanks, man. Let me grab my stuff." The trucker headed back to his rig.

"That was nice." Landry winced.

"I'm sorry you got hurt." He'd rather have cut off his own arm.

Or get shot again.

"It's not your fault, which got me to thinking. Is it possible somebody messed with your brake lines?"

"You know, I thought the exact same thing." It was the only thing that made sense. "I plan to check in at this garage tomorrow morning and find out what a mechanic says about it."

If someone had messed with his brakes, that was three blatant attempts to get him and Landry out of town.

What were they onto?

Chapter Fourteen

The morning sun sliced through the slit in the motel's curtains, filling the room with brightness.

Landry squinted against the light and flung her arm over her eyes. Pain shot out from her shoulder like electrical currents. *Oh, sweet Jesus, make the pain stop.*

She cringed and gently sat up, pulling her arm close to her as if it were in its sling, and stared at the bedside clock.

Really? Nine twelve? Already? She'd slept until after nine?

How long had it been since she'd slept in like this? Months, at least. Must've been those pain pills the nice paramedic had given her. She rarely took even so much as an ibuprofen, so whatever was in those pills had really knocked her out.

She stood and gingerly stretched, taking an inventory of every little ache and pain. Her shoulder hurt, obviously. Her neck ached a bit as she rolled her head to loosen the tensed muscles. The headache she'd gone to bed with last night had eased—no longer throbbing, just a steady, dull twinge. Her left hand felt a little sore as she flexed it. She must've really been holding on to that console with everything she had.

Overall, she wasn't in too bad a condition. Considering. *Thank You, Jesus!*

A quick shower made her feel even better. Not being able to lift her right arm was a bit of an issue in her normal routine. Washing her hair with one arm was particularly challenging. And forget braiding her hair. Even pulling it back into a ponytail was an issue.

No matter how hard she tried, there was no way to center it in the middle of her head. With the third failed attempt, she tossed the band into her bag and pulled out a headband. At least it would keep the hair out of her face.

Dressed and ready with her sling keeping all pressure off her shoulder, she stepped outside and was welcomed by Nickolai standing in the parking lot, talking with the two officers who'd taken their reports of the note.

Nickolai smiled when he saw her. "Good morning. How're you feeling?"

"Better, I think." She couldn't help grinning back at him. "Can't believe I slept so late."

"You were exhausted."

"And the pain pills the EMT gave me really knocked me out." She still felt a little fuzzy. "How's our trucker friend?"

"He made his statement at the police station early this morning, then picked up his rig and headed out. He said he hoped you were okay."

She nodded, regretting moving her neck instantly.

"You remember Officers Hogan and Paxton?"

So those were their names. "I do. Hello, again."

"Sorry to hear you were hurt," Officer Paxton, a.k.a. Winky, said.

"Thanks, but I'm okay."

"They were just telling me that they're requesting a forensics mechanic inspect my truck."

She nodded. "So y'all know his brake lines were probably messed with?"

The older officer, Hogan, shook his head and held up a palm. "We don't know anything right now. We only deal with the facts. Once our team looks over Mr. Baptiste's truck and gives us a report, we'll know more."

How unsurprisingly neutral. At least they were going to check.

"In the meantime, we encourage common sense safety precautions like making sure your hotel room is always locked when you're in for the evening, don't go places alone, always have your cell phone handy. . . stuff like that." Officer Paxton nodded as he spoke, reminding her of a bobblehead figure.

"Of course."

Officer Hogan opened the driver's door of their police car. "We'll be in touch as soon as we get the report."

"Did you find out anything from the note?" she asked.

"Our team's still going over it for any trace evidence. Of course, we didn't dust it for prints since so many of you touched it." Officer Paxton didn't sound hopeful.

"Thanks."

As soon as they drove off, Nickolai moved beside her. "At least they're working the case and not just blowing us off."

She shook her head. "So you feel it, too? Like we're to blame for interrupting their quiet town life? I thought maybe it was just me."

"Nope, I feel it, but I also understand."

"Ahh, you boys in blue take up for each other so much."

"We do, but that's not the case this time. You've got to admit, we do seem to have issues following us all of a sudden."

"Because we're onto something." She so hoped that was the case.

"Speaking of onto something. . . Stan just headed over to Mickey D's Café, not to be confused with the golden arches, for breakfast since the officers said pretty much everything else was closed until the marathon is over. Stan asked that we join him as soon as you were up and the police gone. I told him I'd drive us in your rental. Hope that's okay."

"Of course. I hated not being able to look for Phillip Fontenot last night." She dug the keys for the Jeep out of her purse and handed them to him. She looked around and realized there weren't any other people in the parking lot, and the traffic was almost nonexistent on the main street of town. She'd completely forgotten about the marathon being today.

Nickolai placed a hand on the small of her back and led her to the

Jeep. "I doubt waking anyone up after midnight would put them in a decent mood to answer any questions about Phillip Fontenot."

"No, but I'd still like to know who he really is and why he's here."

Nickolai stopped at the passenger side door and faced her. "And why Stan isn't happy that he's here."

She shrugged, cringed at the burn, and then shook her head. "I think there's more to Stan and Mrs. Winslet and Bartholomew and this Phillip Fontenot than we know. I think we've been so focused on the map that we've forgotten someone was murdered. Now that we've gotten threats. . .well, let's just say that we should probably look into all these connections a little closer."

"I agree." He unlocked the door by the remote and opened it for her.

She didn't resist his chivalry as he helped her up into the Jeep. She wasn't quite sure what she'd have done had he not been there. She couldn't drive with this pain. Well, she could if she had to, but it'd be pretty uncomfortable.

Despite her and Nickolai's truce, so to speak, Landry didn't like having to depend on anyone for anything. Especially one who was, basically, her competition.

Marcie would get a huge kick out of this situation. She chuckled, remembering her best friend's horrified tone last night.

"What's so funny?" Nickolai shut the driver's door and clicked on his seat belt.

"Thinking about my conversation with my best friend last night. She's not amused about the wreck."

"Neither am I." He eased out of the parking lot onto the main road. No cars moving on either side of the four lanes. The couple of blocks drive had no events, thankfully.

"Well, Marcie tends to be a little over the top as far as being cautious and concerned. She all but begged me to come home."

"You might consider that." He glanced at her before turning into the café's parking lot. "Not because of anything other than your safety."

Her back stiffened a little. "What about yours? It was your brakes messed with. I only got a flat and a letter."

"That flat could've caused a blowout and gotten you in a wreck where you just might be in as bad a shape as you are now, or worse." He pulled the Jeep into one of the many empty spaces and slipped it into PARK.

"Now you sound like Marcie." Boy, she'd demanded Landry send her photos last night then made her video call with her. Neither seemed to make her feel better about Landry staying in Apache Junction. "I'm not leaving. No one is going to run me off from a job I took."

Nickolai opened his mouth then shut it before opening his door and stepping out of the Jeep.

She knew he wanted to argue with her but realized it probably wasn't in his best interest at the moment.

Smart man.

He helped her from the Jeep and into the café. Stan waved them over as soon as they entered. He sat in a corner table with another man.

"Good morning." Stan smiled as they sat. "I hope you're feeling okay, Landry. Nickolai filled me in on your accident early this morning."

"I'll be fine; thank you for asking." She wanted to trust him, really wanted to. He was nice and polite and had been nothing but a gentleman on their flight and while here. Yet the implication of something between him and Winifred Winslet left her feeling a bit uneasy.

"This is Phillip Fontenot," Stan introduced the man sitting on the other side of the table.

"What can I get you two?" An older waitress with her hair pulled back from her face interrupted, smiling as she handed Nickolai and Landry menus.

"We've already ordered, but asked them to hold until you joined us." Stan took a sip from his coffee cup.

Nickolai ordered juice and Landry ordered chocolate milk and the waitress left, giving them time to look over the breakfast options. The tension at the table was thick. Surely that's why the waitress rushed off so quickly. Landry hastily decided what she'd have then took a minute to take in the café itself.

Hardwood floors with a carpet overlay, standard café-style tables and chairs with a few booths, a combination of ceiling fans with lights and just plain light fixtures, a TV mounted on a wall, and a smorgasbord of car and truck pictures and items hung on the walls—typical of a local café-diner type of place. What set this one apart was the beautiful, full-wall mural down one entire wall.

The mural depicted the local area, with a blue truck and red sports car on winding desert Route 66 with the Superstition Mountains large in the background. Right smack-dab in the middle was a landmark Landry had come to recognize from all her research and the photocopies she had of the map: Weaver's Needle.

After the waitress returned with their drinks, took their food order, and left, Nickolai caught Landry's attention and raised his brows.

Landry sat up as straight in the chair as the pain shooting down the back of her shoulder would allow. This was going to get interesting. She would take the lead here.

"So, Phillip, how do you fit into the puzzle here?" Landry asked.

Stan's ready grin faltered.

Phillip, however, was all smiles. "I sit on the board of Winslet Industries, but I've been friends with Bartholomew and Winifred since they were dating."

Landry studied him. He was about Stan's age, maybe a year or two older, and they actually resembled one another. Both had gray and silver hair. Both had neatly trimmed beards and mustaches. The main difference was where the top of Stan's hair was thinning, Phillip's had already let loose. But his top-of-the-head baldness wasn't unattractive. It actually added a bit to his overall mature look. Landry could see how Winifred could be attracted to both men. Or either.

"Do you have new information to share about the map? Or the murder?" Nickolai asked.

"No, nothing new. The police in New Orleans haven't told us of any progress. It's actually quite frustrating."

"Then, no offense, but why are you here?" Landry pushed. "If there's nothing new, I don't understand why you're here."

Now Phillip stopped smiling, too. Landry could tell he wasn't accustomed to having his motives questioned. "I'm here to protect Winifred's investment."

"I thought that was your job," Landry said to Stan.

"Stan's here to provide you with what you need on-site. I'm here to check on the overall status of the case."

Landry could almost reach out and touch the hostility between the two men. This was not good at all. "So, Mrs. Winslet asked you to come?"

Phillip didn't respond for a moment. "I asked Winifred if she'd like me to come check things out. She did."

Landry didn't know how to reply. At the moment, she felt like they were smack-dab in the middle of a danger zone.

"It's clear someone doesn't want us to look into this any further," Nickolai interjected, "so we have a right to question everything that's going on with this investigation, including new people showing up and getting involved."

Stan aligned the salt and pepper shakers with the napkin holder. And the jelly packets holder. And the little brown rectangle holding packets of sugar and sugar substitutes.

"Stan's informed me there have been a few mishaps, so I can understand your leeriness of a new person being involved." Phillip offered another smile.

"Mishaps? I'd say more than a mishap or two. There has been a punctured tire, threatening letter, and messed-with brakes. Now you show up."

"I assure you, Mr. Baptiste, that I'm only here to observe and oversee on behalf of Winifred."

"I'm just a little confused as to why you'd think there was a need to follow up since Stan here gives a report to Mrs. Winslet." Landry leaned closer to the table. "Is there something going on we should know about?"

"No, of course not. I'm just helping out a friend."

Nickolai caught Landry's subtle shake of her head. She'd said she'd overheard the two men arguing.

"You're only here as Mrs. Winslet's friend?" Landry asked.

Phillip smirked and nodded. "And as a member of Winslet Industries board, of course."

"The paperwork Mrs. Winslet gave me shows she hired us, not Winslet Industries." Even with her arm in a sling, Landry wasn't to be dismissed.

"Ms. Parker, Winifred Winslet is Winslet Industries. You can't split the two apart." Phillip's smile had lost some of its authenticity.

The waitress returned with their breakfasts and handed out plates. She refilled coffee then returned with more milk and juice for Nickolai and Landry. Just as quickly and efficiently as she'd served them, she left them alone.

Nickolai took a bite of his bacon, but from the corner of his eye, he noticed Landry bend her head and close her eyes. Her lips moved for a few moments before she lifted her fork and took a bite of her biscuits and gravy.

Praying again?

He didn't want to really think about that. Praying was for the weak. A crutch people used when they couldn't accept the truth, usually about themselves or a loved one. Landry had never struck him as a weak person, though.

"Tell me, have you made any progress on the case?" Phillip asked around mouthfuls of pancakes.

Landry nodded. "Some."

Phillip waved his fork in the air, pointing first at Landry, then Nickolai, then back to Landry again. "That's right—you two aren't working together. You're working against each other like in a contest.

Whoever finds the map first wins the monetary prize." He waggled his brows at Landry. "Sorry, didn't mean to put you on the spot and tell any progress in front of the enemy." He grinned at Nickolai. "For either of you."

"Actually—" Landry started.

"I'll bring you up to speed on how much progress I've made after breakfast." He looked at Landry, sending her a look that clearly conveyed he didn't want Stan or Phillip to know they were kind-of-sort-of working together. Nickolai didn't like the way Phillip looked at Landry.

Whoa! He was getting territorial now?

He scarfed down his omelet, anxious to ignore analyzing how he felt toward Landry. Starting to feel? He couldn't explain. Didn't want to. He just wanted to finish his breakfast and work the case. He needed to remember why he was doing this: Lisbeth. Everything had gotten too complicated as it was.

"Yes, let's finish breakfast." Stan took another sip of his coffee. "Did the police have any more information on your accident?"

Nickolai had to agree with Landry in her assessment: there was clearly no love lost between Stan and Phillip. "They're looking into it and will let me know if they find out anything."

"I had just explained to Phillip that I believed you both were wrapping up your leads here."

Wishful thinking, buddy. "I still have some angles to investigate. And now, with my truck being wrecked. . . I don't even know if it's drivable. The mechanic said he'd know more after the forensics mechanic finished."

Stan looked hopefully at Landry. "How about you?"

She slowly shook her head. "I've got a few things to check out myself."

"Since you obviously can't drive in your condition"—Phillip nodded at her arm in a sling—"I'm more than happy to drive you where you need to go. I have a rental car."

That wasn't going to happen. "Actually, Phillip, if it's going to take a few days to get my truck back, maybe you could help me out?"

"Sure. I can be driver to you both."

Landry straightened and shook her head. "Oh, I'm fine to drive. The sling is more of a hassle than it is prohibitive."

"I'd be happy to take you to the rental place and get you a car, Nickolai," Stan offered.

Phillip frowned. "No need for the extra expense. One of us can drive him wherever he needs to go."

Was Phillip really here to keep an eye on the bottom line? Sure, the fifty thousand recovery fee was a big chunk of money, but that was only payable if they recovered the map. If that happened, the fifty big ones would be nothing but chump change. Their expenses so far couldn't be more than a couple of grand. That had to be nothing for a lady like Winifred Winslet.

Unless she wasn't as wealthy as she put on the airs. If she needed the money from the map to keep her business and home, and whatever else.

Nickolai downed the rest of his cranberry juice. He'd call Chris as soon as he could and see what his former partner could find out about the Winslet fortune.

The Vision

Gopan, alone and naked, prayed all night and all day. Thanking for his life. Asking for continued good life and health.

As the sun set on the second day, Gopan stood and faced the eagle feather and conch shell on the altar and prayed, asking for direction. The cold of the desert night swirled around him. Not letting go of his pipe, he wrapped his blanket around him. He continued praying.

As sparks of light, the spirits came, and they came as beings Gopan had known before. Just as was the tribe's history from the beginning. His father, who had died, came. Each whispered in his ear. Images blurred as he weakened, but he stayed upright until dawn broke. He fell to his knees, holding his pipe. Praying. Praying. Praying. The blanket slipped off him, but he didn't move.

Murmurs swirled around him as the Arizona sun heated his bare back. Telling. Coaching. Advising.

Warning.

As the third evening's stars filled the sky with brilliant light, Gopan wobbled to his feet. So tired. So drained. So spent. But he had to continue his journey. His quest. He had no other option. He wrapped himself in his blanket.

Holding tight to the edges of the blanket to keep himself covered, Gopan lifted his pipe high above his head and began to pray. For his protection. His body. His mind. His spirit.

The sky split open, and the sun chased the stars from the sky. Gopan's blanket slid to the ground, but Gopan didn't move. The stillness in his heart calmed the restless spirit inside.

Sometime later, Gopan couldn't really tell when by the sun's location—his mind focused inward and his physical vision blurred—the medicine man with his helpers came.

After standing or kneeling for three days and nights, Gopan's joints were stiff. He felt the burn of pain, the weakness from hunger, and the dying thirst. He had endured scorching exposure to the sun during the day and freezing cold at night. The experience had taken him beyond the physical. It took him to the point of realizing his potential, of seeing what he could do, what he could go through, and still come out in a good way, with his heart and mind clear, and his body still able to function.

The medicine man and his helpers gathered up the tobacco ties, the prayer flags, and the altar, but Gopan continued to pray. Ever so carefully, the medicine man wrapped the blanket around Gopan's shoulders, took him by the elbow, and led him down the hill and back to the sacred fire.

Still holding his pipe in one hand and clenching the edges of the blanket in the other, Gopan reentered the purification lodge tent. Somberly, he sat opposite the medicine man on the west side, Gopan's back to the center. Prayers continued; then the medicine man led them in the sacred songs of their forefathers.

Suddenly, it was silent. Gopan lifted his head and opened his eyes. He looked to the medicine man, who nodded that it was time for Gopan to share the vision that was revealed to him, everyone in the purification lodge tent understanding what is shared is not allowed to leave the lodge.

"Indaa comes." Gopan's voice cracked from the dryness, but he continued in his native tongue. "But the Great Spirit has shown me what to do. How to protect from the white person. How to soothe the Thunder God's wrath."

Quietly, the others in the tent began to chant. Gopan revealed what the Great Spirit had directed him to do. He would meet with the other shamans and do what they must.

It was the only way.

Chapter Fifteen

Awkward silence settled over them.

Landry stared across the table at Stan after Nickolai and Phillip had left the café. Nickolai had volunteered Stan to give her a lift back to the hotel while he took her Jeep. She had started to argue but caught the look he'd given her, so she'd agreed. He must be pumping Phillip for information.

Stan handed a credit card to the waitress, and she rushed away. Now was Landry's chance to do her part.

"I'm not sure I'm fond of Mr. Fontenot," she ventured.

Stan tipped his head. "Many are not. He comes across quite forcefully at times, but he does have Winifred's best interests at heart."

A noncommittal support? Hmmm. Landry tried again. "I guess I just don't understand why he's here. Is he spying on us? Making sure we're not just throwing Mrs. Winslet's money away? You wouldn't let that happen."

"No, I would not." Stan straightened the salt and pepper shakers again.

Time for a different direction. "How, exactly, does he fit into the lives of Mr. and Mrs. Winslet? I know he said he knew them both before they married, but it's a little confusing."

Stan hesitated for a moment then let out a rush of air. "The three of them met in their college days. One of them fell for another. Who fell for whom changes, depending upon who's telling the story. At any rate, they dated then separated. Winifred's family's wealth goes back several generations. You could say she was born with a silver spoon in her mouth, although you'd not know it by her demeanor."

Landry might argue that. She'd thought Mrs. Winslet's air of wealth and entitlement fit her like Landry's jeans—comfortable and well worn.

"Bartholomew went out straight from college, determined to set the world on fire. He started what was Winslet Oil & Gas and over the next five years, built it up as a company of note. I was hired by Bartholomew some thirty years ago, right when his business started booming. Phillip came around soon after and stepped back into the role of Bartholomew's best chum."

"You actually worked for Mr. Winslet before Phillip, then?"

"Oh yes. Phillip didn't actually work at Winslet Oil & Gas." Stan ran a finger over his mustache. "He was just there. I believe Bartholomew put him on his board of directors and let him have a corner office, but everyone knew it was in title only."

"A figurehead, so to speak?"

Stan nodded. "Soon after, Bartholomew ran into Winifred again at some event. They reconnected and began dating almost immediately."

The waitress returned with the receipt and Stan's card. "Thank you. You have a nice day. There's a nice ceremony to award the marathon winners this evening. You should check it out."

They thanked her, and she went to seat another table. Stan signed the check, pocketed the card, and looked back at Landry. "Long story short, Bartholomew and Winifred married months after they reconnected. Phillip was the best man at the wedding."

"So they're friends, but he's on the board still?"

"Once they were married, they merged Winifred's family business that focused on oil and gas with Bartholomew's and created Winslet Industries. It took a lot of hard work, dedication, and many long hours to grow it into the empire it is today."

The corner of Landry's mouth slid up. "The American dream, right? Boy works hard, falls in love with a well-off girl, they marry and merge, and live wealthily ever after."

Stan stood and realigned his chair under the table. "Pretty much."

Landry pushed up from her chair and adjusted her sling. "How does Phillip fit into the Winslet story today?"

Stan motioned her forward and fell in beside her. "For many years, Winifred worked in the office with Bartholomew, and Phillip actually started showing up for board meetings. The three of them spent much time together. Bartholomew and Phillip took trips together in their younger years—hunting, fishing, hiking, climbing—many adrenaline-driven trips. Their friendship never wavered." He opened the door of the café for Landry.

She stepped out, blinking against the sun. The Jeep was gone. Stan led her to his rental car. He unlocked the doors via the remote fob then opened his own door. Landry fumbled the door handle with her left hand and plopped inside.

"I'm sorry. I forgot about your arm," Stan said as he cranked the engine.

"It's fine. I prefer to do it myself." Unless it was Nickolai opening the doors for her.

Ruh-roh, as Marcie would say, she needed to stop thinking like that. Thoughts like that led to feelings, and she didn't have time for those right now. Especially not with someone who confused her.

Plain and simple, Nickolai Baptiste perplexed her.

Back to the subject at hand. "So Phillip really is a dear friend to both Bartholomew and Winifred?" She latched the seat belt and adjusted it around her sore shoulder.

"Pretty much." Stan fiddled with the vents. "It wasn't long after Winifred stopped working every day that Phillip's time in the office dropped to weekly. Then every other week. Then just for board meetings."

That didn't jive. Landry shook her head. "Bartholomew's assistant told me that Phillip came to the office a couple of times a month to have lunch with him in his personal suite."

Stan pulled onto Apache Trail. "I'm sure he did. I meant Phillip didn't come in to actually work in the office."

Landry thought about that for a minute. "He's one of the board of directors?"

"Yes."

"Then what did he do when he worked there? I mean, for all the years you said he worked. I'm assuming the board members don't actually do any work, right?"

"Right." Stan turned on the blinker and whipped into the motel parking lot. "He was Bartholomew's assistant. Until he stopped. That was about the time Bartholomew hired a young woman. She worked for about five years; then he hired Monica." He pulled the sedan into the parking space closest to their room and turned off the engine. He sat very still.

Landry waited.

A minute passed. Then another.

"I don't see Phillip's rental, but the Jeep is here. Wonder if they went off somewhere together." Stan opened the driver's door and slipped from behind the wheel.

Landry was pretty certain that he'd wanted to say something that had nothing to do with a rental. She released her seat belt and eased out of the car. She approached the Jeep and realized it was securely locked. "Oh no. My motel room key is in the console, and it's locked up. Nickolai must have the keys. Guess I'll have to run to the office and get another one." Without waiting for a response, she headed to the office.

She didn't want Stan to accompany her because she wanted to talk to Margaret without an audience present. If she was lucky, her husband wouldn't be there.

She pulled open the door and stepped inside the office. Margaret looked up as she entered.

"Hi. Remember me?" Landry slipped into her chipper voice.

"Yes, ma'am." Margaret rose from her seat at the desk. She glanced over her shoulder as if she didn't want to be caught speaking to Landry.

"How can I help you?"

"It seems I've left my room key in my rental, which Mr. Baptiste has. Is there any way you could give me another key or let me in my room?"

"I'd have to charge you for another key. I guess I can ask Vanessa to let you in. Mr. Hauge isn't in his room?"

Vanessa! Just who Landry wanted to speak to anyway. "Um, I think he is, but if you'll just ask Vanessa to let me in, I'll be fine."

"Okay. Just wait here and I'll get her." Margaret turned and shuffled toward the back. "Don't know why you walked all the way over here when Mr. Hauge could've just let you in with his key," she mumbled under her breath as she moved out of Landry's view.

Wait a minute. . .hold up. Stan had a key to her room?

Phillip Fontenot was actually quite likable.

Nickolai chuckled as Phillip regaled him with yet another story of his and Bartholomew's misspent youth. Phillip pulled the rental car into the mechanic shop's parking lot.

"Ahh, I'm gonna miss making memories with Bart."

"I've not heard anyone else call him that." Nickolai released his seat belt but didn't move. Phillip hadn't turned off the engine, and Nickolai had learned never to cut off a potential suspect when he was on a talking spree.

Phillip laughed and slapped his thigh. "That's because he hated it. With a passion. Would knock someone's block off for calling him that. So, of course, I had to call him Bart all the time. Or Barty. He hated that even more." He eased the car into Park.

Nickolai grinned. He and Chris had that kind of friendship. Knowing what aggravated the other and playing to that. "I've been there." He didn't reach for the door handle. As long as Phillip made no move to get out, neither would he. "My partner and I are like that."

Resting his hands on the steering wheel, Phillip shifted to face Nickolai. "Look, you know that Landry gal is a cutie, that's for sure, but we both know this kind of business ain't for a female. I'm rooting, you know, for you to find the map."

Nickolai smiled, not sure how to respond. Phillip's cluster of "you knows" meant the subject was a sensitive one. Nickolai needed to respond carefully. A week ago, he'd have buddied up with the older man, but now. . .having gotten to know Landry as he had, and feeling. . .what?—he didn't know what to say.

"So where are you on finding it?" Phillip pushed.

"Well. . ." How much should he say? "I'm making strides. I know who sold it to Bartholomew and why. I know there wasn't really another bidder upping the price, but I know who made it look that way. I know a copy of the map is here and it's not as familiar as others from the area."

"I see." Phillip frowned, clearly not pleased with Nickolai's progress. "Do you believe the murderer is also the one who took the map?"

"It's the logical answer." Nickolai studied the older man's facial nuances, called microexpressions. The little ones that he didn't even know he was making but that a cop was trained to pick up on. "I see no other reason why Bartholomew would have been murdered on that exact day, at that exact time he was going into the bank with the map."

Phillip plucked a string from his shirt and cleared his throat. "Ahh. . .well, it does seem like too much of a coincidence."

Nickolai mentally counted off three signs of deception—self-grooming, clearing his throat, and significant pause. Phillip knew more. "I want to make sure I'm thorough, though. That I run down every lead."

"The police back home aren't saying much about where they are with the murder investigation."

With the commander overseeing the case, there'd be no information leaks, or heads would roll. "I'm sure it's hard to be patient, but you want to make sure the right person is brought to justice."

Phillip nodded. "Of course. It's just so much stress on Winifred. It's hard for those of us who care about her to watch."

Nickolai recalled what Landry had overheard. He cleared his throat. "I'm sure it is. I know she's a lucky lady, having so many people to step up on her behalf. Like you and Stan, for example, looking out for her interests." He waited.

"Yes, that's true, you know." Phillip spoke slowly, as if weighing every word. "But Stan was never very close to Bart." His upper lip curled. Just a hair and just for a fraction of a moment.

If Nickolai hadn't been trained to detect microexpressions, he'd have missed it. But he was trained. Well. And he noticed. "Oh, so he was more of just an employee, while you're more of a friend, right?"

"Right. I mean, here's how it is. I also sit on the board of directors, of course, because I've been with Bart and Winifred since before they married. I want you to fully understand, you know, I was there from the start. You know how it is when you're close to people and you want to help them, so I helped build the company alongside them."

Verbal garbage. More concealing of information. "So you worked at Winslet Industries before Stan was even hired?" Nickolai stored all the signs of deception away. He'd process it later.

"Well, he was an employee before I was officially a board member." Phillip's voice rose, and he took a deep breath before unclipping his seat belt, turning away from Nickolai.

Three more signs of deception: voice rising, running out of breath, and breaking of eye contact. Interesting. "I guess Bartholomew and Winifred didn't confide in Stan. Not like they do you."

"Bart never confided in Stan." He tapped his fingers against the steering wheel. "I'm not, you know, positive about Winifred. There were times in the past that there were possible indiscretions. You understand I don't know for certain, but, you know, rumors were spoken."

"About?"

"I'm not sure." Phillip opened the car door. "Let's go see if this mechanic knows anything."

Nickolai followed suit, but he didn't like the way Phillip had muscled in on the investigation, even if he was a fun person. He stretched his strides to enter the office first.

The stench of gasoline and burned coffee filled the small space. Part of Nickolai felt right at home—the station always had a burned-coffee smell.

"Can I help you?" An old, thin man in coveralls stuck his head around the corner. He reminded Nickolai of the old nursery rhyme... the crooked man who lived in a crooked house.

"I'm here to speak to someone about my truck." Nickolai nodded at the large window where his truck was up on the lift. "Officer Hogan told me I could check on my truck's status."

"Oh, I was just finishing up." He wiped his hands on a rag. "I'm Davis Emmerson, lead mechanic."

"Nice to meet you. Nickolai Baptiste." He didn't bother introducing Phillip. "Have you found out anything?"

"You were a lucky one, Mr. Baptiste, that's for sure."

"Oh?"

Davis nodded. "Your brake lines were cut."

Just as he'd suspected. "You sure they were cut?"

Davis smiled. "Mr. Baptiste, I've been working on cars since before I could stand good. I'm the best in town. Trust me when I tell you, those lines were cut. It was clean and straight."

"Have you told Officer Hogan this yet?"

Davis nodded. "He called about twenty minutes ago and I gave him the news. I'll have a written report to him later today."

Nickolai stared at his truck. Landry's tire. The note. His brakes. Who wanted them gone so badly?

"It'll take me a day to get the parts to fix it up, but I can do it. We always take photos for documentation, but you might want to call your insurance and file a claim. Some of them still want to send their own adjusters out."

"I'll do that today. Thank you."

"No problem. Is there a number where I can reach you?"

Nickolai wrote down his cell and his motel room number and slid it across the counter to the mechanic. “Thank you again.”

“No problem. You have a nice day.”

Nickolai stepped out into the dry Arizona air. So much to process. He needed to lay it all out and see what jumped out at him. He had to be overlooking something.

“Where to now?” Phillip asked, clearly excited about being in the investigation.

A fact Nickolai intended on rectifying right now.

Chapter Sixteen

This was Vanessa?

For some reason, in Landry's mind, the motel worker named Vanessa with a boyfriend who collected maps was tall and svelte and couldn't be more than twenty or so. She didn't know why she'd thought that, but the Vanessa waiting on Landry was none of those images.

The motel's housekeeper was fifty if she was a day, stood no more than five feet, and wore her graying hair in a long braid down the middle of her back. Her tanned skin was leathery looking, but her dark eyes were bright. Vanessa's flip-flops flapped across the asphalt as she walked toward Landry's motel room.

She obviously wasn't going to do much talking, so if Landry wanted to find out anything, she'd better ask away. "Vanessa, I understand you took copies of my map to your boyfriend?"

The housekeeper's steps faltered; then she straightened and put her hands on her hips. "I did not steal. Margaret gave to me when I ask."

"I didn't mean to imply you stole the copies. I know Margaret gave them to you." She lowered her tone and moved in closer to Vanessa. "I wanted to know what you did with it. After Margaret gave the copies to you."

Vanessa hesitated a moment then gave a little nod of her head before continuing to Landry's room. "I give to Tarak. He has many maps."

"What does Tarak do with the maps? Does he hang them on the walls? Put them in scrapbooks?"

Vanessa snorted a laugh. "No hanging. No books. Tarak compares them." She stopped outside of Landry's motel room.

"Compares them? To what?"

"Other maps of the mountains."

"Why?"

Vanessa looked at Landry as if she were crazy. "To find the Shis-Inday." She shook her head and unlocked the door.

That was new. Landry stepped into the cool room, opening the door wide enough for Vanessa to step inside. "What is the Shis-Inday?"

Glancing over her shoulder, Vanessa let out a sigh. "The Shis-Inday are the Men of the Woods, fierce Apache warriors. The Superstitions are the home of their Thunder God, and Shis-Inday are protectors of the mountain."

Landry had read some of the myths and mystiques of the area. "That's the legend Tarak believes?"

Vanessa's eyes narrowed. "It is not legend. It is fact. I am from the Chihenne tribe, and it is so. Tarak is also Apache, from the Bedonkohe tribe. Geronimo was Bedonkohe. Some of Tarak's ancestors are Shis-Inday."

"So why is Tarak looking for these Shis-Inday men?" Landry leaned against the door frame.

"Tarak is a proud Apache. We grew up hearing the generations-old stories of the great Shis-Inday warriors, from his own tribe. His name, Tarak, means protector." Vanessa's voice softened.

"He's proud to be Bedonkohe, I'm sure." Landry still didn't understand.

Vanessa shook her head, slowly. "Tarak will join the Shis-Inday. It is his destiny. It was foretold to him by the shaman of his tribe. I will be with him, as foretold by my medicine man." Her eyes brightened. "Tarak must find these great warriors then join them. I will go with him, and we will make home with his ancestors."

Now it was starting to make sense. "Tarak collects these maps, compares them, because he is searching for the protectors of the

Superstition Mountains so he can join them?"

Vanessa smiled wide and nodded. "Yes. Yes. And we will be as one and with the Shis-Inday."

"What, exactly, are they protecting? Just the mountains?"

The housekeeper glanced over her shoulder and actually stepped into Landry's room. She lowered her voice, as if someone might overhear the great secret. "The Bedonkohe ancient ones know of the cave holding the *pesh kitzo*. It was put there by the Thunder God for the tribe to use in emergency."

"Pesh kitzo?"

"Yellow metal. Gold."

Landry's heart quickened. The lost mine!

Vanessa continued. "The Shis-Inday are to protect the yellow metal of the Thunder God. They have since Thunderbird left it there for the Bedonkohe to have in time of great trouble."

"Does Tarak know where the gol—er, yellow metal cave is in the mountains?"

Vanessa shook her head. "Once he finds the cave, the Shis-Inday will reveal themselves to Tarak and he will join them. Then he will call for me, and I will join him."

Sounded more like folklore than reality, but Landry had learned many years ago not to discount Native American customs or beliefs, even if they weren't in line with her Christianity. "Have you or Tarak ever met any of these Shis-Inday warriors?"

Vanessa nodded. "Tarak has had them call to him on his spirit journey. I have seen them, in the distance, in many of my dreams."

So she hadn't even seen any. Landry nodded. "But have you or Tarak seen one here, in town? In person?"

The older woman shook her head. "Once you join them as protector warriors, you live within the Superstitions. Your home is made there."

"Vanessa, if Tarak finds them and joins them, and he isn't seen again here, how will you know where to find him to join him?"

The deep lines across her forehead etched deeper. "The shaman told Tarak he will lead me to him, when the time is right."

Sounded like mumbo jumbo to Landry, but hey, who was she to question someone's way of life? "Did the copies of my map help Tarak?"

Vanessa nodded rapidly. "Tarak says he believes he knows the area where the Shis-Inday are standing guard now. Your map let him get a full view. We are to pray for direction for twenty-four hours; then Tarak will go join them."

Landry's gut tightened. "Tarak believes he knows where the cave is?"

Again Vanessa nodded.

Swallowing against a dry mouth, Landry struggled to keep her emotions in check. "Do you think Tarak could tell me? Or take me there?"

"No." Vanessa shook her head. "I already tell you too much." She backed out of the room.

"Vanessa, please. I just want to see the cave."

"*Dah*. No indaa can go near the Shis-Inday." Vanessa turned and hurried away.

"Vanessa, please." Landry followed, but the older woman moved quite fast to the back of the motel's office. "At least tell me what *indaa* means."

The door slammed shut before Landry could round the corner. No sense going any farther. She headed back to her room, which stood wide open.

"White person."

Landry stopped in front of her open door. Two doors down, a man of at least seventy sat in the chair outside his door, talking to another elderly man and smoking an old but intricately carved pipe. The fragrant smoke seemed to circle around his head. His long braids were white and his skin leathery, with deep etches lining his face. She didn't know whether he was insulting her or trying to get her attention. Either way, his addressing her in such a manner still felt rude.

She really wasn't in the mood. "Excuse me, sir?"

The man he'd been talking to rushed off, leaving the sitting Indian to stare at Landry. "White person."

Landry didn't want to go off on the old man, because his demeanor didn't come across as intending offense. "What?"

He smiled as he exhaled. Smoke moved in puffs of circles from his mouth. "Indaa. It means white person."

Nickolai waited until Phillip had disappeared into his motel room before rushing to Landry's room and rapping quickly on the door.

She cracked it open. "Hey, you still have the Jeep keys."

He glanced at Stan's door. "Let's go for a little walk, shall we?" He nodded toward the end of the motel rooms.

"Sure, now that I have the keys to the Jeep so I can get my room key." She slipped her cell into her back pocket. Pulled her door closed.

"I'm sorry. I didn't realize your room key was in the Jeep." He put his hand on the small of her back. He didn't know why his protectiveness seemed to go on high whenever she was around, but it sure seemed to. He led her past the old man, to the back of the hotel where there were some loungers set up for motel guests.

"It's okay. It worked out for the best, and I'll tell you all about it, but first, what did you find out from Phillip?" She adjusted her sling as she stretched out on the lounger.

He sat on the lounger beside her, sitting sideways to face her. He quickly filled her in on all he and Phillip had talked about, as well as what he'd observed. "And the nonverbal signs of deception. . .there were five or six. Phillip definitely knows more than what he's letting on. I don't know if that's about Bartholomew's murder, the map, or whatever is between Winifred and him and Stan, but the man is hiding something, that much I do know."

"There's something more there, that's for sure. Stan told me that Winifred, Bartholomew, and Phillip were all friends before Winifred and Bartholomew were dating. According to Stan, one fell in love with another, but he didn't specify who fell in love with whom." She leaned her head back a little as the midday breeze skittered across the way.

She tucked a stray curl that had escaped the band-thingy she wore back behind her ear. "He said that he worked for Bartholomew before Phillip did, but once Phillip and Bartholomew reconnected, and Winifred and Bartholomew got involved then married, Phillip became much more involved in the business."

Nickolai nodded. "Piecing together what we know, I'd venture to guess that Phillip fell in love with Winifred, but then she chose Bartholomew. Maybe for money?"

Landry shook her head. "Winifred comes from old money. She'd never have to marry for money." That stray curl of hers moved against her cheek.

That was problematic to his scenario. "So maybe Winifred and Bartholomew fell in love. Maybe Phillip really is just a friend to them, separately and as a couple."

"But that doesn't fit with what I overheard Stan imply." Landry shoved the hair back behind her ear and raked her teeth over her bottom lip.

He wondered what it would be like to kiss her.

Nickolai swallowed and looked away. Guess it'd been way too long since he had a serious relationship if being in such close proximity to Landry made him think such crazy thoughts. "And along with that, what you heard Phillip imply about Winifred and Stan." He ran a hand over his beard and looked at her. "This is getting complicated."

"Complicated and convoluted. Does any of this make a difference in finding the map? Do their love lives matter in our investigation?"

"I don't know, but I can tell you one more thing, my truck's brake lines were cut."

"What?"

Nickolai told her what the mechanic had said. "He's filing a report with Officer Hogan this afternoon, but he'd already given him a verbal confirmation."

"That makes three attempts to get us to leave." Landry shook her head. "I don't think either of us is close to finding the map, so why is someone working so hard to get us to stop investigating?"

"If we find out who's responsible, we can uncover the motive." He stared off blankly into the distance. The Superstition Mountains were a breathtaking sight to behold, even from this distance.

"There's more."

He met her gaze.

She told him she'd spoken with Vanessa, who described why her boyfriend needed the maps to find some hidden warrior Indians who were ancestors from his tribe. Landry explained the legend or folklore, but how Vanessa's boyfriend, Tarak, truly believed it to be real.

"But most importantly, according to Vanessa, the copies of the map helped her boyfriend figure out where the warriors were in the mountains, and they're always guarding the cave with the gold, which has to be the mine." Excitement brightened her eyes until they were sparkling like the stars had been twinkling in the sky last night. "And she said they had twenty-four hours to pray before Tarak will go into the mountains to find the Shis-Inday warriors and the mine."

"Why are they praying for twenty-four more hours? I'm no expert, but why take so long?" He'd never heard about anybody praying over something for a specific number of days.

"I don't know." She looked at him with confusion blinking in her eyes.

"Because it is a sacred number. If the Great Spirit instructed him to pray for twenty-four hours, then he must."

Both Nickolai and Landry jumped at the old man's voice. It was the man who'd sat in the chair a couple of doors down from Landry's room.

"I do not mean to listen, but thought you need enlightenment. I can help you."

Nickolai looked at Landry, who lifted her unhurt shoulder. "He helped me understand something Vanessa said," she said.

Maybe he could shed some light on the situation. Nickolai motioned for the man to join them.

The older man settled slowly onto the end of Nickolai's lounger. "Apache tribes have long called the Superstition Mountains the devil's playground. Some say back before father time kept track, Naiyenesgani, the creator god, settled in the valleys between the peaks. Our people know the Superstitions owe their life to a time of big fire and explosion, born from volcanic explosions larger than imaginable in modern times."

He took a long pull off his pipe then opened his mouth and let the smoke billow out. "Some say Naiyenesgani opened his hand to allow enormous flows of lava to roll across the earth, shooting ash blasting into the stratosphere. They say he opened his other hand and burning avalanches of scorching pumice sliced down the hills, pulling landslides and making the ground quake in fear and awe."

Nickolai wasn't impressed with stories without fact. He opened his mouth to ask the man to get to the point.

The man smiled at him and offered the pipe.

"Um, no thanks. I don't smoke."

"Neither do I." The man took another puff then blew the smoke right into Landry's face.

She coughed and clutched her slinged arm closer to her chest.

"Hey—"

"I know you do not believe in the creation story. It does not change the way the mountains came to be. Once they were formed, Naiyenesgani moved away, to which the Thunder God, Thunderbird, took over. He watched over the tribes of the Apache. Because of him, the Bedonkohe and Chihenne tribes remained."

"And this Thunder God, Thunderbird, will show Tarak where the Shis-Inday are after he prays for a specific number of hours?" Landry sounded as skeptical as Nickolai felt.

"I do not know what any of the gods will do. I do know that if the Bedonkohe shaman has foretold Tarak the protector joining the Shis-Inday, then it will come to pass."

Interesting.

The man struggled to stand. Smoke circled around his head. He spoke to them both but stared straight at Landry. "But use great caution. . .the Thunder God will welcome no white person in his land, and you are not the only ones looking for what the Shis-Inday protect."

Chapter Seventeen

Landry smiled at Nickolai from across their lunch table. Fast food, but edible. There was just something about eating out of cardboard boxes and packets of salt and ketchup. . .always took Landry back to her happy youth, when her daddy would sneak her out to McDonald's without her mom knowing. Her mother had always been a proponent of eating clean and healthy, despite Dad's best attempts to sway her.

"What are you smiling about?" Nickolai wadded his paper napkin into a ball. "You looked so peaceful and happy."

Heat burned her cheeks. "Just remembering my dad taking me to grab a burger and fries when I was younger. He had to sneak me out because my mom was a food nazi."

Nickolai laughed softly. "Your mom never knew?"

"Oh, she probably did. Dad probably even told her, but it was fun for me to think he was sneaking me out."

"Your mom was a food nazi?"

Landry smiled. "In the worst way. She would even try to disguise vegetables to get me to eat them. For the record, cauliflower, no matter how it's cooked, can never be mistaken for mashed potatoes."

"Eww."

"Right? And spaghetti squash did not taste right replacing pasta."

"At least she tried, though." But he laughed.

"Easy for you to say, you didn't have to take a bite of something and then realize she'd done a bait and switch on you." She shook her head, smiling as she recalled. "One time, she pureed broccoli and slipped it into guacamole." She shuddered and stuck her tongue out. "That was the nastiest thing I've ever tasted. I couldn't go to a Tex-Mex restaurant for months after that."

He chuckled.

"Yeah, laugh it up. You weren't the one scarred by her antics. I now have a love-hate relationship with food, and it's all her fault. I don't trust new places to eat."

"It's good you have those memories of them."

She sobered. "Yeah. I'd eat all the crazy stuff she concocted if I could just have her back for a day or two." Tears burned her eyes. "Dad, too." She stared out the window of the fast-food joint. She would. Not. Cry. Here.

"I'm sorry. I didn't mean to upset you." He was so sincere. So caring.

Landry blinked away the tears. "You didn't. I just really miss them sometimes."

"I know."

She took a drink of her iced tea. "You said you lost your parents unexpectedly, right?"

He nodded. "A couple of years ago. House fire."

A grip tightened around her heart. Her hand reached across the table and squeezed his. "I'm so sorry." She couldn't imagine losing both her mom and dad at the same time. That had to be horrible.

"It was one of the worst times of my life."

"I can't even imagine." She squeezed his hand even tighter. *Lord, please comfort him. He'd been shot, lost his job, started a new one from the ground up, and then lost his parents.* And then she remembered something he'd said. "You mentioned a sister. Do you have any other siblings? I'd always wished I had a brother or sister to share the joys and the pain with."

He let out a slow breath. She realized she was still holding his hand. Landry slowly withdrew her hand and took a sip of her sweet tea.

"No. It's just me and Lisbeth."

"That's a pretty name. Are you two close?"

"She's quite a bit younger than me."

Landry raised her eyebrows in question.

"She's about seventeen years younger."

"Wow." Landry covered her mouth with her hand. "I'm sorry, I didn't mean—"

He laughed. "No, it's okay. It was quite the jolt to my parents, too. I think Mom believed she was going through the change, but no, she was having Lisbeth."

Landry grinned. "Bet that was quite the surprise."

"Oh, it was. I'd just gotten my new truck, so I would drive Mom everywhere. I thought I was big stuff when I got to drive her to her doctor's appointment. But she knew it would be a while, so she gave me a list of errands to run." He shook his head and grinned. "When I got back to pick her up, she was waiting outside, looking stunned. She just got into the car and didn't say a word."

"She was probably in shock."

He nodded. "Of course, but my teenage self didn't know that. All I knew is Mom had been to the doctor and now she was quiet and looking white. I thought she had cancer and was dying."

"Oh, you poor thing." What else would a teenager immediately think?

"She didn't say a word, the whole drive home. I was petrified. Terrified. Even as a smart-mouthed teen, I couldn't think of anything to say."

Landry couldn't even imagine.

"As I turned onto our street, I told myself that I'd just ask. Nothing could be worse than what I imagined, so I figured I'd just ask her what was wrong with her." Nickolai looked a little off into the air, lost in the memory. "So I pulled into the driveway and put the car in PARK. I turned and looked at her and just blurted out—'Mom, are you dying?'"

He shook his head, smiling. "That seemed to snap her out of it. She looked me square in the face and told me—'No, son, I'm not dying. I am, however, pregnant.'" He gave a little chuckle. "And do you know how I responded to finding out my mother didn't have cancer, wasn't dying from some horrible disease, and was only pregnant with my little sister?"

Landry smiled, shaking her head.

"I said—'At your age?'" He laughed. "I was mortified that my mom was pregnant. I knew what that meant. What she and Dad had been doing. Of course, I thought I'd just die."

"I bet. Teenage boys are only thinking about one thing, and to have it visible that your mom is still doing that. . ." Landry couldn't help laughing. "Sorry, I can only imagine your embarrassment."

"It was horrible. Especially after she started showing. Man, my friends gave me nine million types of grief."

"But then you got your little sister."

Nickolai sobered. "I did. She was this cute little thing with big ole eyes. And when she wrapped her hand around my one finger. . ." He shook his head. "She had me wrapped from that moment on."

A boulder-sized lump caught in the back of Landry's throat. She'd always wanted a big brother, and the way Nickolai talked about his little sister made her heart skip a beat. Any man who would talk about his baby sister as an infant was a special guy in Landry's opinion.

"I bet she was devastated when your parents passed." The girl had to be no more than fifteen or sixteen. Losing both parents at such a vulnerable age, that had to be extremely hard. "At least she had you."

How was he supposed to respond to that?

Nickolai's memories swirled around him, running out of chronological order and blending together. The fast-food restaurant's background clatter fell away, as did the conversations in the booths around them. He could only remember Mom and Dad and Lisbeth. The night it happened came into clear focus, as if he were reliving those moments. . . .

Nickolai and Chris, at the gym.

Brring!

Chris grabs his cell. "Graze."

Nickolai slips on his shoes. His shoulder aches a little, the constant reminder that he'll never again be the man he used to be.

"Nickolai." Chris's voice is as fierce as his face. "That was dispatch. Fire and EMT have been dispatched to your parents' address following a neighbor's 911 call."

Nickolai's throat tightens as he feels the blood leave his face. Every muscle in his body tenses.

"Come on." Chris yanks him to his feet and pushes him to the parking lot. He collapses into the front seat of Chris's cruiser. Chris speeds down the road, sirens blasting and lights flashing. Nickolai's gut traps his heart as they careen into his parents' subdivision.

Smoke already fills the air. Clouding visions. Fogging the mind.

He jumps out of the car before Chris even comes to a complete stop. Running. Racing toward the house engulfed in flames.

Firemen everywhere. Hoses crisscross over his dad's carefully manicured lawn. Through his mother's prize rosebushes in the front flower bed. Water hissing as it hits the hot flames.

Someone grabs him. He turns, ready to do battle. A fireman shakes his head. "You can't go in there. It's about to collapse."

"My parents are in there. My little sister." His throat burns as he shouts above the din of noise.

The fireman's face falls. Nickolai knows. Truth be told, he knew before he got here that they were gone. He'd felt it in his chest. The burning. The aching. The inability to breathe or think or feel.

"My sister. She's barely fifteen." Dare he hope?

The fireman nods toward the ambulance parked haphazardly on the side yard. "She's in there. We're waiting on the police to get here."

Nickolai turns and darts toward the ambulance. Lisbeth! He has to see her. She has to be okay. She just has to. He can't take losing everyone all at once. Too cruel.

She sits in the back of the ambulance, staring at their burning home. Her eyes wide, pupils totally dilated.

"Lisbeth!" He pulls her into his arms. "You're okay. You're really okay?" He releases her just enough to hold her at arm's length. "Are you hurt anywhere? Burned?"

She shakes her head, still staring at the fire. "Look at it, Nicky. It's eating the house. The flames are licking away the wood planks. It's beautiful."

Chris halts beside Nickolai. "Are you okay, Lisbeth?"

Her eyes brighten as she smiles at Chris then looks back at the burning house. "It's wonderful. So powerful. And grows so fast."

Nickolai's heart clenches. His sister had started rambling to his parents about fire being the source of true power recently. He'd assured them it was all a fad. Just like her cutting herself. Their station had so many reports of teenagers cutting themselves. Over 90 percent of them just did it because someone else did. Surely that's what Lisbeth had done. Just trying to be part of the crowd.

But that sinking feeling in the pit of Nickolai's gut screams that there is more. That he's missed some serious signs. That he's been wrong.

"Lissy, what did you do?"

She stops staring at the flames to look at him. Holds eye contact. "Why, I set the beast loose, of course. I freed him." She smiles and looks back at the fiery rubble that was once his home. "Isn't he truly magnificent, Nicky?"

Nickolai's hands shook. "Are you ready to get out of here?" He knew his voice came out short, and he didn't mean to snap at Landry, but his emotions were tangled and he needed to get out of here.

"Sure." She stood, eyeing him.

He grabbed their tray and emptied the trash then led the way to the parking lot. He had just unlocked and opened her door and helped her climb up into the passenger seat when a man stuck a microphone in his face. "Mr. Baptiste, we understand that you're here on a treasure hunt and that you've received threats if you continue. What are your thoughts?"

"What?" He glanced at another man holding a camera directed right at him.

"The police reports filed show you and Ms. Parker have received warnings to abort your hunt for the Dutchman's Lost Mine. How do you respond?"

"We aren't on a treasure hunt. We aren't looking for the lost mine." Press vultures, they were the worst. He tried to take a step back so he could shut Landry's door.

Landry blocked it with her foot. "Our investigation is based on a private client's need to recover a lost item."

"You've obviously been hurt because someone wanted you to stop investigating. Are you going to?"

Nickolai pushed her foot into the Jeep.

"This doesn't scare me off in the least. It actually makes me more determined than ever to uncover the truth of everything to do with this case."

He shut the door and turned to the reporter. "I realize once the marathon is over, you'll have limited fodder for your news, but you need to leave this alone."

"Is that a threat?" The reporter took a step backward, nearly running into his cameraman.

"Not at all. Just a friendly bit of advice." Nickolai rushed around the car and got behind the steering wheel. He started the engine and set the temperature.

"Well, that was interesting." Landry adjusted the vent.

"They needed something to report on for when the marathon's over. I should've known they'd pick up the police reports and think this was newsworthy."

"It probably is, to them. I doubt Apache Junction sees any crime in comparison to our New Orleans."

He chuckled as he put the Jeep in gear and eased out of the parking place. They passed the reporter and cameraman getting into their van. Landry waved. He sped up. The last thing they needed was a reporter following them.

"I should've just said no comment. I know better."

"You aren't a cop anymore, Nickolai." Landry moved her neck to reposition the sling. "You don't have to be so rigid."

"We shouldn't encourage them. A 'no comment' reply usually kills the story after one airing."

"I wanted whoever is behind all this to know he didn't scare me off. I'm still going to do my job, threats or no."

Nickolai held tight to the steering wheel. How could he make her understand that being public like that put them more at a disadvantage than an advantage?

"Um, do you have any idea where we're going?" She broke his mental argument with himself. "Or are you just trying to get away from the reporter?"

"I thought we'd try to find Tarak and talk with him. Don't know how much we'll learn, but it's worth the time to ask."

She nodded. "According to Vanessa, my copy seemed to help him pinpoint where the mine was. She indicated he seemed very sure. Do you know where he lives?"

He nodded. "When I spoke with Officer Hogan, I asked if he knew Tarak. I figured an officer like himself would know most every local. I was right."

"And he just gave you Tarak's address?" Even she wouldn't have done that, and she played much looser with the rules than the average bear.

"No. But he did mention his last name—Chatto. A quick Internet search later, and I have his street address." He chuckled at her expression.

"Color me impressed. I figured you would find a way around actually looking it up yourself." She wrinkled her nose when she spoke.

Nickolai shook his head. "Should I be offended by that remark?"

"Do you resemble it?"

"Touché." He laughed with her. It felt good. Felt natural. Felt more comfortable with her than he had around anybody except Chris for a very long time.

Nickolai found himself wanting to tell her everything…his parents, the fire, Lisbeth. But a nagging fear cut off his voice. How could he explain? She'd really think he was a jerk when he told her that he was responsible for his parents' deaths. How would she react if he told her he'd left his sister in the hospital because he didn't know what else to do for her?

He grabbed the steering wheel, letting his fingers dig into the cushy leather grips. "Landry, about earlier. At Burger King…"

"Yeah?" Her voice was soft and caring.

He took a deep breath, keeping his eyes on the road as he spoke. "My sister set the fire that burned down my parents' house."

"Oh, Nickolai, I'm so sorry."

She clearly didn't understand. "Lisbeth set it on purpose. She's a diagnosed schizophrenic, who focuses on fire."

"Oh. I'm sorry."

He could hear the pity in her voice and knew he didn't deserve it. "When Lisbeth started showing signs, I misinterpreted. You have to understand, I'd made detective and thought I knew everything. I'd been exposed to extensive training in criminal behavior, as well as behavior triggers and socialist trends. I thought I knew." His throat got tighter and tighter.

Landry put her hand on his shoulder and squeezed.

He couldn't let her think it was minor, just an oversight. "Lisbeth had been cutting herself for months. I knew that was a big fad with a lot of teens in the New Orleans area. Schools had counselors on speed dial to deal with the self-harming. I thought she was just jumping on the 'cool' bandwagon because everyone else was doing it. I told Mom not to worry, and I told Lisbeth to knock it off."

Nickolai focused on his driving but continued to talk. He had to tell her everything. Now that he'd started, he had to let it out or he'd erupt. "All the signs she showed, and there were many—social isolation, aggression, agitation, compulsive behavior, anger, self-harming, rapid and frenzied speaking...I thought it was Lisbeth just being a rebellious teenager. Acting out because her friends were."

She squeezed his shoulder again.

No, he didn't deserve empathy. "I told Mom and Dad not to play into her pity routines. I told them she was just acting out. I discouraged them from taking her to the doctor, telling them it was a waste of money. Even when she burned down the doghouse, I blamed it on her rebellious streak and advised Dad to take away her phone and privileges."

She slowly withdrew her hand. Ah, there it was. The realization of what he'd done...what he'd allowed to happen.

"I didn't know some of the signs she exhibited were classic schizophrenia symptoms: the delusions, how she believed that fire has a special and personal meaning just for her, her strange assertion that her thoughts weren't really her own, so much disorientation, and her false belief of superiority, even over me, Mom, and Dad."

He shook his head as he pulled onto Tarak's street. "I thought she'd snap out of it. I thought if we didn't play into her for-attention drama, she'd straighten up." His lips had trouble wrapping around the words. "I was so wrong."

Nickolai pulled in front of Tarak's address, put the Jeep in PARK, and finally looked at Landry. She had big tears in her eyes. "She set the house on fire after Mom and Dad had gone to bed. Lisbeth sat in the yard and watched it burn down. Watched it kill our parents, and she told me it was beautiful. The fire eating everything was beautiful."

He felt himself blinking against the burning of his eyes, but he had to finish. Had to get it out. "They took her away and had her tested. She was diagnosed with schizophrenia and put in the hospital. She's been there for two years, sometimes better, sometimes not. But every week when I see her, I can only think that she might have been the one to start the fire, but it's my fault our parents are dead."

All. His. Fault.

The *Wopela*

Gopan had much to be thankful for, so he prepared for the wopela custom with a pure heart.

Just as their custom dictated. Just as tradition demanded.

He moved slowly, his joints stiff from the rebirthing time of his guidance journey. He would have to relearn how to use his body. Even though he craved the traditional buffalo soup he could smell that the others in the tribe would eat, he would not. His body would have to adjust to assimilating food. For tonight, the fourth and final night of his journey, he would sip water with lemon and soup broth.

The eldest shaman of the tribe, Paco, ducked into Gopan's tepee.

Gopan bent his head, in respect and reverence for the old man.

"Sadnleel da'ya'dee nzho." By way of greeting, Paco gave the tribe's adage: long life, old age, everything good.

"Yes." Gopan kept his head bent. The visit by Paco was an honor. Not every warrior received instructions from the chief shaman.

"Tonight, your wopela is saying thank you. This is an honoring time. It is a time of giving things away."

"Yes."

Paco continued in his Apache tongue. "Tonight is a time of great celebration as your family tribe celebrates with you that the Great Spirit has allowed you to come back into this world from your journey."

"Yes." Gopan glanced over to the gifts he'd arranged—for the medicine man and the helpers, and for the children of the tribe.

"Stand tall, Gopan."

Gopan did, looking down into the old man's eyes. "Tonight, you will join me, Nantan, and Dyami as the fourth shaman of the Bedonkohe. You now represent the North."

Paco touched Gopan's forehead. "The Rest and Cleansing Moon will rise in the sky tonight. This moon is when you will communicate well within the tribe. Your intellect has risen. The Rest and Cleansing Moon develops your abilities and uncovers your own true being."

Gopan reached for the blanket he'd worn during his journey. Usually given to someone who has been a great helper, Gopan felt he needed to give it to Paco. He wrapped it around the old shaman's shoulders.

Paco shivered, even though it was quite warm in Gopan's tepee. "As a shaman for our tribe, you are also a warrior and must live by the warrior's code of honor."

Nantan stepped into the center of the tepee, almost startling Gopan. When had the other shaman arrived? He didn't have time to think as Nantan spoke, his deep baritone vibrating Gopan's chest. "Warrior, there are no shades of gray in the question of honesty and justice. There is only right and wrong." He placed his hand on Gopan's shoulder.

Dyami joined the men and spoke, his older, softer voice like a salve against Gopan's aching limbs. "Warrior, be courteous even to your enemies. Without this respect, we are no better than the animals." He placed his hand on Gopan's other shoulder.

Paco moved his hand to Gopan's chest. Heat radiated all the way through to Gopan's back. "Warrior, live with heroic courage. This life is risky and dangerous. The warrior way is living life completely, fully, wonderfully."

Placing his other hand on Gopan's waist, Nantan spoke again. "Warrior, there is but one judge of honor, and this is yourself, from whom you cannot hide."

Dyami placed his other hand on the other side of Gopan's waist. "Warrior, be quick and strong, with a power that must be used for the good of all. . .compassion."

Paco shifted under Nantan's six-foot stature to place his other hand on Gopan's back. Tingling pulsated down Gopan's legs, to the very tips of his toes. "Warrior, you are to do as you say you will. No promise need be given. A warrior's word is heavy."

The three men began swaying, sweeping Gopan up into the motion. He closed his eyes as he envisioned an eagle soaring overhead in the evening sky.

"Warrior, stay loyal to those in your care, to those you are responsible for, and in protection of the tribe and gods. Remain fiercely true." The three shamans' voices blended together in perfect Apache as they swayed. Gopan couldn't decipher between their voices.

Their chanting filled the tepee. . .his head. . .his very being.

We are one. We are one. We are one in Shis-Inday.

Chapter Eighteen

"Nickolai, I don't know what to say." Her heart broke. For him. . .for his parents. . .for his sister. A real tragedy.

His face clouded. "There's nothing to say. I just thought you should hear the truth from me." He reached for the door handle. "This is Tarak's address. Let's go see if he's in."

"Wait. Nickolai, I want to tell you how sorry I am that you had to go through that. This." She followed him up the driveway.

"Just drop it, okay? I shouldn't have burdened you with my life story." He stomped up the stairs to the shotgun-style house. A loose board creaked under his weight.

Burdened her? She wasn't burdened. She ached for the pain he'd endured—still endured. But he clearly didn't want to discuss it any further at the moment. She'd bide her time, but she would let him know what she thought when the time was right to broach the subject again.

He knocked hard on the door then looked back at Landry. "It's a weekend, so maybe we'll get lucky and he won't be at work."

She joined him on the steps. "From the way Vanessa talked, I guess I just assumed he didn't have a job."

The door swung open, and a younger Native American glared at them. "What do you want?"

"We're here to speak to Tarak." Even Nickolai's voice sounded commanding.

"He cannot speak to anyone."

Landry leaned against the door frame. "Is he here? Just ask him. I'm a friend of Vanessa's." That was reaching it a little—she and Vanessa weren't friends—but it did soften the young man's intense expression when he looked at Landry.

"Then you should know Tarak cannot talk to anyone. He is in prayer."

Oh, yeah. "Right. The twenty-four hours of prayer."

The young man raised his brows. "You do know."

She nodded. "That's what I need to talk to him about. I'm the one who had the copies of the map." She grinned at Nickolai and decided to wing it. "I knew he was close to finding where the warriors were, so I'm glad my copies helped him locate them."

He nodded somberly. "This has been Tarak's journey since birth. The shaman foretold his destiny."

She had to think fast. "So you understand I'm part of Tarak's destiny. I need to see the complete mapping Tarak compiled."

The young man took a step back. "Tarak did not say this."

"He didn't know I would come. This was foretold to me, not him." She inched in front of Nickolai. "I know that he can't be bothered while he's in prayer. I'm just to look at his work." Inspiration hit. She rose to her full height and squared her shoulders. "I'm supposed to see if he has located the Shis-Inday before his prayer journey is complete."

He hesitated.

"I only need one minute. That's all that I'm required to see." Just long enough to snap a picture with her cell.

The young man nodded. "But not him." He jutted his chin toward Nickolai. "He is not to enter the house." She smiled at Nickolai and tapped the cell in her hand. "I'll be right back."

Landry followed the young man as he led her down a narrow hall. Dream catchers with feathers moving as they walked past and paintings hung on the walls of the hallway. The strong scent of sage filled the house, wrapping around her like a shawl.

He stopped in front of a closed door and nodded. "The maps are inside. I am not allowed to enter."

"I understand." She'd wondered how she was going to get a photo without him seeing. Now she didn't have to worry about it. She reached for the doorknob, a little surprised to find her palm sweaty. She opened the door and stepped inside.

Landry wasn't sure what she had expected, but with the mystique the young man and Vanessa had laid out, she expected more than a plain white folding table with a survey map laid out atop. The best she could tell, it was a modernized aerial map but with great details of landmarks written in.

Keeping her back to the door and using her body as a shield, Landry began snapping photos in bursts with her cell. Every angle she could. She was limited with her arm in a sling, but she used that to her advantage to keep her photo taking obscured from the young man's view from the hall. There, next to what was marked as Weaver's Needle was a funny figure, then a red mark. This had to be where Tarak figured the warrior Indians were.

Where the gold mine was.

Landry took a few more shots for good measure then pocketed her cell before turning back to the door. The young man stared at her intently. She solemnly nodded then joined him in the hall, shutting the door behind her. "Thank you. That's all I needed to do." She quickly led the way back to the front of the house where Nickolai was waiting. The last thing she wanted to do was run into Tarak or Vanessa. She'd have a lot of explaining to do that she wasn't sure she could talk her way out of.

She thanked the young man again at the front door and hustled Nickolai out to the Jeep. "I got all the photos we'll need."

"Does it show where the mine could be?" Even Nickolai sounded excited as he helped her into the Jeep.

She waited until he was behind the wheel with the engine cranked before she replied. "It looks to be right by Weaver's Needle. Drive a little ways away and look at these shots."

He turned left at the corner and pulled into an empty lot.

She handed him the cell. "I took several of the whole map then broke them down into sections. I think the red mark indicates where Tarak thinks the mine is."

"Do we think he might be right?"

Landry raked her teeth over her bottom lip. "All the research I've done indicates he could. And what if he's right? His tribe and his shaman? What if he is supposed to join them? If that's the case, then he would be able to figure it out, right?"

"Tell me you don't seriously think that could even be a possibility?" The incredulity in his voice pushed her to fidget, but she refused.

"What if it is? Think about it. People have searched for this mine for generation after generation. What if it has been hidden in plain sight until revealed to the person whose destiny is to join the warriors responsible for guarding it?"

"You're kidding, right?"

"I'm not saying I believe that; I'm just saying I'm open to the possibility." God worked in mysterious ways and often surprised many by the people He chose to work through. "I don't discount anything."

"Well, I discount all the shaman and medicine man mumbo jumbo, but I do believe there is a hidden gold mine out there. I think it's possible that Tarak has believed this destiny gig his whole life so he has made it his life's work to research the area for possible locations. And if we find it based on his map, then that's the reason I'll believe."

"What if it's divine intervention?"

Nickolai snorted and put the car back in DRIVE and eased back onto the road.

"You don't believe in divine intervention, either?"

"I would have to believe in the Great Spirit or God or something to believe in divine intervention, so that would be a no."

Landry found her words trapped in her mouth, unwilling or unable to escape. What?

He glanced at her. "Oh, I know you're a Christian. I've seen you praying over meals and stuff. Hey, if that's your crutch, more power to you. It's just not for me."

"Crutch? You think Christianity is a crutch?"

"I'm not trying to offend you, Landry. I'm just saying I don't believe in all that. I think people say and do what they want and there are good and bad consequences for everything. There are actions and reactions. That's the world going around. I don't think there's some all-powerful being orchestrating everything." He shook his head as he came to a stop sign. "If there is, it's a cruel being."

Landry's stomach hurt. "Oh, Nickolai. I'm so sorry you've had such tragedy and grief. Yes, there are actions and reactions. . . . God gave us free will, so there are consequences for our choices. But God loves us so much. All of us. He wants us to have eternal life with Him." How raw he had to be to not feel God's love. Landry wanted to pull him into her arms and hold him tight, just to feel a sliver of the care of the Father.

"I'm not going to debate this. You believe what you want, and I'll respect your belief. I just ask that you respect I don't believe." He let out a long breath. "Now, do you want to head to Weaver's Needle and look around? See if we can find the man with the map?"

Landry paused. For a really long moment. Nickolai wondered if he had, in fact, offended her. He hadn't meant to, but he wasn't going to discuss the possibility of God or how He's so good and all that. He'd learned the hard way that if there was a superior being, it didn't play fair.

"Sure. Let's check it out." Her voice didn't sound like she was angry.

He turned the Jeep in the direction of the Superstition Mountains and cracked the windows a bit. The fresh, cool air filled the vehicle. Nickolai breathed deeply. He loved New Orleans, but there was something crisper, cleaner about the air here. And the stars. . .never in his life had he seen the night sky look so amazing and beautiful.

"Nickolai, I don't want to bring up a subject that is obviously painful for you, but I need to tell you something."

He gritted his teeth. She would be one of the ones who had to argue and try to get him to become a believer. Why did every Christian feel they needed to "save" everyone else? It was not only annoying, but also a bit arrogant.

"I'm very sorry for what happened to your family. I can't even begin to understand how heart wrenching and horrible it's been for you." She reached over and took his hand, holding it firmly in hers. "But one thing I do know is that your parents dying was not your fault."

Even though she was so wrong, it lifted Nickolai's spirits to hear her words, like a salve to his wound.

"Your sister's illness caused their death. Not you." She held tight to his hand.

"I discredited Mom and Dad's concern over Lisbeth's behavior. If I hadn't, maybe she would have been diagnosed sooner and the fire could have been prevented. But I thought I knew everything. I thought because of my training that I was smarter than everyone." If only he could go back in time. He'd been so sure it was just a phase. His sister trying to just fit in with the other teens her age who were acting out.

"Nickolai, you can't control everything. Sure, you might have discredited their concerns, but you had no reason to think your sister was sick. From what you told me, it seems like most people would've come to the same conclusion you did. It's time to stop beating yourself up over something you had no control over." She squeezed his hand. Warmth spread all the way up his arm and to his shoulder, warming it more than his PT rubdowns.

Oh, how he wished that were true. "I appreciate your kindness, Landry, I really do." But he knew the truth.

"Let me ask you this, does mental illness run in your family?"

"Not that I'm aware of."

"So was there any reason you or your parents would assume that your sister suffered from any mental disorder?"

"Not really, but still. . ."

"What were your parents planning that you talked them out of?"

"What?" He withdrew his hand to make a sharp turn. The Superstitions loomed before them, big and majestic. Nickolai suddenly felt very, very small.

"Were they going to take her to a doctor? A therapist? A counselor, maybe?"

"No."

"So, what did your opinion stop them from doing?"

"I don't know. I mean, Mom was concerned and talked to Dad, but I don't think they made any plans." They'd been discussing Lisbeth's lack of discipline in the kitchen because she was late for curfew again. Dad had told Mom something needed to be done. "Mom said she didn't know what had gotten into her lately. Even her grades had taken a dive."

"And you said what to that?"

He concentrated on remembering. It seemed like he'd fought for so long to block the details. "I told them they were too easy on her. That they needed to ground her. Take her phone and really stick to a punishment." He shook his head. "My parents were never really great at sticking to any punishment. They were bad at it with me and with Lisbeth. . .well, they doted on her."

"I've had many friends who were parents of teens. Some of those teens were really rebellious and misbehaved. I don't know of a single one whose initial thought when their teen started acting out was to take them to a psychiatrist in case they suffered from a mental illness."

"But she'd been cutting herself. That was a big concern of Mom's."

Landry nodded. "I imagine. Did she talk with any of her friends? Any of your sister's friends' parents?"

He remembered what Dad told Mom. "Dad said one of the boys Lisbeth used to date had done the same thing for a while. His parents had taken him to a counselor who told them not to worry about it. He said all the kids were trying different ways to belong to a group. To relate to each other."

"So you made a recommendation that just about anybody else

would. A trusted friend. Maybe even a teacher or a counselor."

Put like that. . . He shrugged. "Maybe."

"Then it's time you let go of the guilt. You're carrying around something you have no business carrying. It's not yours to have."

"But—"

"No. You don't get to keep the guilt. Keep the grief. Hold on to the feeling of loss if you want, but the guilt isn't yours anymore."

While she really had no authority over his emotions, just her stating that so matter-of-factly sent a release of heaviness off his chest.

Was it really that easy to let go of the guilt? Just because she said it wasn't his to have and keep?

She chuckled. "You feel it, don't you?"

"How?"

Landry smiled. "Because you've been carrying it around like a badge you put on every day. You just needed someone to give you the cold hard facts that you giving your parents your opinion didn't alter their path. You didn't change their minds about taking her to a doctor or therapist." She shifted the seat belt over her injured shoulder. "It's a tragedy. Losing your parents, then having to accept responsibility for your sister and deal with her illness. . .it's no wonder you decided to heap a helping of guilt on yourself."

He didn't reply because he didn't know what to say. He would need to process everything she'd said. One thing was certain, though—he did feel as if his load had lightened considerably. And he owed that to Landry Parker.

If only. . .

"Wow, is that Weaver's Needle?"

The column of rock formed a very distinctive peak that was visible for miles. History explained that the formation was created when a thick layer of fused volcanic ash was seriously eroded. A large split in the side of the formation gave it the appearance of having two tops instead of one, but this could only be viewed from the side. The peak was named after a mountain man, Weaver.

For decades it'd been rumored that the Needle's shadow indicates the location of the rich vein of gold.

"I guess we walk from here." Nickolai turned off the engine. He nodded at Landry's shoulder. "Are you okay to walk for a bit?"

"As long as we aren't going for a full hiking trip."

"I thought we'd just look around. See if anything on that map matches up. See if we discover any signs of the old man. Maybe find where he's camping out and talk to him."

"You mean get the map." She smiled and waited on him to come open her door and help her out.

"Well, of course, we'd get the map." He couldn't explain why her waiting gave him such a burst of happiness. Maybe because he'd been talking about emotional things that he normally didn't talk about. Either way, he was happy for the moment as he led her toward the well-walked path.

She opened the picture on her cell. "Looks like it'd be this way. But, where is that ridge?"

He compared the picture with the actual landscape. "Is it possible it's behind the formation? That's the only thing that makes sense."

"It's a long way to hike there, but what if we got up there?" She nodded to a plateau about fifteen feet above them. "Maybe if we got up there, we could see over the formation and see if this ridge is visible."

Because that would put them closer to the mine, and closer to the map.

He glanced up at the ledge then back to her sling. "I'll climb up there and have a look-see. You stay here."

She opened her mouth, to argue Nickolai was sure, but then she adjusted her sling. "Be careful." It must be aching for her not to argue.

"I'll be back in a flash." He smiled as he started climbing.

It was harder than it looked. Several times his foot or hand slipped and sent small, loose pebbles clattering down.

The sun beat down on the formations—the rocks radiated heat.

"Be careful." If Landry said it once, she said it at least five times.

"Almost there." He reached for the top and gripped with his right hand. He pulled, hoisting himself up. He could just about see—

A sharp jab stuck in the fatty part of his hand between his thumb and forefinger.

He sucked in air. Gulped it. Then he couldn't hold on. His hand released. His heart tightened in his chest.

He fell backward, down.

Nickolai heard Landry scream his name.

Down. Down.

Darkness, nothing but warm darkness.

Chapter Nineteen

Dear Lord, please let him be okay.

Landry raced over to where Nickolai had fallen. He lay on his back, his arms and legs flung out. He didn't move.

She dropped to her knees beside him. "Nickolai."

He moaned and tried to sit up.

"You should not sit up. You had a pretty bad fall." She ran her hands along his legs, feeling for any obvious breaks.

"Maa taagumm feels weerrd." He sat.

Landry turned back to his face. "Oh my goodness." Hives broke out all over his face and neck. She checked his arms. His wrists had welts, too. "I'd swear you're having an allergic reaction." Her own allergy to tree nuts caused this reaction, but Nickolai hadn't eaten anything.

"Caan't bweathe."

She could hear the wheezing in his chest.

Fear gripped her as she watched his eyes widen sporadically. He swayed, as if he'd had too much to drink or had been caught on a fast-spinning amusement park ride.

The wheezing grew louder.

She reached for her phone. No, even if she got through to emergency services, there wasn't time. He wouldn't make it.

Landry grabbed her EpiPen instead. He might not have eaten something, but he was sure enough having an allergic reaction. She knew the symptoms all too well.

She withdrew the medication injector from its case, aimed for his thigh, and stabbed him with the Epi.

The resulting reaction was almost immediate. She breathed a sigh. "Come on, we have to get you to the Jeep. Now."

He let her help him to his feet. He wobbled a little. "What happened to me?"

"I don't know, but I know you had an allergic reaction. I gave you a shot of epi, but we need to get you to an ER immediately. If we don't know what happened, they might need to give you a second injection, and I have no idea how far away we are from a hospital."

"I can look it up on my cell while you drive." He steadied himself. "Can you drive with that sling?"

"Yeah. The pain's almost gone anyway. It's just a precaution to make sure I didn't hurt myself worse." She grabbed his elbow and led him down the trail. "But I won't be able to carry you if you pass out or anything, so at least get in the Jeep."

She helped him into the passenger seat then rushed around the vehicle. *Thank You, Lord, for keeping him alive. And for letting me have the allergy I've resented all my life because it probably saved his life.*

Landry slipped behind the wheel. "Did you find a hospital?"

He held up his phone. "Yeah. Banner Goldfield Medical Center. According to the app, we should get there in fifteen minutes or so." He set the phone to give voice directions.

She buckled her seat belt then roared the Jeep down the road.

"Whoa, I'm not dying."

She cut her eyes at him. "Not funny. You could've."

"An allergic reaction, huh?"

"That's exactly what it looked like. As soon as I gave you the injection, you improved." She paused as the cell's voice gave her directions.

She turned on the next right. "What happened up there?"

"I don't know." He leaned his head back against the leather of the seat. "I was almost to the top and I grabbed the next rock. All of a sudden it was like a piece of hard straw jabbed into my hand; then it burned. Next thing I knew, I was flat out on my back on the ground with my tongue feeling twenty times too big for my mouth."

"Show me your hand. Where it hurts."

He held out his hand, palm up. Right between his thumb and forefinger inflammation and swelling spread from a darker red area. He touched it and cringed. "It's hot and sore."

"Something bit you. I hope it wasn't a snake." Landry hated snakes. With a passion. So many were poisonous. What if Nickolai had been bitten by one of them and she didn't get him to the hospital in time? She bore down harder on the accelerator.

"Slow down. It wasn't a snake. There's one little puncture mark here. Snake fangs come in pairs."

"A spider?" She'd seen documentaries about spider bites. Black widows. Brown recluses. Some of that venom ate flesh and left holes in people's skin. She sped up just a little more.

"Maybe, but if so, it doesn't hurt as much as I thought it would. Must not be one of the very poisonous ones."

She wanted to let out a sigh of relief but realized he didn't know for sure. He didn't know what had bitten him, so he couldn't know the level of danger he faced at the moment.

Oh, Lord, please let me get him to the hospital in time. Please, God.

"Tell me about your dad's business. I heard some rumors, but I'd rather hear the truth from you." Nickolai's head was against the seat and his eyes were closed.

As much as she hated talking about it, she wasn't going to deny him. Not when, number one, he'd shared such personal and emotional details of his life with her and, number two, she needed to keep him talking in case he was about to go into shock. "Dad's memory began slipping more and more, but he refused to back off of working. Said he needed to make sure all the bills were paid."

Oh, the memories of her father's concerns.

Nickolai rolled his head to face her and opened his eyes. "Was there a financial strain?"

"Well, I didn't think so, but I didn't realize how much he'd cleaned out the savings for Mom's care and funeral. He didn't want to worry me, but I wish he'd have told me." It hurt that he'd kept her so in the dark. She could've been helping them financially for some time. Had she known.

"You can't help when you don't know help is needed." He said the same thing Marcie had told her time and again, but from him. . .it was just different.

"Yeah, but I should've known. Especially when he was diagnosed. I should've looked into everything right then and there."

"Why didn't you?"

She cut her eyes to him.

"I'm not judging; I'm really just asking." His tone held no malice, so she couldn't be offended.

"My dad was always a very proud man." Tears stung. "He always took care of my mom. Gave her everything she ever wanted. I never wanted for anything. He took great pride in providing so well for us."

"There's nothing wrong with taking care of the people you love."

"No, but if I'd known. . ." Landry wiped away the tears and concentrated on the road again. "Anyway, when he still had cases to work but started forgetting things, I stepped in and helped. Before long, I was doing the actual work. I didn't mind. I was good at it. Finding insured art items and recovering them challenged me, and it kept Dad working."

"So why was there all this hoopla in the rumor mill about your dad's reputation being tainted or something?" Nickolai's words started to slur.

"Because we never told the insurance company he worked for about Dad's condition. We never told them I was helping Dad at all. I would do the work, recover the piece, have Dad sign off on the report, and take it in as if Dad asked me to bring everything by." She paused and glanced at him. "You okay?"

"I'm feeling a little woozy, but hey, they got their knickers all bunched up because you did your dad's job for him?"

"They said we deceived them, which we did." She knew better.

Always had known it was wrong but kept trying to justify it to herself and even to the Holy Spirit when she felt convicted. "So, they straight-out asked and I told the truth. They fired Dad on the spot, told everybody in the business what had happened, and Dad never had another case before he died." She'd always felt that not having a job had pushed him further into the pit of dementia. Idleness fed his disease.

"Mmm." His head rolled away from her.

"Nickolai, come on, stay with me." She reached for his hand. Her shoulder tinged with pain, but she ignored it. "Come on, stay with me."

Landry glanced at the cell—less than a mile until they would arrive at the hospital. "Come on. We're almost there." *God, help me out here.* "Nickolai! Nickolai!"

The computerized voice telling her to turn right on West Southern Avenue and the destination would be on her right was her only response.

Where was he?

In the recesses of his mind, Nickolai recognized the symptoms of drugs in his system. Understood, on some level at least, that narcotics ran through his veins and altered his perception.

Chanting filled Nickolai's mind. Even though it wasn't English, he understood. He was being told it was okay. Everything was okay.

Nickolai opened his eyes into the darkness. The darkness except for one pinpoint of light. A fire. His pulse thrummed, but the chanting continued. Was he awake or dreaming?

He could feel something close to him. Inanimate, but bright. Yellow. Gold. Lots and lots of gold. The mine. He'd found it.

The chanting stopped, and Nickolai broke out into a sweat. His head burned. He grabbed at his clothes, tearing at them. Hot; so hot. Couldn't breathe.

An Indian appeared from the fire. Taller than him. Wider. Stronger. He pushed the gold from Nickolai's vision. Before he could argue, the chanting returned. So did the peace.

Nickolai exhaled. Inhaled. Slowly. Inhale. Exhale.

He slept, or at least thought he must have, because he was awake now. Awake and feeling like himself again. No heat, no chanting, no fire, nothing but the stench of sickness and bleach mixed making him gag. He struggled to sit up, but there was too much. . .stuff around him.

"Hold on there, buddy." A man's voice seemed to echo inside his head.

Nickolai tried to open his eyes, but the light nearly blinded him. He groaned. The remnants of his dream curled around his mind.

"Hang tight. Let me dim this light for you. It'll help," the man's voice said.

A click blasted in the room, then a steady drone of beeping. Nickolai squinted and opened his eyes again. The light was much dimmer and didn't split his head. The man standing beside his bed wore navy scrubs. He was thin, almost sickly so, with scruffy blond hair.

"Where am I?" Nickolai asked, but his voice sounded warbled and distant, even to his own ears.

"You're at Banner Goldfield Medical Center. You were brought in to the emergency room by a little lady who has worked herself into a tizzy not being allowed back here."

"Landry."

"Yep, that's her name. She was beside herself when she drove up here with you unconscious in the front seat. Then when she was told only family could be back here, well, she almost flipped. She's been asking the nurse for updates every ten minutes. I think the nurses are ready to throttle her." The guy chuckled, but Nickolai wasn't amused.

"Are you my doctor?" Nickolai hoped he wasn't. If this kid was his doctor, he needed to get out of here immediately.

The young guy smiled. "Nope. I'm your nurse. Marvin." He wagged his finger at Nickolai. "Now no rude jokes about male nurses allowed."

He grinned and checked the IV bag Nickolai just noticed hanging next to his bed.

"Landry. The lady."

"She's in the waiting room."

"Bring her back here. Please."

Marvin put his hand on his hip. "Policy is only family is allowed back in the treatment rooms."

"She saved my life. She's my friend." As soon as he said it, Nickolai realized it was true. He did think of Landry as a friend.

"Well, I think that does get her some pull, too. Hold on, I'll see what I can do." Marvin disappeared behind the curtain.

Nickolai straightened in the bed, adjusting the pillows behind him and straightening the covers up to his armpits. He had no idea where his clothes had gone but did his best to cover as much of himself as possible. Why hadn't they put one of the gowns on him? At least he wouldn't be bare chested for pity's sake. He ran his hand over his hair, trying to tame the wildness he could only imagine. He did the same to his beard.

The curtain's metal holders rattled in their groove as Marvin pulled back the curtain and let Landry in the little area. "Now remember, shh." Marvin held his finger to his lips, smiled, and then backed out of the semiprivate room.

"Thank the Lord you're okay. They haven't told me anything except you were unconscious but stable." Landry took his IV-less hand in hers.

"Hey, I heard you saved my life."

"I doubt that, but you nearly scared me half to death."

Nickolai smiled at her. She truly cared about him. The concern in her voice was 100 percent genuine. It'd been a while since someone really and truly cared for him. Well, a woman anyway.

"What did the doctor say?" Landry asked.

"I don't know. I woke up and saw Marvin. He told me you were in the waiting room and I asked him to get you. That's all I know. What happened?"

"You climbed up the rocks, and near the top, you just let go. You fell down, but it looked to me like you were having an allergic reaction. Well, like I do when I eat tree nuts. I didn't know what else to do, so I grabbed my EpiPen and injected you."

He nodded. "Yeah, I remember most of that. I remember getting in the Jeep and talking. You were telling me about your dad."

Her eyes went sad.

He squeezed her hand. "Then I started getting dizzy. We figured out something probably bit me." Nickolai held up his IV hand. Sure enough, there was a big red welt on the palm. He hadn't even realized his hand sat on an ice pack. "I don't really remember anything after that."

"We pulled up here, and I laid on the horn in the emergency entrance until your nurse and others ran out with a wheelchair. I told them what I knew, and they whisked you away. That's all I knew, except the nurses telling me you were still unconscious but stable." She ran her fingers through the top of his hair. "You really scared me."

Nickolai's heart rate sped as her fingers fluffed his hair.

The curtain rattled, and a man joined them. Older, white hair, glasses, and decked out in a nice, long white coat.

"You must be the doctor," Nickolai said.

He smiled. "I am. Dr. McCormack. And you are a very lucky young man, thanks to this lady."

Nickolai squeezed her hand again.

"You were stung by a scorpion, which you are obviously and apparently allergic to. You had a severe reaction. Had this young lady not recognized the symptoms and had an EpiPen available and used it, we might very well not be having a conversation at all."

"A scorpion? I've never been stung. To be honest, I've never even seen one."

"Clearly not from around here." Dr. McCormack grinned. "While the epi took care of the symptoms of the allergic reaction, your body still reacted to the venom itself. It got you pretty good. You're receiving antibiotics in your IV, along with some fluids to keep you hydrated, and we'll keep monitoring your site. As you've noticed, we're keeping it iced to reduce the swelling and further spreading of the venom."

"Wow." Landry's eyes were beautiful in this light.

Dr. McCormack nodded. "We'll keep you overnight to make sure you have no further reactions and monitor the actual site, but I fully anticipate you'll be able to be discharged tomorrow." He signed a chart and handed it to Marvin, who'd returned. "We'll get you moved to a room for the night. I'll check on you in the morning, and of course, the nurses will keep me apprised of your condition." Without another word, he turned and was gone.

"I'll get your admittance started and then come get you." Marvin took the chart and left.

"Well, looks like you're going to be okay." Landry smiled, and it did really strange things to his gut.

Speaking of strange things. . . "Hey, has there been a really tall Indian around? Maybe chanting or something?"

She raised her brows. "Chanting? Not that I've seen. No one like that has come in since we've been here, but maybe someone was back here that I didn't see. Why?"

Now he felt silly. He shook his head. "I probably had a dream because of all the medications."

Landry patted his hand. "Maybe. Or you might have overheard something. Do you remember anything specific?"

"Do you know what 'Sadnleel da'ya'dee nzho' means? Or the word *Gopan*?"

Chapter Twenty

Exhaustion weighed her every move. Soreness tugged at her shoulder. Landry eased out of the Jeep and made her way to her motel room. The bed wasn't as comfortable as her memory foam mattress at home, but it would be just as inviting as drained as she felt.

"I know what you did." The woman's voice behind her caused Landry to turn.

She faced a very angry Vanessa, who pointed her finger in Landry's face. "You used what I told you about Tarak to get into his house. What did you do?" She took a step forward. "What did you do?"

Landry stepped back. "I didn't do anything. I just looked at his map."

"You want to find the treasure." Vanessa spat at Landry's feet. "You will not find anything. You try to interrupt Tarak prayer vigil. You are evil. You stay away from Tarak. And me. You stay away." She spat again at Landry's feet. "The treasure is cursed and those who hunt for it, cursed as well." Vanessa turned and stomped away.

Landry started to call after her, to apologize for upsetting her, then decided to remain silent. It probably didn't matter what she said, the woman would believe what she would. Besides, Landry didn't have the energy to withstand another outburst.

She made her way to her room and went to insert her key into the door, but the door pushed open.

Great. What now?

She flipped on the light and gasped at the sight before her. She leaned against the doorjamb as she tried to take it all in.

Her laptop lay on the floor, smashed. Papers were torn and scattered everywhere. Her clothes were tossed all over the place. Makeup and toiletry items were dumped on the beds, on her clothes. . .everywhere. The room, totally destroyed.

Her heart free-fell to her toes as she went to the bedside table and checked in the narrow space between her bed and the table.

Her gun and case were gone.

She sat on the edge of the bed, fending off the tears threatening to take control. No. She couldn't allow that. *Dear Lord, help me. I don't know what else to do.*

Of course she knew she had to call the police, but everything seemed so overwhelming. It'd been a very long, very emotional day, and apparently, her night would be more of the same.

She called the police from her cell phone, since the cord of the room's phone had been yanked out of the phone, and then called the motel office. Kohl, the owner and manager, hadn't sounded very pleased. He'd offered to send housekeeping to clean up after the police came, but she declined, pretty sure Vanessa wouldn't want to clean up after this mess.

Unless, Landry considered, she'd been the one to make the mess.

Hmm. It was possible. She'd been angry enough, that much was obvious. Angry enough to act on it, too. But would she have destroyed the room, knowing she might have to clean it up? Maybe. Anger tended to render most people unable to think rationally.

"Goodness, what happened here?"

Landry stood and faced the door. Phillip Fontenot loomed in the doorway, surveying the mess that had once been so neat. "Obviously someone broke into my room." Her sarcasm really showed when she was beyond tired.

"Are you okay?" He stared at her face, as if to make the determination himself.

"I'm fine. I wasn't even here. I was at the hospital with Nickolai."

"What?"

She quickly told him about the scorpion sting and following

hospital visit. "But the doctor wanted to keep him overnight to watch him. He should be released in the morning."

"What were y'all doing out in the mountains anyway?"

Something about the way he asked... "Just looking around. Seemed a shame to hear so much about the Superstitions and be so close and not even get closer to see them. It is beautiful out here." Not that she didn't trust him, but. . .well, she didn't trust anybody at the moment. Except for Nickolai.

"It is that. We don't get this much outdoorsy stuff back home, do we?" He smiled.

"That's true."

"Why don't I sit out here and wait for the police with you? I'd feel mighty uncomfortable leaving you all alone right now."

It was nice to have someone care. "I think I'd like that." She joined him outside, sitting in the plastic chair outside her door.

He pulled the chair from beside Stan's door and sat across from her.

Remembering from earlier. . . "While we're waiting, tell me about Stan."

Phillip glanced at Stan's motel room door then back to her. "What do you want to know?"

"You've known him a long time, right?"

Phillip nodded. "Many years."

"Give me your impression of him. As a person. As a vice president for Winslet Industries. As a friend to Mrs. Winslet."

He paused, staring at the ground. "Well now, let's see. He's done a fine job as vice president. As a member of the board, I have no complaints whatsoever with his quality of work. As far as his work ethics go. . .well, he's a good vice president, I'll just say that."

Ah, so she hadn't misheard. "What about as a friend to Mrs. Winslet? She must trust him a lot to not only keep him as an employee, but bring him into her confidence for Nickolai's and my investigation."

He clenched his jaw, the muscles tightening. "I suppose she knows she can trust him based on past experiences."

"Such as?"

"You'd have to ask her, I guess."

"But you know something." Landry didn't mind pushing. She was just tired enough and ready for this day to be over to be more blunt than she'd usually allow herself.

He ran a hand over his head. His bald spot shone in the outside security light's glow. "Let me just say that I believe there are some lines you shouldn't cross. A marital vow is one of those." He crossed his arms over his chest. "I'll leave it at that."

"Are you saying Stan and Winifred—"

Her question was cut off by the police cruiser pulling up and parking right in front of them. Officer Hogan stepped out from behind the steering wheel. "Miss Parker." He shut the car door.

She stood. "Officer Hogan."

Officer Paxton got out, holding a camera. "Miss Parker."

She smiled, her exhaustion threatening to take charge. She sat back down in the chair.

"Why don't you tell me what happened, starting at the beginning?" He held the form attached to a clipboard in his hands, pen poised.

Slowly, Landry recounted the evening's events, ending with Phillip keeping her company until the police arrived.

"Did you see where Vanessa was before she spoke to you?"

Landry paused, trying to remember. She was just so tired. She shook her head. "I'm sorry."

"Did you see where she went after she spat at the ground in front of you?" Officer Hogan asked.

She pointed across the parking lot. "I guess I assumed she went back to the office, but she might've gotten into a car and left. I don't really know. Once I saw my room, I didn't really think about Vanessa at the moment."

"I see." Officer Hogan wrote and then paused, staring into the back of the motel lot. "And the only thing missing is your handgun?"

"That's all I can tell right now. I didn't want to get in there and mess things up if there was evidence."

"Uh-huh. What kind of handgun was it again?"

"Beretta M9. Serial number M9-041802."

"You know your gun's serial number?"

She nodded. "Old habit from my days as an army MP."

He wrote it down. Glanced over at Phillip. "I guess you didn't happen to hear or see anything unusual around Miss Parker's room tonight?"

Phillip shook his head. "I'd been down at Handlebar Pub and Grill having a cold one, and I'd just come back and was walking to my room and passed Landry's. The door was ajar and I wondered if she was okay, leaving the door open and all, so I stuck my head in and saw the mess."

"What about Mr. Hauge? Have you seen him tonight?"

Phillip gave a dry laugh. "He sure wasn't with me."

Once again, clear evidence there was quite a bit of animosity between the two men.

Another thought occurred to her. "There was a reporter earlier who kept asking me and Nickolai about the map. It'd be easy for anybody to find out where we were staying. This isn't an interior hotel, so it wouldn't be too difficult to determine which rooms were ours."

"We'll check that out." Officer Hogan stood as his partner came out of the room.

"Got pictures of everything." Officer Paxton looked at Landry. "Did you call the office to have someone come clean up the mess?"

She shook her head. "I'll do it myself. I'd rather see if there's anything else missing."

Officer Hogan nodded. "Call me if you do."

"I don't see any signs of forced entry." Officer Paxton inspected her door.

Man, how had she missed even checking that out? She must be more tired than she'd realized.

"And you're positive you locked it when you left?" Officer Hogan asked.

"Yes." Well, she was pretty positive. Right now, she was clearly off her game. But when she'd left. . .yes, she always locked her doors.

"Then we'll go speak to Vanessa. She obviously has access to the key. As well as Kohl and Margaret." Officer Hogan slipped his pen into his pocket. "We'll be in touch."

Landry said good night to the police and Phillip then went into her room and shut her door, putting on the night latch. She sighed and picked up her laptop. The bottom dropped off.

Such a mess. As she reached to pick up the keyboard, another thought occurred to her: Stan Hauge had a key to her room.

Every time his hospital room door opened, Nickolai straightened. As soon as he saw it wasn't Landry, he sighed. Strange to admit that, even to himself, but he didn't have time to analyze it at the moment as the cheerfully loud and peppy nurse drew back the curtains. Sunlight spilled into the room. At least now he wore one of the gowns so he didn't feel so naked or vulnerable.

"Good morning. It's going to be a beautiful day." The middle-aged redhead turned and smiled wide at him. "And I hear you'll most likely be leaving us today, which is always good news, now isn't it?" She checked his IV then lifted his chart.

Nickolai had always considered himself a morning person. He always woke well before six, usually exercised for half an hour before settling in with the news over coffee. Yet, in comparison to this woman, he felt like a true grouch, shying away from all things bright and cheerful.

"Let's check your hand, shall we?" She set down the chart and pulled on gloves.

Nickolai set his right palm up for her inspection.

Her fingers were deft but gentle. "Looks like the swelling's gone down considerably. Dr. McCormack said we could go without the ice pack if it was, so looks like you'll get rid of that." She pressed his flesh. "Looks like you might need to finish off your antibiotics before you're discharged to make sure you don't have a residual infection."

"I feel good."

She stepped back and pulled off the gloves with a pop then tossed them in the trash. "You're doing very well. You were quite lucky. Such an allergic reaction. . .out in the mountains. . .well, it could've been disastrous for you."

He smiled to himself. Landry had saved him, in more ways than one. She'd started to heal the wounds of his parents' deaths, without even realizing it. Landry Parker was quite something.

"Well, that smile says it all." The nurse made a note in his chart. "Your breakfast will be in directly."

Nickolai watched her leave, feeling almost as cheerful as her.

He inspected his hand. The redness didn't look as dark as it had last night. It wasn't as puffy, either. There was still a little dark circle around the pinprick where the scorpion had actually stung him. Nasty little creature. During the night, he'd had many nurses and LPNs come in to check on him and monitor his condition. They'd shared their horror stories of the critters. Nickolai considered himself very lucky to have fared as well as he did.

Thanks to Landry.

The door opened and a young Native American girl in scrubs entered, carrying a food tray. She set it on the table beside the bed and moved to adjust it within his reach.

"Thank you." He smiled at her.

She smiled back, her single long braid swaying against her back as she moved. "You are welcome."

"What's your name?"

"Ela." Her smile was easy and honest.

Nickolai immediately liked her. "That's a very pretty name."

"It means 'earth' in Apache."

"Apache. I heard something the other day that I think is Apache. I don't know what it means, though."

"What is it? Maybe I can help you."

"Sadnleel da'ya'dee nzho. Do you know what that means?"

She nodded slowly. "Basically, it means long life, old age, everything is good." She hesitated.

"What?" He sat up straighter in bed.

Ela stood at the foot of his bed. "That phrase is usually used just by shamans in my tribe, and usually during rituals. Where did you hear it?"

"I guess maybe I dreamed it, because I thought I overheard it here."

"You dreamed it?" Ela gripped the rail at his feet.

"Maybe. I heard chanting and that phrase. I think I saw a very tall Indian man." He remembered more of a feeling than what he actually saw. "But I felt safe. Secure. Like everything was okay."

Her eyes widened.

"What?"

"I've never heard of a white man having a dream vision."

"A what?"

"A dream vision. Where a spirit comes and speaks to you. Foretells or warns you."

"I didn't get a warning, and I didn't see or hear a spirit."

"A shaman is very wise in transcendent ways. Their rituals usually lead to vision quests, journeys, and even dream visions. The man you saw was a spirit warrior."

Nickolai wanted to laugh, but he couldn't. He knew the people of this area took this stuff very seriously. In his gut, he didn't see any humor, either. "A warrior?"

Ela nodded. "You said he was tall?"

Nickolai nodded.

"Tall represents strength. Strength of warriors. That you felt safe and all would be okay; that's foretelling that something will happen, something significant and most likely life threatening, but you will choose wisely and all will be okay."

"Like me being stung by a scorpion and having an allergic reaction?"

Ela tilted her head. "Maybe. But if you had your dream visions after you were already here, I think not. Foretelling means you will face a choice. You choose wisely, and all will be okay."

"Hmm." He didn't think he wanted another life-threatening event. The allergic reaction was enough for him.

"Do you remember anything else?" Ela asked.

He shook his head then stopped. "I remember hearing one word. *Gopan*. Do you know what that means?"

Ela stared, eyes wide.

"You do. What does it mean?"

"It means 'protection,' but it's not a word."

Nickolai used his elbows to sit up straight. "It's not a word?"

Ela stood ramrod straight. "It's a name. Gopan was one of the first warriors put in charge of protecting the Thunder God's mountain and all within it." She clasped her hands in front of her.

"Then I guess I just overheard it somewhere else and mixed it in my dream."

Ela shook her head. "No. You see, Gopan lived centuries ago. It is a name of respect. Only warriors reborn to protect are called this. I know of none alive today."

"So how do you suppose I heard it?" Little twinges of discomfort pulsed in his chest as he anticipated her answer.

"You were visited in a dream vision by Gopan. You will make a very important decision regarding the Thunder God. If you choose wisely, you will be okay."

The door opened and Landry stepped inside. "Can I come in?"

Ela backed away. "Remember, choose wisely and you will be okay."

Chapter Twenty-One

Nickolai looked good. Really good. Landry didn't want to really admit to herself how much she'd been looking forward to seeing him today.

"Good morning." Nickolai's smile made something in Landry's stomach quiver then tighten. She'd never felt like this, but she wasn't going to take the time to figure out what it meant. She might not like what she learned.

"How was your night?" She set a paper bag on top of his food tray.

"Good, except they kept waking me up every hour to take my vitals."

"Yeah, a hospital is not a place to get any rest, that's for sure. I brought you something." She nodded toward the bag. "Stopped at Mickey D's Café and grabbed you some breakfast. Figured it had to be better than hospital food."

"You are a saint." He dug into the bag. "Didn't realize how hungry I was until I smelled food. Thank you."

She pulled the chair up beside his bed. "Has the doctor been by to see you yet?"

He shook his head. "Just the nurse. She took me off the ice pack and is having me finish up antibiotics, but said I looked good to be discharged." He took a bite and swallowed. "How was your night?"

She'd debated on the drive over whether to tell him about her room being trashed and finally decided that he'd find out soon enough, so best to tell him herself so she could downplay. "Well, it was interesting, to say the least."

"Do tell." He took another bite.

Landry gave him the important details while he finished his breakfast. His frown didn't give way, even after he'd finished eating and drank the cup of juice that had come with his hospital tray.

"What did Hogan and Paxton say?"

"Nothing yet. They took pictures and were going to question Vanessa and Kohl and Margaret, but honestly, I just can't see it being any of them."

"But Vanessa spit at you."

"Yeah, but she was in my face. I can't see her being direct and also being sneaky to trash my room." She shook her head. "I don't think it was retaliation."

"Then what do you think?"

"I think it's possible it was somebody trying to find out if I knew where the map was."

Nickolai held up his hands and grinned. "Hey, I was in the hospital. Check my alibi."

She laughed. "Yeah, you're good this time. But after the news reporter. . .it could be anybody." She sobered. "Did you know Stan's key unlocks our rooms as well as his own?"

"What?" He bolted upright in the bed.

"Yeah, I didn't, either. The day my room key was locked in the Jeep, Margaret said I should've just asked Stan to unlock my door for me. I didn't really think about it at the time because I got to questioning Vanessa, but now. . ."

"Why would Stan trash your room, crush your laptop, and steal your gun?"

"Well, I had an interesting conversation with Phillip last night."

"Did you, now?"

Landry nodded and repeated the conversation she'd had. "There's definitely something about Stan and Winifred that Phillip doesn't like. Maybe he killed Bartholomew to get Winifred and just stole the map to make it look like a different motive so no one would suspect him." She'd played that scenario out in her head a thousand times last night when sleep refused to come.

"My, you did have an interesting night, didn't you?" Nickolai shifted in the bed. "I guess that would work. I don't know what Stan's alibi was for the time of Bartholomew's murder. Do you remember?"

She shook her head. "And all my documents were destroyed, but I do remember Monica telling me that Stan had been pushing Bartholomew to take retirement. Maybe he was trying to push Bartholomew out of the office as well as out of Winifred's life."

Nickolai straightened the sheet over his legs. "Could be. But then coming here with us defeats his purpose, doesn't it?"

"Have you noticed that he keeps asking if we're done here? How he keeps making a big deal out of the note to leave, making the suggestion that we do? Almost as if everything happened and Winifred asked him to come with us and he couldn't very well say no, but he's doing everything to get us to leave. Maybe he punctured my tire, left the note, trashed my room. He could have even cut your brake lines."

Nickolai laughed. "I can't see Mr. Fuddy Duddy knowing the difference between a brake line and a gas line, much less being able to cut the lines so cleanly."

"You think not? There are videos online on how to do most anything. I checked this morning, and just a random search on my cell for 'how to cut brake lines video' yielded over ten videos. Anybody with access to the Internet and the desire to learn how to do something can find out how. And according to what I saw, it can be done pretty quickly."

"I guess it's possible."

"I'm going to talk to him this afternoon."

"Wait until I can go with you."

She smiled, feeling the heat spread across her face, but she didn't care. It was nice to have someone worry over her. Besides Marcie. A guy. A man. A very attractive man.

Stop it! "I'm here, aren't I? I resisted going to talk to Stan first thing this morning."

"Let me see if they can tell me when I'm going to get released." He hit the nurse call button. When a lady asked what he needed over the intercom, he asked to be discharged. The voice told him someone would be in to see him directly.

"I think while you're speaking with the doctor, I'm going to go find a cup of coffee." She stood, needing to have a little distance from him. She must still be exhausted, because her mind went places it shouldn't. "Do you need anything?"

He shook his head. "But thanks."

"I'll be back." She headed toward the elevator bay, pulling her cell out of her purse as she walked. She pushed the Down button and leaned against the wall. She'd already learned that the elevators in this hospital were slow. Very slow. And one out of order.

"I told you, the white man had a dream vision with Gopan. He told me so himself," a woman's voice wisped down the hall.

Landry froze, holding her breath to focus her listening. She could hear only mumbling in response.

Then the same voice continued. "No, but this means the Shis-Inday are close. Someone is close to finding the mine. Whoever has that map must be stopped. The map must be returned to the Shis-Inday to be destroyed, or we will all suffer the anger of Thunder God."

The elevator dinged, and the car door opened. Landry remained planted to the spot. She still couldn't make out anything but the deep mumbling response to the female voice.

"I know. I will do what I can. I have to go now. I have to get back to work." The sound of shoes squeaked against the freshly waxed floor.

The elevator door closed slowly. Once the hum of its descent sounded, Landry pressed the button again and pushed off the wall. She stared down the corridor where the woman's voice had come from.

The young woman with the long braid down her back who had been leaving Nickolai's room rushed down the hallway. An older man, the same one she'd seen talking to the old Indian at the motel, scurried away.

Nickolai had a dream vision? What exactly was that? What did it mean?

More importantly, who was the man who had the map and was close to finding the lost mine?

"Doctor says I'm good to go." Nickolai jumped off the bed, thankful to be back in his jeans and out of that hospital gown. "The nurse should be here any second with my discharge papers."

"I overheard something interesting." Landry shut his room door.

She wore concern as clearly as her shirt. "What?"

"You had a dream vision?"

He smiled. "Ah, you must have heard Ela."

"The girl with the braid down her back?"

Nickolai nodded then proceeded to explain what she'd told him. "I'm not sure how much of all that I believe, but there you have it."

"Apparently she believes it, because she was talking to someone about it."

"Who?"

"Remember the old Indian at the motel?"

He nodded.

"The first night I saw him, he was talking to another man. It's the same man I saw Ela talking to."

"What did she tell him?"

"Said that because of your dream vision, that meant someone was close to finding the mine. She also said the map needed to be taken to the mountains and destroyed to appease their Thunder God."

He shook his head. "That's crazy, but either way, we're still going to find that map. Before anyone destroys it."

Landry didn't have time to respond before Marvin barged into the room, pushing an empty wheelchair. "I hear you're leaving us." He waved a folder. "Do you need me to go over all these discharge instructions?"

"I think I can figure it out." Nickolai took the folder.

"Well, you have a ride here, so we can wheel you out."

"Is that really necessary?"

Marvin smiled. "I'm sorry. It's hospital policy. But I promise not to crash you."

Nickolai sighed and took a seat. Landry chuckled beside him. "Wanna race?"

Marvin laughed. "I like her."

Nickolai did, too. A lot. A whole lot.

Once they were outside, Marvin said his good-bye and left them.

"Do you want me to drive?" he asked.

Landry cocked her head to the side. "Do you feel up to it?"

"Of course. I've been bored out of my mind having to stay in that bed." He took the keys and opened the passenger door to the Jeep. "Hey, you got rid of your sling."

"I realized I didn't need it." She climbed into the seat and waited until he'd gotten behind the wheel before she asked, "So, what's the game plan?"

"I thought we'd run back to the hotel. Talk to Stan and find out why he has a key to our rooms. I'd like to change clothes. I thought we'd run back out to the Superstitions. See if we can find the man with the map. How's that sound?"

She nodded. "It's a plan."

Funny how quickly he'd become adept at including her in his plans. He'd had a lot of time in the hospital to really think about his life. While he loved his job, he had to admit that he was lonely. Really lonely. Being around Landry Parker made him realize that about his life.

His cell rang. He recognized the special ring tone and answered. "Hey, Chris. You're on speaker with me and Landry Parker."

She smiled and shook her head.

"Oh. Hey. How're you doing? Have you been released from the hospital yet?"

In his boredom last night, he'd called his partner and brought him up to speed on the case and everything, and he'd asked for a few more favors. "Just did. Driving back to the hotel. Did you find out anything?"

"Um, do you want me to call you back?" The questions in Chris's voice were clear.

Landry shifted to look at him, her eyebrows raised in matching questions.

Nickolai chuckled. "Nah, you can talk in front of her." He cut his eyes over to her. "We're kind of working together."

"Really?" The shock in his voice...

Landry burst out laughing. "What did you tell him about me?"

"Horns." Nickolai snorted.

"Horns?" Chris asked.

"I'll explain later. What'd you find out?"

"Okay, here you go. First off, Winslet Industries is doing fine financially. Better than fine, so there's no issue there."

"Good." Well, that eliminated motive to kill Bartholomew so he wouldn't find out money had been embezzled or anything.

"About Phillip Fontenot."

"Yeah?" He glanced at Landry. She had leaned a little closer to his cell resting on the console.

"No record, aside from a couple of speeding tickets and parking violations. Nothing else. His financials aren't anything in comparison to the Winslet fortune, but he's able to make his mortgage."

"Anything else?"

"Never married. No children. Nothing else on him."

Then they'd have to take him at face value. "What about Stan Hauge?"

"Married, no children. Financially, he's sound. Made good investments. Nothing too risky. Comfortable. No record, not even traffic violations. Everyone speaks highly of him. Has a really strong reputation."

"Thanks, Chris. Anything else you can tell me about the investigation?"

"Very little. Some progress has been made. Ballistics report came back. Winslet was shot with a twenty-two caliber at point-blank range. Fleshing by the wounds show the gun was most likely pressed against his back, right at his heart. Two bullets penetrated him from the back and went through his heart and lungs. Both bullets were recovered from the body in autopsy. No fingerprints or DNA not belonging to the victim were detected."

Nickolai stopped the Jeep at an intersection. A ball of tumbleweeds rolled alongside the road.

"You didn't happen to run checks to see if Phillip Fontenot or Stan Hauge happened to have a .22 registered to them, did you?"

"We actually did." Chris laughed. "Imagine that—the police department knowing how to handle an investigation without the great and powerful Nickolai Baptiste."

Landry grinned ear to ear, and he smiled as he shook his head. "Yeah, yeah, yeah. Yuck it up, buddy. Payback will come, my friend."

"You don't scare me. Anyway, to answer your question, neither has any guns registered to them."

"A dead end."

"I didn't say that."

"Do tell." Nickolai turned onto Apache Trail.

"Bartholomew Winslet had a .22 registered. When we went to inspect it, Mrs. Winslet couldn't find any of his four registered handguns. Seems they just disappeared. She has no idea where they are."

"Interesting."

"No pawn shops have any record of any of them. We've run the serials and nothing's come up. If Winslet moved them, we have no idea where."

"Have you spoken with Monica Courtland about them?" Landry interrupted.

"No. Is there a reason we should?"

Landry nodded. "She seems to know a lot about Bartholomew and his movements. If he took them to the office for any reason, she'd know."

"Good to know. We'll check it out. Thanks." Chris sounded surprised, which made Nickolai grin at Landry.

Nickolai stopped the Jeep at the red light just before the motel. "Anything else you can tell me?"

"There are some leads. . . ."

Nickolai recognized Chris's tone. "But you can't share with me."

"Right."

"Okay. Well, if you find anything out you can clue me in to, please call."

"Will do. And, Nick, give me a call later and let's catch up." *Translate to mean: call later and give the scoop about Landry.*

"I will. Thanks." Nickolai disconnected the call and pulled into the motel's parking lot. "Guess that's that."

Landry nodded. "Why don't you go ahead and get changed and cleaned up, then we can try Stan? Just knock on my door when you're ready."

Nickolai nodded, anxious to see if anything was missing from his room before he confronted Stan. Had the man been sneaking into their rooms and going through things to find out where they were with the case? Could he be violent?

Could Stan be a murderer?

Chapter Twenty-Two

Knock. Knock. Knock.

The rapping on her door was faint. She'd expected Nickolai to bang his arrival, larger than life like the man himself. Landry grinned and opened the door then froze.

Stan Hauge stood on the other side. "Hi."

"Hey there." She struggled to not let her shock show on her face. At least she hoped her surprise wouldn't alarm him.

"May I talk to you for a moment, please?" His face was red, and a thin sheen of sweat coated his upper lip.

This was Stan. Nervous and unsure of himself. Not a threat.

"Sure." She opened the door wider. "Come on in." There was no way she could get Nickolai without alarming Stan. Hopefully, Nickolai would show up soon on his own and join in on the conversation.

He stepped inside and sat in the chair by the table.

She glanced outside. No sign of Nickolai. She shut the door, but not quite all the way. If Nickolai came by, he'd be able to overhear their conversation if he didn't want to come in. Landry sat on the edge of the bed facing the table. "What's up?"

"I haven't been completely honest with you, and I probably should."

"Oh?" She clasped her hands in her lap. Was she about to get a confession? Where was Nickolai?

"It's about Winifred. And me." He stared at the floor.

Landry remained silent. She'd learned during her MP training that silence encouraged people to speak more freely and openly than if they were questioned.

"Years ago, Winifred worked in the office with Bartholomew. There were a lot of late nights and long days. We were working to build the business into the empire it is today. It took a lot from all of us—Bartholomew, Winifred, me, even Phillip. We all put in so much time and effort."

She nodded.

"There were times, many times, when Bartholomew had to go out of town for business. Phillip went with him a lot, mainly to party. When necessary, Winifred had to stay there and work. It was, again, long hours and tedious work. I tried to help as much as I could. This was my job, and no matter what, I've always been well compensated for my labor." He took a deep breath.

Landry remained still, not wanting to distract him from his story. He still looked at the floor as he spoke.

"That's no excuse, of course. It was just one night, it was late. . . Winifred and I were alone. We'd been working since seven that morning, not even leaving for lunch, having pizza brought in. We had just finished a big project, one that Bartholomew had been struggling with for weeks. We were exhausted, but pumped because we'd completed it for him. We knew he'd be so happy. We were on a rush of sorts. All the emotions bursting while we were exhausted."

Landry knew what was coming. . .had known it since he started talking, but also knew not to rush him. This was Stan's story to tell, and he needed to tell it in his way, in his time.

"One thing led to another, and before either of us realized what we were doing, we were in each other's arms on the couch." Stan lifted his gaze to Landry's. "It's the one moment of my life I regret the most. It was the biggest mistake I've ever made, and I knew it almost immediately. That doesn't excuse me, or her. We were wrong in what we did. Wrong to my wife and children. Wrong to Bartholomew. Wrong to ourselves."

Stan's face had gone totally red, but the sadness in his eyes gripped Landry's heart.

"We were both so ashamed of ourselves. We agreed it was a huge mistake. Agreed it would never happen again. Agreed we would never tell my wife or Bartholomew." He shook his head. "For months after, we did the best we could to work together without incident, but it was strained. Many felt it."

"Bartholomew?" Landry couldn't stop herself from asking.

"Oh, no. He never knew. He came back from his business trip recharged and rededicated to the business. He dove in headfirst, not really taking stock of anything around him, least of all Winifred."

Landry tried to imagine how blind you had to be not to see the guilt Stan had to show, especially if he still showed it so clearly all these years later. Her parents had always had such a close marriage. Their love had been so evident. . .it was what Landry herself wanted. She couldn't see Nickolai ever being so wrapped up in anything that he wouldn't pay attention to a woman.

Wait! How'd Nickolai jump into her thoughts in such a context?

Stan coughed awkwardly. "Winifred started working from home more and more, coming into the office less and less. Bartholomew didn't notice. Phillip did. I never told him what had happened between us, but I'm pretty certain he figured it out." He rubbed his hands together. "Or maybe Winifred told him."

"Why would she do that?"

"Because Phillip's been in love with her since before she married Bartholomew. She and Phillip actually went out a few times before she went out with Bartholomew. Don't get me wrong—once Winifred dated Bartholomew, she fell madly in love with him and that was it for her."

"And Phillip?"

"He never got over her, I don't think. Back before our mistake, I'd often catch him staring at her when he didn't know anyone was paying attention. You could see the love still in his eyes." He shrugged. "We never had a problem between us, me and Phillip, until he learned about our one indiscretion. After that. . .well, let's just say that Phillip has gone out of his way to push me out of the company and away from Winifred."

Landry tried to absorb it all. "What about Winifred's feelings toward Phillip now?"

"I think she only had eyes for Bartholomew. She loved him. I know that. But she was friends with Phillip. Still is. I don't think she could see he was in love with her. But now that Bartholomew's gone, I don't know what to think. Phillip showing up here. . .I'm not sure what that means. I believe he's still in love with her."

She nodded slowly, thinking about how Phillip had acted very entitled to information on their investigation. On behalf of Winifred. What did that mean?

"For the last several months, I've seen the sadness in Winifred. She loved traveling and was always asking Bartholomew to take time off and travel with her. I'd begun pressing Bartholomew to go. The business is fine. I could oversee the day-to-day operations and bring any problems that needed his attention to him immediately. I wanted her to be happy again. I wanted them to be happy."

So that was why he'd been pushing Bartholomew, not because he wanted to take over the business, but because he wanted the Winslets' marriage to be strengthened. Landry could respect that about Stan. He might have made mistakes, but she had no doubt he'd repented and never repeated his sin. She believed he wanted Bartholomew and Winifred to have a good, strong marriage.

"I'm really sorry for not telling you before. I probably should have, because I'm sure you picked up on something off, at least between me and Phillip. I just wish it had never happened. It almost cost me my wife. The guilt nearly did me in, so I had to tell her." He picked invisible lint off his slacks. "Thank the good Lord she forgave me and took me back, but I still wish I hadn't had that one moment of weakness. It very well could have made me lose everything."

"I'm so sorry." Landry didn't know what else to say. The pain he'd lived with was evident in both his expression and his words. She felt odd apologizing to an adulterer for the pain he'd endured because of his own infidelity, but she did feel sorry for him. It was clear he made a mistake and regretted it.

"I don't deserve your empathy, Miss Parker. I know that. I didn't deserve my wife's forgiveness, or Winifred's. I'm very blessed."

True.

He stood. "Anyway, I wanted you to hear the truth from me. No matter what might be said, I wanted you to have the facts."

She stood as well. Now or never, she couldn't wait for Nickolai. "Speaking of facts, why didn't you tell us you had copies of our motel room keys?"

His face turned redder than she'd imagined possible. "I'm sorry. It's actually habit."

Landry crossed her arms over her chest and raised her brows.

"Whenever I traveled with Bartholomew, I always got a master key for all the rooms in our party. He was the worst about losing his key, and he hated having to notify the front desk. Years ago, he began having Monica request me or Phillip, depending upon who was traveling with him, have a master. It became customary to request copies of the whole party's room keys when we made reservations. I'm sorry. I didn't even think about it until just now."

"But you know my room was broken into. Why didn't you mention it then?"

"I did. I told the police when they came by to ask if I'd heard anything." He glanced around the room. "They said your room was trashed. I'm glad the hotel sent someone to clean it up for you."

"I cleaned it up myself. My gun was taken, Stan."

"I'm so sorry. I assure you, I know nothing and heard nothing."

Landry studied him. The sad thing was, despite his responses sounding so lame, she truly did believe him. She let out a sigh.

"Have you heard from Mr. Baptiste?"

She nodded. "I brought him back from the hospital just before you knocked on my door."

"Has he heard when his truck will be repaired? I think it's safe to say we'll all be relieved when we can leave."

No, she wouldn't. Not if it was without the map. "I don't think they've told him yet. He and I have a lead to follow this afternoon." She watched his face for the slightest reaction.

"You and Mr. Baptiste are working together?"

"You might say that."

He pressed his lips together. "Interesting."

"I'd say." She couldn't tell if the news was a problem for him or not. At this point, she really didn't care. What mattered was she and Nickolai were. . . What, exactly, were they? Friends? Friendly competitors?

All she knew was that when she was around Nickolai, or even just thought about him, she felt happy and all girly inside. She wasn't sure what that meant, but she'd figure it out later. For the time being, she'd enjoy being happy and girly on the inside. It'd been far too long since she felt that way.

Nickolai stuck his wallet in his back pocket, ready to head down to Landry's room. His cell phone chimed. He glanced at the caller ID, and his heart caught in his chest. He slumped to the edge of the bed as he answered the call.

"Hello."

"Nicky? It's Lisbeth." She sounded as happy as she had last time he'd seen her.

He let out the breath that had caught sideways in his throat. "Hey, honey. Is everything okay?"

She let out that little giggle that he'd always adored of hers. Ever since she was a toddler. "Everything is better than okay." She paused for a minute. "Do I only call you when something's wrong?"

Truth was, she rarely called. "I guess not. I was just surprised to hear from you."

"I don't call you often enough, do I, Nicky? That's going to change.

I'm sorry I haven't been a better sister."

"Aw, Lisbeth, I understand." He did, but he didn't. He looked forward to seeing her every week, but he also felt guilty. But now. . . since talking with Landry, he hoped the guilt would leave him alone.

"Nicky, there's a lot we need to talk about. A lot I want to say to you. A lot I need to say."

His tongue wouldn't wrap around the words right.

"But for now, I need to share something with you. Something amazing."

"What?" He hadn't even gotten the payment plan structure from the doctor, so there was no way they were moving her out already. They couldn't without his signature anyway.

"Part of my treatment plan here is to attend some form of church service every week, so I've been going to the Christian service every Sunday morning." The excitement in her voice was something he hadn't heard in her for years. Not since she'd talked about her love of everything to do with fire. "And this morning. . .Nicky, I gave my heart to Jesus and was saved. I'm a Christian!"

"Wow." He didn't know what to say. Was this part of her disease? Another delusion?

"I hear that you're skeptical. I get that. I was, too. When I first started going, I only went 'cuz the doctor told me I had to. If I didn't go, I didn't get any privileges for the whole week. I used to sit there and just think to myself how naive these people were for believing."

Kind of like Nickolai did.

"But something started happening to me, Nicky. I started feeling different whenever I was in the church service. I felt free. Like I wasn't sick. Like I used to feel."

He'd heard all about the feel-good messages from some of the popular preachers on TV. All about how life was good and God had a wonderful life for everyone, everyone just needed to believe that. He'd debunked that a long time ago. If his sister was being fed such a line of cr—

"Something happened to how I felt on the inside. Little by little, I felt a change in me. I started looking forward to Sunday mornings. I started singing in the services. I really listened to the preacher. But most importantly, I got my own Bible and started reading it. Studying.

"Oh, Nicky. I realized I'm such a sinner. All the time. And I've been blaming my illness. Blaming you. Blaming Mom and Dad."

Nickolai froze. She'd never said she blamed anyone. She also hadn't mentioned Mom or Dad in over a year.

Sobs came over the line. "But I'm responsible for my own actions. Me." Her sobs came harder. Heavier. "I set that fire to the house, Nicky. I did it. I knew Mom and Dad were in there, sound asleep, but I didn't care. All I cared about was seeing the fire and setting the beast loose."

His chest tightened.

"I fed my disease. I allowed the illness to control me. I was weak, yes, but I'm stronger now. I know I'm sick. I know I need help. And I know I'm a sinner and need Jesus in my life. He loves me, even with all that I've done. He loves me and forgives me. I don't have to prove to Him that I mean it. He knows my heart."

Tendrils of guilt snaked up his spine. Did he make Lisbeth feel like she had to prove herself to him for him to love and accept her?

Deep in the dark recesses of his heart, the place he didn't want to admit existed, did he feel that way?

"Oh, Nicky, I'll see Mom and Dad again in eternity. They were Christians. Remember, Mom used to make us say prayers before bed? Do you remember that?"

It'd been a really long time since he thought about it, but yes, she had. They'd prayed before eating, too. "I do. I remember." How had he forgotten? Had he pushed all the memories of his family life before the fire down so he wouldn't feel the pain? Had he been so angry at God that he'd rebelled by forgetting the foundation of his mother's faith?

"I'd forgotten. But when I started reading, really reading my Bible, I read the twenty-third psalm, and I remembered hearing Mom recite it when I was little. She'd brush my hair and recite it. I could almost hear her voice starting 'The Lord is my shepherd; I shall not want.' "

He makes me lie down in green pastures.

" 'He leads me beside still waters. He restores my soul.' That's how I feel, Nicky. He's restored my soul."

It was all too much to take in. Lisbeth's excitement. Her happiness. Her accepting responsibility. Mentioning Mom and Dad. Remembering their faith.

"I know you probably think it's not real. You might think it's part of my illness. It's not, Nicky. It's real. But you'll see for yourself. You'll notice I've changed because the change is in my heart. I may still make mistakes, but I'm focusing on following Jesus' example."

"You sound really happy, Lisbeth." He didn't want to diminish this for her. If it was real. . .

"I am." She paused. "Well, I need to get ready for lunch. I just wanted to share this with you, Nicky. I haven't told you in a long time how thankful I am for all you do for me. I really appreciate you. I love you, Nicky."

"I love you, too, Lisbeth." His heart thudded. It'd been so long since she'd told him she loved him. His eyes filled as she told him good-bye and disconnected the call.

Was this for real? Could it be?

The Transition

Gopan turned to the other three shamans. His hands trembled as he set down his pouch and bowed his head against the fire's smoke.

Paco, Nantan, and Dyami answered as one, in their native Apache tongue. "Yes, the earth is our mother and the sky our father."

Gopan had adorned his full ceremonial attire. He beat on the hide drum. "I come to ask for protection to our warriors as we protect Thunder God's mountain and inhabitants."

Paco nodded, standing and facing the eastern sky. He took a long pull off his pipe. His Apache tongue split the silence of the range as smoke seeped out of the corners of his mouth. "Hail to the East, to the new day. To the light. To the eagle. To insight. To the East, we call on you."

Beating harder on the drum, Gopan blinked against the sweat dripping into his eyes. He would enter the trance state soon. The wind whipped the eagle feathers in his headpiece.

Nantan took the pipe from Paco. He lifted it to his lips as he stood and raised the pipe high above his head. "Hail to the South, to innocence. To trust. To the mouse. To the path home. To the South, we call on you."

Smoke filled the air. Swirling and circling. Gopan banged on the drum faster, losing himself in the rhythm as well as the haze of the smoke.

Dyami took the pipe from Nantan, took a drag, and faced the West. "Hail to the West, to the darkened waters. To looking within. Home to black bear. To the medicine path. To the West, we call on you."

Gopan couldn't see. He set down the drum and took the pipe from Dyami. He inhaled, pulling the sage and spices into his lungs. He held it there as he passed the pipe back to Paco; then he took the pouch with the blue cornmeal and faced the North. He raised his arms, exhaling the smoke with his words. "Hail to the North, home of the old ones, and those gone before. To the wisdom place. The place of snow leopard and white buffalo. To the North, we call on you."

All four men knelt as one. In the prone position, each blew into their medicine pouches.

Gopan could no longer make out one brother from another, which was the way it should be. They were to be as one. He closed his eyes, welcoming the nonphysical state. He would ask for protection for the warriors, the protectors who would forevermore be known as the ghost warriors.

Paco's Apache rattled Gopan's chest. "And to mother earth, for the two and four leggeds. For those that fly or crawl and swim. For all children of the mother."

Nantan's voice echoed inside Gopan's head. "And to father sky. Thank you for this day."

Dust mixed with the smoke as they moved, but Gopan stayed in the prone position, his heart open to the spiritual healing he'd undergo. For himself. For the others. For the warriors for all time.

The culture of the tribe ran deep into the veins of the shamans. This was their life. Their history, and their future.

Gopan spoke his heart. "We ask for protection. For those of us who will forever be in the service of the Thunder God. We give ourselves as protectors. As warriors."

Lightning flashed, splitting the darkened skies.

"So be it," said Paco.

"It is a good day to die," all four men whispered. "Sadnleel da'ya'dee nzho." Long life, old age, everything good.

Chapter Twenty-Three

Landry spit out the toothpaste and rinsed her mouth. She wiped her face and studied her reflection in the mirror. She hadn't bothered with makeup in the last couple of days, nor had she been able to really fix her hair since the accident. Thank goodness she'd been blessed with good genes and a flawless olive complexion.

Did Nickolai find her attractive? Was she his type?

She shook her head and turned away from the mirror. She had no business thinking about Nickolai like that. Especially right now in the middle of such a crazy case and not to mention his skewed views on Christianity, which was vital to her very being.

Her cell chirped, the special ring tone for Marcie filling the motel room. "Hey."

"How are you? Anything else happened?"

Landry laughed. "I'm fine. Everybody's good. Nothing's happened today."

"Well, that's good. Seriously, because it's barely after noon. Don't make me get on a plane and come get you."

Landry would laugh, but she knew her friend wasn't really kidding. "I'm fine. Nickolai is out of the hospital. I imagine we're going to head out to the mountains this afternoon to see what we can find out."

"I wish you'd just find the stupid map so you could come home. It seems that every time I talk to you, something else, worse, has happened."

"Not this time." Landry sat on the edge of the bed, smiling into the phone. She really did miss her best friend. "Maybe my luck is changing."

"Funny, but I happen to know for a fact that you don't believe in luck."

"True."

"What? I can hear your hesitation."

Of course Marcie would pick up on her emotional turmoil. They'd been best friends since high school. "Will you just pray for me? And for Nickolai?"

"Certainly, but about what?"

"I just have this sense. . . ."

"Hold up, girl. A good sense or a bad sense?"

"I don't really know, to be honest. Just that. . .I can't explain it." She couldn't. Landry had tried to explain it to herself earlier, before Stan had shown up, but there was just something. . .off in her spirit.

"Landry, I'm not sure you're in a good place, and I don't mean Apache Junction."

"I know, but it's all good. Jesus has my back."

"Now you're scaring me."

"No, it's nothing like that." Landry tried to figure out how to put her feelings into words but couldn't. "It's all good. I just felt like asking for extra prayers is all."

"Now I'm really worried." And it sounded in her voice.

Landry lay back on the bed. "No, don't be. It's not a concerned feeling."

"Are you okay? I mean, really and honestly and truly?" Marcie used their old saying, one they'd reserved for pushing for emotional release.

"I am. Better than I'd thought." As she said the words, Landry realized she meant them. She thought of Tarak and the old Indian man in the motel as well as the Thunder God and the Great Spirit. "Marcie, do you believe God uses anything to do His will? Even things we don't understand or think might be in contrast to religion itself?"

"Give me an example of what you mean."

"There is a lot of history here with Native Americans and their traditional beliefs. Dream visions, questions, destiny, and stuff like that. Do you think God could use any or all of that for His purposes?"

Marcie laughed. "God created everything, the heavens, the earth, all the animals, and us. Why would we think there's a limit on His power in what He chooses to use?"

Landry smiled. Marcie always did fraction things down to the least common denominator. Maybe that's why she was such a rocking CPA. "Thanks, girl. I love you."

"Love you, too. Call me tonight, or before if you need me."

"I will." Landry sat up as she hung up the phone.

Knock. Knock. Knock.

Despite the lecture she'd given herself before Marcie's call, Landry smiled as she headed to the door. That strong and deliberate knock was all Nickolai. She opened the door to find him smiling at her.

"I thought maybe we could grab something to eat before we head out to the mountains. I know I'm starving, and I figured you probably were, too." His gaze dropped to the ground then back up to her face. His cheeks were a little brighter. "I thought maybe we could go back to Handlebar Pub and Grill. That burger is calling my name again."

She laughed. "It was good. I think I'm going to order that this time myself." She grabbed her purse and the keys to the Jeep, handed them to him, and then shut the door behind her. She double-checked to make sure it was locked before following him across the parking lot.

After they were buckled into the Jeep and on the way, Nickolai opened his mouth, paused, shut it again. Clearly something was on his mind. She waited. He did the same thing again, still without saying anything.

"What?" Patience never had been her strong suit.

"My sister called me while I was changing."

Landry's pulse kicked up a notch. "Is everything okay?" Maybe that's why something felt off to her.

"She's fine." He turned into the restaurant's parking lot. "Apparently, she's more than fine. She said she became a Christian today."

Landry smiled. "Oh, Nickolai, that's wonderful. I'm so happy for her."

"How can you just automatically say that?" He parked the Jeep, turned off the ignition, but made no move to open the door. He released his seat belt, turning to face Landry. "You know about her disease. What if this is just a delusion brought on by her illness?"

Landry laughed then saw his frown and covered her mouth with her hand. "I'm not laughing at you, Nickolai. It's just if being saved is a delusion, then there are a lot of us in the world today who are delusional. I can assure you, choosing to become a Christian is not a side effect or symptom of being schizophrenic."

"But you don't know her. How can you be so sure?"

"What did she say when she called?"

"That she'd been going to services. She'd been skeptical, then started in the worship, then listening to the preacher. Said she got a Bible and started reading it. Ended with deciding to become a Christian at the services today."

Landry's heart could've exploded at that moment. "Oh, Nickolai, that's a great testimony. She didn't just jump on a bandwagon. She didn't want to just belong and follow along. She admitted she was skeptical, not buying into any and everything." She undid her seat belt and turned to face him as well.

Heart pumping, she continued. "Little by little—deciding to join in the worship, listening to the message, and finally getting a Bible and reading the Word for herself—all of that was Jesus wooing her. Loving her heart with His. That she made the choice to follow Him. . .that truly is a choice every person has to make for themselves. She made that choice for herself. Don't you see? If anything, this shows she is getting better. She's not just blindly being led, but is thinking for herself and making her own decisions and choices in her own time."

Nickolai stared at her, but it wasn't an intimidation stare. It was. . .oh, goodness, it was a stare of attraction.

Landry's heart threatened to jump out of her chest, and she licked her lips.

Slowly, as if the world had screeched to a stop on its axis, Nickolai leaned toward her. His cologne wrapped around her, drawing her in like a warm embrace. She leaned in as well.

His eyes flickered to her mouth and back up.

Her heart caught in her throat. He leaned in. Closer.

Closer.

Her pulse echoed inside her head. His gaze made her dizzy.

His hand touched the side of her face. His thumb stroked her cheekbone with the gentlest of movements.

Nickolai's breath caressed her lips; then his lips were on hers.

Landry closed her eyes, savoring the sweet tenderness of the kiss. She couldn't breathe, but didn't want to. Didn't want anything but this kiss. Right now. Right here. Until. . .

He drew back, his eyes glued to her face. "Landry." His voice, ragged and rough, yet so soft as he said her name.

It was as if her insides had melted.

A horn honked on the road. They both jumped. Laughed. The special moment between them gone.

"I guess we'd better get inside." He opened the driver's door.

"Yeah." She waited, letting him come around to open her door for her. She needed the minute to compose herself. Every muscle in her body felt weak, as if she'd just run a marathon. Her heart still raced.

He opened the door and cool air swirled around her. She took his hand and followed him into the Handlebar. In that moment, she needed to admit to herself that she wanted to follow him wherever he led.

Amazingly, he could walk.

Nickolai could barely breathe, so the ability to put one foot in front of the other had been a very surprising reality. Quite astonishing he could do anything with Landry in such close proximity. He could smell her indelible shampoo and body wash. He could feel the soft lines of the small of her back under his hand. He could sense her movements just by being close to her.

Everything had changed with one kiss. One earth-shattering, world-spinning, steal-his-heart kiss.

While they waited to be seated, Nickolai couldn't look at her. Had he really kissed her? He felt like he'd lost part of himself, and he didn't quite know how to deal with that at the moment.

The same hostess as the other day sat them out on the patio, as per their request. They ended up at the same table as before. The waitress, again, same as last time, came quickly and took their drink orders. They both ordered the green chili burgers with extra bacon. Déjà vu but not. . .

Except everything felt new. The colors looked brighter, more vibrant. The pecan smoke smelled stronger, almost where he could taste the flavor. The conversations of the other patrons formed a symphony of voices with different pitches and lyrics.

His eyes met Landry's, and while his pulse throbbed, heat burned his face. Did she regret kissing him? Was he making a big deal out of nothing? What if she'd just been excited because of Lisbeth's becoming a Christian?

"Nickolai." Her voice spoke to him on a deeper, stronger level than before.

"I'm so—" No, he wasn't going to diminish his emotions. Not right now. He was raw, and if he got hurt, at least he'd be hurt by honesty. "I'm not sorry for kissing you."

She grinned, her face turning a little pink. "Well, I'm happy to hear that because I'm not sorry for kissing you back."

A strange feeling rose up from his toes and bubbled into his chest. "Okay, then."

The waitress returned with their drinks. "Your burgers will be out soon."

"Oh, Stan came to see me earlier," Landry said as she took a sip of her drink.

"What?"

She nodded and set her glass back on the table. "He told me about his affair with Winifred many years ago. It was a one-time thing and nearly destroyed him. Bartholomew never knew, and Stan respected their marriage vows explicitly from that day forward."

"He told you all that, huh?"

"He did, and I believe him. I'm pretty good at reading people." She reached across the table and touched his hand. Just that one touch made it hard for him to concentrate. "Think about it, Nick; he wasn't hurting for money, your partner told you that. He and Bartholomew hadn't had any disagreements or arguments; no one has said they ever had cross words. Taking all that into consideration, what would be Stan's motive to kill Bartholomew and steal the map?" She pulled her hand back to her side of the table, taking another drink.

Had she called him Nick? Using a pet name indicated intimacy. How, exactly, did she feel about him? Now wasn't the time to discuss, but his mind wouldn't stop circling back to the possibilities.

"But Stan had been pushing Bartholomew to retire, right?"

Landry nodded. "Monica told me he had been. I asked Stan. He said he knew Winifred wanted to travel and spend more time with Bartholomew. That's what he'd been encouraging—Bartholomew to spend less time at the office and more time with his wife."

Logical, but... "What about his and Phillip's argument?"

She toyed with her straw as she talked. "According to Stan, Phillip's been in love with Winifred since before she married Bartholomew. He's stayed around because of her."

"Chris said he'd never married."

"What if he carried a torch for her all this time?"

Nickolai nodded. "But why now? Why murder Bartholomew now? If he's been in love with Winifred all these years, why hadn't he acted before?"

She let out a long breath. "That's the one thing I haven't worked out yet."

"You're saying Phillip is your main suspect?"

"Right now? Yes. Call it a hunch. Gut feeling. Whatever. I just don't trust him."

Nickolai laughed. "I like him, but that doesn't mean I don't think he's a suspect. Then again, there's not an apparent motive for murdering his best friend right now."

"What if he hadn't known about Winifred and Stan's affair until recently? It sent him into such a rage."

Nickolai shook his head. "A rage that made him murder his best friend? Not buying that. He would've killed Stan."

She nodded. "True. Still, I'm not ruling him out as a suspect."

The waitress returned with their burgers. Landry immediately bowed her head and began to pray. Nickolai sat still, wishing he could hear what she said. For Lisbeth, of course. Not for him.

Landry finished and took a big bite of the burger. She closed her eyes as she chewed, clearly savoring every different spice and taste. Nickolai had never met a woman who enjoyed food as much as Landry.

He'd never met a woman like her, period.

Landry wiped her mouth and swallowed. "So, if it's not Phillip or Stan, or anybody else in Bartholomew's personal life, then it comes back to the motive being the map."

Nickolai nodded. "It seems to. Maybe we should have another talk with the original owner, Joel Easton."

"Do you think he knows something you didn't ask?"

"Can't hurt to talk to him again. Maybe something will hit you that I missed."

She smiled and took another bite. He did as well. The chipotle tingled his tongue, but not more than Landry Parker seemed to have tingled deep within him.

Oh, Chris was going to have a field day with this. He'd tried to set Nickolai up on date after date, only to tell him that he was too picky. No woman could meet Nickolai's standards and expectations.

Just wait until he met Landry Parker. Oh, was his former partner and friend in for a surprise. A mighty big one.

Just as she'd blown Nickolai out of the water, leaving him feeling like he flapped about without a hope of recovering.

Chapter Twenty-Four

Landry surveyed the Ironwood Cancer and Research Center in Gilbert, Arizona. It was a beautiful building in a very peaceful location.

"Come on, I know where his mother's room is." Nickolai led her across the parking lot.

"Are you sure this is okay? I would hate to bust in and upset his mother." Landry wanted to get answers, of course, but she didn't want to impose on a woman battling cancer. After what she went through with both her parents and their illnesses, the last thing she would do is intrude.

"Last time we came outside to talk so we wouldn't disturb his mother. He'll most likely want to do the same today."

She nodded and let him open the front door for her.

A blond receptionist sat behind the front counter. She gave Landry the stink eye but smiled as she caught sight of Nickolai.

"Hello again," she greeted him.

"Hi. Hoping I didn't miss Joel." They'd discussed on the drive over that if he wasn't here, they'd just have to wait on him because neither had a good address for him.

"They've finished lunch and I believe he's reading to her."

"Thanks. I remember where her room is." Nickolai flashed a full smile at her. "Thanks."

The receptionist all but swooned. Landry could relate. Did the man have any idea how lethal his smile could be? Mercy!

She almost couldn't believe this place housed sick people. As

Nickolai led Landry to Mrs. Easton's room, she couldn't smell the usual scent of death and illness. She didn't hear the beepings of various life-supporting machines or the painful groanings of patients nearing the end of their life. She'd had enough of all that with her parents' illnesses and treatments. But not here. No, this place had the feel more of an upscale retirement home or faculty housing of some sort.

Nickolai stopped by the door with Mrs. Easton's name. He gave her a quick smile then knocked softly.

"Come in," a woman's voice came from the other side.

Nickolai gently pushed open the door.

A woman sat up in the bed, wearing a bright bed jacket with colorful hydrangeas depicted. Silver hair tips peeked out from under a fuchsia-colored scarf. Her lipstick matched the brightness of the scarf.

Joel Easton, looking just like he had in the video surveillance photographs, sat in a chair beside the bed, holding a very worn, black leather Bible.

"We're sorry for disturbing you." Nickolai looked at Joel. "Perhaps we could talk outside again?"

"No, you can speak in here," the woman said. "I'm Abigail Easton, Joel's mother. He told me about you, Mr. Baptiste." She looked at Landry. "And who might you be?"

Landry pushed past Nickolai and offered her hand. "I'm Landry Parker. It's a pleasure to meet you, Mrs. Easton."

The woman's grip was firmer than Landry had expected. "Please, call me Abigail." She included Nickolai in her gaze. "Joel told me about your visit last time. What is it now?"

"We're very sorry for disturbing you," Landry began.

Abigail chuckled. "Honey, when you're in a hospital, no matter how nice, you look forward to anything that disrupts your normal routine."

Landry liked her. "We're here to see if we missed anything about the map."

"My heavens, that map has been nothing more than a calamity to my family."

"Mom!"

"It's true, Joel, and you know it. Caused so much strife. Brother against brother. Husband against wife. Father against son." She smiled sadly at Joel with her last comment. "I'm thankful we had it to sell for my treatment, of course, but I'm glad it's out of our family." Abigail shook her head. "And now to learn that the poor buyer was murdered. Well, I guess the rumors of the curse might be true."

"Curse?" Nickolai moved closer to where Landry stood beside the bed.

"Please, you two sit down. You're making my neck hurt looking up at you." She waved them to other chairs from her bed.

Landry and Nickolai sat. "You said something about a curse?" Nickolai asked.

"Momma doesn't believe in curses." Joel frowned at his mother.

"I believe in verbal blessings handed down from father to son, as it's written in the good book, so why wouldn't I believe in curses, the opposite?" She shook her head and looked at Landry. "Do you have a son?"

"No. No, ma'am. I don't have any children."

"Just wait. Sons are such a joy, but they are also a major pain in the behind sometimes."

Landry pressed her lips together to keep the laughter inside. Yes, she did really like this woman.

"Anyway, back when our Julia Thomas got the map from Jacob Waltz, legends say the ghost warrior Indians cursed the map. They tried to steal it several times, so I've heard. It's been passed down from generation to generation that whoever uses the map to try and find the mine will meet with imminent death." Abigail fingered the edge of her scarf. "They say the map is to be given to the ghost warriors of the mountain to be destroyed. That's the only way the curse will be lifted."

"I hadn't heard that," Landry barely whispered.

"I've wondered if my cancer might not be because the map came into my possession."

"Mom, that's just plain silly talk. No map gave you cancer." Joel reached over and took his mother's hand.

Landry agreed with Joel. As a Christian, accepting cancer, Alzheimer's, heart disease. . .all deadly illnesses was hard, very hard. She didn't understand it, hadn't since her mother had gotten sick and died. Certainly hadn't when her father's mind and memories had been stolen. But she'd always known that despite the diseases and suffering, God was with them. With her parents. With her. Even with the medical personnel. She had to believe that. She'd felt that.

God could and would use anything for His plans. She had to believe that.

Nickolai looked at Joel. "We were wondering if there was anything you remembered about the map or the sale that you didn't already tell me or the police?"

"I can't think of anything. I told you about Allen and the hacking—"

"I'm still ashamed that you would do such a thing," Abigail interrupted.

"I know, Mom. I'm sorry." He looked at Nickolai and shook his head. "I can't think of anything else."

"What about before you got the map? Who had it before? Had anyone shown interest in buying it before you put it up for sale?" Landry asked. If the map was the motive for Bartholomew's murder, then there had to be something they didn't know. There just had to!

"My father had the map before he passed it on to me," Abigail said. "He and my mother fought over it. My father and his brother were convinced they could find the mine and be rich." She shook her head. "My uncle died out in the Superstitions while hunting for the mine." She shrugged. "It was ruled an accident. . .he lost his footing and fell, breaking his leg. He died from exposure and being bitten by a rattlesnake. But who knows if the curse didn't kill him?"

"Mom, don't get all worked up over this."

"I'm not worked up, son. I'm glad that map's gone. I should've sold it to Phil when he wanted to buy it."

Landry's gut free-fell to her toes. "Phil?"

She nodded. "A couple of years ago, right before I really got bad sick, my family doctor introduced me to my oncologist who hadn't even moved out to Arizona yet. He was finishing up with his patients and still practicing in Louisiana. LSUS Medical Center. Anyway, I met him and we hit it off, and I decided I wanted him to be my doctor. Since I needed to start treatment immediately, I went to Shreveport for treatment until Dr. Martin moved to Arizona as planned. He was getting married to an Arizona girl, which was why he was moving."

"Your doctor is Phil?" Nickolai asked.

Abigail chuckled. "No, I guess I went down a rabbit hole a bit there, didn't I? No, I met Phil at LSUS Medical Center. He was being treated for prostate cancer. We struck up a conversation and became friendly. During the course of several visits over the next few months, our appointments seemed to be on the same day and close to the same times. We would often walk across the street to eat a burger together or just grab a cup of coffee. We talked about many things, but one day I mentioned the curse maybe being the cause of my cancer, which led to me telling him all about the map. On the next visit, Phil said he'd done a little research and was intrigued because he was a treasure hunter."

"Isn't everyone if they think they can make a fast buck?" Joel fluffed his mother's pillow.

But Landry ignored Joel. "So he'd researched the map?" she pressed Abigail.

The older woman nodded. "He said he'd buy the map from me, curse and all, for half a million dollars." Abigail smiled. "I refused of course, laughed him off. He kept upping the price and I kept telling him no. It became quite a thing between us."

"You never told me all that, Mom."

She shrugged. "It wasn't all that important. I got sicker and Dr. Martin moved to Arizona and I didn't see Phil again." Abigail looked at Landry. "He did call me, just after I gave the map to Joel to sell."

"What did he say?" Landry sat on the edge of her chair.

"It surprised me, because it was out of the blue. He didn't really chitchat much. Asked how I was doing. Told me he'd been cancer-free since just after I left. And then he asked me if I would sell him the map again. I told him I'd already given it to my son to sell. He asked why I hadn't given him the first option to buy it, and I told him the truth. That I hadn't thought about him since I stopped going to Shreveport."

"Do you think this Phil is Phillip?" Landry barely waited until they'd hit the parking lot before she asked him.

"I do. It'd make a lot of sense. It'd be a stretch of coincidence, but I've seen stranger things connected by less." Nickolai helped her into the Jeep then rushed to get behind the steering wheel.

"I don't believe in coincidences."

"Then what will you call it? If Phil is Phillip. That Abigail's doctor referred her to an oncologist that hadn't even started practicing in Arizona, but that she just knew was the doctor for her. That she made the trips from Arizona to Louisiana several times and just happened to meet Phillip. That Phillip would be seeing the same Dr. Martin at the same time Abigail was going for appointments." Nickolai shook his head. "The coincidences are stacked up against realism."

"But you said you believe Phil is Phillip."

He nodded again. "I do. I can't explain it, but it would fit and make sense of the rest."

"I don't believe in coincidences."

He turned to her. "Do you believe Phil is Phillip?"

"I think so."

"But not filled with all those coincidences?"

She shook her head, knowing that even if she explained, he wouldn't understand. Wouldn't accept, but she had to believe that God used people and situations for His will. "But Shreveport? There's a great cancer hospital right in New Orleans. Why would Phillip go to Shreveport?"

"I can't answer that one yet." He started the engine and turned on the vents then picked up his cell and called Chris. He put the phone on speaker as he backed out of the parking space.

"Baptiste. You're calling me more now that you aren't my partner than when you were."

"Yeah. Yeah. Yeah. Listen, I need another favor."

Chris laughed over the speaker. "Why doesn't that surprise me any?"

Landry chuckled.

"Oh, is that Miss Parker again? Hello. I'm Chris. Chris Graze."

She grinned as she leaned toward the phone on the console. "Hi, Chris. I'm Landry."

Nickolai didn't want to stop and analyze why he got a rush that these two seemed to hit it off, in a teasing and accepting kind of way. "Okay, now that the introductions are over, about that favor." He pulled the Jeep back on the road toward Apache Junction.

"What do you need, Baptiste?"

"Phillip Fontenot. You said you ran a background on him."

"I did. I already told you what popped up."

"You also said some things had been discovered that you couldn't share."

"I did and there are."

Nickolai grinned at Landry. "Can you tell me if any of that has to do with Phillip Fontenot's medical record?"

"I can tell you, and the answer is no. What's the deal?"

Nickolai rested his hands on the bottom of the steering wheel as he drove. He'd been so certain. "Can you get a copy of his medical records?" He knew before he asked how Chris would react. He wasn't disappointed.

"Man, you know that's a no-no. HIPAA would crawl up sideways if someone's medical records were breached unauthorized."

Unauthorized meant without a warrant.

"Is there reason for me to look?"

"Not enough that a judge would sign off on the request." There just wasn't any evidence that would validate the request for a warrant.

"Sorry. You know I'd help you if I could."

"I know. I'll let you know if I come up with anything you can use."

"Thanks. Bye, Landry."

"Bye, Chris." Her smile reached her voice.

Nickolai hung up the phone.

"So that's a dead end." She leaned back against the seat of the Jeep, her disappointment evident.

"What? You're going to give up that easily?" he teased as he eased the Jeep off the exit for Apache Junction. The Superstitions loomed, huge and beautiful. But did they hold secrets of gold and mines and ghost Indian warriors?

She grinned. "What's your plan?"

He held up a finger then dialed. He didn't put this call on speaker, though. EmmaGrace was only a friend, but she was the biggest flirt he'd ever met. Chris wouldn't even talk to her on the phone when his wife was around, that's how intense some of EmmaGrace's teasing and flirting could get.

EmmaGrace answered on the second ring. "Nickolai Baptiste, what's a girl to think? You're going to turn my head."

Nickolai felt the heat on the back of his neck, creeping around to his face. He resisted looking at Landry, hoping his voice sounded just as even as when he'd talked to Chris. "I need a favor."

"Oh, I'm sure you do, honey. What can EmmaGrace do for you, sugah?"

He ignored her come-ons. That was just her way. He happened to know for a fact she was happily married now but would clam up if you so much as mentioned her private life. He'd made that mistake once and wouldn't make it again. Especially not now. "I need the medical record of Phillip Fontenot from New Orleans. Major medical claim, possibly treated within the last three years at LSUS Medical."

"Oh, you know how to get a lady all worked up." EmmaGrace laughed. "You're going to owe me dinner and a movie."

"Thanks. I really appreciate it. If you could put a rush on this. . ."

"My, my, Nickolai. If I didn't know better, I'd say you had a crush on me."

"Thanks, EmmaGrace."

"I'll call you as soon as I find something."

The phone went dead, and he set it on the console. "We should hear something back soon. Probably not until tomorrow." EmmaGrace was good, but she wasn't a miracle worker.

Landry nodded and turned to look out the window, but not before he caught the microexpressions that crossed her face: inner corners of her eyebrows drew in and up, corner of her lips were drawn down, and her jaw came up.

Sadness.

Chapter Twenty-Five

Monday morning brought even warmer temperatures to Apache Junction, Arizona. Landry almost couldn't believe it was February. Soon, she'd be back home, getting ready for Mardi Gras, but right now, she needed to get a move on. She rushed from the shower to get dressed. She and Nickolai planned to meet at eight and find Stan and Phillip.

Last night, she and Nickolai had been more than frustrated that they couldn't locate Stan or Phillip to talk with them. They had planned to divide and conquer: Landry would see if Stan knew if Phillip had ever been treated for prostate cancer, and Nickolai would talk with Phillip, man to man. Their plan had been a bust when by ten o'clock, there still hadn't been a trace of either man.

Landry didn't want to think what that meant. She'd spent time in prayer last night trying to come to grips with the possibility of this all being part of God's bigger plan. She didn't see it, definitely didn't understand it, but knew from experience that this was often the case.

Her cell rang, Marcie's ring tone filling the motel room.

"Hey, Marcie."

"Landry, are you okay?" Worry weighed every word of Marcie's.

"I'm fine. Why?"

"I just got a call at the office. A man said if I valued you as a friend, I'd advise you to get back to New Orleans where you belonged."

"Oh, Marcie, I'm so sorry." Landry dropped to the edge of the bed.

"This has gone on long enough. This person knew you well enough to know you're my best friend and was able to call my office."

"Did you recognize the voice?"

"Not at all."

"What else did he say?"

Knock. Knock. Knock.

"Hang on, Marcie. Nickolai's here. Let me let him in." Landry opened the door and motioned him inside. She shut the door. "Marcie just received a call about me." She pressed the SPEAKER button and put her cell on the little table. "Marcie, you're on speaker. Repeat what the caller said to you for Nickolai's benefit."

Nickolai sat in the chair at the table while Landry sat on the bed, drawing her knees to her chest.

"I'm at work. A call rang in on my direct line. I answered it, and a man said, and I quote, 'If you value Landry Parker as a friend, you should advise her to return back to New Orleans where she belongs,' end quote."

"Your direct line?" Landry asked.

"Yes."

Landry looked at Nickolai. "That number isn't listed. Only her personal clients, family, and friends have that number."

"Does your phone system at work have caller ID?" Nickolai asked.

"No. I think you need to come back, Landry. This person knows you well enough to know I'm your best friend, and knew my direct line. It creeps me out."

"Could you detect any accent?" Nickolai asked. "Like did he say New Orleans or New Or-leans?" That would give him a bead on where the person called from.

"He said New Orleans, just like we do." Marcie's voice wavered.

"So it's not someone from around here." Nickolai stood and paced. "Have you mentioned this case to anyone, Landry?"

She shook her head. "The only ones who know are you, Mrs. Winslet, Stan, Phillip, Marcie, and my neighbor who is feeding my cat and watching my house." A thought occurred to her. "Marcie, Mrs. McMillian hasn't called you, has she?"

"No. Do you think she might have gotten a phone call, too?"

"Maybe." Landry had a sick feeling. If anyone even remotely distressed Mrs. McMillian, Landry would. . .she didn't know what she'd do. She tightened her arms around her legs, hugging them to her chest.

When her father had died, Landry had thought about selling the family home but just couldn't bring herself to do it. There were too many memories, too much love. But she'd been unable to stay there herself, so she'd rented it out and took out a lease on a condo. Her next-door neighbor there, Mrs. McMillian, was an older widow who had fallen a little in love with Landry's cat, Whiskers. It was rare for Landry to be out of town, but when she was, Mrs. McMillian graciously took care of Whiskers and collected Landry's mail and papers.

"I can run over and check on her and Whiskers, if you'd like." Marcie knew how Landry felt about the sweet lady who'd befriended her and acted as a surrogate mother.

"Thanks, Marcie. I'd really appreciate it."

Nickolai stopped pacing and dropped back into the chair. "Did the caller say anything else?"

"No. I tried to ask who it was, but he hung up." Marcie's tone lowered. "I'm not going to lie, it's really unnerving. Like someone is watching me or something."

Landry dropped her head to the tops of her knees. She'd brought danger right to her best friend's door.

"Marcie, I'm going to call my friend at the eighth district there in New Orleans. I'll give him a rundown on what's happening so he's in the loop. I'm going to have him call you so you can get his cell number. If you have any problems, even a funny feeling, you can call Chris and he'll be there. Okay?"

"Yeah."

"He might want to send a unit to put a trace on your phone if you get another call."

"I'd prefer he didn't. I don't want my firm to get caught up in anything."

"A trace probably wouldn't work with a large system and a short call anyway," Nickolai said.

Landry groaned. "I'm so sorry, Marcie."

"Come home, Landry. Just come home. This is getting out of hand. I'm afraid for you."

Aching, Landry moved to the edge of the bed. "I can't. You know I can't."

"I'll loan you the money you need. I always would have, and you know it. I'll give you anything so you can just come home and be safe."

Landry's cheeks blazed. She hadn't told Nickolai the main reason she took this case was the money. "I know you would, but you know I can't." She swallowed. Hard. "I have to finish this. I have to see it through, Marcie."

"But at what cost?" Marcie's voice rose an octave. "Nickolai, I don't know you, but do you think she's safe?"

Landry met his stare.

"I think she's right—that she does need to finish this. Otherwise, whoever called you wins. We think we're really close to figuring it all out."

"But what about the slit tire, cut brake lines, and trashed motel room? Surely you see those are blatant attempts to get y'all to back off? If that isn't enough, a note telling her to go home most certainly is. I know she's stubborn and hardheaded, but what do you think?"

Landry mouthed the word *please*.

Nickolai let out a slow breath. "I understand what you're saying, I truly do. And I'm worried about her as well." He leaned closer to the phone. "But I promise you, Marcie, anyone will have to go through me to get to her."

Landry couldn't stop the gasp, nor the quickening of her heart. This man...

"I'm going to hold you to that, Mr. Baptiste," Marcie said.

"I expect nothing less. Now, I'll call Chris and have him call you. Let us know if you get any more calls or anything."

"Landry, you be careful."

"I will, Marcie. Again, I'm really sorry. I love you."

"I know. And I love you, too. Call me tonight."

Landry ended the call and turned to Nickolai. "It's crazy, right?"

He was already calling Chris. He quickly gave a rundown before he asked for Marcie's number. He gave it to Chris then tossed his phone on the table beside Landry's. "Do you have any clue who could've called her?"

Landry shook her head. "I've been trying to think and nobody comes to mind." She chewed her bottom lip.

"But?"

"The only people who I can think might be suspect is Stan or Phillip."

"Yeah, me, too. But how would they get Marcie's direct number?"

"I don't—" She had a thought. "Let me see something." She picked up her cell, activated the contacts, and pulled up Marcie's name. Sure enough, her direct number was listed under OFFICE. "If they were able to get into my phone and check my contacts, they'd have the number."

"What's your setting on screen locking?"

"Five minutes, I think."

He took her phone and checked. "Yes. Woman, that's way too long."

She took it from him. "It's never been a problem before."

"Well, it could be either of them. We've eaten with them and spent time. I guess they could've seen it. Or they have access to us through Winifred and probably have ways to get information just like we do. Nothing is a secret anymore."

"True."

Nickolai stood. "Neither Stan's nor Phillip's rentals are here. I guess they either didn't come back last night or they left early this morning."

"I can't imagine the two of them being together."

"Me, either, but stranger things have happened." He looked out the window. "Still not here."

"So what do we do now?"

He looked out the window again then back at her. "I say we can't wait around on them. I think we should take the copy of the map you have, as well as the picture of what you got from Tarak's mapping, and head out to the Superstitions. Maybe we can find the man's camp who actually has the map. We can recover it and get back home, which will make Marcie happy and put your mind at ease."

She smiled. How well he knew her already. "Sounds like a great idea."

"Obviously the terrain is a bit much for what we have. We should probably get some supplies from that military surplus store."

She nodded. "I actually do have my hiking boots with me, and some rugged clothes."

He chuckled. "Of course you'd be better prepared."

"I am former military, remember?" She grinned, enjoying their smooth banter even with everything else going on. "Listen, would you mind going to get supplies yourself? You can take the Jeep, of course."

"Okay. Why?"

"I think I'll feel better if I talk to Mrs. McMillian myself. Just check in and make sure she's okay and my cat is. And I'd like to tell her to keep an eye out. She might be a widow, but she's a pretty strong woman."

"I should've known you were a cat person." He smiled one of those full-wattage smiles of his. The ones that weakened her knees.

"What does that mean?"

"Just that you value independence and originality is all."

She crossed her arms over her chest and grinned at him. "Let me guess: you're a dog person because you value loyalty and wild abandonment."

He looked deep into her eyes until she felt the urge to squirm.

"Oh, I do appreciate those in animals and people. Loyalty, wild abandonment, and passionate zeal for life." He took a step closer to her.

Suddenly his close proximity and the realization of where they were, all alone, washed over her.

She took a step toward the door.

He blocked her path, slowly lowering his head. His lips brushed against her forehead. They caressed her cheek. Were gentle and supple against the soft spot of her flesh just under her lobe. Then his breath was against her ear. "I'll be back soon."

Landry found herself breathless as Nickolai tossed her a smile, grabbed the Jeep keys from the table, and left.

Mercy, this man did things to her emotions. . .made her feel things she didn't even know she could. She couldn't imagine not having him in her life. Was this love? Infatuation? Attraction because of their working together?

She remembered his oath to Marcie, and her heart and stomach switched places. This wasn't an infatuation. It couldn't be.

But was it real?

Landry shook off her thoughts and grabbed her phone. She quickly dialed Mrs. McMillian's number. It rang once. Twice. Three times before the lady answered. "Hello."

"Hi, Mrs. McMillian, it's Landry."

"Hi, honey. How's your trip?"

"I'm okay. How is Whiskers?"

"Oh, she's fine. She acted a little squirrely when I went to feed her yesterday, but she seemed okay today."

Landry froze, gripping the phone a little tighter. "Squirrely?"

"She kept trying to go to the bedroom. Your door was shut, as usual, but she kept trying to claw at it. Like she wanted in. Maybe she saw a bug or something. You know how she loves moths."

Moths didn't crawl under doors. "Did you check my room?"

"Of course not, honey. I respect your privacy."

Someone could've been in there!

"Do you want me to?"

"Oh, no. Not at all." She thought fast. "I just wanted to let you know that a friend of mine, a man, will be coming by later today to get something out of my place. Could you put Whiskers in the guest room for me so he doesn't scare her? Just put her food and water in the guest bathroom. Would you do that for me?"

"Of course. Honey, what man?"

Landry laughed, despite herself. "He's a friend of a friend who happens to be a cop. I'll tell him to knock so you can let him in, okay?"

"Sure. Is he handsome?"

Landry laughed again. She didn't know but couldn't explain that to her neighbor. "He's married, Mrs. McMillian."

"Oh, rats. Well, okay, honey. I'll go put Whiskers in your guest suite now. You just tell Mr. Married to come see me, and I'll let him in. Tell him to bring his badge. I like seeing those."

"I will. Thank you." Landry chuckled as she hung up. Before she forgot, she quickly texted Nickolai and gave him the details, asking him to have Chris go check out her condo. It was probably nothing, but with sweet Mrs. McMillian right there. . .

She set her phone down and checked out the window. Stan's nor Phillip's rentals had returned. She sighed then found her comfortable jeans and hiking boots and headed into the bathroom. Nickolai wouldn't take long to grab supplies and head back. It was warmer than usual out, and being in the sun would be really hot. She should wet her hair and braid it as that would help keep her cooler for several hours. Especially as thick as her hair was. But she'd have to be quick.

Excitement thrummed through her as she jumped into the shower. She drenched her hair then hopped out from under the spray. The tap turned off with a squeak.

Bam! Crack!

What in the world? She dried off and dressed quickly. She opened the bathroom door to red-hot fire.

Orange, red, and blue flames flickered across the floor. Her bed was engulfed in fire.

Dear Lord, help me.

Smoke burned her eyes. Her lungs. She coughed.

Landry put the damp towel against her face. She crouched down and slipped her feet into her hiking boots.

She quickly dodged the fire dancing up the curtains. She grabbed her cell and purse then flew out the open motel room door.

Sirens screamed as a fire truck whipped into the parking lot.

Margaret and Kohl rushed from their trailer in the back to her. Margaret put her arm around her. "Are you okay, Miss Parker?"

Landry coughed. "I'm okay."

The fire truck's ambulance pulled in, and two EMTs jumped out of the front.

"Here. She was inside the room," Margaret hollered out.

The EMTs quickly started her on oxygen. From behind the mask, she assured them she was okay. No burns. Nothing had touched her. She was fine.

Except. . .she wasn't. Someone wanted her out of the way.

Permanently.

Chapter Twenty-Six

Nickolai's heart skipped a beat as he pulled into the motel parking lot. It skipped another as he skidded to a stop behind the caution tape and saw Landry sitting on the back of the ambulance wearing an oxygen mask. He jumped from the Jeep and ran across the concrete.

"Sir, you have to stay back behind the line," a well-meaning first responder yelled.

Nickolai ignored him and kept running straight to Landry. If she was seriously injured...

She pulled off the oxygen mask and stepped into his arms. He could feel her slight quivering, and it pulled at something inside of him. Something that made him want to punch something. Punch it hard.

"I'm okay." Her whisper did little to appease the protective monster roaring in his chest to get out.

He took a step back, still holding her, to take inventory of her and any possible injuries.

She wore very worn jeans, ankle-height hiking boots, and a button-down denim shirt over a white tee. Her face, void of makeup, also showed no signs of soot or ash. Her damp black hair, full of twists and curls, hung freely around her face, over her shoulders, and down her back. Her eyes were a little bloodshot from the smoke, but that looked like the worst of her injuries.

"I'm really fine." She smiled, and his world went back right on its axis.

"What happened?"

"I don't know. I was in the bathroom getting dressed and heard a noise. By the time I'd gotten dressed, my room was in flames."

"That would be because this was thrown in your room." A fireman held a broken glass up. "This is the accelerant, more commonly known as a Molotov cocktail."

"Well isn't that interesting?" Officer Hogan stepped alongside the ambulance, Officer Paxton at his heels. "Seems like you two are becoming quite the people of interest around town."

Nickolai fisted his hands. "I think we've become more of targets."

The fireman jutted his chin out at Landry. "Paramedics say you're okay. Do you want to go to the hospital to make sure you didn't inhale more of the smoke than you think? That happens quite a bit."

"No, thank you. I'm fine. I had a damp towel that I covered my nose and mouth with."

"Smart thinking." The fireman turned to Officer Hogan. "Fire was definitely started by the Molotov cocktail. We'll send the glass to the lab and you'll get a report if they find any evidence."

"Appreciate that." Officer Hogan motioned to his partner. "Miss Parker, we'll need to take your statement."

The urge to punch something hadn't eased any. At all. And right now, Officer Paxton's pearly whites as he smiled at Landry looked like a welcome target.

Instead of acting on the strange and unusual urges, Nickolai released Landry and moved Officer Hogan off to the side. "There's more you need to know."

"Really? What now?"

Quickly Nickolai told him about Marcie's call. "It seems pretty obvious that someone doesn't want us working this case." He glanced over to where Kohl and Margaret spoke to one of the firemen. Vanessa hung back behind them. "She's a prime suspect."

Hogan glanced over to the group. "Margaret? That woman wouldn't know how to hurt a fly with a fly swatter."

"No, Vanessa. She confronted Landry and spat at her."

"Spat at her?"

Nickolai nodded and filled Hogan in on the exchange. "It's clear she has ill intent toward Landry."

"But enough to start a fire at her place of employment? From what I gathered, she and Margaret are fairly close and friendly. This little fire here will cost several thousand dollars to repair. I know insurance will cover it, but there's always a deductible."

Nickolai looked around the dive of the motel. "Maybe they should do a full renovation. They don't even have electronic key cards. It's well into the twenty-first century. . .who still has regular keys?"

"Maybe so, but Kohl and Margaret are good people, and they don't deserve all this." Hogan's tone had hardened a bit.

Nickolai narrowed his eyes. "And Landry doesn't deserve to be threatened and almost burned alive."

"I didn't mean to imply that she did. Perhaps it's time you people thought about heading back to New Orleans. For your safety, of course."

Maybe it was his mood, maybe it was the circumstances, maybe it was just that his emotions felt raw, whatever it was, Nickolai had had enough. "We won't be bullied, Officer Hogan. And you can put that in your report about us people." He turned and marched back to Landry.

"They're just doing their final evaluation for their paperwork, then I'll be done." Landry smiled as an EMT took her blood pressure.

He nodded. "I'll get my stuff and be waiting at the Jeep." He turned and went to Kohl and Margaret. "I'm sure you can understand that we no longer feel safe here. I'm going to go clear out my belongings and we'll be checking out."

"There is the matter of the fee. . ." Kohl stopped talking as he looked into Nickolai's face.

"I'm sure Mr. Hauge will clear the bill when he returns." Nickolai turned on his heel and headed to his room. He shoved his clothes and toiletries into his suitcase.

Where were Stan and Phillip? Neither had been at the motel last night, nor this morning, and Nickolai had checked at seven.

Maybe he and Landry had been wrong. Maybe the murderer and the bully wasn't either of them. . .maybe they were victims as well. Maybe they were in trouble right now. Maybe he should mention that to Hogan. . . .

No, that didn't make sense. Phillip was still the prime suspect, but Nickolai hadn't ruled Stan out of being involved. Landry might believe his song and dance about him and Winifred, but she had a soft heart under that tough exterior.

Nickolai grabbed his charger and the envelope with the case information and strode out of the room. He tossed everything into the back of the Jeep then approached Landry's smoldering room.

A final fireman came out.

"Hey, is there anything worth saving in there? Of the renter, I mean."

The fireman nodded. "The stuff in the bathroom and the suitcase right next to it is all okay." He gave a sheepish smile. "It's all wet, but it'll wash."

"Thanks." Nickolai went into the room. The stench of melted carpet and burned mattress emitted such pungency that his eyes watered. He grabbed her toiletries from the bath and shoved them into her suitcase. He carried it to the Jeep.

Landry sat in the front seat and smiled at him. "Thanks for leaving it unlocked."

"Um, I don't think I locked it when I got here." He glanced at the keys hanging in the ignition. "I don't even remember turning off the engine." He threw her stuff in the back then slipped behind the steering wheel. He took her hand in his. "Are you really okay?"

"I am. Even the EMT said my lungs sounded clear. I used the wet towel over my nose and mouth."

"Smart lady." He lifted her hand and kissed it. The odor of smoke nearly gagged him. He dropped her hand.

"What?"

"No offense, sweetheart, but you stink. You smell like an ashtray."

She laughed. "Funny how that happens since someone tried to snuff me out."

Nickolai didn't laugh. "That's not funny. This is serious. You know, no one would fault you if you wanted to go home."

She stopped laughing. "Do you want to go home?"

"I want you to be safe." He'd been doing a lousy job of that. He'd just promised Marcie he'd keep Landry safe, and she'd nearly been burned alive.

"That's not an answer." Landry shook her head, her beautiful hair settling over her shoulders. "I won't be scared off from doing what I need to do. I started this job and I intend to finish it if I can."

"All right. First things first, we're going to go find another hotel, and we aren't going to tell Stan and Phillip which one. We'll just invoice Mrs. Winslet directly after we get back. Okay?"

She nodded, a smile back on her beautiful face. "Deal."

He drove them down the road to the Best Western. "You stay here. I'll go check us in. I'm going to put both rooms in my name so if someone's looking for you, they'll have a little more trouble deciding which room is yours." He got out of the Jeep before she could argue.

The office of the hotel had fans blowing. The woman behind the counter smiled. "May I help you?"

"I need two rooms, please. Connecting if you can, next door to each other if you can't."

"Just a moment." She clicked on her computer. "I have connecting. For how many nights?"

Nickolai hesitated. Without the Winslet open-ended account, he would have to pay up front for the rooms. He handed over his credit card. "Two nights." That would give them today to rest up and regroup, and tomorrow to search the Superstitions. If they couldn't find the man in that time, even he'd feel like calling it quits.

She processed his card, made notes in her computer, then handed him his credit card and two envelopes with electronic keys inside.

"Thank you." He headed back to the Jeep and actually breathed a sigh of relief as he saw Landry still sitting in the front seat.

Not that he figured she'd bolt on him or anything, but. . .

He didn't even know what he was thinking anymore. Didn't know what he was feeling. Everything about Landry spoke to him on a primal level, and he'd started feeling all crazy and thinking even crazier.

What all did that mean?

"Did you get the rooms?" she asked as he climbed back into the Jeep.

"I did." He passed her one of the envelopes. "We have connecting rooms." He put the Jeep in gear and drove around the building to where their rooms were located.

He caught a glimpse of Landry's face as she fingered the envelope. It hit him—they had connecting rooms. The look on her face said it all. She thought he expected. . .well, something he wouldn't expect of a lady like Landry.

Nickolai parked the Jeep and took her hand again. "I got us connecting rooms for safety. That's the only reason."

Her face reddened. "Well, when you put it like that." She fanned her face and widened her eyes. "You do know how to flatter a lady." Clearly she tried to use humor to ease the awkwardness, but it just made her more attractive. Her giggle was what did him in.

He leaned over and, with the tip of his finger under her chin, turned her to face him.

She sobered immediately. Her eyes big, yet half-lidded.

Caressing her chin line with his thumb, Nickolai leaned in and put his lips on hers. Pressing softly. Moving gently. Deepening slowly.

He felt her breath catch, and he deepened the kiss a bit more.

His heart pounded against his ribs. The blood rushed to his head, echoing in his ears. Every muscle in his body seized.

Nickolai ended the kiss. Wow!

She looked at him from under her eyelashes.

"Make no mistake, Landry Parker, if you were a different type of lady and I a different type of man, two rooms wouldn't have been necessary."

She blinked twice and stiffened.

He chuckled and kissed the tip of her nose. "Now, let's get settled in. You need a shower something awful because you stink."

Her expression made him belly laugh as he got out of the Jeep. She joined him at the back before he could open her door for her.

"Oh, it's soaking wet." She lifted her suitcase.

"Yeah, sorry about that. I got everything of yours, though." He grabbed his own stuff as well as the supplies he'd bought then locked the Jeep.

They'd barely made it to their doors when his phone rang.

"Here." She opened her door and dumped her duffel. He dropped all his stuff on her chair and dug his phone from his pocket. She shut the door.

"Hey, Chris. I'm putting you on speaker." He set the phone on the edge of the table.

"I'm assuming because Landry's there?"

"I am." She sat on the edge of the bed and pulled her hiking boots off.

"Good. I went by your place. Your neighbor is quite the lady." Chris chuckled.

Landry laughed as well. "Oh, she's something, that's for sure. She was okay?"

"Yep. She's fine, your condo is fine, but your cat is possessed."

"What?" Landry smiled at the phone. "Whiskers is a sweetheart."

"You're crazy. That cat howled and meowed the whole time I was there. When I cracked the door to make sure nothing was in that room, a white fluff ball hissed and charged me. I had to shut the door so it wouldn't attack."

"She was a stray that I found when she was only weeks old. She's a sweetheart." Landry laughed and pulled out her phone. She quickly showed Nickolai a photo of a little white cat that might have weighed five pounds soaking wet.

Nickolai chuckled. "I'm looking at a picture of the cat now. That backed you up."

"Bro, it has claws. Long ones. I saw them."

Landry laughed again then sobered. "Thanks for going by and checking on my place and Mrs. McMillian. I really appreciate it."

"Now let's talk about your friend Marcie."

"What?" Landry sat up straight.

"Nothing. She's a funny little lady. I like her. She's fine. I put an app on her cell so it'll record if anyone calls her there."

"Thanks, Chris." Nickolai couldn't help but be extremely grateful that he was in a position to help Landry. "We needed the good news."

"Why's that?"

Nickolai, with a couple of interjections from Landry, told about the fire. "So, we're at the Best Western now, both rooms in my name."

"Look, I shouldn't tell you this, but there's been progress in the case."

"What?" Nickolai looked at Landry, who met his gaze.

"Phillip Fontenot is wanted for questioning in the Winslet murder. We haven't been able to reach him to have him come in and answer a few questions."

"Us, either. No sign of him or Stan Hauge since yesterday."

"We've been in touch with Hauge," Chris said. "He's responded to our messages, but not Fontenot."

"Is Fontenot a suspect?" Nickolai asked.

"Not at the moment, but the captain has found a few inconsistencies with his original statement. Like that he was late getting to the office for lunch, yet in his initial statement, he said he was sure he'd arrived early. This means for the actual time of the murder, we can't verify he was at Winslet Industries."

"That it?"

"Yeah. For now. Watch your backs. Both of you."

"We will. Thanks." Nickolai disconnected the call.

"I wonder where Phillip and Stan are?" Landry asked.

"I don't know." He pocketed his cell and lifted his gear. "I'm going to get settled in and let you take a shower."

She grinned. "Because I stink."

He grinned back. "You do. Anyway, after you're ready, just knock on the connecting door and we'll decide what to do."

"I thought we'd already decided we'd go out to the Superstition Mountains and see if we can find the man and the map."

"I thought it might be better for us to take it easy this afternoon. Have an easy late lunch/early supper, then we could hit the ground to the mountains in the morning."

"Sounds good to me." She smiled.

"Okay. Just knock when ready." He opened the door but leaned back and kissed her forehead and then opened his door and stepped inside.

Very soon, they were going to have to have a talk about this...thing between them. He could get used to kissing her hello and good-bye.

And many, many times in between.

He tossed his duffel onto one of the beds, put his toiletry bag by the sink. His cell rang. He checked the caller ID before answering and felt a surge of gratefulness that he was alone.

"Hey, EmmaGrace."

"Hey, darlin'. I'm just gonna say flat out, you owe me big-time. Dinner has been upgraded to chateaubriand at Antoine's."

Antoine's Restaurant back home served the traditional center-cut tenderloin for two for about 110 bucks a pop, but it was well worth the splurge. It literally melted in your mouth.

And if EmmaGrace named her fee as Antoine's chateaubriand, she'd had to pay some big favors to come through on his request.

He smiled. "You got it, my sweet."

"Ah, I love it when you tease me. Well, I got the medical records of Phillip Fontenot."

"And? Was he ever diagnosed and treated for cancer?"

"You are ahead of the game, aren't you? He was diagnosed almost three years ago during his routine physical, but, he had it kept out of his medical file at his regular doctor's office."

"Really?" That took some doing. And money.

"He showed up as a patient at an oncologist practice up in Shreveport, under the care of Dr. Potter."

What? "Potter, not Martin?"

"Martin was in the practice with Potter, but left and moved to Arizona about six months into Phillip's treatment, but Potter and Phillip were friends from college. Potter kept the records pretty hidden, so I really had to dig for them, then to figure out why they were hidden."

Now it made sense. "Thanks, EmmaGrace. I'll get that gift certificate to you as soon as I get back to New Orleans."

"You do that, sugah. And you make sure you take care. If that man went to that much trouble to hide his condition, I don't think he'll appreciate you knowing the details."

Nickolai hung up. He had to tell Landry. This was the connection that tied it all together!

Now they just had to figure out why Phillip needed the map so badly. So much that he'd murder his best friend for it.

Chapter Twenty-Seven

The shower was luxurious. Landry used almost half a bottle of her vanilla-scented body wash and shampoo, followed with a healthy dose of conditioner. She could feel the smoke and ash and soot gurgling down the drain. She took her time, enjoying the security of knowing Nickolai was just next door and nothing would happen to her while he was on guard.

As she stood under the hot spray, letting it gently pound on her scalp, Landry thought about him. . .and her feelings. How had she become so connected to him so quickly? It didn't make sense. She couldn't explain why she felt what she did. She'd never experienced anything like this before. Just thinking about him made her feel safe and secure. Made her happy, almost giddily so. It was a strange feeling. Good, but unfamiliarly strange.

She'd never been so aware of another human before. When he walked into a room, it was as if her vision came into focus. When he spoke, all her attention went immediately to him, like her ears were peeled on his voice no matter what. Her senses were tuned totally in to his every move, every word. Sometimes, it seemed that her heartbeat quickened just to match his.

Lord, I could really use some wisdom. My heart is telling me one thing, but my head is screaming that he doesn't follow You, so that limits our future together.

Stepping out of the hot shower, Landry tried to clear him from her mind, but it proved a daunting task. She needed to talk to him. Did he feel the same way? He kissed her. Comforted her. Cared about her.

But was that the same? She couldn't imagine his insides being as tied up as hers. Still, she needed to figure out where they stood. Especially before they went back home.

New Orleans with Nickolai would be interesting. Her city. His city. Their city. She'd love to go to Mardi Gras with him. Each of them sharing their favorite haunts and jaunts with each other.

Wait. . .was there a future for them?

God, is he just mad at You because of what's happened to him and his family? She'd been upset when first her mother got sick and died, then her father. There were many nights she'd cried out in anger. Were they so different?

She dressed in the only dry clothes she dug from the middle of her duffel. A pair of jeans and cotton shirt. With ruffles. Goodness, had she really packed that? She quickly pulled her hair back into a french braid, thankful her shoulder only had a twinge of discomfort occasionally. With a deft hand, she applied eyeliner, mascara, and a little lip gloss. She surveyed her reflection. Not bad. Especially not bad considering she'd been caught in a fire hours ago. Not bad at all.

If I'm not supposed to love him, Lord, please take the feeling away from me. I don't think I can be tested on this one. I'm not strong enough.

Nerves bunched in the pit of her stomach as she approached the connecting door. This felt like a date, which both thrilled and terrified her.

Her cell phone rang. She checked the caller ID, a little scared she'd see UNKNOWN but didn't. Instead, it was Stan. She knocked on the connecting door and answered at the same time. "Hello."

Nickolai opened the door as Stan replied. "Miss Parker? Are you okay?"

"Hi, Stan. Yes, I'm fine." She put her finger to her lips at Nickolai then set the phone on the table and activated the speaker. She sat in one of the chairs while Nickolai sank into the other one.

"I was so worried. I just got back to the hotel and saw your room and learned what happened. I spoke with Officer Hogan, and he seemed to be concerned for your safety. Not many people have any information on where you've gone. Some said you were taken to a hospital. Some said you just left. I didn't know what to think."

"I'm sorry to have worried you, but I'm fine. I've moved to another hotel, obviously. You weren't there when I left, so I couldn't tell you."

"Where are you? I'll come put the charges on our credit card. I was planning on moving us to the Best Western down the street."

Nickolai shook his head.

She understood what Nickolai meant. "I'd rather not say, Stan. No offense, but I seem to have a target on my back, and the less people who know where I am, I think it's better." But if Stan was at the same hotel anyway. . .

"Is Mr. Baptiste with you?"

Nickolai again shook his head.

But she couldn't lie. "I'd rather not give out any details about where I am, Stan. I know you can understand. I'm sure you could call Nickolai and speak with him."

"I'll do that because I just got off the phone with Winifred and gave her an update. She's most distressed about the events that have occurred to both you and Mr. Baptiste. She feels responsible."

"Unless she's hired someone to do these things, then she's not responsible."

"I understand that, but you wouldn't be here, facing all of this, if she hadn't hired you and pitted you against Mr. Baptiste."

"We each chose to take the case for our own reasons. Either or both of us could have refused. Let her know I don't blame her for any of it." A thought occurred to Landry. "And she needn't worry about either of us claiming she put us in danger. We aren't going to sue her or anything." She didn't know if that was even a possibility, but surely Mrs. Winslet would worry about the chance if it was an option.

"I can appreciate that, Miss Parker, I assure you. As I am confident Mrs. Winslet feels the same way. However, in light of all the horrible events going on, Mrs. Winslet is choosing to terminate this project."

"What?" Landry couldn't believe this. She stared at Nickolai, who looked just as distressed as she felt.

"Don't worry. Mrs. Winslet is a fair lady and will generously compensate both you and Mr. Baptiste for your time and trouble."

No! "But we're so close." They'd go to the mountains tomorrow and, Lord willing, find the man who had the map.

"I understand your distress, Miss Parker, I do, but this is Winifred's choice."

Nickolai shook his head as well.

"Look, Stan. . .we're really close. Give us twenty-four hours."

"I don't know. Winifred was very adamant."

"Let her know we're so close. Twenty-four hours. That's it. If we don't recover the map by tomorrow night, then we'll accept her withdrawal of the investigation. But please, give us another day."

"I just don't—"

"Stan, I need this recovery fee. I'll lose my business if I don't." She choked on the words and refused to look at Nickolai. She never intended to let him know how much she needed the payday. Now, considering how she felt toward him, she was embarrassed for him to know her weakness. What must he think?

"Just twenty-four more hours?"

"Yes." She let out a sigh but still almost choked on her own pride, even though she knew being prideful was wrong. *Oh, Lord, please help me. I'm beyond confused and emotional.*

"I'll see if I can talk Winifred into giving you one more day."

She smiled as relief swelled. "Thanks, Stan. I know you can convince her." If he didn't, but they still found the map, would they still get paid?

"I'll call you after I speak with her. I'll call her before I phone Mr. Baptiste." Stan paused. "Are you sure you're okay, Landry? Kohl said you seemed a little disoriented when you left, but the paramedics report you were physically fine."

"I am fine. I just wanted to get away from the motel. I'm safe now, and focused on finding the map." She paused. "Stan, are you with

Phillip? Or have you been?"

"What?"

"Well, last night I planned to talk to you, let you know how close we were to locating the map, but your rental was gone. So was Phillip's. And this morning, after the fire, neither of you were there again, so I just thought maybe you two were together." Doing what, she couldn't even imagine, but both of them being gone last night and this morning was quite the coincidence.

Seemed like a lot lately was coincidental. For someone who didn't believe in coincidences, she was running out of logic and leaning toward divine intervention.

"I don't know where Phillip is. I met my wife's relatives over in Phoenix last night and stayed there until this morning."

"Oh. I didn't realize you had family here." He hadn't mentioned it. Was that something to make a big deal out of?

"It's my wife's cousins. We weren't sure how long I'd be here, so I didn't make plans to visit with them until yesterday. My wife had spoken to her cousin who called me and invited me to supper. We had a nice visit and it got late and I didn't feel like driving the hour back, so I stayed in their guest room." Stan paused. "You haven't seen or heard from Phillip, either?"

"No." She remembered what Chris had said. "I have a rather personal question about him that you might know the answer to. It seems personal, but I promise you, it's related to the investigation."

"Okay." Stan's voice trembled just a little.

"Do you know if Phillip was ever diagnosed or treated for cancer?"

Nickolai shook his head at her, but she'd already asked the question. He must've heard back from his source. That EmmaGrace woman he flirted with on the phone. All of Landry's confidence seemed to dissipate like the steam from her shower.

"Why would you ask that?" Stan asked.

"Trust me, it has to do with the case."

"I don't think so, but he wouldn't exactly tell me something like that. If he has, then he has my sympathies. My mother had breast cancer. She had surgery and chemo and lived in remission for many years, but I know what a battle it can be."

"I'm sorry." She chewed her bottom lip. If Nickolai already had confirmation. . . "Stan, do you know of any reason Phillip would want the map?"

"Enough to kill Bartholomew for it? No." He paused. "Are you saying you think Phillip killed Bartholomew?"

Nickolai shook his head and waved his hands.

"I'm just trying to get to the truth, whatever that is." She cleared her throat. "I really appreciate you getting us just one more day. I feel pretty certain we'll have the map by tomorrow night."

"Well, okay. I'll call you later, but if you need anything, just call me."

"Thanks, Stan." She disconnected the call and rubbed her hands over her jeans and looked at Nickolai. "Well, guess we have twenty-four hours."

He nodded. "We should probably eat, then come back here and lay out our plan for tomorrow. Since I've already gotten supplies from the surplus store, I suggest we get a very early start in the morning."

"I agree." She grabbed her cell and slipped it into her purse and stood. "I'm guessing you got Phillip's medical details?"

He stood as well. "I did. They found the prostate cancer at a routine checkup. Apparently he wanted to keep it quiet, so there's not an official record on his medical chart at his physician's office. He chose the oncology clinic in Shreveport because his friend from college, Dr. Potter, is one of the oncologists there."

She opened her door and stepped onto the balcony. "So he wasn't seeing Dr. Martin like Abigail? Just another doctor in the same clinic?" She shut the door behind him then checked to make sure it locked before following him down the metal stairs.

"Right."

More being at the right place at the right time than so coincidental. She followed him down the stairs and to the Jeep in silence, her mind slowly laying out the facts.

Phillip meets Abigail at the oncology clinic. She tells him about the map. He offers to buy it—she didn't know why yet. She declines. Months later, Abigail gives the map to her son to sell to pay for her cancer treatment. Bartholomew just happens to bid on the very thing his best friend had wanted?

"In all the information in the packet, did you see anything about how Bartholomew became aware of the map in the first place?" Landry clicked her seat belt and shifted to look Nickolai in the face.

He started the engine and cocked his head. "I don't think so, and Mrs. Winslet never said." Nickolai shrugged and backed the Jeep out of the parking place. "I just assumed since he was a collector he had people keeping an eye on those types of auctions."

"Maybe." But what if he didn't? What if when it came up for sale at such a high price and Phillip knew he couldn't afford it, he turned his best friend onto it, knowing he'd probably get the chance to get the map?

Which brought her right back to her original question. . .why did Phillip want the map so badly?

Nickolai pulled into the parking lot of Los Gringos Locos. "We haven't tried this one yet, so I thought you might want to. I don't even know if you like Mexican food. We can go somewhere else if you'd like." He rambled. He found he often did when extremely nervous. He couldn't be sure why he was so nervous right now with Landry, but it was almost as if he could feel a change.

"This is fine. I love Mexican food."

They were halfway to the restaurant before he realized he'd taken her hand this time.

This woman had him all messed up. He acted crazy. Couldn't think clearly. It was almost as if he had a bug of some sort.

The restaurant welcomed them with its dulled yellow paint on the top half of the walls and wood-planked bottoms. The aroma of rich

Mexican spices mingled with peppers and onions enveloped patrons as they entered.

They were seated at a booth with yellow vinyl that creaked as they sat across from each other. He waited until they'd placed their orders and received their chips and salsa before he spoke again. "Landry, I know we're in the middle of this case and we need to discuss it and make a game plan and all. . ."

"Yeah?"

"But I need to be honest with you, too. We both took this case for financial reasons. I didn't miss what Marcie said to you about loaning you money, and I can't ignore what you told Stan. Is your business really going to go under if you don't get the recovery fee?"

She picked up her silverware rolled up in a brightly colored paper napkin and unwrapped it, putting the red napkin in her lap.

"I'm not trying to embarrass you or make you uncomfortable. I just want us to be honest and open with each other."

"Let's just say I'm apparently a better recovery specialist than I am a business owner." She straightened her knife and fork beside the little green appetizer plate.

"I understand. Trust me, I understand. I had to hire an office manager who keeps everything running at We Find It."

"I should've done that, but I was too hardheaded. I'd been doing it for Dad, so I thought I could just do the same. I didn't know a thing about advertising budgets or projections or anything." She shook her head and rearranged her knife and fork. "I'm ashamed to admit that I've driven his company into the ground."

He reached over the table and took her hand. "You couldn't know. Just like I couldn't. I can give you the names of some really good office managers I interviewed. There were a couple who have sterling reputations."

"Thanks, but I don't know. I'm starting to question everything. Maybe I should close the business and just go to work for someone else. Get rid of all the business-owner headaches." She pulled her hand free and grabbed a chip. "Are you hiring?"

He smiled, imagining how cool it would be to work with her. Every. Single. Day. "I'd hire you any day of the week and twice on Saturday."

"Why did you change your mind and decide to take the case?"

Turnabout was fair play. "Lisbeth's doctor thinks she's a candidate for a halfway house–type program. I'm still not too sure about it, but she's all hyped up about the possibility."

"That sounds awesome."

If it would really help her. . . "But because it's a trial program, our insurance won't cover any of the fees, which is approximately forty thousand a year."

"Wow." Landry's eyes widened.

"Yeah. My thoughts exactly."

"But if it helps her. . ."

"And that's the thing. Will it? Will this help her any better than medications and therapy? Will she ever be able to just live a life on her own, without me having to worry about her hurting herself or others? Is this a stepping-stone to her moving out from constant medical observation and involvement to just outpatient treatment?"

"But her doctor thinks it will?"

He shrugged. "Who can say, really? Doctors can't commit one way or the other on prognosis because of fear of a malpractice suit, and who knows if they get financial compensation from pharmaceutical companies? Even trial programs. . .do they get a kickback?"

"I guess I never really thought about it that way. I know with Dad, Alzheimer's is so prominent in the public eye that most people have a lot of knowledge about it before they ever get a diagnosis in the family." She took a sip of her soft drink. "But I do know that if there had been even the slightest of chances that I could have done something to help Dad have better days or more of them, I'd have done it in a heartbeat."

Now it was his turn to be embarrassed. "I sound like a self-centered jerk, don't I? Worrying about how much it costs, if it's worth it. . . Will it be any better than the regular treatment our insurance does pay for."

"No, I didn't mean that at all." Her voice cracked. "At least your reason for needing the recovery fee is noble: to help your sick sister. Mine is to save my dad's business that I mismanaged. How selfish is that?" She let out a sigh.

He chuckled, which brought her head up. "What's funny?"

"Us. Feeling sorry for ourselves, but beating ourselves up for it. Almost like playing the game of who is the worst person."

She smiled. "I see your point."

The waitress delivered their order. It smelled amazing. He'd ordered the Mucho Grande Burrito, served with refried beans and rice. The burrito itself was a huge tortilla stuffed with rice, whole pinto beans, guacamole, grilled veggies, cheese, and pico de gallo. He took a bite and savored the goodness.

Landry had ordered the Diablo Enchilada lunch special, red chili pork wrapped in a corn tortilla and topped with red sauce and bubbling cheese. She cut into the enchilada, blew on it, and then did that thing she did when she enjoyed the food—closed her eyes and chewed extremely slow. His gut tightened. Now was the time.

"Landry?"

She opened her eyes and swallowed.

"I think we need to talk." Why weren't the words coming?

She took a sip of her drink. "Okay."

"About us. You and me. Aside from the case."

"Oh." She folded her hands on the table in front of her. Defensive gesture.

Maybe she didn't feel the same way. Nickolai licked his lips and swallowed. It'd never been so hard to talk to a woman before. Not like this, but he needed to know where he stood, and he'd learned the best way to do that was just to come at the problem face front. "I like you."

It took maybe one twenty-fifth of a second for the microexpression to cross her face: wrinkled crow's-feet, pushed-up cheeks, and movement from the muscle orbiting the eye.

Happiness.

His heart threatened to explode.

"I like you, too." Her voice sounded more husky than usual. Throaty. Almost raspy. "Very, very much."

"I want to see you. Date you. Be with you."

Her smile brightened the dim room. "I'd like that as well."

"I mean, not just the dating game. I haven't felt this way about anyone in a very long time." He grinned. "Not sure I really like it."

"I feel the same way. Confused. Happy. Elated. Bewildered."

He reached over and took her hand. "I almost can't explain how I feel when I'm with you. And I want to be with you all the time." He rubbed his thumb over her knuckles. "I want to hug you, hold you, kiss you. . .talk to you for hours on end and just stare at you."

Her face reddened. "It's the same for me."

The waitress came to refill their drinks. He released her hand but knew, in that moment, she'd stolen his heart.

Chapter Twenty-Eight

Landry held the map they'd drawn all over the night before in her lap as Nickolai drove the Jeep toward Weaver's Needle. She'd overlaid the information from the copy of Julia Thomas's map with the markings of Tarak's main map. Last night, she and Nickolai had marked five different spots that were the best chances of where the man could camp on his way to where the mine was marked. There wasn't a key to the map, so figuring distance wasn't an option. They'd have to follow the markers depicted on the map and do their best.

They agreed on the plan: find the man, find the map, recover it, and get out. If it got to be three or four, a couple of hours before sunset, they'd start heading back whether they had found the map or not.

Yet, Landry knew that if the map had really led to the mine, she wouldn't be able to resist checking it out. Even if she only looked. National parks were closed to prospecting, but everyone close to the Superstition Mountains looked for the mine. Or a cache of gold left there.

Tuesday morning had turned out beautiful, with temperatures in the seventies. Landry had been able to find the laundromat at the hotel and wash and dry her clothes. Redressed in her denim shirt and comfortable jeans, with her hiking boots, she was ready.

Nickolai had packed the backpacks he'd bought with bottled waters, almonds and granola bars, flashlights, first aid kits, ropes, and a couple of other things Landry had no clue what they were used for. It didn't matter—they were almost to the mountains.

Almost to the map. And the mine.

Nickolai chuckled as he reached for her hand. "You can barely sit still."

"I'm so excited. I just know we're going to find it today."

"The map or the mine?"

"Either. Both." She laughed. "Stan called. Winifred said she'd give us until the end of today to find the map. After that, we are to return back to New Orleans or any further charges here are at our cost."

"Good thing my truck's ready, then. They called this morning."

"I have a feeling Stan checked on that before he spoke with Winifred." She pulled her sunglasses from her bag and slipped them on. "I asked Stan if he'd seen or heard from Phillip and he hadn't."

Nickolai shook his head. "Can't imagine what's going on with him. I called Chris and told him what we'd found out. He's going to look for a reason Phillip wants that map so badly. He said he'd call as soon as he knew anything."

"Even if he's not supposed to?" She could never be a cop. All the keeping secrets would drive her insane. Luckily, she hadn't had to do that as an MP. Military was much more transparent in their investigations.

"Yes. He knows we've given him a lot of information, so he'll share with us. And with all the attempts to scare us off, he's more than a little cautious."

"Marcie is thrilled I'll be home soon. She all but begged me to come back immediately. Told me she'd give me the fifty thousand recovery fee if I'd forget about this. The fire really freaked her out."

"Freaked me out, too." He lifted her hand and kissed it.

Oh, she was so going to get used to this. "I'm fine."

"Just out of curiosity, why don't you take a loan from Marcie?"

Pride? No. She'd come to terms with that. "I just think it's a bad decision to have a loan between friends. It can ruin a friendship."

"If you say so." He sounded skeptical.

"Would you take a loan of that amount from Chris?"

"Hmm."

The breeze from the cracked window lifted his hair, making her want to run her fingers through it.

"Maybe. I don't know. For my sister? Yes. Not that Chris has that much money, and certainly not to loan."

"If he had it, and it wouldn't put him in a bind, would you take the loan to save We Find It?" She caught her bottom lip between her teeth.

"I don't know."

"See." Although Marcie had argued this over and over because she came from money. Not that she flaunted it—no way, Marcie had earned scholarships for college and worked hard to get the job she had. That didn't diminish the value of her trust fund, though.

"It's a tough one, that's for sure." He pulled into a dirt area where several other cars were parked. A couple had horse trailers attached. "Looks like we need to park here and hike in the rest of the way."

Seeing the other signs of people…"I guess I forgot how populated the area can be." She let him take her hand and help her out of the Jeep.

"Especially on pretty days. And that reporter that got in our face the other day didn't help." He eased her backpack over her shoulders. "Tell me if this is too heavy for you."

"No, it's fine." It was actually a lot lighter than she expected. Landry noticed the bulk of Nickolai's pack. Such a gentleman, taking more of the weight so she wouldn't have to carry a full load.

She started to unroll the paper map they'd created, but Nickolai put his hand over hers to stop her. He nodded toward a group of people coming back up the trail on horses.

Right. No sense feeding anyone's curiosity. She kept it rolled in one hand and held tight to Nickolai's with the other. They made their way down the trail, past the plateau where Nickolai had been stung by the scorpion.

"I have another EpiPen with me, just in case." She smiled as she teased.

"I'm hoping we don't need one."

They walked hand in hand down the trail. Landry enjoyed the comfortable silence between them and the majestic beauty around them. Tumbleweeds rolled by, just like in the movies. The pungent scent from the creosote bushes wafted on the breeze. Their yellow-green waxy leaves were popular with the natives as antiseptics and emetics. The ones they passed on the trail had already bloomed—their inch-wide, twisted yellow petals opened to the sun.

"Have you talked to your sister since Sunday?"

Nickolai shook his head. "I plan on calling her this evening. I hope to have good news to tell her."

That moment Landry knew. She cleared her throat. "I've been thinking."

"Does this mean I'm in trouble?" Nickolai teased as he reached for the map and unrolled it slowly.

"I'm serious."

He looked up from the map. "Okay."

"If we recover the map, I want you to have the recovery fee. For Lisbeth's treatment."

His face went blank.

She closed the space between them and reached her hands up to rest on his shoulders. "I'm dead serious. That's what I want."

He pulled her into a tight hug. So tight she could feel the pounding of his heart against hers. He nuzzled her neck then kissed just below her ear before releasing her. "That's very sweet, but I can't let you do that. If we recover the map, we'll split the recovery fee."

"But I want to do this. For you, yes, but mainly for her."

He put a hand on his belt loop. "Why? You don't even know her. You only know what I've told you. What if I'm lying? What if I made it all up just to get you to feel sorry for me? What if I don't even have a sister?"

Could he. . . No, there'd been too much pain in his face, his voice, his very being. She chuckled. "You aren't that good an actor. Sorry."

"I still can't let you do that."

"But I want to." She held up her hand. "She's my sister, too."

Nickolai shook his head and lifted one corner of his mouth. "What?"

"She's my sister in Christ." There. She'd said it. He could argue it all he wanted, but there it was.

He stared at her. A moment passed. Then another.

Landry shifted her weight from one foot to the other, not breaking eye contact with him. She could win a staring contest hands down.

"I don't even know how to respond to that," he finally said.

She grinned. "Good, then, it's settled. If we recover the map, the fee goes to Lisbeth's halfway house treatment."

"I didn't say I agreed to any of that."

She pushed up on her tiptoes and kissed his cheek, just above the clean line of his beard. "I'm glad we agree."

Was she serious?

Nickolai held one side of the map while Landry held the other. He was supposed to be studying it to lead them to one of the five places they'd marked where they might find the man with the map, but he couldn't concentrate. Not when Landry had offered what no one else ever had: hope that his sister could and would get better.

Who did that for people they didn't even know? Sisters in Christ?

He wanted to shake Landry and tell her not to be so naive with people, not to be so trusting, but he'd been around her enough to know that while Landry Parker might have a soft heart, she wasn't foolish.

So what could he do?

"This one is the closest." Landry tapped one of the places they'd marked.

"Yeah." He studied the map before shifting his focus to the terrain. Following the map, they'd be off the trail and into the uncharted area. "You ready?"

"Lead on, McDuff." She grinned, took a swig of her water, and then shoved the bottle down the side pocket of her backpack and hoisted it back over her shoulders.

He pulled on his own backpack and led the way. The hike wasn't too much, thankfully, but they had to move single file. That was okay, because it gave him time to think.

Nickolai knew he wanted to be with Landry. He was pretty sure his feelings were the forever kind, but would wait and see how their relationship played out. They had a lot stacked against them. They were, after all, competitors, so to speak. If they got serious, how would that work?

That was getting the cart before the horse, as his mother used to say.

What about her Christianity? Remembering that his mother had been a Christian brought up all sorts of memories and emotions. He'd blocked so much out because he hadn't wanted to remember. Remembering meant allowing the pain access. Now Lisbeth claimed the faith. Landry had given good reasons why he should believe his sister. Could he?

And Landry. She was strong in her faith. Praying over meals. He'd seen the Bible in her belongings when he'd gotten her duffel. He'd seen the scripture app on her phone when she'd shown him the settings. If there was a forever for them, what about her faith and his lack of it? How would that work? Christians weren't supposed to be with non-Christians, right?

"Nickolai, look," Landry whispered and jerked on his arm.

He followed where she pointed to a little makeshift lean-to. Remnants of a campfire, embers barely smoldering, just in front of it.

"Looks like a possible campsite," she whispered.

"Let's check it out." He pulled his gun from his backpack and slipped it into the waistband of his jeans.

"I wish I had my gun."

He did, too. Seeing Landry with a handgun would be a rush, he just knew it. "Shh." He led the way to the lean-to. Drawing his gun, he nodded at Landry to open the flap. She did, and he widened his stance.

Nothing.

"I have to admit, I'm disappointed. I thought we'd found him." Landry moved around the small space that housed an imprint of a sleeping bag or bedroll, a circle where a can or bottle had been, and footprints of a man's boot—Nickolai put his size-twelve foot against it. "About a size eleven."

"But there's still some heat from the fire here," she said as she moved to the rough fire pit. "So whoever was here hasn't been gone long."

Nickolai studied the dusty desert ground. He pointed at the footprints alongside hoofprints, leading down an incline. "Looks like that's the way he went. And he has a horse."

"Probably a mule, so I've read is more popular here to haul things." Landry popped her hands on her hips. "Do we follow his footprints, or do we move on to the next place we marked on the map?"

He pulled out the map again, studying it. "The next place on the map is down there anyway, just over several hundred yards, thereabouts. What do you say we follow the footprints until we get down to this mark right here?" He tapped the part where it looked like the terrain evened out a little. "If the footprints don't veer left toward the mark, we can decide then which to follow. Sound good?"

"Yep." She smiled and nodded. "Lead the way."

If he had it his way, she'd follow him everywhere.

Chapter Twenty-Nine

The sun moved higher in the Arizona sky, pulling the temperatures up with it.

Why hadn't she thought to ask Nickolai to buy her a hat when he went to the military surplus store? Even with her sunglasses, the brightness of the sun's rays over the grains of sand was nearly blinding. Just when Landry was sure she should tell Nickolai she needed to take a break, get a drink of water, he stopped. Stopped so suddenly she almost ran into his back.

His gun was in his palm before she could see what caused him to halt.

"Whoa, there, friend." An older man stood beside a mule loaded down with bags and rolls. "You don't need no firepower here."

Landry took quick stock of the old man. "I've seen you. You were talking to the Indian at our motel. And again, at the hospital talking to Ela."

He remained silent, neither confirming nor denying, but he looked like he could clam up from now until the end of days.

She laid a hand on Nickolai's shoulder. "Forgive us. You can never be too careful, can you?"

"Guess not, little lady."

Nickolai slowly lowered his gun but kept his eyes narrowed and locked on the man.

"I'm Landry Parker and my friend is Nickolai Baptiste."

He stared at Nickolai warily. "Jediah Kyle."

"Nice to meet you, Jediah. Perhaps you could help us with something."

The old man squinted and held a hand over his eyes to block the sun. "If I can."

"We're looking for a map of the area. A very specific map." Landry watched Jediah's expressions. She might not be as trained as Nickolai, but she was pretty good at detection, and she detected a mix of fear and surprise with his tensed lower eyelids and thinned lips stretched over his teeth.

He knew about the map. This was the man who had it, Landry could just feel it.

"Little lady, there are many maps of this area. You can stop at any of the souvenir shops lined up in town and buy several." But he didn't smile.

"Sir, no disrespect, but I think you know exactly what map I'm referring to. I think you have it."

Landry carefully stepped around Nickolai but still left his line of fire to Jediah clear. "I know you were hired to find the mine. I know you've been talking to people about me and Nickolai. I'm positive Phillip Fontenot gave you the map and told you to find the mine for him. He probably warned you about us." She glanced at the pack mule. "I'm sure he told you to sneak out some of the gold you found and he'd reward you handsomely."

"I don't know what you're talking about." Yet the old man eased up closer to the mule.

"That's far enough," Nickolai said in a tone that left no room for misinterpretation. "Step away from the mule."

"Friends, you've got the wrong idea here about me. I'm just out here camping with ole Bessie here." He reached up and patted the mule's neck.

"I said, step away from the mule." Nickolai's voice demanded adherence.

"Fine." Jediah stepped closer to Landry.

"I'm sure you are camping, sir. I know you purchased your gear at the military surplus store recently, after you got the map from Phillip in Cobb's Restaurant and Lounge."

The old man opened his mouth then shut it.

"Why does Phillip want the gold so badly?" Landry asked.

"I don't know; I'm just a professional prospector and gold hunter." He held up his hands. "Look, the man contacted me over the Internet a couple of weeks ago. Said he had a map come into his hands that he believed to show where the Dutchman's Lost Mine was hidden. Agreed to pay me twenty-five thousand dollars to spend a week looking for it." He sat on a large boulder and took off his hat, wiped sweat with his shirtsleeve. Put the hat back on his bald head. "Twenty-five grand for one week? Count me in."

"So you agreed?" Landry lowered herself to a smaller rock. Nickolai moved in behind her.

"I agreed to meet with him. We met on Thursday late afternoon, at Cobb's, just like you said. He showed me the map." Jediah spit on the ground. "I've lived near these mountains all my life, grew up chasing the lost mine as a teen before I expanded my hunting grounds. I gotta tell you. . .the map has markings and details like I've never seen. It looks pretty genuine. I thought to myself, what the hey? Besides, twenty-five big ones just to look was a great motive. I talked to some of my old contacts here, like you saw, but they only warned me to stay away."

Landry shook her head. "I'm confused. People have looked for this mine for generations. People have had maps before. This is a national park. If there were really a mine, don't you think someone would've found it by now?" That was rational. . .logical. . .but still, Landry held out hope that there really was a mine.

Jediah spit again. "It's been said over and over that the old Dutchman hid the cave in plain sight. Said you could drive a pack train over the entrance and never know it. That's what makes professional hunters so frustrated. We should be able to find this mine. Whoever does. . .they'll be king in the business."

"So you believe it's here?"

"I do. And I think the map will lead me right to it."

"Now see, that's where we have our problem." Nickolai stood and moved in front of Landry.

Jediah stood up and faced Nickolai, doing his best not to look intimidated. "I don't see that as a problem. The man gave me the map and hired me to do my best to find the mine using the map. That's what I'm doing."

"But Phillip stole that map, Jediah. We've been hired to recover it for the rightful, legal owner." Landry moved beside Nickolai. Her right hand almost ached for her gun.

"So you say." The old man lifted his chin in defiance.

"So we say." Nickolai jutted out his own chin.

"Don't suppose you'd have any actual proof of that, now would you?" Jediah wasn't going to back down.

Mercy, but the testosterone had grown as thick as the sultriness of the desert. "We do, actually."

Nickolai shot her a baffled look.

Had the old man not been there, she would've laughed. Instead, she pulled out her cell phone and pulled up the news report of Bartholomew Winslet's murder. "Here, read for yourself." She handed her phone to Jediah, who spit before he took it.

She glanced at Nickolai as she eased her backpack to the ground and pulled out her water bottle. It'd gotten downright scorching. If this is how it felt in the middle of February, she couldn't imagine how smoldering it would be in the summer. Then again, unlike the humidity back home in Louisiana, this was a dry heat, so despite being warm, she wasn't sweaty and sticky.

"Hmm. Doesn't say Phillip stole it." He handed the phone back to Landry.

"But here's the connection." She pulled up the website for Winslet Industries and loaded the page with the board of directors. "Check this out." She kept hold of the phone this time, just moved closer to Jediah so he could see the screen. "See, that's Phillip, right?"

He didn't have to answer—his eyes verified Phillip gave him the map. "That's him."

"So now you understand we aren't making anything up, we'll need that map. Mrs. Winslet hired us to recover it and return it to her."

"It's right here." The man reached for one of the packs on the mule.

"Slowly." Nickolai leveled the gun at the man. "I don't want any surprises."

Jediah reached into the pack and pulled out the map, still in its protective sleeve but rolled. "I did my best not to damage it."

Landry took the map from him. "Do you really believe the mine is here?"

"I do." He nodded at the map. "I think I finally figured out what all the symbols mean. When I take that into consideration, the map shows only a couple of places where the mouth of the mine could be. I've checked out three of them. There are two others."

Landry wouldn't lie—the idea of finding the lost mine...

"But I gotta warn you." The old man spit. "There are some natives who want that map. Really bad. I've been having to move and search primarily in the middle of the day. Early morning and nights...well, those Indians can move through here like ghosts."

"Ghosts?" The stories of the ghost warriors and Shis-Inday scratched against Landry's spine, prickling her arms with goose bumps.

"They chant so low you can't understand what they're saying, but you can hear them. Always chanting. Sometimes there's a drum in the mix." Jediah shook his head. "The way they move...it's like they're mists."

"Chants?" Nickolai asked.

Landry remembered he'd talked about an Indian chanting when he'd been in the hospital. The hospital worker had been sure he'd had a dream vision.

"Do they want the map?" Landry asked.

"I'm pretty sure they do, which makes me know the map will lead us to the mine."

"Us?" Nickolai asked.

Jediah loosed a stream of dark juice from his mouth and wiped his lips with the back of his sleeve. "Well, yeah. I can be your guide. You might have the map, but if you can't decipher the markings and know the area, you'll never find the mine. Just like the legend says."

He had a point. Landry started to speak, but Nickolai interrupted her thoughts. "We found you, didn't we? Without the map."

Although they did have copies.

"Not too hard to find an old man and a mule."

"We found where you spent the night, then tracked you to here."

Jediah laughed. "Well of course you could. That should be easy. I haven't been trying to hide my whereabouts, except from the natives. A child could track me."

Landry pressed her lips together at Nickolai's frown. "So you want to find the mine so Phillip will pay you, right?"

Jediah shook his head. "My fee was never dependent on me finding the mine. If I did and brought him proof, then I'd be given a bonus, but the twenty-five thousand is paid just for me looking. I already got a ten-grand deposit."

Here was proof Phillip was the murderer. He'd killed his best friend for the map and hired Jediah to locate the mine off the map. Obviously money was the motive, but Phillip's records didn't show him in dire straits. It just didn't make sense.

"Come on," Jediah said. "You know you want to see if the mine's really here. What is it gonna hurt to let me guide you?"

Nickolai wasn't sure this was the best idea, but he'd agreed to Landry's request—what could it hurt just to take a few hours and see if they could find the mine? The map was secure in his backpack. The worst that could happen was they not find the mine and have to hike out with dejection hanging on to them.

"Hey, Jediah." Landry moved right behind the older man leading the mule.

"Yeah?"

"The waitress at Cobb's didn't recognize you, but you grew up around here, right?"

Good point. Nickolai reassured himself that his gun sat securely against the small of his back, tucked into his waistband.

"I don't go into the local businesses very often. Never did. My family was from the poorer parts of town."

After seeing the condition of many area places, Nickolai could understand that.

"I spoke with the salesman at the surplus store and he told me you asked about camping out here. If you grew up here—" Landry pushed.

"Then I should know, right?" Jediah finished.

"Exactly." Her tone was even, inoffensive, even as she questioned.

Nickolai had to give her credit. He'd seen very seasoned detectives who couldn't walk the fine line of interrogation as smoothly as she had.

Jediah spit but kept leading the mule down around the offshoot of Weaver's Needle. "Rules at national parks are always changing. I haven't been camping out in these mountains in many moons. Most surplus store employees are more up to date on the current regulations."

"Makes sense," Landry said.

Snap!

Nickolai drew his gun and spun around to face the sound behind him.

Nobody was there.

"What was that?" Landry asked. She and Jediah had stopped, so Nickolai knew he wasn't hearing things.

"I don't know."

"It's the ghost Indians." Jediah moved faster down the incline. "I told you they want that map."

"Why would a ghost want a map?" Landry asked.

Nickolai stared behind him for a few more seconds then stuck his gun back in his waistband and followed them.

"Rumor has it that their spirit or whatever needs all legit directions to the mine destroyed." Jediah quickened his pace even more. "Some say those spirits are what happened to the Dutchman and why he couldn't recover from his illness."

"Hmm. What's interesting to me, and I don't know the history well enough to have an answer, but what was a bread maker from Louisiana doing in Phoenix during the big flood?" Landry stumbled as she stepped on a rock. She grabbed the side of the mule and regained her balance.

"That I don't know, but the stories I heard growing up, Julia's husband had deserted her in Phoenix, and when she took care of the Dutchman, he paid her in gold, which further proved to everyone that there really was a gold mine. Some of the stuff you don't hear in the legends is that Gottfried Petrash, a friend of both Julia and the Dutchman, was supposed to have destroyed the map."

Nickolai listened carefully. If Julia's husband deserted her, then did she really have descendants passing down the map to eventually get into Abigail Easton's hands?

Jediah continued. "After the Dutchman died, it's said Julia looked for the mine but couldn't find it. Desperate, she supposedly fell in love with a fire worshipper named Alfred Schaffer and married him. It's said she learned to speak to the fire spirits and then tried to convert many of the local Indians to her religion. There was some talk that some of them came to recognize her as a shaman. She and her husband left Phoenix, had children, and she later died. Heard tell some of her kin returned to the area generations later and settled back in Arizona."

"That's fascinating." Landry slowed to fall in step beside Nickolai. "Isn't it ironic that Julia was originally from Louisiana and we're from Louisiana, and we're possibly following in her footsteps at this very moment?"

Jediah chuckled. "I hope not. She never found the mine."

"Well, there is that little fact." Landry grinned and took Nickolai's hand.

This was what he wanted from this point forward—to walk beside Landry, even into the unknown, holding hands. Despite the heat and uncertainty, at this moment, he was content.

"What's even more ironic is that it's February, and the flood believed to have given the Dutchman the pneumonia that killed him happened in February of 1891."

"That is quite a coincidence." Landry spoke softly, as if her thoughts were somewhere else.

Nickolai squeezed her hand. She looked up at him and smiled.

"Some think that when she died, she joined the ghost Indians to protect the mine, since she could never find it in life." Jediah slowed.

Nickolai squeezed her hand again. "It's okay. I'll protect you from any ghosts, Indian or otherwise."

She shook her head. "I don't believe in ghosts."

"Here's where we need to start turning." Jediah brought the mule to a stop. "We need to change direction toward the next markings on the map."

They had hiked around to the side of Weaver's Needle, where the large split carved dual peaks into the rock. This needlelike structure could be seen only from the side of the formation. Several crevices and crannies circled the area. A tree. Clumps of mesquite bushes and tumbleweeds. Cacti tall and thick. Small openings into dark places.

"What are we looking for?"

Jediah pointed. "That's what's marked on the map as water, and those are marked as the three pines."

Nickolai pulled out the map and compared. It all matched up perfectly. Excitement shoved down his skepticism. "Which, according to the map, means the mine should be. . ."

"Along this way, between here and the Salt River."

"How far is that?" Landry asked.

"Going this way, without the trails"—Jediah spit and wiped his mouth with the back of his hand—"about eight to ten miles, give or take."

Landry's eyes widened and she smiled. "Then what are we waiting for? Let's go."

Nickolai couldn't resist smiling back at her. Her enthusiasm wasn't only contagious, it was endearing.

Chapter Thirty

"How far have we gone?" Landry hated to sound whiny, but she was tired. All the workouts with Marcie hadn't prepared her for hiking in the Superstitions.

"According to my GPS, about four miles." Nickolai handed her a bottle of water then raised his voice. "Hey, Jediah, do you need some water?"

The older man turned, his eyes wide. "I think we're close."

Fatigue forgotten, Landry shot forward. "Really?"

"Yeah. Let me see the map again."

Nickolai pulled the map out and held it out for Jediah to study.

"See this dark zigzag mark here?" Jediah pointed on the line that went from Weaver's Needle almost to the marks before Salt River.

"Yes," Landry said.

"Those are little tree lines. Or they were back when this map was drawn. But erosion and time has made them taller and thinner. If we compare them to the other row on the right by three pines, then right around here should be the mark Julia had circled." Jediah looked up from the map and pointed in front of them. "Right in this area is where she has it marked."

Nickolai put the map back in his backpack. "So what are we looking for?"

"Remember that the clues were given back in 1891, so the terrain has changed."

"Right." Landry leaned against the mule.

"But this is what's important in the way of directions that the

Dutchman gave to Julia, at least as the story goes. Two landmarks are pointed out: Weaver's Needle and a two-room house in the mouth of a cave on the side of a slope near a gulch." Jediah pointed to an area just to their left. "Right there used to be a small shanty years ago, but it was torn down sometime during the early 1900s."

"You're saying that shanty was the house he told Julia about?"

"Maybe. But more importantly, he supposedly said that about two hundred yards across from the gulch and house, there was a tunnel that was well covered with bushes so it couldn't be seen. He said that some distance above the tunnel, on the side of the mountain, is a shaft that isn't too steep but is concealed. The Dutchman said, again supposedly to Julia, that the shaft led right down to the mine."

Jediah shielded his eyes from the sun with his hand. "Which, taking into account what I know about the terrain of the past, and erosion and other elemental details, I'm going to say that I think the entrance to the tunnel is right over there, by those old bunch of mesquite bushes."

About eight or ten clumps of mesquite bushes, some grown full into trees, sat in the area he indicated.

"They look uninterrupted," Landry commented.

"Well, if that's the entrance to the tunnel that leads to the mine, and the mine has never been found, I would expect the old bushes to be unhanded. Do you know what the mesquite bushes are commonly called when they grow into trees? Devil trees. Fitting, wouldn't you say?" Jediah smiled. "Shall we go check it out?"

Landry's entire body tingled as she surged forward, holding Nickolai's hand and keeping up with the surprisingly spry older man.

"What if we find the mine? People have looked for it for years without finding it, but what if we do?" she whispered to Nickolai.

He kissed the tip of her nose. "Let's see what's what first."

"Spoilsport." She stuck her tongue out at him, dropped his hand, and practically skipped to be beside Jediah.

The older man stopped by the bushes. "Keep in mind, this entrance has been hidden for many, many years."

She nodded, smiling at Nickolai as he joined them.

"Be very careful." Jediah bent beside the first clump of bushes. He pulled a walking stick from his pack on the mule and began jabbing it into the ground by the bushes.

Landry looked around and found a stick. Not as big or long as Jediah's, but it would do. She moved to the next clump of the mesquite bushes or devil trees. . .whatever, and started poking the ground in between the bases of the plants. She'd never felt so alive.

Nickolai had found a little larger stick than hers and approached one of the other clumps of bushes. With the three of them looking, they could easily find the mine. If the map was right, or if Jediah had read it cor—

"Whoooaaaa."

She and Jediah both straightened and looked to where Nickolai had just been standing seconds before. They couldn't see him any longer. Landry rushed forward.

Thud.

"Nick! Nick!" *Oh, Lord. Don't let him be dead. Please, don't let him be dead.*

"Wait." Jediah grabbed her arm. "We need to approach slowly. The ground might give."

She nodded then inched her way forward, keeping an eye on the ground. She approached carefully.

A hole, two and a half or three feet in diameter, had opened at the base of the mesquite bushes Nickolai had been inspecting.

"Nick?" She carefully crept to the edge.

"I'm okay. I think."

Thank You, Jesus!

"I think I might have twisted or broken my ankle, though." Nickolai's voice sounded so far away.

Jediah joined her at the mouth of the hole and peered down. "Can you stand?"

Groans and grunts traveled up the hole.

"Not without leaning on something," Nickolai finally said.

"Let me toss a rope down to you and we will pull you up. Bessie will help us," Jediah said.

"Wait," Nickolai replied. "Hang on."

Zip. Click.

Light shot up the hole.

"Let me look around here for a second."

Landry pulled out her own flashlight, lay on her stomach, and peered over the edge of the hole. She could see Nickolai below her. Just being able to see him made her heart stop, threatened to choke her.

"I think I'm in the shaft of the mine." He shined his light up at Landry. "I think we found the mine."

"Oh my gosh. Oh my gosh." Landry didn't know whether to be more dismayed that Nickolai was hurt, or excited that they'd found the mine.

"We need to go get help for him," Jediah said. "I can take Bessie and go if you want to stay with him."

"Yes."

"Jediah, wait. You need to see this," Nickolai called up. "I think I can actually see some gold flecks on the walls here. Something's sure shining in the light of the flashlight."

"Might be quartz." Jediah shook his head. "But we'll still need help to get you out of there since you're hurt."

"But then everyone will know where the mine is located," Nickolai said. "Not that I don't think it shouldn't be a national treasure, but I'd like us to be sure before we get everybody excited. It might be nothing more than quartz in an old shaft."

"It's more important that we get you out safe and sound; then we can decide what to do about the mine," Landry said. "Let me get the rope."

"Actually, it's more important that I get the gold, and you don't move, Miss Parker. I'd hate to have to shoot you with your own gun."

Landry looked over her shoulder and met the cold eyes of Phillip.

"What's going on?" Nickolai shined the flashlight on Landry, who hadn't moved.

"Um, Phillip's here." She sounded funny, but maybe that was because he was down in the shaft.

"What's he want?"

"The gold. He has my gun." Landry's face had paled, even by the awkward lighting of the flashlight. "Wait a minute." She looked over her shoulder then turned back to him a few seconds later. "Nickolai, is there enough room for us to come down there with you?"

There was, but what if he said there wasn't? Maybe that would stall Phillip. But then Landry would be up there, with Phillip, while he was stuck down here. Nickolai shifted, putting too much weight on his right ankle. Pain worse than when he'd been shot fired up his leg. A groan escaped him.

"Are you okay?" Landry looked over her shoulder again. "He's hurt. His ankle is most likely broken, so just give him a minute." Her voice was harsh. She turned back to Nickolai.

"I'm okay. Just hurts like the dickens."

"Okay. Is there room for us down there with you?"

At least if they were here, he could protect Landry from Phillip. "Yes."

"Okay. Hang on." She disappeared from the mouth of the hole.

Nickolai forgot all about his ankle. What was happening? Where was Landry? If Phillip hurt her. . . "Landry!"

She leaned back into view. "Just a second. We're working something out." She disappeared again.

Nickolai had never wanted to be able to jump up and punch someone so badly as he did right now. The thought of Phillip, with Landry's gun, up there with her. It made his stomach turn and balled his fists.

"We're tossing down a rope. It's attached to Bessie's saddle horn. Phillip will climb down first, then me, then Jediah. Stay clear." Landry backed away, and moments later, a new nylon rope hung beside him, almost reaching the bottom of the shaft.

It was a new rope, one of the ones he'd bought, which meant he'd gone into Landry's backpack.

Pack. . .phone.

Nickolai pulled out his phone. He dialed 911 and waited. There was enough battery, but not enough of a signal to get the call out.

"Nick, Phillip says to toss your gun to the other side. Now."

Nickolai took the gun from his waistband and tightened his grip.

"He says throw it now, so we can hear it, or he'll shoot me." Landry spoke louder.

He threw the gun to the other side. It clanked against the shaft wall.

"Phillip's coming down. Don't try anything, Nick, or he'll shoot me. I'm coming right along so I'll never be out of his view or range." Landry's voice wobbled a little.

He checked the cell. Still not enough of a signal to get a call out. But maybe enough to send off a text?

Phillip's form replaced Landry's at the top of the hole. "I'm coming down, Nickolai. No funny stuff or I'll shoot Miss Parker here. I think you two have gotten sweet on one another. Would hate to have to kill her."

Nickolai quickly flipped his phone on silent then sent a text to Chris.

PHILLIP FONTENOT MURDERER. PROOF. HAS US AT GUNPOINT. SUPERSTITION MOUNTAINS. USE GPS TO LOCATE US.

Phillip was only about five feet down when he hollered at Landry to start descending. So much for Nickolai's hope that maybe he could just knock Phillip out as soon as he got down and not put Landry in danger.

He glanced around. Needed to find a place to hide his cell. Where Phillip wouldn't find it. Needed to keep it on so Chris could track him.

If he got the text. . .

Phillip hung about six feet above him. Landry, four feet above Phillip.

There, that rock. Small enough not to be really noticeable but big enough not to be kicked out of the way.

Phillip was four feet above him.

Nickolai shoved his cell under the back edge of the rock, the side closest to the shaft wall. He stepped back to where he'd been before.

"Look out, Nickolai." Phillip jumped, landing beside Nickolai and leveling his gun at his head. He lifted Nickolai's gun and put it into his waistband.

"Now, hand me your cell phone." He spoke out of the side of his mouth. "You just stay right there for a minute, Landry."

"I didn't bring my phone. I left it in the Jeep." Nickolai almost choked on the lie, but he had to protect Landry as best he could.

"Now why don't I believe you?" Phillip held the gun steady on him.

"I don't know. The battery was almost dead because I forgot to charge it last night, so I just left it in the Jeep."

"Toss me your backpack."

He did. Phillip kept the gun trained on Nickolai as he went through the backpack. He slid it back to Nickolai. "Show me your pockets."

Nickolai did, moving slowly more for his own injury than to be cautious for Phillip.

"Come on down and join us, Miss Parker."

Landry jumped to the ground. She stood and immediately went to Nickolai. "Are you okay?"

"I'm fine. Just my ankle."

She looked at it. "Oh, mercy, Nickolai. Let me splint and wrap it."

"Yes, let Nurse Parker fix you right up."

She ignored him and unzipped her backpack, pulling out the first aid kit. She looked around and grabbed the stick Nickolai had been using to poke the ground. It had broken into three pieces, but one was straight enough for her to use as a splint on his ankle. "Oh, Nick, this has to be killing you."

"It's not so bad. Not now that you're here." It sounded cheesy, yeah, but he meant it.

She leaned over and kissed his cheek.

"Hey Jediah," Phillip called up.

"Yes?" He stuck his head over the hole.

"Come on down here."

"You know, I don't think so. You haven't paid me yet."

Before he could move away, Phillip lifted the gun and shot.

Bam! Bam! Bam!

Thunk. Thunk.

Jediah hit the ground beside Landry with a thud.

"Sweet Jesus, help us," Landry said.

Phillip laughed, flat and humorless. "I told you people I wasn't going to play around with y'all."

"You didn't have to shoot him." Nickolai reached over and felt Jediah's neck for a pulse. Nothing. He pulled his hand away. His fingers were wet and sticky. He moved them into the beam of the flashlight. Blood. He shook his head at Landry.

She glared at Phillip. "You killed him."

Phillip shrugged. "I gave you all warning." He waved the gun at her. "Now, help him up so we can look down the shaft. I want to see my gold."

Nickolai struggled to his feet, with Landry's help. The splint helped with the pain. He leaned close to her ear and whispered. "I texted Chris to send help. If the text went through."

"Come on, you two. Secrets don't make friends." Phillip turned to them and dug the end of Landry's 9mm into her side.

Nickolai reached out and put his hand over the gun, yanking it from her side and pressing it against his own gut. "You want to poke that thing somewhere, you put it on me."

"A bit testy, are we, Mr. Baptiste?" Phillip laughed but dug the gun deeper into Nickolai's ribs. "Let's get going."

He tried not to lean on Landry too much, but with Phillip shoving the gun in him, he was off balance.

"It's okay." Landry must have noticed him not putting weight on her. "I've got you." She gently rubbed his back.

Just her touch, her words, and knowing how she cared made all the difference to him. With renewed energy, he picked up the pace.

"That's the spirit, boy."

They'd made it about a hundred yards down the shaft, and Landry slowed. "I don't understand, Phillip. You're on the board at Winslet Industries. You're in love with Mrs. Winslet. Bartholomew was your best friend. Why?"

"I've asked myself many times how I got to this place, and I always come up with the same answer. It's Bart's fault."

"What?" Nickolai couldn't imagine how Phillip would think that. Not with what they knew.

"Guess it doesn't matter now if you know or not."

Which meant they weren't going to get out of here alive. Not unless they outsmarted him. Nickolai tightened his hold on Landry and slowed their pace.

"I met Winifred first. Fell in love with her as soon as I saw her. Asked her out and almost died when she agreed. After we went out a couple of times, I knew she was it for me. No other woman would ever do. And then I introduced her to Bart." Phillip shook his head, lost enough in thought that he didn't seem to realize Nickolai had slowed the pace a little more.

"He stole her from me, but I loved her enough that I wanted her to be happy, even if it wasn't with me. So I stood by Bart as he married the woman I loved. I bit my tongue when I gave Bart advice over and over again that helped him achieve higher levels in his business. I could've gone out on my own and made a lot of money, but I didn't because I wanted to be near Winifred. Needed to be." He pulled the gun out of Nickolai's side.

Nickolai knew he'd have to make a move of some sort before they got to the gold. Phillip would surely kill them there.

"So what changed?" Landry asked very softly.

"Winifred had an affair with Stan Hauge. Stan. Out of everyone, Stan? She should have known I loved her. I could hold my tongue about her with Bart, but Stan?" Phillip shook his head and shoved the gun back into Nickolai's ribs. "I found out years after it happened, but when I did, I was so disappointed in her. I decided I needed to live my life for me, so I asked Bart for a loan to get something going."

Ahh, so that's where the money part came in.

"He loaned it to me, but with official loan documentation and everything. To charge me interest. After all the advice and help I'd given him, he wanted me to pay him interest." Phillip shook his head, easing the gun off Nickolai's side again.

"I need to rest a second." Landry stopped and leaned against the wall of the shaft. "I need some water." She pulled her water bottle and took a long sip. She grinned at Nickolai as she did.

She was stalling. Trying to buy them more time.

Nickolai slipped to the ground and took the water bottle she offered him.

"Just for a second." But Phillip sounded a little winded as well.

"So you got the loan. Why didn't you leave?" Landry asked, resting her hands on her knees as she bent over.

"Things had changed and investments weren't the income maker that they had been. I made several different types of investments I couldn't recover. Then I had some bad personal news, but that's when I learned about the gold." He waved the gun. "Let's get to moving."

Landry straightened and helped him to his feet. Nickolai wrapped his arm around her shoulders. Taking a second to snuggle her, he looked at Phillip. "That's when you met Abigail and learned about the map, right?"

"So you know that, huh?"

"I'm so sorry you had to battle cancer, Phillip. That's a horrible disease." Landry spoke softly as they made slow progress.

"I've been in remission, so I'm good. I don't need your sympathy." He shoved the gun into Nickolai's side.

"I'm guessing you're the one who told Bart about the map?"

"Yeah, when Abigail's son got a higher bid than mine, I had to do something. So I turned Bart onto the whole story. Soon, he was bidding until he bought it."

Nickolai noticed the shaft was getting wider. He slowed their progress, trying to figure out how to get the gun away from him.

"The day he bought it, he told me he was calling my loan. If I didn't repay him immediately, he would have no other option but to turn it over to his legal department for collection satisfaction. Me. His best friend. A sitting board member." Phillip shook his head. "Just proves what a self-centered, egotistical, arrogant blowhard he was."

Even though Phillip was a criminal and Nickolai wanted to knock his block off, Winslet did sound like a jerk.

"Wow, that's really rude." Landry slowed even more.

"I know." Phillip slowed with them, but without argument. "I couldn't be humiliated like that. Not at work. Not to Winifred. Bart left me no choice. I had to kill him. I figured if I stole the map, found the mine. . . I'd finally get the financial windfall I deserved. I could forgive Winifred for her affair with Stan and sweep her off her feet. She's always wanted to travel. See the world."

Before Landry or Nickolai realized it, they'd turned and the shaft opened into a cave.

A cave whose walls were filled with gold flecks shimmering against their flashlights.

"Oh my gosh." Landry leaned Nickolai up against the wall and stepped into the mine. "It's amazing."

"And it's all mine."

"You don't know how to mine this, and you shot the one person who did." Landry put her hands on her hips.

"We'll figure it out." Phillip turned his back to Nickolai to survey the mine.

Now or never.

Nickolai dived for the gun. Phillip turned just as Nickolai fell forward. Landry screamed. Phillip lifted the gun and pointed it at Landry. Pulled the trigger.

Crack!

Landry screamed. Crumbled to the ground. A red blot seeped across her denim shirt, growing and spreading.

Noooo!

Nickolai lunged for Phillip. The gun skittered across the floor of the mine. Nickolai crawled for it. Phillip kicked him in the ankle.

He growled. Fell. Spots danced in front of his eyes.

God, if You're there, I need help. Landry needs help. Save her, God. She loves You. I don't know if You can hear me, but if You can, please save Landry. I love her. Please, God.

Phillip reared back his steel-toed boot. Brought it forward like a football kicker. Nickolai raised the gun and pulled the trigger. Pain ricocheted down Nickolai's head and neck. The world spun.

Everything went dark.

Chapter Thirty-One

The drum's cadence echoed inside his head.

Nickolai fought against the smoke burning his lungs. The overpowering scent of sage accosted his nostrils. The chanting filled his ears. . .head. . .mind.

Chanting.

He struggled to open his eyes. They were heavy, so very heavy.

In the smoky haze, the tall Indian again stood in front of him. There was no right or left, just darkness except for the big man filling his vision.

In one of the dark recesses of his mind, recollection snapped, like an overused rubber band. "Gopan?"

"Remember before. Sadnleel da'ya'dee nzho."

Long life, old age, everything is good.

"Now is your time to choose. Will you forget this place, forget what you've seen, forget what you've learned. . .to save her?"

He couldn't see Landry but knew she was there. Sensed her. Could almost feel her heartbeat weakening with every passing second. "Yes!"

Everything went dark again.

Beep. Beep. Beep.

Landry slowly opened her eyes.

"Hi there." Marcie smiled, but her eyes were bloodshot like they always got after she'd had a long crying jag. "Don't you ever scare me like that again."

"What. . .what happened?" Landry struggled to sit up, but pain screamed through the left side of her chest. She dropped back onto the pillow. "You were shot." Marcie wiped another tear away. "I told you that you should've come back home."

Memories flooded her. "Phillip shot me. Nickolai!"

"He's okay. He's in a room right down the hall."

"Jediah?"

Marcie's brows furrowed. "The old man?" She shook her head. "I'm sorry; he died."

"In the mine."

Marcie shook her head. "Honey, you must've bonked your head. You weren't in a mine. Y'all were on a trail near Weaver's Needle. All four of you."

"I'm confused."

"I'm sure you'll remember everything once you start feeling better."

"Landry!" Nickolai rolled into her room in a wheelchair, his right leg stuck out in front of him with a cast around his ankle. He rolled beside her bed and took her hand. "They wouldn't let me see you after your surgery, and I was sick with worry."

"Surgery?"

"To remove the bullet from your chest." Marcie held up a little clear vial and shook it. A metal slug rattled inside. "I figured you'd want to keep it."

"I do." Landry squeezed Nickolai's hand. "What happened? I remember being in the shaft then the mine. I remember getting shot. But how did we get out? How did we get here?"

He gave her a crooked smile. "What mine? What shaft?" He squeezed her hand back. "We were right by the rocks across from Weaver's Needle with Jediah when I fell off the rock and broke my ankle. Remember, you put a splint on it from the first aid kit?"

What? "You broke your ankle when you found the shaft to the mine and fell in. I splinted it in the shaft."

Nickolai shook his head, shooting Marcie a look. "No, I fell off the rocks just before Phillip showed up and demanded the map." He frowned, and the lines around his eyes deepened. "He shot Jediah, killing him."

Landry nodded. "Yeah, he shot Jediah because Jediah was going to go get help. Phillip shot him and he fell down the shaft beside us."

"Honey, there was no shaft."

"So how did I get shot?" None of this made any sense. Why didn't Nickolai remember what happened?

He rubbed his thumb over her knuckles. "Phillip grabbed my backpack and I lunged for him. He shot you then kicked me. We both lost consciousness." His eyes widened as he spoke. "Apparently Chris got a text I sent him, and sent police to the coordinates of my cell phone. Officer Hogan found us and had us airlifted to the hospital here."

That made no sense. Had she hit her head? "What about Phillip?"

Nickolai gave her a sad smile. "I remember getting the gun from Phillip and pulling the trigger. Apparently my aim found its mark. He didn't make it."

Landry fought to remember the details as Nickolai told them. She couldn't.

"What do you remember?" Marcie asked.

"I remember Nickolai finding the shaft to the mine and falling in; that's how he broke his ankle. Phillip had my gun—apparently he's the one who broke into my hotel room and stole it—and he made me climb down the rope into the shaft with them. . . ." Saying it out loud made it sound fanciful in comparison to Nickolai's version.

Maybe she had hit her head. Or maybe when she lost consciousness when Phillip shot her, she had a crazy dream that mixed fact with fantasy.

"Landry?" Nickolai whispered her name with his rough and coarse voice.

She smiled. "I just realized I'm probably mixing parts of what's real with a heavy dose of imagination. All that matters is we made it out safely, and we're okay."

"Amen to that," Marcie said.

"Amen," Nickolai added.

She frowned at him. Maybe she'd hit her head a little too hard.

Marcie cleared her throat. "I'm going to go find me a cup of coffee. I'll be back." She leaned over and kissed the top of Landry's head. "Try to stay out of trouble while I'm gone, will you?"

"You got it, Mom." Landry smiled as her best friend left the room. She turned her head to look back at Nickolai. "I must've really had some imagination working overtime, because I thought I just heard you say amen behind Marcie."

He smiled, pretty wide, showing off his perfectly straight teeth. "You aren't imagining that."

"What?" She squeezed his hand. "Tell me about that."

"When you were shot. . .well, I thought I'd lose my mind."

"Oh, Nickolai." She enveloped his hand with both of hers.

"No, it's okay. I mean, it isn't okay that you got shot, but. . ." He shook his head. "Anyway, when you were shot, I prayed. I didn't know if God was listening to me at all anymore, but I begged Him to save you because you love Him so much. And He did. I'm feeling pretty thankful at the moment."

Landry was pretty certain she could die of happiness right at this moment, even having been shot and having had surgery. *Thank You, Jesus! For saving him for me!*

"What?" His smile had to match hers.

"Can you get up here and kiss me?"

"Oh yes, ma'am." He pulled himself up to sit on the side of her hospital bed. With a callused but gentle hand, he ran his fingers over her lower jaw, easing his head lower.

When he was just a breath away, his nose almost touching hers, he looked deep into her eyes. "I love you, Landry Parker."

Her heart raced, and she parted her lips to tell him that she loved him, too, but his mouth covered hers, claiming it in a kiss. Claiming her heart forever.

Epilogue

Gopan stood silently in the back of the church, lurking in the shadows of the corner. The wedding was more beautiful than he'd witnessed in his many, many years. A beautiful bride madly in love with her charming groom, whose heart and devotion to her had been tested and found to be true.

"Shaman," the man beside him whispered.

He turned and raised a brow at his young apprentice.

"We've destroyed the map. Burned it just like you said. But she"—he nodded at the bride—"could remember the location if she tried hard enough." Tarak was so eager to please, yet needed to learn so much.

"Enough time has passed that she's forgotten. They were paid a handsome fee, even though the map wasn't recovered. The woman felt bad that much of the events were caused by a man's obsession with her." Gopan nodded toward the couple kissing. "They are getting on with their lives."

The bride turned to the two women standing at the front of the church with her. She first hugged the short redhead who'd been crying ever since she'd preceded the bride down the aisle. The bride then hugged the young lady on the cusp of womanhood, who looked very much like her brother, the groom.

The groom turned and hugged the taller African American who stood beside him before returning his bride comfortably to the crook of his arm.

Gopan stepped back farther into the shadows as the bride and groom walked down the aisle, now as man and wife.

They both hesitated for a minute when they passed the shadow Gopan and his apprentice stood concealed in.

The groom cocked his head for a long moment then whispered, "Sadnleel da'ya'dee nzho."

Gopan smiled as the groom led his bride away.

Long life, old age, everything is good.

About the Author

"I love boxing. I love Hallmark movies. I love fishing. I love scrapbooking. Nope, I've never fit into the boxes people have wanted to put me in." **Robin Caroll** is definitely a contradiction, but one that beckons you to get to know her better. Robin's passion has always been to tell stories to entertain others and come alongside them on their faith journey—aspects Robin weaves into each of her twenty-five published novels. When she isn't writing, Robin spends quality time with her husband of twenty-six years, her three beautiful daughters and two handsome grandsons, and their character-filled pets at home. Robin gives back to the writing community by serving as executive director/conference director for ACFW. Her books have finaled/placed in such contests as the Carol Award, Holt Medallion, Daphne du Maurier, RT Reviewer's Choice Award, Bookseller's Best, and Book of the Year. You can find out more about Robin by visiting www.robincaroll.com.

Discussion Questions

1. Landry was a bit of a rebel in her following of rules. Do you agree with her actions and reasoning? Why or why not?

2. Mr. Winslet was a collector. What do you collect? Why are those items important to you?

3. Nickolai's little sister was responsible for their parents' deaths, but it was due to mental illness. Share your feelings about that. How do you think he should have felt toward his sister?

4. Phillip had been in love with Winifred for a long time. What advice would you have given him to help him deal with his emotions in a more productive way?

5. Stan had an indiscretion with Winifred years ago. His wife forgave his infidelity. Discuss your views on forgiveness.

6. Marcie was a "mother hen" to Landry. Friends are vital to our well-being. Discuss ways you can show appreciation to those friends closest to you.

7. Nickolai had a difficult faith journey, but Landry and others who lived their faith in their daily life were a witness to him. Share ways your spiritual life is a witness to others.

8. Landry lost both her parents to different illnesses. Discuss the importance of compassion and how we can show our sympathy to those grieving.

9. Greed was an underlying motive for all of Phillip's actions. Discuss ways we can focus less on materialism in our daily lives.

10. The Native American culture is somewhat different from Christianity. Discuss how you feel about religious differences.